FERRY TO WILLIAMSTOWN

FERRY TO WILLIAMSTOWN

A Novel by
Colin Heston

HARROW AND HESTON
Publishers

AUSTRALIA, NEW YORK & PHILADELPHIA

Library of Congress Control Number: 2019955431
ISBN: 978-0-911577-45-7

CONTENTS

1. Willy's Kitchen

Babs slammed the phone down. "You're the daughter from hell! That's what you are!" she muttered, yet again. Every Friday night at seven, she called Lizzie, and every time, Lizzie answered the same thing. "I'm not coming Mum, I've told you a thousand times. The men get drunk, they can't keep their hands to themselves."

"Thinks she's too good for us, and she lives on a bloody Winnebago," muttered Babs to herself as she carefully lifted a tray of sausage rolls from the oven and slid them on to a plate. Why couldn't she be like Ryley, she asked herself, why does she have to be so difficult? We did everything we could to make her happy. And the more we did the more trouble she gave us.

Holding the plate of sausage rolls in one hand and a bottle of ketchup in the other, Babs stood in the kitchen doorway. Only a skinny five feet tall, if that, she filled the entire doorway, narrow as was the rest of the house. Husband Sandy rummaged in the refrigerator for more beer.

"Come on, you bastards, if you want something to eat you better come and get it!" Babs yelled, unheard.

Even if the noise were in a large room it would have been deafening, but in their little living room, crammed full of old worn furniture, two easy chairs and matching sofa, all padded with floral designs aping those in stained glass windows, a tiny round rosewood coffee table, two dark wooden dining chairs (they had no dining room) a foot-stool to match the sofa, and satin covered cushions distributed all over the floor between the furniture legs, the noise filled the room even more than the furniture. And in the far corner, the one just below the front window, sat the centrepiece of the room, the source of the racket, the radio and LP record player in a curved cabinet, speakers built into the streamlined face. There were maybe a dozen people crammed into the room, all talking, beers in their hands, a few trying to sing along with the record.

Babs tip-toed forward, trying to step between the legs of bodies on the floor, grabbing the arms of furniture to keep her balance, proffering the sausage rolls as she went. She didn't drink. It was the one big thing that Sandy had to work hard to forgive. Otherwise, in his eyes she was perfect. He came up behind her with a bottle of beer, extending it out to top up the blokes' glasses.

"Come one you buggers," he said, "we've got another dozen to knock over yet."

No one answered. The buzz and chatter had stopped, though. And in its place the crescendo of two hundred male voices filled the room, probably finding its way down the street to the Methodist church, because Ryley, their son and proud university student, had reached over to the record player and turned up the volume to the max.

"Listen!" he called, waving lanky arms around like a drunken conductor, "this is what Marx is all about!"

Sandy, embarrassed, quickly filled up glasses, banging the neck of the beer bottle against their rims as he went. Babs leaned forward with her sausage rolls. "Ryley, darl, turn it down a bit will you? The Methodists will be calling the cops 'cos we're disturbing the peace or some bloody thing."

The lyrics were absolutely clear, two hundred male voices in unison:

...No ne grusten ya, ne pechalen ya,
Uteshitel'na mne sud'ba moya...

Ryley stood tall, all six feet of him, his long black wavy hair fluttering as though to sound waves, his hand extended like Caesar's, lip-sinking the Russian in English:

...All zat is best in life zat God gave us,
In sacrifice I rrre-turned to the fierrry eyes!
(Vsyo chto luchshevo v zhizni Bog dal nam,
V zhertvu otdal ya ognevym glazam!

"Ryley, stop showing off!" cried Babs, proudly.

"It's the Red Army Choir!" he yelled in response.

Then a voice, a rough female voice at that, fired off from somewhere on the floor, maybe behind the sofa.

"He's got it wrong. Since when did Marx believe in God?"

"Get stuffed, Monie," answered Ryley, "*Dark Eyes* is just an old Russian folk song. It's how they sing together that's important."

"Two hundred male penises spouting together," Monie joked as she stood up from behind the couch.

"Don't you see? There's no harmony. There's no upper and lower parts. All the singers are equal," countered Ryley.

"So there's no class distinction. I get it."

"Ryley, turn it down," called his Mum.

Simone Crenshaw, Monie for short, drunk as usual every Friday night, dropped down behind the couch and lit a cigarette. Bobby, Babs's youngest brother, number four that is, was trying unsuccessfully to make out with her as he did every Friday night when he also got drunk. But when Monie got drunk, all she wanted to do was argue, her tongue splattering saliva everywhere, especially on her thick glasses. His brothers, Babs too, made fun of his infatuation, if that is what it could be called. More like lechery. No one knew her age, but Babs reckoned Monie was in her early forties, whereas baby Bobby was late thirties, thirty-eight to be exact, coming on thirty nine next month. Babs leaned over the couch.

"Hey Bobby, you want the last sausage roll?"

"Piss off, sis, can't you see I'm busy?"

"Yair, a sausage roll will take care of that mouth of yours." Bab's picked up the sausage roll from the plate and popped it into his mouth just as he was about to answer. He tried to talk, but nothing came out except bits of sausage roll sprayed all over.

"Bloody hell, Bobby. I'm getting out of here," said Monie as she struggled up and fell over the couch on to the cushion then onto the floor. "Where's my bloody husband?" Her husband, Lennie Stalinsky, rarely showed up to these weekly booze-ups. Every Friday they all came together down at the Steam Packet pub around five. Drank till six, then retired with the appropriate amount of booze to Sandy and Babs's narrow little town house at sixty eight Cecil street and boozed on.

"Hey Mum!" Ryley called, "did you make any of those party pies?"

Babs turned, a cross grin on her face. "'Course not. Who do you think I am, your lackey?"

"Aww, Mum! Don't be so crabby."

"Of course I made party pies."

"I knew it. Good-on-yer Mum! You're a beauty!"

"Yair, yair. When are you going to marry someone who'll cook them for you?"

"Don't start on that again, Mum. She'd never cook as good as you, now would she?"

"Depends who she was, don't it?"

Monie staggered up then fell against Ryley whose long arm hit the turntable. There was a screech and the crooning of the two hundred throbbing penises was no more. Cries and moans went up from all the blokes. Ryley placed the turntable arm at rest. "Shit, Monie, get the fuck out of here," he mumbled as he carefully picked up the LP and examined it for a scratch, "go on, get off home to Lennie."

"I'm not bloody leaving. I'm staying here to teach you some Marx. What do they teach you at university these days anyway?"

"Get stuffed, Monie. Go on, get home to your useless hubby. He could do with a refresher course on Marx anyway."

"So you've joined the intelligentsia, have you, you smart-ass?"

"The Russian *intelligentse* never went to university, you don't know anything. Go on, get!"

Bobby stood up and grabbed one of Ryley's waving arms. "Leave her alone," he said, "I'll take her down to the ferry. She lives in Richmond, for Christ sake. She can't get there all by herself in her condition and she doesn't have a car, does she?"

"She can take the train, can't she?" asked Ryley, shaking his arm free.

"She could, but I wouldn't do that to her. The hooligans will be out in force with all their antics."

"They climb out the window while its going, and they maul the passengers too," said Babs, "Ryley darl, don't you ever read the papers?"

"It's a bit early to be calling it a night," said Bobby, "but hey, there's time to get her on the ferry and across to Richmond."

Bobby grabbed Monie by the arm, trying to be tender, which for him it was, except that he had huge hands, puffed up they looked, but with solid muscles and knobby tendons as a result of his working with ropes and pulleys all day on the Williams-town ferry.

"Let go of me!" cried Monie.

"You're coming with me, you silly bitch."

"Bobby, watch your language!" ordered big sister Babs.

"So is anybody else going to take her?"

"Go on, get! I'll phone Lennie to meet her at the ferry terminal," called Babs.

Bobby half dragged, part carried Monie out through the front door, thrusting the screen door open so hard it banged against the house, then dragged her behind him as he limped down the little steps and through the old gate to his Hillman Imp.

Babs turned towards the kitchen. The party pies would be ready. To think that was how she'd be remembered when she was dead. The pies and all the stuff she cooked to feed the men. She turned to face the old wood stove. Sandy had promised to get her a new gas one when a big deal went down very soon.

That's what he thinks I want. I'm gripping the old oven glove and I want to put it in my mouth and tear it to pieces with my false teeth. Of course I'd like a new stove. But is that all I'm worth? I cook and wash dishes and clean up the house after Sandy's mates have gone, and I wash and iron his clothes. That's all I did for twenty years or more. And what about our two kids? While Sandy was at work, lording it over the wharfies, I'm stuck at home with two little brats, chasing after them, doing everything a good Mum is supposed to do. I'm not complaining, mind you. Don't get me wrong. Sandy and I, we've never had a bad word between us. Well, that's not saying much, because Sandy is the strong silent type, everyone says, and I knew it before we were married at Saint Mary's just down the street from us. And Ryley and Lizzie, they're doing all right now. Ryley at Melbourne Uni doing a P-H-D whatever that is, but they say you have to be really smart to do it. And Lizzie, well, I better not say too much about her. I think she's all right. I don't see much of her, to be honest. She drops in from time to time, but I hear of her from Bobby who sees her on the ferry quite a bit. He says she's doing great. Runs some kind of consulting service in Melbourne for smart-ass executives, he says. Then last year—it was only a year ago, around Australia Day I think it was, I decided to do something more. I went out and got a job. Well, I didn't exactly go looking for one. It kind of fell into my lap. I was walking down Nelson Place, going to drop by the barber shop, the one that J.J. Liston owned, now owned by my brother, number three, christened Lauchlan by my mother to emphasize our Scottish heritage and demonstrate to everyone that we weren't Irish but Scottish, and solid Catholics none the less. She was a piece of work, my mother, but that's another story. Anyway, Lauchlan was too big a word for anyone to say, so we all called him Lockie, though many changed that to "Lucky" on account of he loved the horses, the dogs and anything else he could bet on, and I'd say he's probably worth a lot more than J. J. Liston when he owned the barber shop.

The slight smell of burning pastry wafted up from the oven. Babs shook her head and stooped to open the oven door and pull out the pies, just in time.

"Hey Babs, you're not burning the bloody pies, are yer?" someone called out from the living room, amidst lots of laughter. Sandy was right behind her, though, grinning. He knew his mates got on her nerves, but he said nothing. Babs lifted the tray of pies on to the top of the stove. They were a little over done, just how he liked them. The smell was better than any smell he ever knew.

"Get out of the way, you old bugger, and hand me the big plate," rattled Babs with a big smile, "and you'd better ring Lennie to tell him to pick up his missus at the ferry."

*

Bobby pulled his Imp into the small parking lot under the solitary street light. Monie was snoring beside him. He looked over at her and wondered why he kept after her. Amazing what the booze will do. Bloody awful hag, that's what she was. He climbed out into the faint drizzle that hung in the air making the late season moths and insects glimmer in the single street light above. The ferry was moored and there was no sign of any cars, save that of Eurie the abbo, his co-ferry captain. But there were people crowded at the gangway, calling out, shouting to each other. Something had happened. He limped over as quickly as he could, leaving Monie to her slumbers.

"What's going on?" he called as he got closer and saw Eurie with one of their biggest boat hooks trying to drag something out of the water.

"There's a body!" someone called, "it's a rotten body!"

"Probably from the meat packing plant down by North Shore."

"Nah. It's a human, that's for sure."

Bobby pushed his way into the front of the crowd to help his mate pull in the body. They managed to get it up on to the landing and with a splat it landed on its back, the head banging on the concrete, causing a mass of little crabs that had been sucking on the lips and eyeballs to break free and run for the water. "Shit!" the crowd said almost in unison, as everyone tried to decide whether to turn and run, or lean further forward to look at the ghastly thing, a sight that each and every person there would remember for a lifetime.

"Someone phone the cops!"

"Is there a phone on the ferry?"

"Of course not. There's a phone booth at the end of the car park."

"I'll phone them. My brother's the local cop," called Bobby as he made off, skipping with his limp across the car park, taking a quick look on his way to see if Monie was still out to it, which she was. He knew that Shooter, his big brother, the second eldest of the boys, wasn't at the police station but at Sandy and Babs' place, of course. It was Friday night after all. He dialled Babs's number looking out at the ferry as he waited. The Winnebago was parked on the far corner, as usual. He could see a faint light on inside, and thought he saw the dim shadows of someone, or two. This time of night, he didn't expect any ferry riders. When he was on the late shift he often closed up if there was no one around.

Babs's phone rang.

"G'day!" someone yelled, "whatdya bloody want?"

"Lockie, you silly bugger, it's Bobby."

"Yair, well so what, Gimpy."

"Stuff you too."

"So what's up? Monie spewed up in your car or something?"

"Nah. She's still out to it. But something's happened. Is Shooter there?"

"Yair, he's had a few though. What's happened? You had a bingle?"

"No. We fished out a body from the water, just near the ferry."

"No kidding? I bet you I know who it is."

"Bugger you Lockie, put Shooter on."

"No, I tellya. I bet I know. A tenner? Bet you a tenner?"

"Lockie you hopeless bugger, put Shooter on."

"Hey Shooter, your gimpy little brother wants to talk to you!"

"Lockie, how many times have I told you, don't call Bobby Gimpy. Think yourself lucky it didn't happen to you," cried Babs.

"There, there Mum. I'm only fooling around. Shooter, can you get Shooter?"

"Shooter! Bobby wants you! He says it's urgent," she yelled trying to make herself heard over the Red Army choir. "And Ryley, for Christ sake," Babs crosses herself, "turn that Red Army down!"

Shooter, quite sozzled, struggled up off the couch where he had been in deep conversation with Ryley.

"Take it from me," says Ryley, "there's going to be trouble. The unions won't stand for it. Ask Dad, he'll tell you." He ran

his fingers through his brimming black hair, thick as a mop, so
thick that the kids at school called him Dago, the Italian, even
though he was as Irish—well Scottish—as anyone in Williamstown knew. But Ryley was a big kid even then, so not too many
were game to call him that except behind his back.

"I know, I know. You think I don't know what's going on?"
said Shooter, "I talk with Sandy all the time."

Shooter reached the kitchen and took the phone from Lockie
who grinned, unable to contain himself. "I bet it's the prime
minister, I bet you a tenner," he said.

"What are you bloody talking about?" asked Shooter.

"Shooter? Is that you? It's Bobby."

"What's the problem? I can't hear you. Hey, Ryley, turn down
the record. Turn it down!"

"There's a body."

"Gimpy? What did you say? A body?"

"We just fished it out of the water next to the ferry."

"Yair? You know who it is?"

"Nah. Body's all shrunk up. Horrible sight, I tellya. You better
come down. They was gunna call the cops so I said I'd do it."

"I'm on my way. Babs where's my cap?"

"Where you left it. How would I know? I'm only the cook
and bottle washer around here."

"Now Babs, don't be so touchy."

"I'm not your mother, lucky for you."

"All right, all right!"

"If she was here she'd quickly fix you up, cop or no cop."

"Major Mum! You're just like her. Now where's my cap?
Can't go out on official duty without it."

"It's over here, you were sitting on it," called Ryley, "I hope
you can shoot straight," he grinned.

Bobby was still talking, describing in detail what the corpse
looked like. But then he realized there was nobody on the other
end. Shooter had hung up. He banged the receiver down,
actually more than banged it, he was angry. They all treated him
like he was a half-wit just because he limped. "Bastards!" he
yelled, and banged the receiver several times at the booth
window until it cracked and bits of the Bakelite hand-piece
broke off. He thrust open the door in time to see that Monie had
woke up and was meandering towards the ferry. He skipped
across to catch her before she got to the bunch of men still
talking and pointing at the corpse. Her thick rimmed glasses

hung down on one ear, her hair all ruffled, and lipstick smudged. She looked even more of a mess than usual. He grabbed her by the arm and steered her back to the car.

"Better wait in the car. There's been a body found in the water."

"Let me see it! Let me see!"

"It's nothing a woman should see," said Bobby, now calm again.

"You fuckn bourgeois Willy people. There's nothing a real woman shouldn't see!" she yelled, shaking off his grip and staggering towards the spectacle. "I'll decide for myself what I can look at!"

"You can't even walk straight, you're so drunk," snarled Bobby.

"Yeh. You should talk," and she staggered off, leaving Bobby fuming once again. But he pursed his lips and contained himself as he approached the small group of onlookers.

"I called the cops. They'll be here any minute," he announced to the group. But then he saw that there was someone else in charge, all very official, a large rotund gentleman in an impeccable uniform, lots of stars on his cap and stripes on the sleeves.

"All right. Stand back everyone," he ordered quietly, turning to Bobby, "so you've called the local police?"

"Yes sir, Shooter, I mean senior constable Frank Frost, will be here any minute."

Bobby looked around for a police car and wondered how this bloke got here and who he was. Then he felt Monie tugging at his arm. "Now what?" he asked belligerently.

"It's the fuckn Commissioner!" she blurted thinking she was whispering, but everyone there heard her.

"That's right Madam. I am Gordon Trinity, Chief Commissioner of the Victoria police, at your service. It's fortunate that I happened to be here when I saw the disturbance. I must now ask you all to stand well back, this is a serious police investigation and crime scene."

A siren sounded and lights showed up in the distance, probably coming from Douglas Parade. The Commissioner busied himself herding the onlookers back, his short arms poking out, looking a bit like Humpty Dumpty. Then Shooter appeared on the scene, and just as quickly, the Commissioner disappeared. Bobby thought he saw him, a dark shimmering

shadow returning to the ferry, walking in the direction of a
Winnebago.

*

Lennie Stalinsky was no hero, but he felt deeply for the
impoverished condition of all workers everywhere and from a
very young age he had devoted his life to the cause of ill-treated
workers. His father, a holocaust Jew as he called himself, lost
his entire family to Hitler's gas chambers, with the exception of
his twelve year old son Lennie, and by a series of escapades
ended up in Australia via Cuba. He repeated many times to
Lennie that he'd brought with him on that Ulysses-like journey
the only two possessions that he had left: his son Lennie, and
just one book, his bible of sorts, Frederick Engels' *The
Condition of the English Working Class*.

Lennie now sat in the dimly lit alcove of his tiny rented flat
on Jessie street in Richmond, clutching the book in his hands.
Its old red cover was well worn and deeply discoloured from
the dirt and grease of constant handling, the pages frayed, the
colour of rust on their edges, so brittle they were difficult to turn
without tearing or even disintegrating in his fingers. It had
helped him over many a crisis even though it had itself been the
source of perhaps one of the most traumatic events in his life, a
nightmare of sorts.

We've just come down the gang plank of this old freighter
and I'm hanging on to Dad's hand. He's got this old leather bag
in his other hand that has all our possessions in it. There are
rows of ships, all looking rusty and broken, moored along the
pier, Port Melbourne as I found out later. We're herded into the
customs house and there's a row of officers standing there
waiting to interrogate us. We're dressed in our ragged coats and
jumpers even though it's a hot summer day, we have no other
way to carry them and we've learned that you have to keep your
things close to you or you lose them. An officer singles us out
and points to the leather bag. "Open it," he says, and my father
struggles to undo the latch. I pull away from his hand and go to
help him, but it's too late and he drops the bag on the floor and
some of the contents fall out, among them *The Condition of the
English Working Class*, which I of course quickly grab up and
hold close to my chest with both hands.

"Let me see that book," demands the officer.

I stand frozen. My Dad starts to put things back in the bag.

"You speak English?" asks the officer, in a really loud voice.

I wait for my Dad to answer but he doesn't. He's still rummaging in the bag.

"Yes," I say.

"Good. Then let me see the book. It's got a red cover, so I think I know what it is and you can't bring that book into Australia. It's against the law."

"It's just a book," I say in disbelief.

"Let me see it. I know it's a communist book, so give it up."

I don't move, keep hugging the book to my chest. "It's not! It's not!" I cry, "it's the only book we have. Please let us keep it! Please!" Tears are running down my cheeks.

The officer moves towards me and I cringe, and in a flash he swipes the book straight out of my hands. "If you're coming to live in this country you have to learn to obey its rules. Books by Karl Marx are banned and that's that!"

This rouses my father. "But sir, it is not Karl Marx. Just an old historian who lived his life in England."

The officer flips through the book, and not seeing Marx as the author, hands it back to me. It's in German anyway. "You read this book, son?"

"No Mister, sir. My Dad reads it to me in English."

A quiet knock on the door was enough to snap Lennie out of his reverie. "It must be O'Shea," he thought. Then the phone rang. "Just a minute," he called to the door as he picked up the phone on the stand in the hallway.

"Lennie Stalinsky speaking," he said.

"Lennie. Sandy Malley. You better come and get Monie. She's had a few too many. Bobby's taking her to the ferry."

"Why doesn't she take the train?"

"She's too far gone. The hooligans on the Willy train will maul her."

Lennie sighed and muttered to himself, "as if I don't have enough to worry about," but he could hear the Red Choir rising above the chatter in the background and it gave him heart.

"You there Lennie? You hear me?"

"Yes, yes. It's just that someone's at the door. I'll be there to get her. About when do you think?"

"I'd say about half an hour or a bit more. Everything all right? No cops banging on your door or anything? I know what it's like."

"No, nothing like that. Or at least not yet. But you know that things are a bit dicey with what's happening with O'Shea."

"Yair, I heard—Hey! Turn that bloody noise down!—If there's anything I can do to help, let me know."

"Thanks, Sandy. You're a great comrade."

"Comrade? Enough of that commie talk. We're good mates, right? This is Australia, not Germany."

"Yes, yes, comrade Malley. Got to go."

Lennie hung up the phone and opened the door. There stood O'Shea, a shocking sight. He'd lost so many pounds in just a few weeks, his once jolly square Irish face seemed to have narrowed, the lines deep, the skin sagging into thin jowls, grey and sickly. His hair, grey at an early age, now turning white, was combed back from high on his forehead, just enough hair to show some waves. His eyelashes were already a stark white, and there were no eyebrows to speak of. Lennie, around six feet tall, towered above him. They shook hands, and Lennie was pleased to feel a tight grip. "He hasn't lost his will yet," he thought.

"Clarrie, you beauty. Come right in. I've only got a few minutes. Got to go to the Williamstown ferry to fetch Monie. What's up?"

"I'm going on a hunger strike."

"Shit, Clarrie, you look like you already started."

"Nah. Just been so busy, haven't slept in I dunno how long."

"What can I do for you?"

"You're good mates with Sandy Malley, right?"

"Funny. I was just talking to him. He phoned me to pick up Monie from one of their Friday night shin-digs."

"Do you think he could get the wharfies to go out on strike to support me?"

"Why? Things have got so bad?"

"That bloody asshole Kerr is threatening to send me to gaol if I don't open the union books for inspection and have my blokes pay up the $8,000 fine the Industrial Court levied against the Tramways Union. He claims I'll be in contempt of court."

"He can't do that!"

"I know they're following me around all the time. I wouldn't be surprised if there was someone right outside the door ready to grab me."

"But there'd have to be a court hearing, right? They can't just put you in gaol, can they?"

"They can do what they like, that's the way it looks to me. But a court hearing has been scheduled for next Thursday."

"The fifteenth?"

"I s'pose so."

"That gives us six days."

"Right."

"Isn't the Trades Hall doing anything? Surely they should be on your side?"

"Bloody typical. They're just sitting by watching it all happen. They're not supporting us."

"You know, I've long suspected that they've been paid off. They're not on our side, that's for sure."

"You're right there."

"Clarrie, you can depend on me. I'll call a meeting of the Party and get in touch with Sandy right away."

"You'll phone him?"

"Too risky. I better go see him in person."

"I better be off then. Have more stops to make, getting a lot of support from a lot of other unions.

"I'll wait a while before I go out. I think I'll take the train to Willy. And I'll talk to my blokes. We're a national party now you know. We have a lot of contacts with unions all over Australia. We'll have to keep it quiet. If the *Age* or *Sun* know we're collaborating, they'll call it a communist revolt, and you'll lose popular support right away."

"Rightee-o. Thanks Lennie."

They shook hands, a firm determined hand shake, then Lennie let him out the door, both men looking furtively up and down the street. It seemed deserted. He closed the door and immediately went to his desk to retrieve his diary. It awaited him in a small drawer sitting atop the old writing desk he had bought some years ago at the auction house a few blocks down Swan street. It reminded him of the desk his father had in their Berlin apartment. Dark rosewood, or that was its colour, round except for one straight side so that it would fit in the little alcove flush against the wall just below the front window that looked out on the street; that is, when the curtains were opened, which was not often because Monie didn't like windows, thought people were sticky-noses. She liked it dark inside. He didn't know why, even though he'd asked her often enough. She never gave a reason. After a while he stopped asking her. She had her secrets, lots of them he suspected, though he thought that by now he ought to know them all. After all, he picked her up off the street, where she was half-begging, half-sleeping, homeless —although it turned out she wasn't homeless, far from it. Instead, she'd decided to live like the homeless to see what it was like, so she said, and it was then that she got started on the plonk, and maybe worse, smoking cigarette buts, and became a smoking addict, her voice now beginning to crackle like potato chips in a paper bag. But you couldn't believe anything she said about her past.

Lennie and Monie had been together now for several years, Monie coming and going as she pleased, working as a social worker for the Victorian Education Department. A bunch of them drank at the Royal down on Punt Road. A lot of them were communists, or commo sympathizers as the *Sun* would call them.

*

Bobby helped the ambulance blokes and watched as Shooter started to herd the onlookers away, barking at them to go home. Boy! Did he like to give orders. He'd been like it all his life, no wonder he became a cop. That, or a school teacher, but then, that was left for Tommy the eldest who, until he left for the war, gave the orders with great gusto. That left the two poor buggers at the bottom of the food chain, the slaves of the clan, Lockie and the "baby" Bobby who everyone treated like a little kid and never would let him grow up. He was the pathetic one, the one who always had something wrong with him, was always sick, was always whining and after all he had that limp, none of his doing, the real victim of Major Mum. Though, as often happens, God had worked his fair and balanced magic and saw that Bobby would grow up to be the biggest of all the boys by far. And in a scrap, which still occurred from time to time, especially on Friday booze nights, he came out the winner every time.

"All right, get away from the ambulance. Come on! We haven't got all night!" yelled Shooter, "there's nothing more to see. Go back to your homes. There's nothing more."

"Who is it, then?" asked someone.

"How should I know? Now get going, all of you!"

Bobby grinned to himself. It was nice to hear him ordering someone else around instead of himself. But the thought came too soon.

"Bobby! Come here, I want you to take some notes for me while I talk to your ferry mate."

"I'm no constable's lackey," he growled.

"Where's your sense of duty? You're a citizen, it's not much to ask."

"All right! All right! I'm coming."

Bobby limped slowly across to the gangway where Shooter stood, interviewing Eurie. He handed Bobby a notebook and biro pen.

"Name?"

"Eureka Smith."

"What? That's your name? Are you sure about that?"

"It's not my fault, is it?"

"There's a severe penalty for lying to a police officer you know."

"All I did was fish a body out of the water, and you're threatening me already," replied Eurie belligerently. "You cops are all alike, you treat us abbo's like we're all drunks and thieves."

Shooter ignored the remark. "All right. At what time did you first see the body?"

"When I was tying up the ferry, about half past seven."

"And what did you see, exactly?"

"I saw this thing floating on top of the water, big, a big white bloated thing."

"You getting this down Bobby?"

"Yair, sort of." Bobby didn't like writing much. He wasn't that good at school.

"Then what did you do?"

"Well, it was wedged between the ferry and the pier. As soon as I got the gang plank down I got the boat hook and that's when Bobby helped me drag the body up onto the jetty."

"I see. Was there any clothing?"

"Only what was on it that you already saw. Pants all torn, clinging to his ass and one of the legs."

"You knew it was male?"

"I kind of guessed I suppose. It was, wasn't it? I mean it had pants."

"Right. Did you touch the body in any way?"

"Only enough to get it up out of the water. Wouldn't touch it with me hands, that's for sure. Bloody horrible!"

"About how long did it take you to get it out of the water?"

"I dunno. About ten or fifteen minutes I s'pose."

"You get all that down, Bobby?"

"Most of it. Not much to say about it, anyway, is there?"

"You leave that for the police to decide."

"Yessir!" grumbled Bobby, feigning a salute.

At that moment, Monie lurched forward and snatched the notebook from his hand.

"Hey! What the hell you doing?" yelled Bobby.

She hung on his arm, almost pulling him off balance. "Where's Lennie?" she pleaded, "what have you done with him? That wasn't him they put in the ambulance, was it?"

"Of course it wasn't," said Bobby.

"You're fuckn lying!" she screamed and threw the notebook into the river.

"You better get Monie out of here," ordered Shooter, "get her on to the ferry."

"Aye! Aye! Captain," chided Bobby, "but what about the precious notebook?"

"Get stuffed!" snorted Shooter.

"Come on Monie, let's get on the ferry." He turned to Eurie. "You going to start her up?" he asked.

"Well, now you're here," answered Eurie, "why don't you do it and I can go home? I knocked off an hour ago, anyway."

"But Eurie, it's not my shift. I don't come on till seven in the morning."

"Too bad. I'm going home. I've had enough of this." And he left.

Bobby grabbed Monie and started to walk back to the car. "Bugger it!" he muttered to himself, "I'm not going to drive the ferry out when it's not my shift. It's against union rules anyway. They wouldn't pay me overtime either. And now I'm stuck with Monie. Lennie will just have to come to Willy to get her."

But now, the ambulance was gone and Shooter in his police car, siren blaring, took off as well. He was about to open the door of his Imp to cram Monie inside when out of the drizzling gloom emerged the Commissioner. "You're the ferry captain for tonight?" he asked.

"What's it to you?"

"I need you to drive the ferry across. It's important police business.

"But I don't come on duty till seven in the morning. It's against union rules."

"You realize that disobeying a police officer of any rank is a serious offense?"

Suddenly, Monie's crackling voice came from inside the Imp. "Mister Commissioner!"

"Who is that?"

"Where's my husband? They've taken my husband away!"

The Commissioner turned to Bobby. "Who is this, what is she saying?"

"Don't mind her, sir. She's had a few too many."

Monie climbed back out of the car and shook her fist. "You bastards!" she yelled, "I know what you bastards are up to. Just because he's the Chairman of the Communist Party of Australia you treat him like he was a murderer or something. Where have you put him?"

"Monie! You're drunk! Get back inside the car and I'll take you back to Babs's place."

"What is she talking about?" asked the Commissioner, amused, yet curious.

"She's drunk, sir. I'll take care of her."

"Is Stalinsky her husband?"

"Yes, that's right. You know him?"

"No, but everyone in Melbourne has heard of him," lied the Commissioner. "And you are with her?"

"I was just taking her across the ferry where Lennie should be waiting for her. But it's got too late now, so he won't be there."

"Are you also a communist?"

"None of your business."

"I think it would be in your interest to start up the ferry and take her across."

"If you say so, Commissioner."

Bobby leaned down and hauled Monie out of the Imp. "Come on you silly bugger, let's get on the ferry. Commissioner, sir, you'll have to watch her while I get the ferry up and running," said Bobby in his most obedient manner. But the Commissioner was gone. Nowhere to be seen. Bobby looked around. All that was there was the huge black chimney of the nearby power plant towering above the gloom of the car park. The drizzle turned into heavy rain. They were predicting floods and high tides. "He must be in the Winnebago already," smiled Bobby.

*

At Flinders Street Station, Lennie stepped out of the Richmond train and rushed over to the platform where the Williamstown train was about to depart. It was the last train, he thought. As he entered the dilapidated carriage he caught a glimpse of himself in the mirror, cracked of course, that was adorned with fancy floral scrolls and an advertisement for Haig's Scotch Whiskey. That bald head with protruding forehead, ringed by black hairy fuzz, the little beard pulled to a point by the constant stroking of nervous fingers, the very dark eyes, almost black, peered back at him. This was Lennie Stalinsky, chairman of the communist party of Australia. His comrade mates, the dyed-in-the-wool communists that is, called him Lennie, short for Lenin because they reckoned he was the spitting image of him. He didn't mind the nick-name, in fact kind of liked it. Lenin was a man of action, unlike Marx who was, after all, just a theorist trying to convince others to act in his stead. He peered into the mirror and saw a tiny bead of sweat appear on his shiny forehead. He wiped it off with his hanky and looked around for a seat. The naked female bodies entwined in the floral borders of the mirror ached for attention but to no avail.

The carriage was, thankfully, empty and remained so all the way to Williamstown, no hooligans to deal with, not even any drunks which was unusual this time of the evening. If you want to see how the poor people live, take a train trip, he thought as he looked out the window at the back yards of the many houses, full of junk, gutters falling down, trash piled up and strewn around the yards, beer bottles stacked up just outside the back doors. And barely any space between one house and the other, grey wooden fences separating them none the less, and those weird matched pairs of houses built by the housing commission. As the train slowed down in its approach to Williamstown Beach station, the new high rise flats came into view, the latest in housing for the poor, built by the Victorian government housing commission. It was a new idea, copied from the pommies of course, moving people out of the slums and into nice new flats.

The trouble is they were already finding out that if you put all the poor people in one place, for some reason they stay poor. That's what he'd heard about the Gorbals in Glasgow. But the Gorbals had always been awful, full of crime and violence, so you couldn't blame the high rises for that. Not like here. Of course, there shouldn't be any poor people in the first place. And the locals complained too that the government demolished the old bluestone buildings to make way for it. What about preserving the historic buildings of Williamstown they complained. A typical bourgeois argument. The demolition of history was inevitable. Marx has shown that, incontrovertibly. Get rid of the old, the products of primitive capitalism anyway, and built by convicts to boot. At least the government was doing something for the poor, even if it was a bourgeois government. And you had to remember, it was right now conducting a war against the unions. And that's what it was, a war, a very one-sided war. The cheap houses and flats for the poor were just a charade, the government didn't really care, he knew that. Marx had warned about getting duped by the ruling class. They offer salves for the wounds they themselves cause, making them seem magnanimous and generous. But they didn't care one bit. They didn't really, seriously, give two hoots for the working class. They did just enough to keep them quiet. Well, this time they were going too far. O'Shea was resolved, solid as a rock. We comrades will do everything we can to support him. And the unions, all of them, I'll get them to come out in full force. A national strike, that's what is needed!

The loud whine of the brakes sounded as the train pulled into the station. Lennie thought briefly of Monie. Hopefully she would be back at Sandy's place once they realized he wasn't at the ferry. He walked out of the dim lights of the station and on to Parker street, past the primary school, an old bluestone monstrosity that ought to be demolished and replaced with something modern and functional, around the corner to Cecil street, and then to Sandy's little place. He'd done this walk often, always to get Monie, but in the dark of the evening, with little street lighting, it was a bit risky, not only because some drunken hooligans might be wandering about, but the footpaths were unkempt, the roads disintegrating, there was always the chance he could trip over. There were only a couple of houses on the street that still had their lights on. Everyone else had probably gone to bed. But Sandy's, of course, was always open, people showed up there any time of day or night. Everyone in the hood knew that. The wire door was swinging back and forth in the cool breeze as he walked up the tiny footpath to the door of sixty-eight Cecil street. All was quiet. No blaring noise of blokes half-pissed arguing about the football or whatever else. He knocked lightly on the door and heard a faint call from the back of the house. "Come on in!" Sounded like Babs.

"It's only me," he called, "Lennie."

"Oh! Lennie, come on out back, We're in the kitchen. No room in the lounge room, they've all flaked out on the floor," called Babs. "What are you doing here? You're s'posed to be picking up Monie at the ferry, aren't you?"

"I phoned Sandy to say I'd come directly here instead. Didn't he tell you?"

"Yair, didn't get round to it," said Sandy who was sitting with Babs at the kitchen table, having a cup of tea.

"Where's Ryley?" asked Lennie.

"Dunno. He went off somewhere an hour or so ago. He's probably got a girlfriend hidden away somewhere," answered Sandy.

"Yair, that would be the day," muttered Babs.

"Want a beer, or I've got some Corio somewhere, and there's always some red lying around now that Ryley's at uni. You know how they like to drink the red."

"A glass of red would be good."

"So you don't have Monie?" asked Babs.

"No. I thought she'd be here by now when she saw I wasn't there to meet her."

"Bobby's not back either. He took her to the ferry, so I s'pose he'll bring her back. But there was some kind of incident at the ferry."

"Really?"

"Yes, they pulled a body out of the river. Shooter went down to take care of things."

Lennie took a sip of the red. "Very nice," he grinned. "So Sandy, I need your help."

"Tell me."

"On Thursday, they're going to put Clarrie O'Shea in Pentridge prison."

.

2. Winners and Losers

The flat above the barber shop had seen many a game of cards and not a few games of two-up, of which Lockie preferred the latter. Two-up was a simple game, the two pennies either came up heads or tails. It's true that you could make it more complicated by adding more pennies to each throw, or betting on runs of heads or tails, but he never went for that. It was like betting red or black in roulette, not that he had ever played that, mind you. As far as he knew, there wasn't anywhere in Melbourne that had fancy betting machines like roulette. He'd only seen them in the movies. But tonight, after a brief warm-up session of two-up played in the corner of his living room that had a stiff rug on the floor so the pennies wouldn't make a noise when they hit the bare boards, he and his mates were all set for their monthly poker game. Lockie went to a lot of trouble to get in a brand new pack of cards each month and he had scoured all the second hand and auction houses in Melbourne to find a round table big enough for six players to sit comfortably and not have to worry about others peaking at their cards. More important though, was to have plenty of booze—most of them went for scotch and soda, a couple for good old Fosters (these days they preferred the large cans). Ever the gamer, Lockie would join them to play a few hands, and continue if he was winning, but most often he would sit it out and tend to their needs. He saw himself as the manager of his little upstairs casino. They all happily agreed to pay him twenty percent of the winnings, because, after all, as Lockie said, it was he who was taking all the risk for hosting the gambling on his premises.

This was a dark night, and Lockie busied himself arranging the dim lights and drawing down the heavy blinds and curtains to block out any light that might filter through to the street. He ran downstairs to check that the gate was unlocked at the back of the yard. The escape route was there in the unlikely event of a police raid. Unlikely because brother Shooter knew all about their game, but pretended not to, and Lockie pretended that he did not know that Shooter knew. That was all a game as well. Everything was a game to Lockie. It had been so for as long as he could remember because that was what his father, who taught him two-up when he was three or four years old—old enough to count—did all his life. Oh how he missed his Dad, killed in a pub brawl one night down at the pub near the racecourse where he took bets on the horses. Lockie, always good with numbers, was his Dad's tick-tack man, computing the odds on the fly, communicating them at the speed of light with the hand signs which he eagerly and effortlessly learned from his Dad and became a master at them. He discovered at an early age that money came and went, and if you were prepared to take a few risks, it came more than went. Most of the blokes who waged their bets didn't have a clue what they were doing. It was easy to give them long odds, compute the chances of them losing. True enough, though, lady luck had her way, and occasionally he would have a disastrous day and do the lot, but just as soon, if there was time to recoup, lady luck would endow him with riches again. He made an exception with the poker game though. Poker was a game of skill, or at least there was more skill than luck, and a few of the blokes were pretty good, a few of them big timers from Melbourne, a judge, a Q.C., a big deal politician, depending on who could come on any particular night. They liked coming to Williamstown to play, because they thought that Willy was a backwater that everyone else in Melbourne had forgotten. The perfect place to lose oneself and indulge in an illegal game of poker. Its being illegal made the game even more attractive to them, that's what Lockie thought. Anyway, there was no way he was going to compete with them, what with his having left school at fourteen, not that he went to any school for much time anyway because most of his childhood the family was constantly on the move with the rough and ready circus his Dad owned. And rough it was, no tent, no stands, nothing. Just a couple of horse-drawn wagons that served to carry the props he used to show off his acrobatic antics at horse-riding (something that Lockie never took to), his Mum playing second fiddle, dressed in silly short frilly skirts, handing him hoops and whips, and he, Lockie, working the onlookers, hat in hand, collecting money. He was good at that. And when the show was over he and his brothers, supervised by big sister Babs, nestled together in the wagons that became their bedrooms for the night.

Lockie switched on the light in the barber shop briefly so he could check himself out in the mirror behind the barber's chair. He insisted on formal attire for his guests, suits and ties upon arrival, though if they wanted to loosen their ties as the game progressed that was fine. He himself dressed much more formally, dress suit, bow tie, the works. He tugged down the bottom of his jacket, turned slightly and nodded with approval. Some would say he was old fashioned. His plentiful black hair was carefully combed with a perfectly straight part on the left, a small wave coifed in front, rather like Superman, all of this kept in place with a sweet smelling hair oil which he still used, even though it was rapidly going out of fashion. He switched off the light and walked out back to stand by the gate. His guests would be arriving any minute. It would be good if the drizzle would let up.

*

"Where are you two going? You up to no good?" asked Babs with a grin.

"We're going for a walk down to the pier," said Sandy, grabbing Lennie's elbow as he lightly steered him through the bodies on the floor and out the front door.

"What for?"

"I need to walk off the booze and we have some planning to do."

"So you're leaving your wife to the mercy of these drunks?"

"They're at her mercy, more like," quipped Sandy.

The old screen door slammed shut and Babs turned back to the kitchen to make another cup of tea. She lit up a Dunhill and took a long draw, fingering the packet, admiring the elegant letters of the "h" and two "l"s. It was the main reason she liked them. Silly really. Though they did have a nice sweet aroma, she thought. The kettle came to a boil just as someone in the front room let out a big snore. There wasn't one person in that room now that she knew. People just showed up, uninvited a lot of the time.

It's because of Sandy. They all look up to him. He's so quiet, so solid. All right for them, but what about me? He's quiet, all right, but that means I have to guess what's going on with him. It's like I'm a piece of the furniture a lot of the time. Not to mention washing his clothes, doing the ironing, making the beds, cleaning the house, cooking his meals—and his mates' meals a lot of the time as well. Still, it's what Mum did and more, so I shouldn't complain. But Sandy has much more, his union thing, and all those wharfies who look up to him, think the sun shines out of his ass. And what have I got? Just what my own Mum had—nothing except the kitchen and now a washing machine. That she didn't have, how could she when we were constantly on the move trolling all over Victoria. And in a horse and cart, no less! Mum barking out her orders at us. How else could she have done it? And then when Dad came to his sudden end. I don't know how she coped with us all. How she got this house, that's right, this house was hers, you know. I always reckon it's why Sandy married me, to get his hands on the house because he was here so often and he loved it. And I still don't know how she came to own this house and passed it down to me. She even had a will, would you believe it? And I don't think she could read hardly at all. And the will said I had to get the house. The boys weren't too happy with it, because after the house there was nothing left to pass on. But Mum reckoned that they were boys so could always get good jobs, not like girls who couldn't get a good paying job except in just one profession, if you see what I mean. Besides, the boys drove her up the wall. Not me, being the eldest, my job was to make all the beds, such as they were in the carts most of the time and later when we were in this house, and tidy then up, and later do all the cooking when Mum was too sick to do much. Trouble with the boys was that they were always hungry and Mum didn't have quite enough food to go round a lot of the time, whereas I didn't eat that much, so I was always giving some of mine to them.

One good thing about always moving on with the "circus" as we called it—it wasn't really a circus, more a one man acrobat and horse-riding show—was that there were always open paddocks where the boys could run wild and in summer, winter too, Mum saved up and bought them a cricket bat and balls, so they spent a lot of time running around the paddocks, bare feet on tough dried grass. They didn't care. And that's how Bobby got his limp, at least that's what I think. He probably has a different story. It was Major Mum at her finest, well, depending on how you look at it, maybe her worst as a Major.

Bobby, the youngest, was always the spoiler. He wasn't quite old enough to play the games, even cricket, cried when he went out, and they made him do a lot of running if the ball was hit for a six. It was middle of summer, somewhere near Horsham, a little place called Rupanyup, I think, we stopped for a couple of weeks while Dad did a bit of shearing for one of the local farmers. We all went to one of those little rural schools, but I don't really remember much about it. We were most of the time running around in the stubble of wheat fields. One day, Bobby came running up to me crying that he cut his foot. Looked like it was his little toe. There wasn't much blood that I could see so I just gave it a kiss and told him to run off and play. He must have been about five or six, I think. He kept on whining about it, so each time he came to me I'd sprinkle a little bit of salt on it to stop it getting infected. Of course, each time I did that he wailed and screamed that it stung, so eventually, he decided not to whine to me, but to go straight to the Major, which was a big mistake. We were all scared of her after all. It must have been hurting him pretty bad to go to her. She must have put salt on it too, because he came running out of the caravan, still wailing. And I heard her yelling after him that if he came back whining she'd cut the bloody toe off! He ran back to the cricket game, just in time to see Shooter hit the ball for a six to the excited yells of the others, and Shooter standing there like big-time cricketers do, nonchalantly leaning on his bat, spitting out orders to Bobby to go get the ball. Which he did, but then came running back, hopping a little every few steps, crying that his toe hurt.

"Hurry up and throw the ball, or I'll cut the bloody toe off myself!" Shooter yelled.

Bobby threw the ball only a few feet, then went running in to the Major. "I want a bandage, Mum. It still hurts!" he cried. There was a brief silence then I heard the Major talking to him, then all of a sudden he bursts out the door of the caravan, screaming, his face all red, and, hopping, arms waving.

"She cut it off!" he screamed. "Me little toe! It's gone!" We were all used to his screams, but this time it was deafening. We all ran to him.

Bobby was sitting, hugging his knees, rocking back and forth. I looked closely and couldn't see any blood coming through the old cloth that Mum wrapped around it.

"Let me see," I said, leaning down to pick at the bandage.

Bobby cringed and cried, "Leave me alone! Don't touch it!"

Major Mum appeared at the door of the caravan. "Let that be a lesson to you all, you little buggers. No whining or you get what's coming to you!"

I looked more closely at the bandage and saw some blood oozing through. I really wanted to take off the bandage, couldn't believe that she really had cut it off. None of us really believed it. But Bobby wouldn't let us get anywhere near it. A day or two went by, Dad would come home full of booze and sleep it off in the caravan, and us kids would play out in the fields, sleeping in our beds made up carefully by yours truly, in the carts, under the stars. And Bobby would lay there, curled up in a little ball in a corner of the dray, whimpering until one night I saw him shivering, and he was pale as a ghost. I tried to talk to him, but he just kept shivering and saying his leg hurt. So at last I got up the courage to go knock on the door of the caravan until Dad stirred and groaned, "What's the matter?"

"Bobby's sick," I called.

And for the first time ever, Dad staggered out of the caravan and I pulled him by the hand over to the cart where Bobby lay shivering, and his eyes all glazed over. I produced a torch from under the mattress and Dad looked him up and down. "Gees, he looks like old Daisy the day she dropped down dead!" he said. Daisy was our old draft horse.

"It's his leg," I said.

Dad tried to get a look at it but Bobby was curled up so tightly in a ball that he couldn't pry him open. Feeling very grown up, I said, "Dad I think we have to take him to the hospital." How that could happen I didn't know as we didn't have a car or a phone. Just a couple of horses that pulled the carts. A bloke picked Dad up each morning, if he was with us, to take him to the shearing shed.

"Run down the road to the pub and ask them to phone an ambulance," Dad said.

So I ran the half mile to the pub, banged on the door. I don't know how late it was, must have been after midnight. There were still some drunks lolling about, and the publican, Mickey they called him, a jovial bloke with a round face and little grey whiskers poking out of his cheeks in all directions came to the door.

"Call an ambulance, quick! Me brother Bobby's dying," I cried.

"Dying? What? You sure? Where's your Dad?"

"He's back there with him. He sent me to call an ambulance."

"It'll take forever to get an ambulance out here, luv. I'd better get the car and we'll go down and see what's wrong and take him to the hospital in Horsham."

"Gee, thanks Mickey," I said, all coy and I really was thankful. I thought Bobby was going to die, just like Daisy did. Really I did.

Mickey drove Bobby to the hospital where they said, according to Dad, but you could never really believe him because he loved to spin yarns, they were all ready to cut Bobby's leg off, but Dad grabbed the saw out of the surgeon's hand and told him he wasn't going to let any butcher take off his son's leg. In the end, things ended up all right, because the doctor prescribed antibiotics or something, maybe it was penicillin, whatever, but anyway it fixed his poisoned leg, though they said he'd be a cripple all his life. Dad said his little toe was nowhere to be seen, and Mum forever insisted that she never cut his toe off. I don't believe her. I know what she did, you wouldn't believe it. I'm the only one who really knows what she did. Not even Bobby knows. It's a miracle, though. Of us all, Bobby's the sweetest, and he's suffered the most. It's Jesus at work, that's what I think. And it's why he's the only one who could talk with Lizzie, my daughter from hell. She's always looked up to him. And I can tell you, she has never looked up to anyone else in her life.

Babs reached for the tea-strainer and poured herself another cup of tea. The Dunhill was down to its last draft, which she took, then stubbed it out on the old Corio whisky ashtray that someone had lifted from the pub. She went to the front room and began prodding the bodies on the floor. "Come on you buggers," she called, "it's closing time, off you go."

*

In the midst of the excitement, Eurie, before taking off, thinking they were done for the day, had turned off the ferry's old diesel engine. Apart from running the ferry, the engine generated electricity, enough to run the hoist to raise the gangway. Bobby climbed up the ladder to the bridge that formed a bulwark on one side, opposite a lower bulwark on the other, which was the engine room. The ferry was tiny as ferries go, fitted about 20 cars so long as they were guided into place properly. He turned the switch to prime the engine, and waited patiently, poking his head out the small porthole to look for any signs of movement and saw none on the ferry, though he thought he saw a figure dart across the car park. It was hard to tell in the drizzle. He looked back across to the other shore of the Yarra and could see only the faint glimmer of lights. There was no movement on the ferry that he could see, though he would look again once he got the engine started and the lights of the ferry switched on. There was a faint light inside the

Winnebago. He pressed the starter button and after those few moments of silence, the whine of the starter motor struggled to turn the engine, which, sounding half dead, suddenly sprang to life and the loud pulsing grumble of the diesel motor flexed its muscles. It was a comforting sound Bobby carried with him even to bed, a relaxing, reassuring blanket that closed down his busy brain each night. He really liked his job.

The lights came on and Bobby struggled down the ladder, his gammy leg having difficulty finding the right rung. He did the rounds of the deck, checking for stray persons and seeing none, raised the gang plank, unhooked the hawser, and carefully coiled it around the cleat. With everything set he returned to the bridge and looked for signs of any boats in the vicinity but saw none. With satisfaction, he opened the throttle and the chains creaked and rattled as they slowly pulled the ferry across on its ten-minute journey. The light in the Winnebago flickered, and Bobby smiled to himself knowingly, but then he remembered. He had forgotten all about Monie. He dashed down the ladder and ran, to the extent he could, all around the deck looking for her, calling out "Monie! Monie! You silly bugger, where are you?" finally realizing that there was only one place she could be and that was in the Winnebago. But surely not! And if she were not, there was only one other place. In the Yarra river!

He knocked lightly on the door of the Winnebago. His big worry was that maybe the Commissioner was in there, though he was fairly certain he saw him sneak off across the car park along with everyone else.

"Just a minute," came a muffled voice. "Who is it?"

Hearing Lizzie's voice, Bobby was relieved. She sounded happy too, more reason to be relieved.

"It's just me."

"Uncle Bobby?"

"Yair. Come on, open up will you?"

The door opened and Lizzie peaked out, dressed provocatively in expensive lingerie, her face at this hour absent of any make-up, a rare sight for Bobby who gulped every time he set eyes on her because he knew what she was up to and also found her incredibly, voluptuously attractive. She stirred in him feelings that one should not have for one's niece. They were, after all not that far apart in age, he being the youngest of his clan and she being the oldest of hers. They were maybe only ten years apart if that.

"Uncle Bobby! What's up?"

"You got anyone in there?" he asked.

"Nah, been a slow night," she grinned.

"Gees, Lizzie, I wish you wouldn't..."

"Now uncle Bobby, no sermons please, that's reserved for your big sister Major Mum number two."

"OK, OK. But that's not why I'm, here." Bobby glanced across to the approaching shore. "Look, I've got to run up and drive the ferry. I've lost Monie. You haven't seen her?"

"Monie? What are you doing with Monie? Isn't she married to Lennie the commie?"

"She got drunk back home, you know, the usual Friday night shin-dig. I was taking her to meet Lennie on the other side. And then Eurie found this body—"

"What? What body?"

"A body, he dragged it out of the water on the Williamstown side. Happened just as I got there with Monie. Then the police Commissioner—"

"What? The Commissioner? What was he doing there?"

"Well, you'd know about that, wouldn't you?"

"Gees, there you go again, uncle Bobby."

"I gotta run back up. We're getting close to shore."

Bobby turned and ran to the bridge.

"Whose body?" Lizzie called after him, her contralto voice rising above the throb of the diesel and rattling of the chains, "whose body?"

*

Lockie heard the dull mutter of voices approaching. He gave his tuxedo a tug to make sure it was straight, then quietly unlatched the gate that was set into the high paling fence. He could tell that one of them was the Commissioner because he always dug his heels in when he walked, you could hear him a mile away. And probably the other was his mate the judge. The drizzle let up briefly. Must be the influence of the Commissioner, he grinned to himself.

"Good evening gentlemen, sorry about the drizzle," he said, standing as tall as he could, towering above the Commissioner, level with the judge, clicking his heels lightly and offering a very faint bow. He had seen a movie with Jeeves in it, and did his best to copy that character. It softened up these toffs like you wouldn't believe.

"Good evening Lockie," smiled the Commissioner, "sorry if we're a bit late. Had an urgent police matter to deal with."

"Oh, sorry to hear that sir. I trust everything is all right now?"

"Everything's jolly good now," answered the judge, "we are both well satisfied. Your brother did a special trip on the ferry to bring us over."

"Indeed, Ambrose, indeed he did."

"Oh, you mean little Bobby?"

"He's not so little," observed the judge.

"Well, you know what families are like. The youngest is always the little bloke even if it turns out he is the biggest of us all. I'm pleased to hear he treated you as you deserve, gentlemen." Since Bobby had been at Sandy's for the usual Friday night's shin-dig only an hour or so ago, he wondered how he could have driven the ferry across like they said. "Let's go right up and I'll get you your drinks, scotch on the rocks as usual sirs?"

"Sounds good to me," said the Judge.

"Me too," said the Commissioner.

Lockie ushered them up the creaky stairs and they seated themselves at the big round table, covered specially with a fine felt cloth, green of course, and very card-friendly.

"Now if you will make yourselves comfortable, gents, I'll go back down to wait for the rest of our guests. The scotch and ice and everything are behind the bar. Help yourselves."

Lockie wasn't sure they would all show up. Tim Furst, Lord Mayor of Melbourne had promised to come last he saw him when he ran into him on the ferry, as did Freddy Farselit, Q.C., and chairman of the labour party of Victoria. But the one he really hoped would show up was Harry Nolte renowned race horse owner, gambler and real estate agent who controlled most of the property sales in Williamstown and beyond. Harry had turned up in Lockie's barber shop below a few weeks ago and, with a wink, had given him a huge tip and said he'd like to join the game. Lockie made a big show of writing in his name on a special card he had for "special customers" and gave it to him, the time and date written on the back of the card. "This is your appointment reminder for your next visit and I will reserve a special chair for you upstairs. You may use the private entrance around the back. I'll be waiting to greet you there."

It was not long before a car pulled up in the lane out back. Lockie hurried to the gate and opened it in time to welcome Harry, always first in line, followed by Freddy, a jovial man with flabby jowls that shook when he spoke which was constant, and a little later by Tim Furst, nicknamed Timber because he was tall and thin like one of those narrow gum trees you saw in the Otways rain forest. He was about to shut the gate when a faint voice from across the road called "wait-a for me," in an unmistakable Italian accent. It had to be Father Zappia from St. Mary's around the corner who graciously watched over the proceedings and enjoyed the Scotch as well.

"Welcome Father, I was beginning to think you weren't coming," said Lockie.

"Oh no, wouldn't-a miss it for anything."

"You haven't been in the shop for a while. Isn't it time I trimmed up those nice Italian curls of yours?" joked Lockie.

"I've-a been so busy." He walked directly up the stairs and went straight for the scotch as if he owned the place.

"Help yourself Father," said Lockie, "I'm glad you're here to offer us God's guidance."

Father Zappia seated himself with the other players, all of whom knew him well of course, since he was a regular player. Lockie obsequiously tended to their every need. "Is the ice OK sir? Would you like some more soda water? Is there anything else I can get you sir? A cigar perhaps?" Finally, seeing that all were seated and ready to go, Lockie went to a special cabinet that had a large lock and key. He retrieved two sets of playing cards, still in their wrappers, of course, and placed them on the table. He also took out a two-up paddle and with a flair, brandished it around announcing, "we will keep the best for last for anyone who wants this."

Two-up was Lockie's favourite. He would not join the poker game. There was much more money for him to make from the twenty percent of the winnings he charged for overhead, and that amount didn't depend so much on luck, as someone always had to win, even if most lost. But later, when they were all primed for it, having won and feeling lucky, or lost, hoping to make it up, they would be easy targets. Now all that remained was for his unofficial bouncer, Buck Hamilton, currently star Collingwood football player, a fact that Lockie, a Geelong supporter, tried his best to overlook. Most of his clients were Pies supporters, so it made sense to employ Buck to whom he paid one percent of the house take for his services which had never been needed. But, it was worth it for the sense of security and well-being his celebrity and his presence provided. He heard footsteps on the stairs. Buck was here, having let himself in through the back gate.

"G'day all. Sorry I'm a bit late. Training went a bit over."

Buck squeezed into the only place left at the table. The other players, pleased to be in the same room as such a sporting celebrity, grinned and welcomed him, joking about winning and losing, an experience all too familiar to a Collingwood player this season.

"Then let's get started," said Lockie, looking directly at Father Zappia who made a small cough and placed his hands together in the position of prayer, the signal for all to bow their heads. "Before Father blesses our game, may I remind you to ante up your tithes for him to play. I recommend a minimum of $500 each which gives him enough to play a few rounds. Father is not a gambler of course, though he has told me that the bible does not condemn gambling. Anyway it's a nice way to include him in our group, and whoever wins I hope will donate a part of his winnings to the charity that Father Zappia chooses, which is our tradition."

Father Zappia began. "May the Lord look over us-a tonight, as we enjoy His bountiful love and the fruits of our earthly endeavours, and we beseech-a You O Lord, we Your humble servants, to bestow on us the good fortune that only You in Your great wisdom can provide." He reached out and placed his hands softly on the unopened packs of playing cards. It was a signal for all to also place a hand on his. "Bless these cards and bless all these hands that do Your divine bidding here on earth for the good of mankind. Amen."

*

Sandy had led the way to Pascoe street, then on to Nelson Place where they crossed the road to the park. They had walked in silence, Sandy, as usual, saying nothing, until at last, Lennie broke the ice.

"Sandy, we need your help."

"I know, I guessed that."

"Can you get your wharfies to strike in protest?"

"That's a bit drastic. What do we get in return?"

"Gees, Sandy. What is there I can promise? We're just a small party. We don't have much money."

"You see? That's what I'm always telling you. How can a little party like yours get anywhere without any money?"

"Money is the root of all evil, you know what Marx said."

"I don't know what he said, and I don't care. You sound like Ryley. He's always going on about Marx. The airy-fairy stuff they fill their minds with at Uni."

"That airy-fairy stuff brought on the revolution in Russia and in China. Surely you know that."

"Look, Lennie. I can get my wharfies to back you, but I can't call a strike for a little issue like this, even if Clarrie is a fair-dinkum bloke, which I know he is. There's got to be money or working conditions to go on strike over. There's got to be something the blokes will get out of it, something they will thank me for."

"But there is money in this, or at least, if Clarrie loses and goes to gaol all the unions lose because the precedent will be set and no one will be able to strike because of the enormous fines the government can levy against the unions, and back them up with the threat of Pentridge if the unions—yours included—don't knuckle under."

They turned on to Gem pier, a light breeze from the bay bending the chilly drizzle under the occasional lights along the pier. Sandy stopped briefly and looked back. He scanned the shops and houses along Nelson Place. There were still a few lights around the couple of pubs that were still open, and there was, he thought, a light above the barber shop. Lockie must be at it, he grinned to himself.

"So what's so funny?" asked Lennie, immediately regretting it.

Sandy ignored the remark and turned back to the pier. The cool breeze would make both of them cold, their clothes already quite damp from the drizzle. Sandy liked the cold, it helped him think. He purposely had not put on a jacket when they left the house. Lennie was already cold and now miserable, even though he was still wearing his turtle neck jumper that Monie had knitted for his fortieth birthday.

"You want to turn back?" asked Sandy.

"Oh, no! Let's continue and get the death of cold," said Lennie, trying only a little to hide the sarcasm.

They walked in silence once again. It was Sandy's way. Lennie was kicking himself for getting annoyed and showing it. They reached the end of the pier, having managed to avoid tripping on the debris lying everywhere, fishing tackle, rope, old pieces of machinery, you name it. The old pier, the first ever built in Williamstown, was crumbling away. And now, at its end, it was agreeably cold. Sandy looked across to the lights of Melbourne, Lennie hugged himself trying to keep warm, looking down at his feet, the old patent leather shoes soaked wet.

"Tell you what," said Sandy, "this is what we should do."

"Tell me, please."

"All the unions should get together and have a big march down William street, big banners, chanting FREE CLARRIE and end up in front of the court house where Clarrie will be tried."

"But isn't that a strike?"

"No. It's a demonstration. It's a stop work action.

"But how will we get them all together?"

"That's for you and Clarrie to manage. Clarrie knows all the union people. And with your help, getting on the phone and telling them all where to gather at the bottom of Swanston street, starting at Flinders Street Station where there are lots of people, then marching to the court house, banners waving, shaking fists, yelling all together like the Red Choir, FREE CLARRIE! FREE CLARRIE! The TV cameras will love it."

"I don't know, Sandy. I don't know if we can get them all together."

"There's six days till Thursday. Of course you can do it."

"I'll have to find Clarrie, get him to use his contacts."

"For Christ sake, Lennie, you're a bloody commie! Marches and demonstrations are what you bloody-well do! Right?" exclaimed Sandy in what for him was a loud voice, one of exasperation.

"Not really. That's for the workers to do. The commie's as you call us, work behind the scenes. We're the strategists, or at least that's what I am as the leader of the party.

"So strategize then, whatever that's supposed to be. There's no substitute for action, Lennie. Pull your finger out."

Sandy led the way back to Nelson Place. The light was still on above the barber shop. Lockie's doing all right for himself tonight, he thought with satisfaction. But Lockie was full of surprises. You didn't know what he was going to do next.

"Clarrie should be able to get his tramways union on board," said Lennie, "I'll have to talk with him. And the miners' unions too. Maybe there'd be time for them to come down from Newcastle. And there's the liquor trades people."

"And the nurses, and the teachers' unions, though they're a piss-weak lot," added Sandy.

"You know what? This might work," chirped up Lennie.

"I'll put the word out to my boys on Monday. They'll love it. A march up William street will be a good break from the hard work of loading and unloading ships all day."

Sandy looked to Lennie as they carefully stepped over an old anchor lying in their way. He could see that Lennie was struggling to keep up enthusiasm. He was a pitiful soul. The terrible experiences he'd had in Germany, the escape from the death camps, his father dying of a heart attack not long after they got off the ship in Melbourne, his complete and utter devotion to communism, laudable for sure under the circumstances, but hopeless none the less. It seemed like he wanted to be harassed and pursued by the authorities just as he was in Nazi Germany. It was the only life he knew. It was no wonder that Monie drank so heavily in between doing her good deeds of social work. Living with Lennie would be like living in a mouse hole, too frightened to go out because of the cat, and for her, pretending that she could thumb her nose at it, knowing that one day, the cat would pounce. "We had better get back. Monie and Bobby should be there by now," he said looking back.

Lennie had slowed, carefully stepping around the puddles, trying to keep his only pair of leather shoes dry, his head bent down almost below his shoulders. The drizzle accumulated on his bald head and trickled down his forehead. Sandy took a deep breath and sighed. Water started to collect above his brow but he quickly wiped it away.

*

They had gone through a couple of bottles of scotch, and plenty of peanuts and finished up the card game with some hot party pies that Babs had insisted on cooking for the event. She was a great sister, no doubt about it, even if she was a bit bossy, grinned Lockie to himself as he took the pies out of the oven. But you couldn't blame her, given what she had to put up with, her uncontrollable young brothers and having buckled under to the Major all her childhood. These pies, though, they always went over well, just the thing to soften up his clients.

As expected, Harry Nolte had won big, Lord knows how he managed to do it. All the other players pretty much lost the lot and the judge heavily. "Now gentlemen enjoy your pies, there's a cold beer to go with them if you want, and for the *pièce de résistance* I hold here in my right hand the historic two-up paddle owned by none other than J.J.Liston, the famous Willy racehorse owner and benefactor of the last century, and once the owner of the very barber shop below us.

Lockie gathered up the cards, stuffed them in a paper bag and placed them in the rubbish bin for all to see. "They'll be burned to a crisp in the kitchen oven downstairs first thing in the morning, gents. And now, who'll be the first to play?"

"What about you?" said judge Turner, annoyed at having lost so much, "it's about time you lost a bit, isn't it?"

"Right you are!" answered Lockie. "The tradition is that I play the winner of the spoils. So here you are Harry, the paddle and two brand new pennies, almost extinct now that Australia has switched to dollars and cents."

Harry took off his jacket and rolled up his sleeves. The others stood and lifted the card table to the front of the room, leaving plenty of space to toss the coins.

"So how do you want to start?" asked Harry.

Lockie couldn't hide his devilish smirk as he said, "what about all your winnings?"

"You mean everything on one toss?"

"Yair, why not?" called the Commissioner, with others chiming in.

"How much you got?" asked Lockie.

"Gees, I dunno, but there it is all in a pile at the edge of the table. I'd say about thirty thousand dollars."

"Good grief!" cried the Mayor, "we lost that much?"

"Well, you must remember it was $1,000 a bet," announced Q.C. Farselit as though he were in court.

"All right then, let's get on with it, asserted the Commissioner who had a little too much to drink and lost heavily. "Here, let me examine the weapons to make sure everything is above board."

Lockie handed over the paddle and two pennies and then went to a small safe under the locked cabinet where he kept the playing cards. "Here's my lot," he said as he opened the door of a small safe and pointed to neatly stacked piles of $1,000 bills, "so if I lose, we can count up the pot and then I'll match it. Fair enough?"

"You're on!" cried Harry with bluster.

"Everything's in good order," announced the Commissioner. "The weapons are in pristine condition. Who's tossing?"

"As the *maître de,* I do the toss," said Lockie. He took back the paddle with his right hand and the coins in his left. He began turning the pennies over and over in his hand, a nervous mannerism perhaps, but also with considerable agility, the fingers of a string player.

"Hand them over," demanded judge Turner, eyeing Lockie suspiciously, "loser tosses."

"Of course, Ambrose, it's only fitting that you toss and be the judge as well."

Lockie handed the paddle and pennies over and the judge, who with some difficulty, placed the two pennies in the small indented circles on the paddle. He coughed nervously.

"Don't tell me you've never done this before," chimed in Mayor Furst, who prided himself on his lowly place of birth, lack of education and his record in the Guinness book of records for downing a yard of beer in eleven seconds, not to mention his reputation as a swimming champion of the 1956 Olympic games, a gold medallist, no less.

"Matter of fact I haven't, not with these fancy instruments. When I played it as a young student at Melbourne University, we threw the pennies against a wall."

"Hey, Judge, this is a classy joint, we do everything spot-on here," joked Lockie.

"So how high do you want me to toss them?" asked the judge.

"Here, give them to me," said Buck. "You buggers don't know what you're doing. I'll toss them and the judge here, can announce the result and the winner." Buck took the gaming tools from the judge who resisted slightly as he asked haughtily, "what are the rules, so I can adjudicate impartially and correctly?" Buck laughed, and pretended to throw a punch at him.

"There are no rules," said Q.C. Farselit, "does that make you nervous judge?"

"We must agree on a couple of rules," interrupted the Mayor, with authority. "First, each player must take it in turns to call."

"But we agreed that we'd only bet on one toss, didn't we?" said Lockie.

"That's what Lockie and me agreed on," said Harry, "and I'm right with that. But it just remains that we have to decide whether Lockie calls or I do."

"Are you two blokes sure that's what you want?" asked Buck.

"I'm OK with it," said Lockie.

"Me too," said Harry.

"Why not do two out of three. I mean, it's not much fun all that money going on one toss. It'll be over before we know it."

"That's the whole point," said Q C.

"For Christ sake get started," complained the Commissioner.

"As a matter of fact," said Lockie, "now that you've all had your say, as I am the *maître de* of this establishment, I will tell you what the rules are. In this house we play by the Anzac rules."

Lockie firmly reached over to Buck and firmly took the implements from him. "First of all," he said, brandishing the paddle, "this is the kip, it's not a paddle though it looks a little bit like one. Second, the pennies are placed on the kip by me, the spinner, and they're put down one head up and the other head down."

"So who calls out evens or odds?" asked Buck.

"No one. Although the judge can be the referee who announces whether its two heads, two tails, or odds. If it's odds, the spinner tosses again. If it's two heads, the spinner wins. If its two tails Harry wins."

"Seems complicated," complained the Mayor, "but since it's not my dough, do what you like."

"House rules, as I've said," replied Lockie firmly. "So are we ready?"

"Toss 'em," said Harry, "go to it!"

Lockie carefully placed the pennies on the kip, signalling everyone to stand back. He deftly flicked the kip up and the two pennies flew into the air, the one from the front of the kip leading the way. They almost reached the high ceiling, but then gravity had her way and they dropped quickly on to the stiff rug where they bounced on to the bare floor, and settled, one not quite flat over a crack in the floor boards. The judge stepped forward peering down. The pennies had settled close together, less than a foot apart. "Two heads! Spinner wins!"

Lockie smiled broadly. "Thank you gents," said,. "I may be able to buy a very nice racehorse with this take." He moved to rake in the money sitting on the table. "Anyone else want in?" he asked.

"Double or nothing," said Harry, unperturbed.

"Make it triple!" grinned Lockie, a glint in his eye.

"Well, now, young man," said Harry, standing straight, shoulders back, chin pushed forward, "let's quadruple it!"

"Now gentlemen," intervened the Commissioner, "I can see where this is leading. I don't want to have to deal with any policing matters here, you know."

"You coppers are all the same. Leave them alone. It's up to them. They know what they're doing," said Buck, not a little belligerent.

Lockie straightened his tux. "Look, gents. All I want is for my customers to be satisfied and hopefully return for another wonderful night's game. So if you don't want to go on with this, so be it. But I'm still game."

"Well you should be," said Q.C. "You've got nothing to lose. Harry stands to lose a fortune."

"That's for him to decide, isn't it?" argued Buck.

"You buggers, stop moaning, you're like a bunch of pommies. I know what I'm doing. In fact the odds are in my favour, the longer I play," answered Harry.

"Are we ready?" called Lockie.

"We are!" cried Harry and a few of the other blokes.

Lockie deftly tossed the coins, the judge eager to announce the result. "Two heads! Spinner wins!"

There was a faint cheer from someone who stopped prematurely, for fear the others would not approve. It wasn't clear who was cheering for what or whom.

"Sorry, mate," smiled Lockie. "Guess it's my lucky night."

Silence reigned. As of now, Harry owed Lockie a lot of money.

"I think we'd better call it a night" said Lockie cautiously.

"You're not going again? asked Buck, clearly fooling around.

"Yair, go on! Go again!" urged the Commissioner, having lost all control of himself after tossing down the last of his whisky.

Harry looked around at this tough crew, and that's what they were. He knew that. But so was he tough, that's how he got to where he was now. "So we're up to about $120,000 right?" he asked, eyes wide, cheeks flushed.

"That's right, Harry. You don't have to if you don't want. I'm more than happy to call it quits," said Lockie slyly.

"If I'm not mistaken," said Q.C., "you really do have nothing to lose and Harry has everything to gain so long as he keeps betting."

"Right you are," answered Harry. I have really no choice."

"There's only one thing, Harry. I need to see something that guarantees you can pay up if you lose again," purred Lockie.

"I won't lose. The odds are in my favour. Q.C. said it right."

"An IOU will do." said Lockie.

Harry waved his arm as if to a crowd of spectators. "I'll do better than that. I have a large property in Werribee that I'll put up. It's worth much more than $300,000. Will that do it?" He looked across to Father Zappia who was standing by the Scotch bottle, finishing off the last few dregs.

Lockie did not hesitate one second. "Let's do it!"

"My son," said Father Zappia, "are you-a sure you want to do this? Have you asked God for his permission?"

Harry ignored him. "One small condition, if I may ask?"

"What's that?"

"You give the kip to someone else to flip the coins for you."

"Are you implying that— "

"Implying nothing. It's just that, in anticipation of a big win or loss, we can be sure that nothing untoward has occurred. See my point?"

"He's right," intervened Q.C., "it's a reasonable precaution."

"I agree," said the Mayor. We're all mates here and enjoy our little games. We don't want any hard feelings."

"Fair enough," said Lockie and he handed over the kip and pennies to Buck, the acknowledged gamer of the group anyway.

Buck placed the pennies on the kip and showed the kip around the group to confirm that they were placed properly. Father Zappia stepped forward, scotch and soda in hand, and placed his free hand over the kip, closed his eyes and mumbled something. "Out of the way, Father," ordered Buck, "it's too late for divine intervention now." He tossed them high, so high that one of the pennies hit the ceiling and then seemingly wafted down to the floor where it landed on its mate, causing both to jump and twist before settling down in their own space. They had rolled towards a chair and one had settled under it so that it could not be seen easily from above. The judge, a little old for crouching down because of his arthritis, was unable to get down low enough to pronounce the result. Lockie was about to, but was held back by Buck. Lockie looked around the room. The Commissioner was too drunk to entrust to this small task. The Q.C. a bit doddery as well. So it had to be Timber the Mayor, since Buck seemed to think he had to hold Lockie in an iron grip. "Mister Mayor, would you do the honours please?" he asked.

The Mayor, used to being on his knees for reasons we shall not divulge at this point, quickly knelt down to examine the coins.

"Two heads! Spinner wins again!"

Father Zappia downed his scotch, tossing his head back, looking up as though to Heaven itself. "God has spoken!" he pronounced.

*

Bobby made it to the bridge just in time to cut the engine to idle and glide slowly to shore. There were no cars waiting and no pedestrians either. He wondered now, why the Commiss-ioner had made him bring the ferry across. And Lennie wasn't there, he must have got tired of waiting and gone off. He didn't even bother to lower the gangplank, but revved up the old diesel and started back to Williamstown. Once the ferry was in motion, he ran down the ladder and again looked everywhere, behind every nook and cranny, but found no trace of Monie. He was tempted to return to the Winnebago to ask Lizzie if she'd seen her, but thought better of it. The light was out in it anyway, so she must have decided to turn in. No doubt she'd had a big day, Bobby muttered to himself, disapprovingly. He stood briefly at the gangway surveying the shore ahead, few lights glittering in the drizzle now, a dim half-moon trying to show itself through the dense clouds that hugged the great chimney of the power plant, its black smoke rising then winding its way through the clouds like the mustard gas they showed in the movies of World War I. His leg throbbed, it always did when he was worried. If Monie were lost, or worse, something happened to her, it would be his fault. She was in his care, he should have watched her more closely. But she seemed to be coming out of her drunken stupor when she spied the Commissioner. It was she who told him who it was. So she couldn't have been all that drunk, could she? She was slurring her words, though, but then she only needed a couple of drinks before that happened. He limped back to the bridge and prepared to pull into the Williamstown mooring. He looked across to the car park and saw only his little Imp sitting there under the dim street light. Maybe she was in the Imp fast asleep, he thought.

But it was not to be. She was not in the car, and nowhere to be seen around the car park. He drove around a few of the narrow streets nearby, got out and walked along the chain link fence that surrounded the power plant. It was well kept, no holes in it, so she could not have strayed in there either. Maybe some-one gave her a lift, maybe she went back with Shooter. In any case, he drove the long way back home along Douglas Parade to look for her. Home it was. Still living at home, the one where he had spent most of his childhood after his Dad kicked it, still living there with his sister and Sandy. He pulled up outside the little house on 68 Cecil Street just as Sandy and Lennie were arriving back from their walk.

"G'day Lennie," said Bobby, "long time no see. How come you weren't at the ferry?"

"G'day Bobby. I didn't get the message. I was already on my way here by train. I had to see Sandy on urgent business.

"So she's not with you then?" asked Sandy.

"Nup. She was really sozzled and when we got to the ferry, they were hauling this body out of the Yarra, and after Shooter showed up and there was a big crowd milling around, Monie was making a nuisance of herself...

"As usual..." interrupted Lennie.

Bobby took a deep breath and continued, "...and I told her to get on the ferry because the police Commissioner was there, would you believe it, and last I saw she was walking to the ferry, and the Commissioner ordered me to start up the ferry and drive back to the other side, but then when I did, Monie disappeared and so did the Commissioner, though I think he may have gone back in the police car with Shooter. Maybe she's with him." Bobby sighed and breathed deeply again.

"Not likely," said Lennie, "he's not her favourite person."

"But she's OK with Shooter, isn't she?"

"Yes of course, why wouldn't she be? He's one of your clan and we all love you blokes," said Lennie, almost smiling, a rarity for him.

"She's probably inside with Babs," said Sandy. "Let's not get worried just yet."

Bobby limped along the crumbling concrete footpath to the house. His leg hurt really badly now. Sandy noticed, but said nothing. Lennie was lost in thought, thinking how he would organize all his union contacts to join the big march on the court house to save Clarrie.

But Monie was not inside and Shooter was. He had indeed driven the Commissioner and dropped him off at the Steam Packet pub where he was staying, so he had said. Shooter, of course, had asked no questions. And he had not seen Monie.

"I'll put out a missing person bulletin for her," offered Shooter.

"No, she'll show up," said Lennie, "too early to declare her missing yet. She's done this before, lots of times."

3. Babs' Kitchen

Babs stood at her usual Saturday morning post in the kitchen, cooking bacon and eggs for the men in her house, this morning Sandy and Bobby, and probably Ryley if he could get up early enough and leave his sweetheart whoever she happens to be. Maybe even Lockie would show up, depending on how his card game went. And Lizzie, she showed up once in a blue moon, even though bacon and eggs was her favourite. There was no point phoning her. And if she made a thing of it she knew that Bobby would want to go get her. She stared blankly at the frying pan.

Bobby was limping badly last night, so there must be something worrying him. I can always tell. It's such a tragedy that leg of his. Such a strapping, healthy young boy he was, and to think that our Mum, bless her soul and she needs a lot of it, cut off his toe, just because his whining got on her nerves. But she denied it until the day she died, right in this house in the front room were we all party. She was lying on that old couch, and she feebly beckoned to me with her dreadfully thin arm, the empty skin of it hanging several inches down like a pelican's bill, and when I bent down, she grabbed me by the ear and pulled me down to her mouth. "Don't ever tell Bobby about his toe. Remember, you promised, it's our secret, please, I know we've had our differences, but you were like the sister I never had, I love you so much, please don't tell." Her hand let go my ear and flopped to her side, hanging down from the couch, her dead fingers just touching the old wood floor. And that was it, she was gone. And good riddance. She made life hell for us all, but especially Bobby. What she did to him was truly unforgivable.

The smoke rising from the toaster jolted Babs back to life. She caught it just in time. The boys liked it a little burnt anyway.

She turned back to the eggs and flipped over half of them, the others she carefully removed with her old spatula on to a plate warming in the oven. She heard the toilet flush and Bobby shuffled into the kitchen, rubbing his eyes. He hadn't changed one little bit, just like a little kid. But Babs had decided that it was time to tell him the truth. What he'd been told was that he had cut this toe on a metal tent peg and it had sliced through the bone. So he was running around the paddocks, no shoes of course like all the others, playing cricket, with the toe just hanging on by a bit if flesh. So at last when he went to Major Mum, she decided to fix it properly and just cut off the toe hanging there by a piece of skin. That's what she said. But the thing was, we never did find the toe that she says she "set free." None of this is true, except for the part that she cut the toe off. It wasn't hanging by a piece of skin. She cut the whole damn thing off with a carving knife. That's what she did. I saw the knife with the blood on it there on the folding table in the caravan. What I didn't see was the toe.

"You want your eggs over or what this morning darl?"

Bobby plopped down on one of the old chrome chairs, his head buried in his hands, his elbows on the table.

"Well, what is it? What's the matter with you? Drank too much last night after I went to bed?"

"Leave me alone, sis. No, I don't have a hangover. I went straight to bed as soon as I got back from the ferry."

"Then why is your leg acting up?"

"How'd you know?"

"I know you like you were my own son—and speak of the devil, I think I hear him coming in."

"Mum?"

"Ryley?"

" Got any eggs for me?"

"What do you think?"

Ryley squeezed his lanky body on to a chair at the table. His gorgeous hair was all over the place, just how Babs liked it. How she and Sandy produced such a handsome boy and voluptuous daughter were two of God's miracles.

More people began to show up. Sandy's union mates came and congregated in the front room, woke Lennie, asleep on the couch, and he wandered into the kitchen following the rich aroma of bacon, once forbidden to him, now his favourite.

"Ryley, get everyone a cup of tea, please. And would you check the toaster?" asked Babs, trying not to sound like the Major.

Sandy, already dressed in his old jeans and hip *El Che* tee-shirt appeared at the kitchen door.

"Darl, would you turn the toast, please? And you want your eggs over, right?" asked Babs.

"OK. Thanks luv," he answered, "so has Monie shown up yet?"

"She's missing? I thought uncle Bobby took her to the ferry last night?" said Ryley.

"I did," mumbled Bobby, "but I lost her."

"Wasn't Lennie there to pick her up?" Ryley asked.

"I'm here," said Lennie. "I wasn't there, came here on the train."

"Oh, sorry, Lennie, didn't notice you, too busy shovelling in my eggs and bacon."

"Not to worry."

"So why are you here and Monie isn't?" insisted Ryley showing the brashness of youth.

"That's the big question," came a loud voice from the living room.

"That you Shooter? Come for some breakfast?" called Babs.

"If you don't mind."

Of course Babs didn't mind. She didn't mind being the chief cook and bottle washer, did she? "So hadn't you better go and find her? That's your job isn't it?" she asked.

"I was waiting till I got here, thought she'd be here with the rest of you. I'll put out an all-points bulletin as soon as I've had me brekkie."

"She'll show up, I'm, sure of it," said Lennie. "She probably flaked out under a bush somewhere down near the ferry road. Anyway, that's where I'd suggest you look for her."

Shooter looked askance. "Isn't that what you should be doing?" he said as Lennie passed him his bacon and eggs which he began to eat from his lap, sitting cross-legged on the floor.

"I can't. Have to get our march on the courthouse organized this weekend. It's going to be a massive demonstration."

"The cops can't do everything for you, you know," lectured Shooter."

"I thought it was the opposite," said Ryley with a grin, "they can't do anything."

"Ryley, that's enough of that uni talk," said Babs, trying this time to sound like the Major.

"Your mother's right," said Sandy, "Shooter does all right by us, don't you Shooter?"

Ryley pushed his empty plate forward and unwound himself from the table. "Yair, trouble is you lot all stick together. Can't trust anyone over thirty, that's what we say."

Sandy as usual said nothing. Babs was about to speak up, but Lennie chimed in.

"Ryley's right. You can't trust the police. They just do the bidding of the bourgeoisie. They're the lackeys of the ruling class."

"Here! Here!" cried Ryley, raising a clenched fist.

"That's enough! No politics in the kitchen!" said Babs, this time really sounding like Major Mum.

Shooter had already gulped down his breakfast and was wiping his plate clean with his last mouthful of toast. "Lennie, you're a shithead. You're asking me to go look for your missus while you do your union organizing." He rose to his feet and moved purposefully to the kitchen sink where he rinsed his empty plate.

"You think I'm not aware of that? The union work is more important, especially this march. It could be the beginning of the revolution, but you wouldn't understand that, would you?"

There was no love lost between Lennie and Shooter. In fact, Lennie despised all cops, regardless of who they were, even Shooter who was his best friend's brother-in-law. All cops reminded him of his childhood and escape from Germany. They unquestioningly did Hitler's bidding, and after the revolution, as Mao made so very clear, they would do the bidding of the workers.

Ryley made his way out of the kitchen, but as he did so, he turned to Lennie and said, "sorry, Lennie, I'm with you most of the way, but you know as well as I do that Marx and Lenin were critical of the unions—they too do the bidding of the bourgeoisie, it's a clever ruse for making the workers think that their condition is improving, when it's really not. They'll always be at the bottom until the revolution. Bye all! Thanks Mum for the brekkie. Got to go to the Baillieu to do some research."

Sandy handed his empty plate to Babs and walked around the table to Lennie who looked down, morbid. "You were young once, remember," said Sandy quietly as he lightly touched his shoulder. The trouble was that Lennie was thinking of his youth right then and that was why he was morbid.

"What's the Baillieu?" asked Shooter as Ryley left.

"It's the library at Melbourne university," said Babs proudly.

"So isn't anyone going to ask me about the body?" asked Shooter as he made to leave.

"We're interested in live people, not dead ones," snapped Lennie, still preoccupied with his internal past.

"Oh, yes," said Babs, "is it anyone we know?"

"Don't know," answered Shooter. "CID moved the body to the city morgue for an autopsy. It wasn't anyone I knew, but its face was half eaten away, so I couldn't really tell."

*

Babs was left with the dishes. The men had departed, Sandy had arranged to meet his union mates at the meeting room at St. Mary's church precinct just down the road. They would have more room there and Father Zappia always let them meet to plan their activities and make the signs for demonstrations. He even provided them with some of the paper and paint needed to make the signs. Babs turned to the kitchen sink. "I'll go down after I've cleaned up here, as usual," she muttered to herself. "Those blokes can't do signs properly anyway. I'll have to do a lot of it all over again." She carefully placed the clean dishes in the rack to dry, wiped her hands on the tea towel, then went to the loo. Pensive, she dawdled here and there, doing a little dusting, straightening up the furniture. Going down to the church, which she still did every Sunday morning for Mass, always made her depressed, though that was not quite the right word, regretful, maybe. She missed her colourful childhood but at the same time wished that it had been different—more like her own two kids' childhood, who wanted for nothing, had fun times with their friends at kindergarten, a stable home and bedroom to come back to each day. She had made sure that their childhood was not a constant battle for survival like hers was. Theirs was a happy childhood, wasn't it? Though she had to admit that she had never asked them whether they thought it was. And now, what was there to show for those happy times? Ryley as a know-all uni student and Lizzie, she'd rather not think about whether she was happy or not. The fact was that Lizzie hardly ever showed up home any more. Hadn't since she quit high school at fifteen. Bobby had kept in touch with her, and always said she was doing great, had a marvellous business of some kind, an event manager for high-flying big shots or something. That's what he said she did. But Babs didn't even know where she lived. Somewhere in Melbourne, Bobby said, but she was always on the move, organizing special functions. On the move all the time. That described Babs' own childhood until her Dad died and they settled here in this little house. She sauntered out of the house and turned towards St. Mary's. You could almost see it from their front gate. It was here that she stood with Major Mum when the priest met them right at the gate, well there's no gate there now, fell off years ago.

He was this handsome priest, I remember him as elegant, tall, carefully combed black hair, flat with hair oil, a perfectly straight part on the right. He was fresh from Italy, spoke beautiful English though with a lovely Italian accent. I can say that now, of course, I didn't have a clue when I was a kid. I just knew it sounded beautiful and wished I could talk like it. Major Mum adored him too, I could see that. She went all silly and tried to speak like she grew up in Toorak. With a plumb in her mouth, as Dad used to say.

"Mrs. Malley," he purred, "nice to-a see you again. I was just coming to see you. I got your message that you-a wanted to speak with-a-me?"

"Oh, Father Zappia, I did. After you told me the story of Saint Catherine, I have something that I want you to see."

"Of course. What is it?"

I tugged at the Major's arm. "What story, Mum? What story?"

"You have not told little Barbara the story of Santa Caterina?"

"She's just a girl, Father. She wouldn't understand."

"I'm thirteen Mum, I can understand a story for God's sake."

"Barbara! How dare you speak like that in front of the Father!" growled the Major.

"Now, now. In fact, there are many stories about Santa Caterina. I just told your Mum one of them because she was very interested when she saw the relic in our church, the only true relic of the church as a matter of fact. Not like in Italy where I come from, where every church even the tiniest has a relic."

"What's a relic?" I asked.

"It's something that is very old, sometimes as old as Jesus himself, something that is-a special, a piece of Jesus' clothing for example. And later, the churches-a collected relics of the Saints, you have-a heard of many of them? Saint Peter? Saint Paul? Saint Francis, many more, and then Saint Catherine."

"They were all killed, weren't they? Had their heads chopped off and hung on a cross too?" I asked with relish.

"Some of them. But in the case of Santa Caterina, she was not killed, but lived a life of chastity and self-denial, said-a she was married to Jesus, and performed miracles. She once floated up the stairs of her house without-a her feet touching the floor. Amazing!"

"That's the story?" I asked, disappointed there was no blood and gore. Mum squeezed my arm till it hurt.

"But it is why I am here, is this not so, Mrs. Frost?"

"It's nice of you to come," said Mum. I started to giggle because she talked so funny.

"And what is it you want to tell me? Perhaps you would rather do it in confession?" We can make a time for it. Little Barbara of course could not come to that."

"I wanted to show you something and ask a very big favour," said Mum.

Father clasped his hands and said, "then show me, if that's want you want to do."

Mum looked down at me, I could tell she didn't want to say anything in front of me. "You remember how you told me of Santa Caterina's thumb?" she said.

Pulling at Mum's hand, I pleaded, "Mum, what are you talking about?"

"Shhh! Go back inside and play."

"I do indeed-a remember. I was telling you that my first priesthood was at the beautiful Basilica of San Domenico in Siena, where they have many relics, including that of-a Santa Caterina's thumb," the priest waggled his thumb in front of my nose, "and also her head."

"Really?" I asked. "They cut them off? Was she still alive?"

"Barbara! Stop it! Go back in the house and play!" ordered the Major.

"Mrs. Frost, I don't mind. It is good for her to-a learn of Santa Caterina. She was a wonderful woman, girl really, who is an excellent example of chastity for all young girls."

I was about to ask what 'chastity' meant, but Mum squeezed my arm so much I yelped instead.

"I wanted to ask you," continued Mum, "how did they manage to preserve the thumb so it did not rot away and leave just the bone?"

"That is the miracle, Mrs. Frost. The people of Siena wanted something to remember her by, so after she died, they cut off her thumb and placed it in a special glass jar, sprinkled it with holy water and placed it under the altar."

"And it never rotted?" I asked, spellbound.

"Never. The flesh is still on the thumb, it looks like the day it was cut off."

Mum suddenly let go of me and rushed back inside the house. I persisted with Father Zappia. "What happened to the rest of her body? Did they cut off other bits as well?"

"Yes, they did, though we do-a not know where all the parts are now. Her head is still in the special chapel of the Basilica of San Domenico, though over the centuries it was kept in a lot of-a different churches, especially one near Rome. And in Siena there is a procession every year on her birthday when the priests carry the head—it's in an ornamental glass-a jar encrusted with jewels—from the Duomo of Siena through the winding streets-a back to the Basilica of San Domenico.

Mum came back, treading carefully, carrying an old Vegemite jar. It was filled with a liquid the colour of water with a touch of lime, looking rather like my pee I thought. She held up the jar in front of the priest's nose.

"This is what I wanted you to see," she said proudly.

Father Zappia squinted and took the jar from her so he could hold it away to focus more clearly. I could see a small object, about the size and colour of a baby witchety grub. I was as puzzled as was the Father.

"What is it?" he asked, dumbfounded.

"I thought you'd guess, Father, after my confession last week.

"Some kind of insect or beetle?"

"Father! How could you? It's my son Bobby's little toe!"

Well, Father Zappia went red from his ears down to his neck, and I'm sure it went a lot further than that, if only I could have looked behind his collar. I stood there, frozen, my mouth wide open, unable to scream or cry.

The story doesn't stop there. Later, after I found out the rest of what Major Mum did, I stopped going to church and only went back after she died, which was a few years ago now. She lived too long, must have been almost ninety. We didn't really know because there was no birth certificate and she always lied about her age. I still remember Father Zappia's blush and he's still at St. Mary's. Sandy teases me about him. Of course, Sandy never goes to church, even though that's where I met him.

Babs bit her lip and sighed deeply. She turned away from the church and headed for Nelson Place instead. She would drop in at the barbershop to see Lockie. That would cheer her up. It took some time to navigate Nelson Place because Babs had lived in Williamstown for so long that she knew just about everyone she met on the street and had to stop and yarn with each one. She knew all the shops and offices intimately, could even tell when a window display had been changed, went inside and chatted with the shopkeepers. They weren't a happy lot. You could tell by the dirty windows and the peeling paint that surrounded them. Nobody came to Williamstown any more. The place might as well be tucked away in the outback. Melbourne has forgotten all about us, she muttered to herself. Thank goodness they have, that's all I can say. And it's just horrible that they're building this ugly high rise supposedly for all the new people moving into Willy. It's right on Nelson Place too. And I know what they're doing. They're going to cram it full of all the new Aussies that never made it out of the migrant hostels that the government in its bloody wisdom decided to close.

The shop right next door to the barber's was the only one in the street that looked like it was thriving. It wasn't a retail business, it was a bookbinders, of all things. It suddenly popped up back in 1963 or thereabouts, run by a nice old man and his wife. The windows were spotless, the black paint shiny and fresh, fresh as it was when first applied just after they moved in. Why they chose Williamstown for this business was anybody's guess and Babs had never asked them. But she always stopped by to chat with Phil and Doris, liked the lovely smell of the glue and freshly cut paper. According to Phil, business was booming now that Monash University was in full swing, and Latrobe Uni was also getting going. The Universities had big and growing libraries, they needed all the journals they acquired bound into volumes. So there was plenty of work. On this morning, though, Doris was not there. It was a few weeks since Babs had popped in. Husband Phil sat on a high stool working on a book cover, applying the glue to attach a solid buckram to what would be a fine, sturdy spine.

"G'day Phil. Where's Doris today?"

"She's not here, they took her away to hospital yesterday." Tears welled up, Phil's eyes red-rimmed. He had been crying a lot.

"Oh, I'm sorry Phil. Is it serious? Is there anything I can do?"

"She had a stroke. They said she wasn't going to make it, or if she did she'd be a vegetable." Phil put down his tools, his hands shaking too much.

"Hey, Phil, here let me help you," said Babs as she moved around the work table and, standing on tip-toe she reached up and placed her arm around his hunched shoulders. It was times like this that she wished she was taller and not the shorty like her Mum.

"I'm sorry, I'll get over it. I have to anyway. Have a lot of work backed up already. Don't know how I'm going to manage it."

"Maybe I could help?" said Babs before she had really thought about it.

"But you don't know the business."

"I could learn. I'm very good with my hands, you know. I've been cooking with them all my life."

And that was how Babs started in her job. Doris passed away in just a few days, and Babs learned the bookbinding trade. Her deft fingers, experienced from mixing and kneading dough, peeling vegetables, crafting pies and pasties, carefully icing cakes, had prepared her well for this trade that demanded flexible fingers, durable hands and strong arms. And as well, she just loved the smell of the glue and fresh paper. That's really what it was.

*

Major Mum had really wanted Babs to name her first child Caterina. She lay on the little cot out in the back sleep-out, the little add-on room that Sandy and Bobby built for her to see her through her last days. It ran almost the width of the little house, which was not much more than a half dozen paces long, and only a few paces wide, like a miniature railroad car. Her emphysema was so bad in the last months she could barely get out of bed, and finally, she just couldn't or wouldn't make the effort. Her voice, that piercing commanding sound of authority, was now just a whisper. Her face, wrinkled into a thousand small folds like those on the squashed silver wrapper of a Cadbury's bar of chocolate, was the colour of dirty washing, the skin stuck directly to the cheek and jaw bones, no flesh there at all.

Babs hurried home from the bookbinders for a bite of lunch and to check on her Mum. She sat beside her in the sleep-out holding her hand, and sipping a cup of tea with the other.

"It's all right, Mum. I'm here," she said, squeezing her bony fingers lightly. And to her surprise they were squeezed firmly back. "What is it Mum?" she asked, "what do you want to tell me?"

"Caterina. I want to see her."

"Mum, her name's not Caterina, it's Lizzie."

The Major tried to lift her head, but had not the strength to do so. But her eyes were wide and alert, unusually so.

"You want to sit up?"

"Yes," she whispered.

Babs found an extra pillow and managed to tuck it behind her back and prop her up. "There, how's that Mum?" she asked.

"Babs, get me that priest."

"Priest? What priest?"

"The one that knows about Bobby's toe."

"The Italian one, Father Zappia?"

"Yes. Is he still there at St. Mary's?"

"Of course. I can get him if you like."

"No, don't leave me. I want to tell you. I can't die before I get it off my chest.

"But we know what you did, Mum. You showed us the toe in the jar. The priest forgave you on behalf of Jesus a long time ago. What else do you want to tell me?"

"Father took it away, didn't he?"

"The toe? Yes, I was there, don't you remember? We met him out the front of the house that day."

"The next day, I went to see him and asked for it back."

"You did? What happened?"

"He told me it was sinful of me to want to keep it and I said that it couldn't be because he told us that day of Saint Caterina's thumb and even her head kept in the church in Siena. You remember that?"

"Mum! I remember of course. What a Saint she was and Father worshipped her, didn't he?"

"Well I said what's the difference and why can't I keep my Saint Bobby's toe?"

"Mum, you didn't!"

"And he said that if I kept it I would go to hell and I said that I couldn't live without it and I didn't care if I went to hell."

"Mum, you didn't! What did Father say?"

"Promise me you won't tell anyone else about this, Babs. Promise?" Her voice, thin and trembling, pleaded in a way that demanded compliance.

"I promise, Mum, really I do."

"I told him he was the one who would go to hell for taking away from me my one cherished possession that meant more to me than anything else in the world. But he said Santa Caterina was a saint and your Bobby isn't, and I said he is to me, and I ran out of the church and he ran after me."

The Major sank back into her pillow, exhausted.

"Mum, take it easy. Here, take a sip of water," said Babs.

"I want you to promise me—"

"What, Mum? Promise you what?"

"That you'll go and get the toe from that bastard of a priest."

"He still has it?"

"Yes, because I went back the next day and asked to see the toe he took from me and after I called him a hypocrite I did confession and made it up to him but I asked him a very big favour, well not so much a favour but offered a solution to our disagreement."

"What, Mum? What?"

"I told him to bless the toe with Holy Water and then it couldn't be sinful to keep it, and especially if he would keep it in a special place in the church."

"Really? Mum, did he do it? I'm amazed he hadn't thrown it away."

"That's the miracle, isn't it? Jesus spoke to him to keep it for me."

"Really? Father told you that?"

"Yes, otherwise why would he have kept it?"

Mum turned her head to the side. Her eyes told me everything. I have never seen such eyes before or since that day. They moved me to tears. I squeezed her hand but it was limp and lifeless. I leaned over and turned her head towards me so I could look into her eyes, tell her I loved her. She moved her lips but her voice was gone, her confession had sucked the life out of her, just like in those medieval wood prints I've seen in the books I've worked on at the bookbinders. The words, the spirits good and bad were streaming out of her open mouth, like I could see them. "Don't worry Mum, I'll take care of it all. I love you, you know that." But I think she was already gone and didn't hear anything I said. It was the first time in many years I'd told her I loved her because the truth is I wasn't sure I did, especially after what she did to Bobby.

And then I wondered. Was there something I did that Lizzie would never forgive me for? Something that caused her to stay away and hardly ever see me? And Bobby. She loved him.

Loved him a bit too much. Maybe she knew all about the toe? And blames me for it?

*

"Good morning! Mrs. Malley, isn't it?"

Babs looked up, startled. She had been sitting on the little front porch, wrapped up in her favourite blanket, one that Major Mum used to have on her bed, thick wool and heavy. She squinted through the light drizzle and saw a tall, lithe man, jogging on the spot, very short shorts, like a footballer's. She rubbed the dark rings around her eyes unable to make out who it was. He didn't look like any of the men she knew around here. He was too thin, not an ounce of fat on him.

"You live around here?" she asked in a most unfriendly manner.

The jogger stopped and stood at the front gate, or where it used to be, now hanging by just one hinge. He breathed deeply, his hands on his hips.

"Mrs. Malley, right?" he repeated.

"Yes, and who are you?"

"May I come forward?"

"No. Stay where you are. I'm not buying insurance, if that's what you're up to. But then I never saw an insurance agent dressed in shorts," she said, trying not to grin at her own joke.

The jogger stopped and took one step towards her. "I'm Detective Striker, Melbourne C.I.D." Striker put out his hand.

"Then you better get going. We don't talk to coppers around here," she said, thinking again of her Major Mum who most certainly didn't like cops, and of course, her Dad had beaten many of them up in his time, and received many beatings in return.

Striker persisted, "your husband is Sandy, is that right?"

"Go on! Get!"

"Your brother, the ferry driver, he fished a body out of the Yarra, that right?"

"Go on! Get!"

"He was the last person to see your friend Monie before she disappeared, Mrs. Malley. Doesn't that concern you?"

"Piss off, copper!"

4. Web of Suspicion

It takes at least a week to organize a demonstration, at least that was what Lennie always said. But Sandy knew better. He could get his people in line in less than a couple of days and it didn't matter whether it was a weekend or not. Preferably, of course, a weekday so they would get time off work, and the powers-that-be didn't dare dock them pay for the time off to demonstrate or they'd get hell from Sandy's boys and threaten a strike that would cripple the docks, cause shortages of staple products, you name it. So when they all met down at St. Mary's meeting room, there wasn't a lot to talk about, except that Sandy told his boys that on Thursday they would be joining their union mates in a march and demonstration up William street to the courthouse. Lennie tried to make a speech about Clarrie and all the great things he'd done, but the blokes got restless. Lennie was a boring bugger, as Sandy knew only too well. And he was full of talk that none of his boys could care less whether it was Marx or Lenin or whoever else. They just jumped at the chance to make trouble and squeeze a few more cents out of the bastards that ran the docks. All they needed to know was that the government, the one they elected to protect the working men like themselves, was in cahoots with the bastards that made money off of their backs. It was trying to take all the money Clarrie's union had collected from his members, and break the union. And if they didn't stop the bastards right now, it was only a matter of time when they'd start in on the wharfies.

"We won't allow it, will we mates?" yelled Sandy, his voice, rarely heard above a mumble, bounced off the plastered stone walls of the old meeting room. "I'll let you know where we'll assemble and at what time after Lennie gets his crowd together," he continued looking across to Lennie. "What we have to do now is make some really good signs so they'll see them on the telly, and practice what we'll call out as we march. Any suggestions?"

"Save Clarrie, kill the cops!" someone yelled.

"The cops are our friends," grinned Sandy. "We can't be saying that on the telly."

"Let's each of us write out on a card what we should chant and then we can go over them and discuss what ones are best," offered Lennie, but this met with cries of derision and Sandy gave him another look as if to say, "I told you so."

Lennie finally got the message. He whispered to Sandy, "I think I'd better go. There's a train in ten minutes leaving from Williamstown Beach. I'd better get back and start doing the phone calls around all my union contacts. Once we get then all together, I'll leave it to your boys to lead the chants and the rest of us can join in."

Sandy was about to ask whether he was going to do anything more to find Monie, but he thought better of it. Anyway, she'll probably be home when Lennie gets there, he thought.

*

Babs pressed her nose against the shop window of the bookbinders. The neat display of rare books, the rich leather bindings, she had spent a couple of days getting it just right. And she'd made some nice curtains light cream lace, fine gold threads woven into them, carefully draped around the edge of the window. She looked forward to Monday when she would arrive early, Phil would be out front sweeping the footpath, keeping everything tidy. "We don't want dust getting into the glue or between the pages," he'd say proudly and they would both get down to work, stitching, cutting, gluing.

She turned towards the barbershop, there was noise, a lot of talk. She noticed Shooter's police car there. Something must have happened. Maybe Shooter had found out whose body it was that Bobby had dragged out of the Yarra, or maybe Sandy had decided to meet with his union boys at the barbershop.

"All right, all right," she yelled as she entered the shop, aping Major Mum, "what's going on? All of you shut up and Shooter tell me what's happened."

Lockie was sitting in one of his two barber chairs, Sandy was standing at the back at the foot of the stairs, holding a beer, Shooter was standing in the middle of the shop, his big frame reflected from the mirror, his face contorted with anger. There must have been a dozen men crammed in the small shop, all holding beers in their hands. They'd been at it for a while, the place had the same atmosphere as the public bar in the Steam Packet pub.

"They're sending me to Geelong," said Shooter.

"Well, what's wrong with that?" said Babs.

"I've been transferred."

"You mean for good?" asked Babs, shocked.

"Right. And it starts tomorrow."

"But that's ridiculous," offered Lockie, "they can't do that."

"The Commissioner can do whatever he likes," said Shooter. "I thought you might be able to do something. I know you know the Commissioner, and I know the Commissioner was sniffing around here the other night."

Lockie adjusted his chair and sat upright. He was particularly cheerful this morning, in contrast to the rest of the crowd crammed in the shop. He'd had an unbelievably good night, some of it at the expense of the Commissioner. But he wasn't about to get involved in this. There was something else going on here, he suspected.

"I did chat briefly with the Commissioner late yesterday evening. He came by for his haircut as usual. I opened the shop just for him. He likes to have his hair cut in private. And he didn't say anything to me about your transfer. There must be some reason, though. He wouldn't do it for no reason. He's a good bloke."

"I bet it's got something to do with this march you bastards are planning," said Shooter, looking around the room, looking for Lennie, but he wasn't there. The room went quiet. It was a signal for Sandy to say something. "We've done lots of marches and demos before, Shooter, there's nothing unusual about all this," he said.

"I don't understand it. My replacement is showing up tonight, and I start my new duties in Geelong first thing in the morning."

"If you don't mind my saying," said Babs, "the only unusual thing that's happened in the last twenty four hours is the body that Bobby pulled out of the Yarra, and you're the cop who attended the scene."

"And the Commissioner was there too," said Shooter.

"And by the way. I had a visit at home from a bloke called Striker, said he was from CID."

"He came to our house?" asked Sandy, dumbfounded.

"He was wearing shorts, would you believe?"

"What did he want?"

"I don't know. He asked about Bobby and the body. And Monie too. I told him to you-know-what."

*

Every Sunday morning Babs got up early, lit the oven and stoked the fire until the temperature was just right which she determined by putting her hand in the oven. She then peeled the potatoes, arranged them around the leg of lamb and put it in to roast while she went to church. Bobby rarely went with her, dismissing church as a place for the sinful, so he didn't need to go. Instead, he took his Sunday morning walk around the block, walking their greyhound that Babs had insisted they take from Lockie who had raced her almost to death, and having lost some money was about to dump her. Babs reckoned that the dumping would be into the Yarra or Hobsons bay, so had taken the animal in, fed her too much, until she was informed by a that you had to walk greyhounds a lot or they got arthritis and died. Surprising her, Sandy offered to take care of the dog and, even more surprising and not a little annoying to Babs, they became quite close friends. In fact Sandy talked much more to the dog than to anyone else, including herself. He had even insisted on naming her Nellie after the famous opera singer, though he had never listened to opera as far as she knew.

On this morning, there occurred a small incident, out of the ordinary because Sandy had done this walk for several years and nothing ever happened that was out of the ordinary. He said good morning to the same people, the same people came past him walking their dogs or on their way to church. He had just turned the corner on Pascoe street and saw across the road in front of the Manchester Unity Hall, an old man, dressed in a tweed suit no less, walking an Irish terrier. It yapped and snapped and made Nellie a little skittish. Not recognizing the couple, Sandy guided Nellie across the road to meet the new dog on the street. The old man looked furtively at him, and began to walk away, dragging the dog that clearly wanted to stay and meet Nellie. By the time Sandy and Nellie came within sniffing distance, the old man was clearly upset with his dog. He pulled and tugged at the dog until the collar choked its bark out of him. Nellie strained to get closer, and Sandy allowed her to take a good sniff.

"Leave my dog alone," the old man cried, "or I'll call the cops!"

Sandy reigned Nellie in, but said nothing.

"Go on! Get out of it!" the old man screamed, then, horribly, he yanked so hard on the leash it pulled the terrier off all fours, yet the old man did not stop there. He let go the leash, ran forward and booted the terrier so hard it flew several feet in the air and landed on top of the small picket fence that lined the Manchester hall. And there it hung, its neck wedged in between the fence palings, kicking in vain to pull itself free. Instead of running to its aid, the old man fled, yelling, "Police! Police! This bastard's killing my dog!" By this time, the terrier was gasping for air, choking to death. Sandy let go Nellie and raced to the fence to free it, but it grappled so hard with its sharp little claws it scratched his hands and arms. Sandy grasped the dog's little torso trying to free its neck from the fence. And at that moment a police car, siren blaring, came screaming around the corner, skidding to a stop. Sandy, taken by surprise, let go the dog and the officer ran over to free it. But it was too late, and the dog expired in the officer's hands.

"I'm arresting you for the wanton and callous abuse of an animal," said the officer.

*

When Babs returned from church Nellie, her leash still attached, was waiting for her at the front door, panting, her thin tongue hanging out the side of her mouth. Until now, Babs had stayed away from Nellie. She was Sandy's girlfriend, you might say, and she enjoyed watching Sandy talk to her, though it still annoyed her that he spoke more to the dog than he did to her. She took Nellie's leash and they walked through the house calling for Sandy "as though he were a dog," smiled Babs to herself. She opened every door until she came to Bobby's room. At first she hesitated, but then said to Nellie, "come on Nellie, your mate might be in here, God knows why, but we better look." She ferreted around in a kitchen drawer and found a key and unlocked the door. Bobby's room was the same he had since he was a kid, he just never left home, the small single bed the same one he had as a boy. Sandy wanted to buy him a new one, but Bobby refused, even though his long legs poked way out the foot of the bed. But what really surprised Babs was that there was barely any room to enter because the entire room was packed full of shoe boxes, every inch of the floor covered except for a narrow passage to the bed, right up to the ceiling. "Holy Jesus," she exclaimed to Nellie, "he's been at it again!" She returned to the kitchen, closing the door behind her.

Sandy was not to be found. It wasn't like him. He could hardly wait for Sunday roast, as could the rest of the family who no doubt would drop by any minute. Babs was about to call Shooter, but then remembered that he was gone to Geelong already. She took the roast out of the oven, worried that it would be overcooked, waited half an hour and finally decided to go look for him. Maybe he'd had a heart attack or something. She looked down at Nellie who returned a knowing look. "If only you could talk," said Babs. They walked out to Cecil street just as Bobby's little blue Imp pulled up.

"Sandy's gone!" Babs cried, "Nellie's here but he isn't."

Ryley stepped out of the car and ran to his Mum. "It's OK Mum, there's nothing to worry about."

"What do you mean? What's happened? Has he had a heart attack?" pleaded Babs.

"Nah, nothing like that. He's in gaol," answered Ryley trying to be calm.

"How'd he get there? What's he done?"

Ryley looked to Lockie. "Tell her, Lockie. The bastards!"

"Looks like the cops are trying to frame him," said Lockie.

"What for?"

"Animal abuse and cruelty."

"And he's in gaol for that?" Babs said angrily.

Lockie had more to tell. "And they reckon he's been stealing stuff from the docks. They're holding him until they formally bring charges in court tomorrow. I was there when the J.P., a friend of mine, signed off on it. That's how I knew. I phoned Ryley and we went right down to the police station."

"And Bobby?" asked Babs. "Where is he? How'd you get his car? I have to speak with the bugger. All this is his bloody fault, I know it."

"Bobby was here, wasn't he?" asked Ryley, that's what Dad said."

"Bobby's not in his room, I can tell you that. He's been there though. They beat Sandy up, didn't they? I know those bloody cops. Dunno what we're going to do now with Shooter down in Geelong."

"Dad's got a bit of a black eye, but I think he's OK," said Ryley, "at least that's what the J.P. told us. They wouldn't let us see him."

"It's because of the demo on Thursday," said Babs.

"Your guess is as good as mine," said Lockie, "but they seemed more interested in the stuff they reckon he stole from the dockyards."

"No guess needed," said Ryley always looking for a conspiracy, "the bloody cops are tools of the ruling class. They're trying to stop the march by making all these false charges, but it won't work. There's going to be a national strike now, whether or not Dad's in the lock-up."

"So where's Bobby, then?" persisted Babs.

"He stayed back to talk with Sandy about some deal they were working on," said Lockie.

"There's something going on," said Babs. "They're up to something, the two of them, and I know what it is."

"What, Mum?" asked Ryley.

"Never you mind."

*

At Monday morning Magistrate's Court, Sandy was brought before the J.P. The new senior constable, Stanford Lane, stood up, tugged at the bottom of his policeman's jacket. All of five feet eight, it was a wonder he had made it past the height requirements of a police officer. As if aware of this handicap, he constantly raised himself on to the balls of his feet and back to his heels, as he accused Sandy of the callous killing of a defenceless little dog, on a public street in broad daylight no less, grabbing the dog away from an old man who was minding his own business, then breaking its neck on a picket fence.

The old man, deliberately unshaven no doubt, still dressed in his tweed suit, sat forlornly beside Constable Lane, his mouth drooping, eyes red from crying, or so that was the impression intended.

"The poor old man sits beside me, your honour, and I have here for the court his signed affidavit that attests accordingly."

The J.P. peered out from his rimless glasses to look down on Sandy, standing in the dock. Sandy had been here many times before, so it wasn't as though he was scared by the proceedings.

"What do you have to say for yourself, Mr. Malley?"

"It's all a pack of lies, your honour."

"A pack of what? Speak up man."

"Lies! It's all lies, as usual," mumbled Sandy.

"And you deny the charges as usual, Mr. Malley. Senior Constable Lane, what physical evidence do you have?"

"None present, your honour."

"The dead dog?" asked the Justice.

"It's been disposed of, your honour, for sanitary reasons."

"No doubt. It's a matter of he said–he said," mumbled the J.P. straight faced. "Case dismissed."

Lockie, sitting at the back if the court, smiled and left. Things could be made to work, even with Shooter gone.

*

Bobby went to his bedroom and found it locked. He considered breaking it down, but then remembered that Babs kept all the keys in the kitchen cupboard, in the tin marked flour. He tipped the keys on the kitchen table and began trying each one in turn. But none of them worked. It was midday and Eurie was covering for him at the ferry. He opened the fridge looking for something to eat, but found nothing except beer, so he opened a can and sat, glum, sipping it out of the can, a large one at that. Babs would be home any minute, he mused, then there would be hell to pay. She had always threatened that she'd have Sandy kick him out of the house if he ever brought stuff home. But it was such a great opportunity he couldn't resist, and anyway, he couldn't have pulled it off without Sandy's help. Unfortunately, someone had tipped off the cops and he had to find somewhere quick to unload it all.

It all happened when Banger, Sandy's brother and enforcer, signalled to him as the ferry pulled in to the Willy side. Bobby came down from the bridge to give Eurie a hand with the moorings. Banger ran up the gang plank dodging the cars as they came down.

"Banger? What are you doing here? I thought you and Sandy were busy with the demo," called Bobby.

"G'day Bobby. Yair, we are, but an opportunity came up to make a few bucks and we couldn't resist it."

"Yair, sure. What's going on?"

"Sandy said you may be able to help me."

"Do what?" asked Bobby.

Banger looked around to make sure there was nobody listening. "You see that van down there?"

"The white combie van?"

"Yair. Well it's got a few thousand dollars' worth of merchandise in it."

"So?"

"It came straight off a ship this morning, avoided the customs house, and now we need to hide it while Lockie finds a buyer."

"So why doesn't Sandy store them?" asked Bobby, annoyed.

"He said his missus wouldn't allow it," replied Banger.

"Well, I dunno what he's talking about. I live in his house, what can I do?" said Bobby, perplexed.

"You could keep them on the ferry, and we could send buyers to you," suggested Banger.

"What kind of merchandise?"

"High end, very classy Italian shoes," announced Banger proudly.

"There's no room on the ferry. Surely you can see that."

"What about the Winnebago?" asked Banger.

"What about it?" Bobby replied, still annoyed.

"Sandy said you know the owner and could make a deal."

"And what if the owner drives off the ferry?" asked Bobby.

"Look, I got to get rid of them. The cops from Melbourne have been snooping around. And the combie van is hot. We swiped it just for the job. I reckon someone has snitched. They've suddenly transferred Shooter to Geelong, so we don't have his cover any more. If you don't help me, Sandy's going to get caught as well."

'They moved Shooter out?" Bobby was incredulous.

"Yeh. He's bloody crooked on it," said Banger.

"Sandy knows, of course?" asked Bobby.

"Well, that's another story," said Banger with a sigh.

"What do you mean?"

"He's in bloody gaol."

"What? You're kidding!" Bobby gasped.

"Nope. They got him on animal cruelty of all things, said Banger."

"This is ridiculous!" cried Bobby again.

"Lockie's trying to get him out right now."

"All right then. Bring the van on to the ferry, park it next to the Winnebago," sighed Bobby.

There were only a couple of cars waiting. He signalled them on and guided them to park on the west side away from the Winnebago. Banger drove the combie van up and parked it right by the Winnebago. In no time, Bobby had the gangplank up and the ferry was on its way. He ran down and hopped in big strides across the deck to the Winnebago. He knocked and a faint voice answered, "just a minute."

Lizzie opened the door and poked her head out. "Bobby, I'm busy right now," she said.

"No you're not. It's too early in the day. We need your help. Your Dad said to ask you."

Lizzie opened the door further and saw the combie van crammed full of shoe boxes. "Don't tell me Dad's been up to his tricks again," she said, amused but annoyed.

"G'day Lizzie, lovely to see you again," smiled Banger, who, running his finger through his close cropped hair, like most men, couldn't help surveying the entire length of her body as she stepped down from the Winnebago.

"Bobby," she said, ignoring Banger, "I've told Dad I'm not getting involved in any of his crazy schemes. It's too risky for me as I'm sure you understand."

"Of course I do, luv, but he's your Dad and he's in a fix."

"Well he'll have to get out of it himself this time."

"They've got him in bloody gaol," said Banger.

"Too bad. What's he done this time? Swiped a car from the docks or something?"

"It's shoes," answered Banger, nodding to the van, "lovely shoes too, ones you would like."

"Not a van full of them. You mean they already got him locked up for pinching these shoes and you want me to take them? You're a pair of bloody idiots!" complained Lizzie.

"Nah, they got him on a trumped up charge for kicking his neighbour's dog in the guts and strangling it or something like that, so the boys down the pub told me."

Lizzie burst out laughing. "Has Williamstown gone mad? Dad wouldn't hurt a fly! He's the gentlest man I know, and believe me, I know men."

Bobby, embarrassed, went a little red in the face. He almost said, "I bet you do," but managed to hold it back. "Please Lizzie, we've got to get these shoes out of the van. The cops are surely looking for it as we speak."

Lizzie was about to pull back and close the door when a muffled voice came from inside. "You better help them out Lizzie, he's your Dad after all." It was Lockie.

"Lockie, what the hell are you doing in there?" asked Bobby, now really annoyed.

"Lizzie and I have been transacting some business that need not concern you, at least not yet. Come on let's get the merchandise loaded."

Lockie pushed past Lizzie who looked askance, shrugged and said, "I give up. You blokes are impossible. But it's only this once, and it has to be driven off immediately we get back to the Willy side."

Bobby returned quickly to the bridge to manage the approach to the Port Melbourne side. Once there, he dashed down to tie up the ferry and drop the gang plank. They furiously worked to transfer the shoes to the Winnebago. Lizzie, unusual for her, walked across the ferry and watched the cars roll off. She stood at the edge of the ferry, her tall slender figure, poised as always on high stiletto shoes, a light beige raincoat hugged tightly around her body, the chilly breeze and occasional spots of rain pushing against her face, pale from lack of sunlight, hair blowing in the wind. The beauty of his niece reduced Bobby to water, his knees buckling under him as he tried to carry armfuls of shoes, eyes fixed on her figure rising to the sky, a match to the tall chimney of the power plant across the other side of the Yarra.

"Bobby. Come on. She's your niece, remember," prodded Lockie.

"No kidding? And what were you doing in there with her?" retorted Bobby, clearly upset.

"Nothing you wouldn't do," teased Lockie.

"Asshole. You better not have—"

"Just kidding, Bobby. Calm down. We were doing some business, that's all. I'm helping her out with her finances."

"I bet you are." Bobby plonked down an armful of shoes and turned to grab Lockie by his collar.

"Bobby, for Christ sake!"

Banger stepped between them. "Come on mates, let's get this job done. We don't want to draw attention to us, do we?"

Bobby stepped back, pushing Lockie just a little. "This isn't over," he said, then hopped on over to raise the gang plank and collect fares from the cars parked neatly on the deck.

But it was over. By the time they got back to the Williams-town side, Bobby had calmed down and Lockie had remained standing at the front of ferry, the wind blowing into his face, the salt water from Hobsons Bay spraying him from time to time. Since his big win at two-up the world had been very good to him. Once the ferry was moored, he shook hands with Bobby and walked off across the car park and down one of the small streets.

Banger drove the combie van away and would dump it some place. Bobby walked to the phone box in the car park and phoned Eurie to come and take over. And after one more trip across and back, Eurie was there and Lizzie drove off the Winnebago, Bobby sitting beside her in the cabin. He could think of nowhere else he'd rather be.

"Where are we taking this crazy load, then?" Lizzie asked as she shifted gears.

"The only place I can think of is where I always used to stash my merchandise."

"Where's that, then, uncle Bobby?"

"In my bedroom back at your place."

"You mean Mum and Dad's place. I don't live there."

"Yair, of course you don't. You know what I mean though."

"Yes, of course I do," she grinned, "but Mum's not going to be pleased. I remember her laying down the law to you and Dad that you were never to bring stuff home into her house, because she wasn't going to gaol even if you two were."

"Yeh. She did. That was a long time ago, when you were a growing girl," said Bobby still eyeing her over.

"All right then, it's home we go!" Lizzie changed gears again and the Winnebago tilted as they turned the corner into Douglas Parade.

5. Hairless Bodies

Tuesday morning. There had been a small disagreement. A lot of Sandy's boys did not want to march all that way from Flinders Street station to the courthouse. If they were going to have a day off work, they wanted to have a good day off and go to the pub or visit relatives, just like they do weekends. Doing the march all that way as well as a demonstration outside the Industrial Court wasted a good day, they said. Sandy had informed them that O'Shea was due to appear in court at 11.00 a.m., so they wanted to sleep in and have a leisurely breakfast, then show up at the courthouse five or ten minutes before the hearing. Sandy did not resist, even though Banger, his younger brother and enforcer wanted to flex his muscles against Sandy's wish. He forbade any physical coercion, a prohibition that Banger routinely ignored, once Sandy was out of sight. So the boys would show up at Flinders Street station and march the whole way. Besides, Banger well knew that Sandy never went to these things. His job, he always said, was to work behind the scenes. Besides, Sandy was sure after having met with Clarrie on the ferry this morning, that the really important part of this union uprising, its show of solidarity as Ryley kept harping on about, would be the days following the trial, especially if they put Clarrie in Her Majesty's infamous Pentridge prison. This was certainly what Lennie was banking on.

The meeting with Clarrie that morning on the ferry had been brief. Sandy, accompanied by Ryley who insisted on being there, not only promised all his boys would show up and make lots of noise like wharfies were expected to do, but that if they put Clarrie in prison, he would call a national wharfies strike which would remain in effect until they released him. He should tell that to the press and repeat it as often as he could, especially if one of the TV people interviewed him.

"Solidarity! That's what it's all about. Solidarity!" announced Ryley.

"Don't say that to the press," advised Sandy, "it sounds too commo-like and they'll paint us all as communists."

"But we are communists," said Clarrie.

"You are, but I'm not and neither are most of my boys. The press and most Aussies don't like communists, as I'm sure you know, Clarrie."

"It's totally unfounded," said Ryley.

"We're not a threat. We're out to better the lives of the working class which is most Aussies," replied Clarrie.

"If I'm to start a national strike and keep it going, commo talk has to be kept out of it, otherwise we'll lose public support and the national strike will fail."

"That's if a strike is necessary," said Ryley.

"Believe me son, Clarrie's going to Pentridge and if Lockie were here he'd bet on it."

Clarrie and Ryley shook hands with Sandy and walked down the gangplank to the waiting bus full of protesters, some still working on their signs. Sandy, remaining on the ferry, waved and looked up to the bridge where Bobby stood looking down. All the cars and bikes were loaded and Eurie was already raising the gang plank. He eyed the Winnebago and took a step towards it, but changed his mind. Instead, he made for the bridge where he would chat with Bobby, see if there had been any more news on Monie and the dead body.

*

On Thursday 15th of May, the morning of the Great March, Lennie was pecking away at his tea and toast when he heard a knock at the door. Still in his pyjamas, he gulped down a mouthful then went to see who it was. The arrangements were that they would all meet at Flinders street right outside the station at ten o'clock. They would then march down Flinders street and up William street to the Magistrate Court where the Industrial Court met. And there, they would give them hell. Expecting one of the union bosses from Sydney or Newcastle he opened the door, but instead he was confronted by a uni-formed police officer.

"What do you want? Have they sent you to stop the march? You can't arrest me for anything," snarled Lennie, licking a piece of scrambled egg stubbornly clinging to the corner of his mouth.

"Sir, are you Mr. Leonard Stalinsky?"

"What's it to you?"

"Sir, said the officer politely, a small notebook in hand, a small hand for an officer, an officer almost too short to be one. He opened the notebook, withdrawing a photograph and asked again, "sir, are you Leonard Stalinsky?"

Lennie saw it was a very old photograph of Monie, taken some years ago, probably one from the files of *The Age* on a day he remembered well, one of Monie's rare appearances at one of his marches, the huge demonstration against the Vietnam war.

"I'm Lennie. And I don't think that's my wife Simone. It's a very old photo if it is. What's it to you? Is she all right? She's been gone a few days. Have you found her?" His face went red with a mixture of anger and grief, the tell-tale beads of sweat appearing on his shiny forehead.

"I'm sorry to have to report, sir, that we found a body that we think is the person in this photograph, washed up on the shore of St. Kilda beach, well, not exactly that beach, the beach more towards Port Melbourne, along Beaconsfield Parade."

Lennie's demeanour suddenly changed. It was a biological condition that returned him to his childhood, possibly something learned in those dreadful days in Berlin. All emotion was gone, his brain and body became robotic.

"You're sure it's her?" he asked mechanically. "Would you like to step in for a cup of tea?"

"No sir, thank you. We are not sure it's her and that's why we need you to come down to the mortuary to identify her."

"But I can't. I'm just finishing my breakfast, and I have a lot of things going on this morning, all day in fact."

"I'm well aware of that," said the officer with a slight air of superiority.

"I'll come down at eight o'clock this evening. In any case, the photo doesn't look like her."

The officer stared at Lennie's bald head and the beads of sweat, which Lennie now wiped away with his arm. He opened his mouth to speak, but nothing came.

"Come on in for a cuppa," continued Lennie, "you look like you could do with one. And if you like you can stay and meet some of the demonstrators who'll be congregating here very soon."

"Well I—"

"Come on!" Lennie grabbed the officer by his arm and ushered him in. "You blokes don't have a union yet, do you? I bet you've got plenty to gripe about. Overtime pay, working conditions, low salaries, no women on the force..."

*

Flinders Street Station was jammed full of people on any weekday morning, let alone with hundreds of demonstrators milling around the big stone steps at the Flinders street entrance. The bus from the ferry stopped right on the corner, effectively clogging the traffic at the intersection, backing up cars all the way to Spencer street and who knows how far both ways on Swanston street. Banger was first out of the bus followed by Ryley. Then Clarrie appeared and immediately there was a roar from the crowd and the chant began. "Free Clarrie! Free Clarrie!" Banger surveyed the crowd looking for cops. There was just one, probably the regular one who was there every weekday morning. He looked for troublemakers, there were usually a few no matter what the demo, sent by that bastard Bjelke-Petersen from Queensland. And sure enough, he spied a bunch of them, still wearing their shorts as if they were still up there in banana land, their heavily sun-tanned faces with big smart-ass grins.

Clarrie raised his hand to speak. The crowd went quiet. That was easy, thought Banger. It was going to be an easy crowd to work with.

"Workers! Mates you are!" Clarrie shouted, "I thank you for showing up today! It's not just me that Gorton and that cur Kerr want to put away, it's all of us dinkum hard working blokes. They'd chain us to our jobs and pay us nothing if they could get away with it!"

"Rah! Rah! Free Clarrie! Free Clarrie!" Came the chant.

"We love our country! We despise its rulers!" Clarrie shouted again, "follow me to the battle!"

"Rah! Rah! Free Clarrie! Free Clarrie!"

Clarrie stepped down from the bus and Sandy's boys followed. Banger grabbed Clarrie and steered him through the crowd, around the bus that had already nosed its way into the traffic, out to the middle of Flinders street on to the tram tracks.

"This way," he called, his big frame rising above the fray. He gave Clarrie, who wanted to address the crowd some more, a bit of a nudge along the tram tracks. Frail, weak from starvation, Clarrie's steps were uncertain, even timid. And he didn't like crowds, they scared him. But Banger loved them and managed them with great skill. "Move it Clarrie," he called. "We need to get up momentum, get them marching forward. There'll be plenty of time for a speech when we get to the courthouse. Lead on Clarrie!"

They marched as planned, down Flinders Street along the tram racks, forcing trams to stop, until they turned into William Street. Banger sent a couple of his men forward to direct traffic, waving red handkerchiefs to stop the cars, move them to the side. The drivers were not happy, tooted their horns, yelled at them telling them to go back to work like everyone else. Ryley screamed back at them calling them scabs and all sorts of nasty names. He brandished a sign that said GUT GORTON. Banger told him to shut up or he'd get run over and that would mess up the whole point of the demonstration, especially for the TV people. "Go to the back. See if you can find Lennie, he always brings up the rear," he commanded Ryley with a grin. "You're the only bloke who can understand him anyway."

The chill of the May morning was beginning to lift and Clarrie was getting a little over heated. He felt the sweat trickling from his arm pits, ran his hand through his thinning grey hair and felt the sweat even there. Reluctantly, he removed his suit coat, slung it over his back and walked faster than he would have liked. It revealed more fully his white shirt that his wife had carefully ironed for him this morning before breakfast, and the black tie with the thin red stripe and his old Christian Brothers School crest, the tie he wore on every special occasion.

Banger now raced ahead and stopped at Lonsdale street, directing the mob towards the Supreme Court. "We'll assemble at the Supreme Court and you can make your good-bye speech in supreme surroundings," he informed Clarrie.

Clarrie did as he was told. They assembled outside the Supreme Court complex and Clarrie stood up on a folding stool that one of Banger's boys had brought for the purpose. The crowd filled the entire intersection of William and Lonsdale streets, completely blocking the traffic, chanting in unison, nearly as good as the Red Choir.

"Free Clarrie! Free Clarrie!"

Banger called for silence, cars honked in the background. Clarrie raised his arms in a V, his palms facing out. He had seen RFK, his American Hero, do that on the news just before they shot him.

"Workers! Fellow Workers! This is a great day! This is the day when we unite and say No! No! No! We will *not* be threatened, we will *not* be silenced, we are *not* insects! We are workers!"

The mob nearly became a mob right then, and Banger had to signal to his boys to control some of the more boisterous. They had already quietly removed Petersen's bunch of idiots by giving them money to buy themselves a few beers at one of the pubs along the way. Clarrie continued.

"Let me walk alone across the road to the court house. There, I will speak for all workers. I will refuse the oath, I will refuse to present the union books, I will call the proceedings for what they are, a disgusting demonstration of Gorton's tyranny and Kerr's duplicity!"

Amid cheers and chants, slaps on the back accompanied by "G'd-on-ya mate" Clarrie jumped down from his stool and pushed through the crowd across the road to the courthouse on William street. He stopped, turned to the crowd, once more raised his arms high, and called, "wait for me at Pentridge!"

This was the moment that Sandy's boys had been waiting for. Sandy had disbursed to them, out of union funds, a generous demonstration allowance that they planned to spend at the Metropolitan pub a few hundred yards down William street. Ryley quietly disposed of his sign by sliding it under a parked car, and headed off to the Uni where he had a political science tutorial. Out of the corner of his eye he saw Lennie talking to a bloke who looked very much like a plain-clothes cop.

On this historic day, Thursday 15th of May, Clarrie did all he said he would in court and was promptly arrested and transported to Pentridge prison. The boys at the Metropolitan pub had tossed down quite a few by then, and they announced that they would march to Pentridge and demand Clarrie's release. But when Banger informed them that Pentridge was way out in Coburg, they decided to stay put. It was what Sandy wanted, because there were bigger things in the air.

*

Thursday was Albert Park day. Every Thursday Paul Striker, renowned detective of Melbourne's crack C.I.D. jogged from his house on Page Street, Middle Park turned left on Armstrong Street, crossed Canterbury Road and into Albert Park, then around the lake, past the golf course and back home again. A quick shower, followed by tea and plain yoghurt with wheat germ and he was ready for work. Striker loved his work, and every morning during his run, he cherished the time to be alone with his thoughts, plan his next moves, should such planning be necessary, depending on the case. The trouble was that, after talking with the Commissioner, a rare event when just a washed up body was involved, he wasn't sure what exactly the case was. The Commissioner had opened their meeting yesterday with questions about the body fished out of the water beside the Williamstown Ferry, but had quickly moved on to the pending demonstration by the unions and a bunch of rebel-rousers. In particular, he seemed to be most concerned with Lennie Stalinsky's role in it. Why should this matter, Striker wondered, since it was no secret that Stalinsky was a communist which wasn't a crime in Australia anyway. He would much rather be down in Williamstown interviewing people about the body. The Commissioner had insisted, though, that there might be some connection, and that Stalinsky should be taken to the morgue to identify the second body that washed up on the beach near Beaconsfield Parade, which, the Commissioner theorized, might be the body of Stalinsky's wife, Simone who had gone missing.

As he and Lennie Stalinsky stepped out of the unmarked car in front of the Melbourne metropolitan morgue, Lennie asked, "do we really have to do this detective? I told the officer that the old photo didn't look like her."

"What officer was that?" asked Striker, puzzled.

"I don't know. Officer Lane, I think. That was his name. He came to my door and asked me to identify her from a photograph and I said I didn't know because it was an old worn photo and couldn't tell."

"But your wife is missing, isn't she?"

"I suppose so."

"What do you mean by that?"

"Well, she goes missing ever now and again. She's an alcoholic, you see."

"So you never reported her as missing?"

"No. I did not. She usually turns up. Officer I don't want to look at this dead body. You have no right to make me."

"Mr. Stalinsky, I know this is difficult for you. But I have to cover every possible avenue in any investigation."

"Of what? Me and the communist party?"

"No. Not at all. A body has been fished out of the water by the Williamstown Ferry. And now another one by St. Kilda pier. We are simply trying to find out who they are and whether they are connected in any way."

"And the first person you come to is me?"

They were about to enter the morgue when a voice from across the street called out, "Mr. Stalinsky? I'm Ernie from *The*

Age. Is it true that the communists are organizing a national strike to force the government to release O'Shea?"

Lennie stopped, but Striker squeezed his elbow and eased him forward. "We need to get this done," he muttered.

"The body they fished out of the Yarra at Williamstown, was it a union boss?" called the reporter, now almost beside them.

"I don't know anything about that," replied Lennie.

"The identity of that person is still unknown," said Striker.

"What's going to happen now that O'Shea's in Pentridge?" called the reporter.

"How would I know? I have nothing to do with the unions," said Lennie, a slight smirk on his face. "Now if you don't mind, I have to accompany the officer here." For once he was glad to be taken by a cop. Striker opened the door and ushered Lennie through. The reporter tried to follow, but Striker held him at bay saying, "sorry, reporters not allowed." The reporter meekly obeyed.

They walked through a set of swinging doors, down a long passage, to the receiving room. then into a cavernous room, cold as a refrigerator. Striker showed his ID to the assistant at the desk who said, "the boss is inside. He's got the new one. That makes three, in just a few days. Tickled pink he is."

Lennie shivered. "Striker, you can't do this to me. I know you're only doing this for effect, whatever it is you want."

Striker ignored him. "Wait here," he said and Lennie obeyed, but he wanted to turn and run.

Police medical examiner and coroner Dr. Borst Cordner stood poised over a body, his saw at the ready. "You're just in time to see the fun," he said, a grin from ear to ear, and they were tiny ears connected to a fat round face, sitting on a squat rotunda, draped in a tightly fitting dark green hospital gown. "We've got a new one just came in."

Striker looked down. It was the body of a young woman, her hair totally shaved off. "Did you shave her head or did she?" he asked, immediately realizing the foolishness of what he said.

"Paul, don't be a dumb-ass. If I shaved it, there would be no nicks. It's a rough and ready shave, in fact looks more like a sheep looks after it's been sheared. Someone else did it, and it was done after her throat was cut, so I doubt that she did it."

"Slit with a razor, then?

"Probably."

"And before her head was shaved?"

"Yes.

"She was fished out of the Yarra, right?"

"Close. Actually off the end of Gem Pier in Williamstown."

"OK. I'll look to that one in a minute. We're here to see the other one washed up at St. Kilda beach."

"That was number sixty-three, I think. Over here. As a matter of fact, I have some new information about her."

"What's that?"

"I think that she was probably dumped in the Yarra somewhere near Williamstown too. There was mud in her gut and under her finger nails. I'd know Yarra mud anywhere, especially the dark black mud that's more common on the Williamstown side of the Yarra towards Hobsons Bay."

"Mr. Stalinsky," called Striker, "over here please."

Cordner pulled out the big drawer and out came the body. Striker held Lennie gently by the elbow as the coroner pulled back the sheet.

Lennie remained expressionless, his lips drawn tightly together. Beads of sweat appeared on his shiny forehead as usual. "It's not her," he said, "It's not Simone."

"You're sure, you're very sure?"

"Even without the hair. I'm sure."

"Any idea how it might have happened, Mr. Stalinsky?"

"Her throat was cut, obviously," answered Lennie facetiously, "how would I know? I told you, it's not Monie. She was supposed to show up at the Willy ferry, but she didn't show. I know she was very drunk, that's what one of my mates told me. Anyway she's always drunk on Fridays."

Striker turned to the coroner. "Done by the same killer as the other, then?"

"Probably, but not definitely, Paul. I need to look more closely at the nicks and cuts on the scalps. But the angle and depth of the throat cuts are close to identical, so I'd say they were done by the same person."

"With a razor?"

"A very sharp razor." He closed the drawer and motioned to the body that he had been working on. "Hadn't he better look at that one too? Might be his missus?"

Lennie stroked his beard as he often did, out of habit more than anything else, and Striker noticed.

"You shave with a razor Mr. Stalinsky?"

"What is it to you? Why aren't you out looking for Monie, instead of chasing after an imaginary communist conspiracy?"

Striker took Lennie lightly by the arm and guided him over to the other body. "So this one showed up by Gem pier?" he asked Cordner.

"That's right. A fisherman hooked her. Thought he'd caught a shark."

Lennie looked away.

"Mr. Stalinsky. Please take a look and confirm that it is or is not your wife Simone."

Lennie glanced briefly at the hairless corpse. His brain leaped ahead of him, wanted to say that it was too good looking to be Monie, a horrible thought.

"It's not her," he said.

Striker asked in his best copper's tone, "where were you that Friday night?

"On my way to Williamstown," answered Lennie a little too quickly.

"On the ferry?"

"No, on the train."

"And why were you going to Williamstown?"

"I don't think that's any of your business," said Lennie looking Striker in the eye.

"I could arrest you, you know." Striker rattled the handcuffs attached to his belt.

"Not for refusing to answer a question that is an invasion of my privacy."

"You're the chairman of the Australian Communist Party, are you not?"

"I am and proud of it," answered Lennie still looking Striker straight in the eye.

The Coroner coughed politely. "Well I have other bodies to attend to. If you don't mind, Paul, could you conduct your interrogation outside?"

"The head of the wharfies union resides in Williamstown, does he not?" continued Striker.

"So now you're going to do the usual thing and blame the union demonstration to free O'Shea on a communist conspiracy?"

Belligerence was in the air. Lennie could not help himself. Besides, he found Striker repulsive because he had that gaunt, boyish Germanic face, perfectly trimmed short and thick blond hair, low forehead, slender upright build, long arms, lithe body. He expected a click of the heels and a Nazi salute any time. And worse, he detected a very faint Germanic accent, so faint he doubted whether anyone else would have noticed it. There was a cadence to his talk, a slight softening of the "w" sound, it was the way he said "wharfies" that was the give-away and he held on to the 's' sound a little too long. But Lennie was wrong about this. The fact was that Striker's so-called accent was a speech defect he had since childhood or at least that was what his teachers had told him. He grew up in an orphanage, after all, and had no memory of any parents.

"I'm conducting what looks like a serial murder investigation, Mr. Stalinsky, I am not the slightest bit interested in politics, least of all the communist party," he lied. His boss had only this morning told him to keep an eye on Stalinsky because he reckoned that the communists were going to incite a national strike. The directive had come down from the Commissioner himself.

Lennie gritted his teeth to stop himself from saying something he would regret. He wanted to call Striker a Nazi. Instead, as soon as they stepped outside, he turned his back on him and walked away.

"Mr. Stalinsky!" called Striker, but Lennie quickened his pace. No matter, Striker thought, there wasn't a thing the commies did without the Federal Police knowing about it and they would tell him all he wanted to know, should he need it. After all, he and the Commissioner of the Federal Police were good mates, sort of. They had met in police training school years ago and kept in touch. It was the Commissioner who got Striker into Melbourne C.I.D, a move consistent with his and the Victoria police commissioner's policy of filling top jobs with good protestants. They regularly attended services at St. Paul's, though Striker kept a low profile, usually only nodding to the Commissioner as they passed. The Commissioner, of course, was all show. A strong public presence of a good protestant was important for the people of Melbourne to see. And it sent a message to the Catholics to keep them in their place.

*

Down at the Steam Packet pub Sandy stood at the far end of the bar sipping his usual pot of beer. The pub was in a bit of a shambles because it was undergoing renovations extending the "Ladies Lounge," as it used to be called, to provide a lot more seating, to be renamed the "Bistro Lounge" and encroaching on the public bar space which would end up half its original size. The extension of pub closing times to 10 o'clock had changed everything. Lots more families were showing up and staying late, especially as now they put on entertainment in the Bistro.

Sandy and the rest of his mates hated it. That's why every Friday night they decamped back to Sandy's place at around six, pretending as though the pub was closing like it used to.

"Sandy," called the barman, handing the pub phone across the counter to him, "one of your mates, I think."

"Sandy here, who's this?"

"Sandy, it's Lennie. Got some good news and bad news."

"Tell me the good."

"I've got pretty much all the unions across Australia lined up. The miners, nurses, tramways, stevedores, service industries, railways in every state, and your wharfies of course. The only ones I couldn't get were the teachers."

"And the bad news?"

"Monie's still missing and that bastard Striker's accusing me of killing her."

"What? That's ridiculous!"

"Striker's been following me around most of the week, took me to the morgue straight after the march and I had to identify what he reckoned was her body."

"Bloody hell, Lennie! The bastard!"

"He showed me this body, not the one that Bobby pulled out by the ferry, but one that washed up on St. Kilda beach, and another one that popped up at the end of Gem pier.. Their throats slit, hair all shaved off. But no Monie."

"Shit! Lennie!"

"They showed me this old photo of what might have been Monie, and the body looked a bit like her, but I'm sure it wasn't."

"You're sure?"

"Well I'd know, wouldn't I?"

"Of course, you would. Sorry, mate."

"But don't worry, Sandy, Monie will show up. She's probably gone on one of her benders. None of this will interfere with our national strike. When are you going to announce it?"

"One of my mates from the *Age* is coming to the Steam Packet, should be here any minute. All my boys are crammed into the bar."

*

"We're going to Pentridge, D Division entrance," said Sandy. "We'll make the formal announcement there. My son, here," Sandy nudged Ryley who was leaning on the bar sipping a glass of red, "will lead a small but select group of blokes from a bunch of different unions, but most of them will be my boys."

"Pleased to meet you," said Ernie, *The Age* journalist, as he shook Ryley's hand. Ernie's real name was Graham Everest, but everyone called him Ernie because he boasted his uncle in America was a close friend of Earnest Hemingway, the greatest novelist of the twentieth century, according to him. Ryley had seen him around Melbourne Uni. when Ernie was the editor of *Farrago*. But they had never met officially.

The din of the crowded bar descended on them. Ernie, an occasional drinker at most, had hardly entered a public bar since he graduated university. The noise was deafening, much to the satisfaction of Sandy who liked it this way, especially when talking to the press.

"OK. So what's the beef then?" yelled Ernie, trying to be heard.

"You want a beer?" Sandy called.

"Oh, er, a glass of red like Ryley's got would be good."

Sandy beckoned to the lone barman who was making his way down the bar, filling empty beer glasses and collecting money as he went. "A glass of red for our visitor," called Sandy.

"Simple," yelled Ryley, "we announce a national strike and we'll all stay out until that bastard Kerr frees Clarrie, gives the union a complete pardon and abolishes the penal powers."

"Penal what?"

"Powers. Penal powers. That's the law that Kerr reckons justifies his Draconian actions."

"That's not so simple, is it? I mean, abolish the penal powers? Won't parliament have to do that?"

"Who cares how they do it? It has to be done, or we stay out."

"Mates, is this really that important? I mean, this could ruin Australia's economy. A lot of people, poor working people too, are going to suffer," said Ernie, stoking the fire.

"Too bad! It's not our fault, it's that bloody Justice—that's a misnomer if ever there was one—Kerr and the rest of those hypocrites in the government, the capitalist leaches who suck the life blood out of the workers!"

Sandy nudged Ryley's elbow. "What he means is that all the unions are completely committed to this strike action. They will all stay out as of today, being Friday, until the government backs down."

"If you really want a good story," said Ryley, "you should come with us now. We're taking a bus to Pentridge and going to camp out in front of the D-Division entrance until they free Clarrie."

"It will make a great picture, that's for sure," grinned Ernie. "I better phone them at the office and get them to send a photographer. I always wanted a picture of myself standing in front of those awesome bluestone towers."

"OK. So drink up, and off we go!" said Ryley.

"One more question, though. My editor is sure to ask me this. Are the commies behind all this? Did they orchestrate this national strike? It's straight out of the Communist Manifesto, isn't it?"

"Look around you, Ernie," answered Ryley. "These blokes never heard of the Communist Manifesto. They couldn't care less. All they want is to be treated fairly, not ripped off every day they go to work."

Ernie rested his notebook on the bar and tried to jot down a few notes. The bar was wet and the pages stuck to it, the biro ink running all over the page. He ripped a few wet pages out and in the end gave up. At that moment, the bar became suddenly quiet. Ernie looked around and saw standing in the doorway of the bar, silhouetted against the bright light of the street, a small woman, a glint in her eyes, holding up signs. It was Babs.

"All right! Listen up you buggers!" she called. "Here are your signs. Don't get them dirty or crumpled up. Never know, we might need them again some time."

Sandy grinned at Ernie. "That's my missus," he said proudly. "It's not a communist conspiracy, it's a family affair."

Babs had borrowed some spare cardboard from the bookbinders and made enough signs to go around. She knew enough not to enter the public bar and to stay at the entrance. It was hallowed ground to these blokes. Women just did not go in there. Ryley pushed his way through the crowd and helped take the signs and pass them out. They read simply in plain Sans Serif script, FREE CLARRIE. Ryley clasped Babs' hand and raised it high. "Mates, this is my Mum, she's a beauty!" he announced with a big grin, "and she's why my Dad over there is so bloody great."

Ryley and the wharfies, Sandy's boys as he liked to call them, camped out in front of Pentridge all weekend until Tuesday, when the dam broke. Ryley was ecstatic. Australia's economy had ground to a halt. Its government had been reminded that Australia's economy depended entirely on its workers, that the insatiable haves could not feed their greed without the have-nots, the workers who were happy so long as they had enough money to feed their families and put a roof over their heads.

That's all they wanted. Compared to the haves, it was a tiny need. But all was not roses, Ryley mused. According to the *Financial Times*, a benefactor had stepped forward and paid all the fines demanded by Justice Kerr's Industrial Court, so Clarrie came walking out of D-Block, a big smile on his face, and was quickly rushed to the nearest pub where he was treated to a big counter lunch and a beer. Yet, the penal powers had not been repealed. They'd better be, mused Ryley, they'd better be.

*

Striker decided to start the week with a run through a neighbourhood where he thought his quarry might reside. This morning, he would drive to the Williamstown Ferry, ride across, then leave the car in the parking lot and jog down to Williamstown along Douglas Parade, cut across to Williamstown beach, back to the little centre where the churches and schools were, then to the parking lot, and through some of the local streets to get the feel of the place. The Williamstown ferry also seemed to him to be a strange place for the Willy people wanted to cross to Melbourne. The drive was through a bit of traffic, but it was, all-in-all quicker than taking the ferry that didn't have a timetable, only ran when the drivers felt like it, or so it seemed, and by the time you waited for it to arrive and for all the cars to be loaded on, and get to the outer side, you could just about be there by car.

Dressed in his running gear, he drove down Williamstown Road to the ferry. It was just leaving from the other side. He saw it packed with cars, and small vans, messenger or delivery vans. The Winnebago that sat on the back end—actually the front corner once the ferry returned to his side stood out, a lumbering vehicle if ever there was one, always looking as though it was going to tip over any time, especially if there was any kind of wind or wave to toss the ferry about. It had always been there as far as he could remember, certainly every time he had crossed by ferry which was once or twice a year. But now he rode the ferry to meet the people who used it and the drivers who no doubt would know the regulars. Maybe they had seen something. And that Winnebago. Probably had nothing to do with the likely murders, but its ubiquitous presence was good cause for suspicion, and he already had some hints as to what was going on there. On this trip, though, he would feign ignorance. Would talk just with the ferry hands and any incidental travellers.

The aboriginal ferry hand let down the gang plank and the cars drove off, scurrying like ants on a mission. He was three cars back, so was soon beckoned on and guided to a place forward. The ticket collector knocked on his window.

"Three dollars, mate," he asked.

Striker wound down his window. "Three dollars?"

"That's right mate. If you've got the right change that would be good."

"Here you go. What's your name? Have you worked here long?

"Eurie, they call me. Worked here for about four years, maybe more."

"And what about the other bloke, the one driving up there in the cabin?"

"What about him? Look mate, I got to attend to the other cars."

"How long has he been working on the ferry?"

"I dunno, mate. As long as I've been. Thanks mate, I've got to go."

Striker wound up the window to keep out the drizzle that seemed like it would never stop. He looked back and saw that most of the cars were loaded. They were jammed close together, he could hardly even see the top of the Winnebago. He should really get out and go talk to the ferry driver whom he knew was Bobby Frost, but he didn't want to get wet and cold before he started his run.

The windows began to fog up a little and he hugged himself to keep warm. The first body, the one that Eurie probably fished out of the water by the ferry, was older, had been in the water a lot longer and was male. Nothing to show it was defiled, had all its aging hair, no slit throat. It had to be unrelated to the two female bodies. Those two had to be the victims of a weirdo, defiled as they were, the hair shaving a tell-tale sign. And the murderer probably lived in Williamstown. Why else dump the bodies by the ferry or around Williamstown? Surely the murderer would not go to the trouble of moving his victims to Williamstown, a place not easy to get to from Melbourne. Unless the murderer lived in Werribee. It was the first principle he had learned in detective school. Criminals always like to commit their crimes close to home. It's because they are very familiar with the environment; makes them feel safe in what they are doing, even if it is a crime.

He wiped off the inside of the windshield just as he felt the jolt of the ferry reaching shore. He followed Eurie's hand signals, drove off and parked at the far corner of the parking lot, turning the car around ready to embark when he returned. Stripped down to his running shorts and shirt, off he went, his body taut from the shock of the drizzle and cold. He felt invigorated, jogged faster than usual, straight down Douglas Parade, then to Nelson place, and by the time he reached Gem pier he was pleasantly warm, if not a little hot. He crossed over the road and started along Nelson place past the shops and the iconic sign of the barbershop. And as he jogged past, he noticed through the window, Lockie Frost talking with one of his customers, who was laughing, as a young lad, probably an apprentice, carefully shaved the back of his neck.

The penny dropped! Where else, these days, does one find sharp razors? They are almost relics, now that there are new blade razors you don't have to sharpen every day. And there were even electric razors now. The murders had to be committed by someone who had access to, or preferred the old fashioned razors. Of course! The owner of that barbershop is a Frost, if he remembered rightly. One of *them*! And the Catholics were covering it all up! Looking after their own as they usually do!

6. Criminal Justice

It's amazing how much you can store in a Winnebago, mused Lizzie. She had all the props stored in five separate cupboards suspended above the small double bed that, when converted, became the kitchen table. What did not match the confines of the cabin was Lizzie's size, which was, for a woman of beauty, overwhelming, larger than life. She had inherited an inverted triangular build from her grandfather, a tall, sinewy man, with broad square, sharp shoulders, and at the height of his powers, a contour that tapered down to narrow feet, which when snapped together, formed the inverted apex of an isosceles triangle.

Amazing! Ryley wouldn't believe that I remember what an isosceles triangle is. Except for Bobby, they've all forgotten how good I was at maths and English. All they remember is the bloody evil things I did, and I admit I did some terrible things and gave the nuns hell. But they deserved it.

It's why Mum never liked me. Though she says that's not true, that I was the apple of her eye. It's a lie of course. She doted on Ryley, two years older than me, so it's only natural he'd be the favourite. Though the one she really has a soft spot for is uncle Bobby, but then, so do I. I can tell you I feel much, much closer to uncle Bobby than I do to Ryley. I've never really figured Ryley out. He was just too boy-like, which is not what he's like now, by the way, and I suppose that's the way Mum saw him too, being brought up in a house of boys. And he was nothing like I was. I mean, he was easy going, more like my Dad, always quiet and compliant, never once raised his voice, always did what he was told, though quite frankly, he didn't even have to be told to do things. For Mum he had to be the perfect son. And, unlike yours truly, Ryley was very studious, right from as far back as I can remember. He loved books, came home with armfuls of them from the library, and read all the time. No wonder he ended up at university. I have to admit, though, that he was closer to Dad than was I. Probably because he liked to go with him down to the wharf—though I did too, Dad always took us both—but the wharfies took to Ryley whereas they looked at me like I wasn't supposed to be down there with them. I was kind of a mascot, whereas Ryley was one of the boys. So pretty soon, I stopped going. And Ryley never seemed to be close to Dad until he got to university, and then he started with all the commo talk, the Marxist lingo, and suddenly he and Dad had a lot in common. I could have gone to uni too, but the fact is I was never one for books. Ryley is a reader and thinker. I'm a doer, not a reader. I am a thinker though. I have learned everything I know from the men I've slept with. So there.

Fact is, I'm sure I inherited grandpa's body and free spirit and Mum's domineering personality. I don't know what Dad's genes were doing at the instant of fertilization. All I can say is that they must have got there too late to do their bit. Anyway, Dad's a bit slow off the mark isn't he? Though Banger always tells me that Dad's really the brains of the family. Otherwise how could he be the big shot down on the wharf? He's just a labourer but they all do what he says. Well, I'm a labourer too in my own way, and my clients all do what I say. That's the fun of it, and the most amazing thing is they love being bossed around and they do exactly what I tell them, although I'm careful to order them around in the way that they want.

I am also very strict about appointment times and being punctual. That's something I did get from Major Mum Two. She was and still is a stickler for punctuality. Anyway, I couldn't run my business as well as I do unless my clients were absolutely punctual. I allow only twenty minutes between appointments, allowing for washing up, clean-up, careful storing of props, changing the bed linen and so on. That's all factored in. A few years ago one of my clients was a dentist. He showed me how to schedule appointments and especially how to apportion your time so you don't get exhausted from too many clients in one day. So I gradually managed to charge enough money so that I only had to work with a small number of high paying clients, just one or two a day. When I was younger, I did all clients in three days straight, but now, I'm more mature about it, so I have a leisurely schedule, weekdays only, and occasional weekends if one of my top paying clients asks for something special.

Lizzie was always the independent one, never on good terms with her mother whom she called Major Two when she was angry, which was often. She was precocious right from the start. Head and shoulders above all the other girls in Williamstown Catholic Primary School, she talked back at the nuns and was soundly beaten for it with a thin leather strap around the legs, reached puberty as soon as she moved on to high school. There, she drove the nuns to the point of distraction. She was an excellent student, learned so quickly, wrote wonderful stories, and drew fascinating pictures, but she had a foul mouth, from which came much abuse directed at any person close by, but especially the head sister. Babs had worn a track to the Diocese to receive embarrassing reports of Lizzie's unacceptable behaviour. The head sister assumed, of course, that the foul and hostile things that came out of her mouth—she even spat at the nuns on many occasions—were the result of her upbringing. It didn't help that Babs took Lizzie's side against the nuns and became angry when the head sister implied, and eventually told her outright, that she was an unfit mother. Babs explained that Lizzie had been like this from the day she was born, when she refused to take her nipple, spat out the formula, and cried constantly, so much so at one stage that Sandy announced that he would not sleep in the house. She finally found a way to quiet her, by lacing the formula with a little brandy and sugar. Sandy never questioned how she did it, and she never told anyone. "Just a mother's charms," she said when asked.

But when Lizzie was almost walking she suddenly refused the bottle and began to search for Babs's nipple whenever she was held, which was not often because she squirmed and wriggled making it almost impossible to hug her. Babs had to work on generating her milk supply which at last came, only to lead to an incessant demand by Lizzie for more and more, a suck that almost swallowed the nipple, all the time squirming and grabbing with strong little hands, pushing her little feet into Babs's body. But at least it was a bond between them, even if painful. It was better than nothing, so Babs told herself over and over again.

There is little point in recounting Lizzie's boisterous and adventurous childhood. Her behaviour was such that Babs turned into her own mother and adopted a sergeant major style, hoping that enough fear could be generated to give her and Sandy a little peace and quiet. And since Williamstown was a small community where Babs knew everything that was going on, whenever Lizzie was on the edge of the precipice Babs was there, ready to catch her. Lizzie was probably the first kid in her high school to take the pill. It was the only solution as far as Babs was concerned. And to this day Sandy never knew, though at times it was difficult to keep it from him because the pills cost so darned much. And, thank you Jesus, Babs said every morning, taking the pill regularly was the one and only thing that Lizzie could be relied upon to do. It meant, though, that by her last year in high school—tenth grade probably—Lizzie had moved out of home and was shacked up with some star footballer. Babs had difficulty explaining all this to her friends, and especially to her brothers who were never backward in telling their big sister that she was up shit creek. But she stuck to it and over the years, she and Lizzie developed a pleasant enough relationship, even though Lizzie did not drop by to see her as much as she would have liked. And the good thing was that her young brother Bobby, the nicest of them all, became very good friends with her, and more or less looked after her, making sure she was all right. It was he who had bought her the Winnebago. And it was he who made it possible for her to "run away from home."

Trouble was I didn't really have anywhere to run to. Mum and I had a row because I wasn't doing my homework and I was staying out late, sometimes not coming home at all. I had been flirting something terrible with the boys at school and we frolicked around in Robertson Reserve after school and often later at night when we'd all sneak out of our houses and get together and smoke, and the boys would bring a few cans of beer. We'd generally have a good time. I came close to letting them get into me, especially Buck Hamilton who I found just adorable, strong and muscly, but I hadn't got there yet. Then word spread around the town that Buck and I were a "couple" and of course it got back to Mum who went crazy and screamed at me telling me that I wasn't to go out ever again. As if she could stop me!

Uncle Bobby, whose room was next to mine, overheard everything and quietly came into the kitchen.

"Would you like me to talk with Hamilton?" he asked Mum.

"What good would that do?" she asked angrily.

"I can tell him to piss off. Simple as that."

"Uncle Bobby, don't you dare. How could you?" I cried.

"Like your Mum, I don't want you to get into trouble," he said.

I yelled back at him, "I'm just seeing him, OK? Bloody hell!"

"That's not what I've heard," said Mum.

"You bloody old busybodies are jealous of me, that's what, I growled."

"Have you slept with him?" asked Mum, tight lipped.

"How dare you?" I screamed and ran to my room, slamming the door behind me, all the time thinking that this is how a teenager is supposed to act. There was no lock on the door so Mum and uncle Bobby just followed me in. Mum stood at the doorway, in her usual major Mum pose, hands on her little hips. One of her edicts was coming.

"You're going on The Pill," she said.

"What?" I asked, dumbfounded.

"The Pill. It's the only way I can protect you from those young bastards out there."

Uncle Bobby quietly withdrew and went back to his room. I summoned up the courage to ask, "what's that?"

"You'll see," said Mum, not realizing that it would change my life forever, in ways that none of us could imagine.

*

The Commissioner always comes on a Friday. He says that the stress builds up so much over the week that it is unbearable by week's end. Frankly, I don't believe him. How could being a police commissioner be so stressful when you don't have to actually solve a case of murder or whatever? You just have to tell your detectives to get it done. It's my guess that it's always more than what they say. For the Commissioner, I think he's all screwed up inside, and I'm guessing he has a wife that orders him about. Which is really silly I know because that's what he wants me to do, only a lot more of course.

I keep the Commissioner's paraphernalia in the top right hand corner of the cupboard above the bed. The handcuffs are the most important. Every now and again he brings me something extra, but it's mainly the same things he likes me to hit him with over and over. There's a switch of an old peppercorn tree that I really hate because although it's old and dried up it still every now and again oozes sap and it gets all over my hands and it won't come off without a thorough scrubbing. And when I grab him with my sticky fingers he yelps but asks for more.

"You disgusting murdering bastard," I mutter in low tones.

"Commissioner," he pleads, "I didn't do it."

The Commissioner, resplendent in his bright white short sleeved shirt, bedecked with badges and patches, his bullet head well-scrubbed and shining, hair cut down to the shortest of crew cut, is standing just inside the door and I pull it shut. "Show me the knife!" I demand and he cringes as he backs up against the bed. I let my gown fall to the floor and he licks his lips and gulps.

"Honest, sir, I didn't do it. I don't have a knife," pleads the Commissioner.

I raise the peppercorn switch. "Show it to me or you'll get the beating of your life!"

"I know my rights! You can't do that! I want my solicitor!" he whines.

"It's a strip search for you, then, you filthy scum! And we'll search your every orifice!"

The Commissioner takes off his shirt and pants and he's down to his underwear.

"Come on! Everything! Get it all off!" I grab his shirt and pants and put them on. I must look really funny, the pants too short and the shirt too long, but a good fit for my wide shoulders. I've done this scores of times and I still have trouble holding back a laugh. I must look ridiculous. I raise the switch.

"Come on! Get it all off!" I give him a couple of stripes and he screams.

"Please, Commissioner! I didn't do anything wrong. Please!"

"Of course you did. There's never any doubt. Come on where's the knife?" I whack him again and he whimpers. "Come on, show me. It's up your ass isn't it?"

Now he's on all fours and I'm beating him mercilessly. He's removed his singlet and he's struggling to get his underpants off. They're all stained. Truly disgusting. "You disgusting filthy shit!" I say in a very serious tone, my low voice resonating against the Winnebago roof. He pulls them off and rolls on to his back and spreads out his arms. I already have the handcuffs in place, so I reach and snap them on each wrist. His tits are as big as mine almost, and I know he has a pulsing erection, though I can't see it because of his protruding beer belly. All my clients except one have big beer bellies. He rolls on to his back and lies with his legs dangling down over the edge of the bed. Now I can see it, red, no foreskin, squat and thick, its helmet reminding me of a London policeman. One day I'll paint it black.

"You cunt of a Commissioner," he snarls, "you have no right to torture me. I'll report you to the authorities!"

"I *am* the authorities," I say with a cruel grin, "and you're about to find out who's the boss!" I land a dose of the switch right across his belly and he screams, but presses his back further into the bed, his buttocks now thrust forward. His prick peeps out from under his beer belly. I land another stripe right across his prick, and this time he really screams. There's even a crimson slash on its shank where I struck my mark. I throw down the switch and jump on to him, my legs apart and I reach up to the shelf above the bed for the lubricant spray. I have to time this exactly right or he'll go off and we would have to start it all over again, even then I could lose him. Now I have him in me and I start slow, rhythmic strokes, but I feel him softening up. "You pathetic little insect," I growl, "I'll crush you. You're nothing but a useless, despicable criminal who deserves everything he gets!" I slap him over the face a couple of times, he makes a kind of whimper but moves his head from side to side to soften the blows. "Take it like a man!" I say, "you criminals, you're such cowards, snivelling little cowards. You deserve to be crushed, beaten down to your proper place at the bottom of society."

"You can't treat me like this!" I'm the Commissioner!" he cries.

"What world do you live in?" I snarl, "You're in my world, and I'm the Commissioner." I reach for his underpants, "this will show you who's boss!" I yell, and I rub the disgusting underpants into his face.

"Aaagh!" he cries. He's coming back. We're almost there. I push the underpants into his mouth and he struggles to breathe. I reach for the small knife under the pillow. I wave it in front of his eyes. "Oh No! Not that, Commissioner! I'm sorry, I didn't mean what I said!"

"You are a disgusting creep," I snarl, "say it! Go on! Say it!"

"I, I am a disgusting creep!"

"That's better!"

And now we're right at the big moment. It's when that look comes into his eyes, the moment of truth, they look past me to who knows where, but he is transfigured, his arms spread out as fixed on a cross. I flourish the little knife that Lockie gave me as a moving-in present when he and Bobby got me the Winnebago. I keep it sharp and thoroughly sanitized, like Lockie told me. I look down at his belly and swipe the blade across it, drawing a slash, bright red, that radiates out from his navel, adding to the other scars that make his belly look like the rising

sun. He screams and his buttocks rise and convulse up and into
me. And for that climactic moment we are joined at the hips like
Siamese twins.

Now this is the really hard part. As he softens up, I lean back,
my knees astride him. My hands are on my hips. I'm looking
past him, already thinking about my next client. But he stretches
out his arms, wanting to hug me. They say that in business you
should have respect for your clients, but it's hard to when you
see how pathetic some of these big shots are. Besides, it's not
love that I give them, only sex, and they should surely understand that. They're very important people, after all. They're not
dumb. Yet I don't think they come for the sex either. It's as
though they're not comfortable in their world. They yearn for
another.

*

Monday. The judge liked to start off his week on a good
footing. He's a little man, his face grey like that of a corpse,
though I've never seen one of course, except my grandfather
when he died, but that was different, he was freshly beaten to
death on the footpath outside the Steam Packet pub. It seems
like the judge was once bigger, but shrunk and his skin didn't
shrink along with his body. There are deep furrows in his brow,
a wrinkled face like no other, jowls hanging down that shake
appropriately, I bet, when he pronounces a poor bugger's
sentence. And he's got a mass of white hair that sits up like three
clumps of cotton candy.

"Morning Judge," I say.

The judge steps up into the Winnebago and I grab his hand
so he won't slip. He seems frail, but I know he isn't, I can tell
you that. I already have on the silly wig that they all wear. And
I've got the jar of black facial paint all ready. I allow the judge's
robe I'm wearing to slip open and his eyes immediately take in
my fulsome body. I'm wearing only a G-string and I take off the
wig and wedge it under the G-string. He stands there waiting
for me. I have to do it all, undress him slowly, folding up each
garment carefully and placing it in a neat pile on the driver's
seat of the Winnebago. I lift him on to the bed, he's light as a
feather. I then start to paint his face with black body paint, then
down circling his tits, then further to his nether regions. It's a
painfully tiny little prick that sticks up like a daffodil at the first
sign of spring. I'm chewing liquorice and I spit its black chewed
up muck on to his body and he shudders and cries, really cries,

"You cruel bastard! Let me go! Let me go!" But he lies passively
on his back.

"You filthy little pig, abbo trash!"

"I'm not trash! Please don't send me to gaol," he whimpers.

"You're going to gaol, you black little abbo shit, where you
can hang yourself like all the others"

"Please! Have some mercy! Please, your Honour!"

I open a little Vegemite jar of petrol. Its fumes immediately
fill the air. "Come on! Sniff this, it's all you scum can do! Sniff!
Sniff!" I push it into his face and hold it under his nose. He
raises his head as far as he can and takes a deep sniff. "Aarrgh!"
he says, and tosses his head from side to side. Now I'm dipping
my finger into the jar and tracing light lines down his body,
down to his little daffodil. He begins to writhe and squirm. I've
got him where I want him. I place the lid back on the jar. His
whole body now smells like a petrol station.

"Please your gracious honour! Give me one more chance! I
promise I won't do it again!" he whimpers.

"You people are the wretched of the earth," I pronounce with
as much arrogance as I can, "you belong in caves, gaol is where
you must go." I push myself into his little daffodil that is about
to bloom. I've got him ripe and ready. He lets out a deep sigh
as the wig, made of the finest silky human hair imported from
China, so he told me, rubs against him. And in a wink its done,
and he lies lifeless under me, groaning, looking into my eyes,
it's that look again that all my clients give me. I stare through
him and smile, knowing that my bright red lipstick smile will
be imprinted on his brain forever.

*

Wednesday. Kewcy is what I call him, the most famous
Queens Counsel in Victoria, maybe Australia. Uncle Lockie
sent him to me like he has most of my big money clients. He's
a rough and tumble sort of bloke, jolly most of the time, but he
can drive me crazy with his talk. That's pretty much all he does.
Talk, talk, talk. He gets me to read to him and a lot of the time
he wants to recite poetry to me. Weird stuff, like I'm sure nobody has ever cared about. Most of it I never heard of before. I
can't believe they would have taught this stuff in school
anyway, the brothers wouldn't like it, least of all the nuns.

He's an average sized sort of middle aged bloke, his face and
body pudgy, his cheeks and nose puffed up reddish like a lot of
heavy drinkers. I try to keep on top, in fear he might crush me.
His breath is always sweet, he chews spearmint gum before he

comes to me, I'm sure of that. And his voice is always gravelly, and when he speaks it's always with a smile even if what he's saying is horrible or hostile (which is rare). And his mouth is so large, larger in proportion to his big body, even larger in proportion to his head which is quite small really, his hair thinning at the front, but still full at the back, full waves, brown tinted with grey, his skin as white as any white man could be; it's smooth though, for a man of his age, few deep wrinkles. His brows full and thick, constantly moving and tilting in unison with his talk and his smiles. His lips, wide and the shape of a seagull's wings, are constantly in flight, struggling to keep ahead of his stream of words and I suppose there's thoughts behind them, though I confess I don't know what they are. He keeps calling me "My Dear" which, for the first few years, I found offensive and patronizing, but now I see it as a term of endearment. He knows he's much smarter and better educated than me, and it's of course obvious to me too, but that doesn't matter. I'm his match none the less, and he knows it. I have something—and I don't even think it's sex any more—that he either wants or needs and maybe he doesn't know what or why. And now I'm starting to get to like him, a rush of words popping out of my mouth, or more precisely, out of my head because my mouth, behind its bright red lipstick, doesn't say such things.

He's sitting on the edge of the little bed and I'm unbuttoning his jacket. I take from my cupboard the old rolled up barrister's gown that he gave me last year for my birthday, though he doesn't know when my birthday is and he said that it didn't matter, it was for my birthday whenever it might have been or would be. He licks his lips, and starts to talk but I gently place my fingers over his lips and say, "sshh" and he smiles and gives his head a toss back as though he was tossing the hair out of his eyes. And his eyes seem a paler grey than usual, but I suppose I'm imagining it. I guide his hands to his pants and get him started at undoing them while I stand back and drop my clothes and slip into the barrister's gown. Now I pull him off the bed and he's standing straight, his head almost touching the roof of the Winnebago. It's time I moved to a new place, I say to myself. There is a mound of grey curly hair bedecking his chest, his nipples barely poking through. At last, I get him naked and I push him lightly against the bed and he slides back, his big legs dangling over the edge. I help lift them up on to the bed and he only just fits, his feet pushing a little against the side of the Winnebago. Then I'm at last astride him, where I want to be. He has my head in both his big hands and pulls me towards him. I let him slobber me with a kiss, then I pull back. It's the signal to begin, and here it comes.

"*All men, in law, are equals,*" he says in a booming voice, "come on my dear, you must say your part."

"Which is?"

"Say 'in any case' after everything I say."

"In any case," I say and he smiles and I feel him move his hips, getting into position.

"*Free of tyranny--* " he mouths.

"In any case."

"*We choose a knave or a eunuch—* "

"In any case."

"*To rule over us.*"

"In any case.

"*These fought—* "

"In any case."

"*And some believing—*"

"In any case."

"*Some for love of slaughter—* "

"In any case." I'm riding him now.

"*Some in fear—*O God!"

"In any case!" I'm almost screaming.

"*There died a myriad—*Christ Almighty!"

"In any case—Go! Go!"

"*For an old bitch! Gone in the teeth!* Oh God no!"

"In any case, in any case!"

"*For a botched civilization!* Forgive me! Please forgive me! Arghh!"

"In any case."

"*Smiling at the good mouth —*"

I lightly touch his fluttering lips. "In any case."

"*Eyes gone under earth's lid—*"

I lean forward, lightly stroke his closed eyes, run my fingers through his hair. "In any case."

"*For two gross of broken statues—*"

"In any case."

"My dear Lizzie—"

"In any case."

"*For a few thousand battered books—*"

I lean down and rub my nose on his. "Go on! Say it!" he mutters.

"In any case," I say, and I kiss him on the forehead.

And now it's over, and Kewcy rolls off the bed, nearly toppling me over.

"Kewcy, watch out! You trying to do me in or something?"

"You know who that was?" he asks with a grin.

"Who, what?" I answer, showing off my ignorance.

"The poet."

"Does it matter?"

He looks down at me and sniffs. "I suppose it doesn't," he says.

"Choose a happier bloke next time, Kewcy" I smile, a little smile, a superior smile, my red lips puckering a little.

"You know that wouldn't work," he says, seriously. He grabs me in his arms and kisses me hard and full till it hurts.

"Kewcy!"

"Lizzie my dear!"

*

Thursday run. Striker stopped briefly at the gate of his house on Page street to tighten his shoelace. This was a big run day, his Williamstown run. He ran up Page Street, left on Phillipson, then right on Beaconsfield Parade, ran all the way to Williamstown Road, followed it to the Ferry and jogged on the spot until it arrived. This morning he would continue on the ferry combining business with pleasure. He would interview the ferry driver and talk to any others who were frequent travellers on the ferry. Maybe they saw something. The Winnebago was always there. He had long suspected there was something not quite right about that. The whole idea of a ferry after all was to get across and go somewhere else. Not to stay on the ferry all the time. Nor was the scenery especially attractive.

As he ran, he recalled yesterday's visit to the morgue.

"This one came in from Geelong," said Cordner in his droll voice. The body washed up at St. Helens beach, right near the meat packing plant."

"Hair, throat and toe?" asked Striker.

"The same as the other two. Head shaved, throat slashed after death, and right little toe removed. All done most likely with a razor-sharp knife, same as all the others. This one was a male, though."

"Does that mean that we're not looking for some kind of twisted mass murderer?"

"How would I know? That's your job."

"It makes two male and two female, so sex isn't what's driving the killer."

"Depends what kind of sex, doesn't it? replied Cordner with a wry smile.

"Can you get all four bodies out so we can look and see if there's anything else that's common about them?"

Cordner had his lab assistant bring out the bodies and lined them up side by side. "There is one thing that sticks out," he said.

"What?"

"Well, can't you see?" teased Cordner.

Striker had seen lots of bodies in his time, many often scarred and mutilated. The putrescent grey of the skin always got him down. He wanted to press on the flesh of each one with his finger, but could not bring himself to do it. He imagined it would be like pressing down on foam rubber, the kind they make for top class bed mattresses, not that he could ever afford them.

"How old are they?" he asked.

"You mean how long have they been dead, or what's their age?"

"Both."

"The first one that was fished out at the ferry, old. Probably seventy. The others forties and fifties."

"And the one that Stalinsky denied was his missus?"

"Forties."

"And how long have they been dead?"

"Up to the time they were fished out of the water, I'd say about three to four weeks. I'm still doing tests on that. There's something else."

"Well, come on. What is it?"

"All the bodies do have bite marks, probably from a shark. But they are very minor, as though the shark had a nibble and decided it didn't like the taste.

*

Saturday. Mayor Tim Furst, star swimmer of the 1956 Olympic games, had worked hard to retain his swimmer's build, the massive muscles across his chest, an almost non-existent rear end, slender long torso and legs, arms and fingers that extended just about to his knees if he let them hang loose. He still swam every day in his private swimming pool behind his house on Brighton Beach, though for publicity's sake, he made it a point to show up at the old Melbourne public baths most weekends to work out, and of course dropped in at the Olympic pool every now and again to sign autographs and give some pointers to the youngsters who were coming along.

Lizzie was very good to him, shifting her schedule around whenever he needed it, since his own schedule was crammed full of events, meetings, and ceremonies that often without notice changed time and place. On her side, Lizzie was well used to top sportsmen, their competitiveness always a challenge, not to mention their athleticism that often tested her own endurance to the limit. So it was always with some apprehension that she opened the Winnebago door to Mayor Furst, always careful to address him as Mr. Mayor, never by his first name, which he disliked, saying that it was too girl-like, the name of weaklings. What she did like about him was his cropped crew-cut, kept no more than half an inch long, glistening gold stubble that resisted her fingers when she ran them through it. It matched his nick-name Timber, which he liked because it denoted strength, and which she reserved for special moments.

"Mr. Mayor. Welcome to my humble abode," she said with a smile, reaching out to ruffle the stubble of his golden hair.

"Lizzie, my love, how I've missed you. I've been so busy, sorry I had to cancel last week."

"I'm always here for you, Mr. Mayor."

"It's that damned bridge. It will never get built the way we're going."

"I'll have to change my business plan if it does," smiles Lizzie.

"You'll find another ferry, no doubt."

"Maybe I could set up shop at the end of Gem pier and everyone could come to me by water taxi."

"You'd have to get a permit first," joked the Mayor.

"Speaking of which, did you bring your permit today?"

"I'm the Mayor of Melbourne. I don't need a permit. I *am* the permit."

"Of course you are, Mr. Mayor. And what style would you prefer today?" Lizzie reaches around into her cupboard above the bed. "I have a new item just off the boat from Paris, according to my source. It's a pale pink bikini, handmade lace of the finest Chinese silk. I have made a few small alterations to the bottom part, since I know how big you are, don't I?"

The Mayor has already disrobed and stands as if poised at the edge of a pool. While they have done this countless times, Lizzie always draws a sudden breath when she sees how big he is. It's enormous and quickly growing. She holds out the two fragile descendants between the thumb and forefinger of each hand, her big red-lipped smile and big eyes drinking in his David-like shape, allowing her own gown to slip down revealing her inverted white triangular body, curved at just the right places. He edges toward her, his cheeks and mouth pursed as though to blow into a balloon. He breaks open his lips with a light blow, takes the top piece and holds it against his breast.

"How does it look?" he asks, tilting his head, bending his body to the side.

"It looks marvellous! Here let me help you put it on."

Lizzie takes it from him, turns him around, rubs her belly into his buttocks, then slips the bikini top around his chest and ties it in a fine bow at the back. She has set up a mirror on the back of the Winnebago door, so they stand there, admiring themselves, she running her hands under his arms, through to his nipples, stroking them lightly through the openings of the bikini made specially for fondling. Their hips sway gently in unison. Then she slowly turns him around to face her and dangles the bikini piece, so fine it's almost a G-string with a big O in the middle through which she will thread his enormous presence.

"Shall I dress you, dear?" she asks, dangling the bikini from her index finger, its long red nail shaped almost to a point.

"Oh, please do mummy, please do," squeaks the Mayor in a boyish voice. He lifts one of his long legs and Lizzie reaches down to slip the bikini over the equally long foot, then the other. She slowly pulls the bikini up to his groin, then pulls it forward, its elastic stretching to its limit, fitting it snuggly over his crown jewels, the bottom of the O pressing up, pushing everything outward and upward, creating an enormous handful of tension and slack. With one hand holding him there, she turns him around slowly and presses her belly into his buttocks once again, now both her hands caressing his bunched jewellery.

"Let go, mummy! I want to see!"

Lizzie lets go and stands back, running her hands down his slim back, running her nose across his broad shoulders, admiring his massive chest muscles in the mirror.

"Mummy! Mummy! Quickly, it's time!"

This is the part that Lizzie hates. She reaches behind her for the dildo that lies waiting under the pillow.

"Mummy! Mummy! Hurry! I can't wait!"

"Shut up, Timmy, be patient," Lizzie says sternly, "Little boys must wait their turn."

"But I'm a big boy, mummy! Please! Please!"

Lizzie straps on the dildo, applies the necessary lubricant, then with a huge lunge of her hips, thrusts it into the Mayor who stands astride, half bent over, no longer looking in the mirror.

"Aaargh!" he cries in agony and ecstasy, "mummy, you're hurting me!"

"And I'll hurt you more if you don't stop whining, you little bugger," sneers Lizzie.

She pulls his buttocks into her hips, then with one last thrust, she yells, "take this!"

"Ohhh!"

"And this!"

"Oh, mummy! Thank you mummy! I'll be good from now on, I promise!"

"Timberrrr!" she calls.

Lizzie feels his body go limp to her touch. Thank goodness that's over, she says to herself. She removes the dildo and throws it in the bucket placed in the corner for that purpose. The Mayor collapses back on to her and she falls back on to the bed, her arms wrapped round him, lightly squeezing his sleeping jewels.

"Careful, now," he says.

They lie quietly, motionless. Lizzie glances at the clock she keeps wound on the wall above the tiny kitchen stove. Bobby is coming to pick her up this morning. She doesn't like him seeing her clients, although of course, he has known what she does for a living since the very first day she started. He has never once openly expressed disapproval, a matter that made her thankful for his understanding, but in a way, wishing that he would show some resentment. If he really cared for her, wouldn't he nag her about her professional life?

"Are they really going to build a bridge to Williamstown?" she asked.

"Believe it or not, eventually, yes."

"So I should be buying up houses and land in Willy and make a killing when the bridge is built?"

"If you can wait ten or fifteen years, probably."

"I'm getting tired of this Winnebago. I think my business has outgrown it. Don't you?"

"You're not thinking of moving off the ferry, are you?" asked the Mayor, understandably concerned.

"I am. Why, would it be bad for you?"

"Not if you set up shop on my side of the river."

"Not likely. Bobby says it is too expensive on your side."

"Then I'd have to rethink my arrangements. Thing is, I can come to you without anyone noticing. I just park my car right next to your Winnebago, open my door, and slip into yours. Completely out of sight. The only person who knows anything is your uncle Bobby, right?"

"Right. That's all, and Bobby is such a sweetie, he'd die rather than give me away."

"Maybe if you found somewhere close to the ferry on the other side?"

"I could. But won't the bridge eat up all the land around there?"

"You have a point there. But there is another place that would work for me."

"Where?"

"You're not going to like it."

Lizzie sits up and slips her finger under his bikini bottom and snaps it back.

"Ouch! Stop it!" he says, enjoying the playfulness none the less.

"Where?" she says, her finger under the bikini top this time.

"Above your other uncle's barber shop."

"But that's where you play cards, isn't it? And some of your mates are also my clients, I hope you know."

"Of course I know, but that doesn't matter, does it?"

"It matters a lot. Maybe you blokes talk about me among yourselves, but I don't want to facilitate that."

"We have never talked, at least I haven't. What we do is completely between you and me."

"Well, I think it would be too risky, especially if you blokes get boozed up as well, as I've heard you do. Uncle Lockie treats you pretty well, I hear."

"He does and we have a good time. He does all right himself, in fact very well. He won pretty big at our last game."

"Really? I wondered why he seemed so happy recently. How big, exactly?" she asked sneakily.

"Tut! Tut! None of your business," said the Mayor putting his finger to her lips.

He suddenly rose off the bed, turned for Lizzie to untie the bra, and in a flash he was dressed and ready to go, without even a kiss good-bye. The door slammed behind him and Lizzie and the ferry shuddered as it slid into the jetty, which felt like the St. Kilda side. She cleaned up the bed, dropped down the folding table, washed the dildo clean, using the expensive disposable gloves, and packed everything away. She made herself a cup of tea and switched on her new transistor radio that one of her clients had bought at the tax free market in Aiden on his way back from London. She always tuned into 3 AW, for no special reason. Just habit she supposed. The midday news came on.

"There is still no information on the identity of the unconscious woman who was pulled out of the water by a fisherman not far from the Williamstown ferry last Friday. Still unconscious, she remains in critical condition. The police medical examiner Dr. Borst Cordner, says that she had almost drowned, and there were no indications of foul play. Police have yet to establish her identity. They describe her as a toothless woman in her late forties, about 5 feet 4 inches tall, thin build, a shrivelled face dark red in colour probably caused by alcohol use, heavily stained nicotine fingers, dressed in a brown tweed suit and cream frilly blouse."

7. All in the Family

Bobby entered St Mary's church, trying unsuccessfully to hide his limp. He held Lizzie's hand as they walked quietly down to the front row and slid into the pew next to Babs. The church was almost empty, people filling the first few rows, an occasional straggler sitting alone further back.

"I cancelled an important client to be here. Are you sure we need to do this?" Lizzie whispered. Bobby didn't answer, just squeezed her hand. It was the best way he could think of to make things up with Babs after the fight they had about the shoes in his bedroom. They looked across at the tiny coffin, decked with flowers. Babs came to every funeral for a child, regardless of whether she knew the family, though it was rare that she did not, because she knew pretty much everyone in Williamstown. Father Zappia was officiating as usual, his deep, accented voice floating up to the whitewashed ceiling and bouncing off the walls.

"Who is it?" asked Lizzie.

"Sshh!" replied Babs.

"A little kid got run over when he ran across the road from an ice cream truck, I think," said Bobby.

"Oh, that's terrible," said Lizzie, "so sad. And only six years old."

"It's the parents' fault. They shouldn't let a little kid run around the streets," mumbled Babs.

Lizzie was about to say, "yair, like you kept me and Ryley off the streets, like hell you did," but managed to hold it back. Bobby squeezed her hand. He knew what she was thinking. The familiar squeeze from Bobby—uncle Bobby he was to her then —took her back to those crazy days of her affair, not quite the right word. Even then she always knew exactly what she was doing, even though it may not have appeared so, especially to Major Mum Two. Things would have been different if Bobby were not Babs's favourite brother. She doted on him as if he

104 COLIN HESTON

were her own child. And except for his bad temper, it was understandable, because uncle Bobby was, and still is, a kind and considerable bloke, a gentle giant like they say, a huge fellow, as big or bigger than grandpa, certainly as tall, and definitely heavier, solidly built. There's no way Bobby could have done the acrobats on the horses like grandpa did, too big and heavy. He often looked me over and said I was so like his Dad, you couldn't believe. I was his size, had the agility to jump up on the horses and dance around on their back, that's what he often said. He'd loved to see me do it. And I would have too except that I was only about five or six when grandpa died and the circus antics died with him. The fight that caused his death was relived over and over among my uncles as they argued in the kitchen, me climbing on one of the old chrome chairs, hanging on to uncle Bobby's arm, sometimes crawling around under the table and pulling at his pants.

Every Sunday Mum cooked a roast and everyone came back from church to have it. She cooked the best roast you could imagine, always roast lamb from Sandy's wharfie mate turned butcher, golden brown roast potatoes, just a few of them slightly burned on the corners that Mum would pick out for me, plump green peas from our veggie garden that Bobby tended with great care, roast parsnips and carrots, all cooked in the natural fat of the lamb. Hardly a word was spoken during the feast. Just the noise of smacking lips, the occasional "bloody delicious, sis," and Dad sitting in his chair at the head of the table, quiet, cheeks flushed from the white wine drunk only with Sunday dinner, and he'd raise the glass and say, "to the greatest cook in the world," and we'd all say, "here, here!" And when every plate was clean, every sign of gravy wiped up with bread, Ryley and I would start to gather the dishes until one of us dropped something, which was the sign for Mum to say, "all right. Who's washing and who's drying?"

Uncle Bobby would always say, "I don't mind washing, but the rest of you buggers better keep up with me and don't waste time arguing."

That was the cue for Dad, Lockie, and Shooter to make a grab for the tea towels that hung on the oven door. Mum and grandma would leave and go to the front room and sit at first in silence, grandma doing her latest piece of crochet work, her eyes failing, Mum then telling her she wasn't doing it right, and they'd argue over what was the right stitch.

Uncle Bobby prided himself on being a fast dish washer. The others would wipe the dishes and place them in a pile on the kitchen table. Shooter, though, would often pass a dish back to Bobby and tell him it wasn't clean. Then Bobby would say, "you wouldn't do that if Dad was washing, would you?" And then it would start.

"He's bloody not here, is he? Shut up and wash the dishes. And do them properly."

"Dad never washed a dish in his life," mumbled Lockie, "what are you talking about?"

"He did too!" said Bobby.

"We never had Sunday dinner then. We were always on the road somewhere," argued Lockie.

"He was never here anyway. He was always down at the pub," said Shooter.

"And that's what killed him, that's what," said Bobby.

"Shut up you buggers," Mum called from the living room, turning to grandma, "we can't concentrate on our crochet work, can we Mum?"

Major Mum would not answer. In her old age she had become almost mute when in the company of her boys. She spoke only in whispers to Mum, as though she had worn out her voice barking orders all her life.

"He was in lots of fights at the pub, and not just that pub, any pub," pronounced Lockie, claiming to remember much more of their Dad than did they.

"He was a drunken oaf," muttered Shooter.

"That's our father you're blaspheming about," grinned Lockie, half serious.

"We were much better off after he kicked it. He spent all his money on booze, there was nothing left for Mum and us kids. He gave her a terrible life, came home—we didn't even have a home most of the time—and pushed Mum around," said Shooter, full of resentment.

"He never hit me!" called the Major.

"They should have gone after the bastard that killed him," said Bobby.

"It was an accident," said Shooter, "I was there."

"Yair, and so were a hundred others. That bloke clocked him with a haymaker, and down he went like a sack of spuds," retorted Lockie.

"Everyone was drunk anyway," said Bobby.

"How would you know? You were too young to be there," said Shooter.

"I might have been too young, but I was there all right."

"When he went down, his head hit the corner of the gutter. That's what killed him," said Shooter, sounding like the cop that he was, "we're all better off for it."

My Dad Sandy, always the peacemaker, coughed a bit and raised his tea towel. "OK, let's call a truce. He wasn't my Dad, but he wasn't all that different from mine and lots of boozers. He's gone, let's make the best of it."

Uncle Bobby pulled the plug in the sink and I listened to the dirty water gurgle away as I squatted holding on to his legs. He was only a teenager then, but seemed like a giant to me and was even then bigger than any of his brothers.

*

Father Zappia moved to the coffin and muttered incantations as he sprinkled holy water over it. The scattering of people in the church became restless. I'm sitting there nestled into Bobby.

Father Zappia is a piece of work, I can tell you that. Of course, I've known him all my life because he Christened me, naturally enough. But I really got to know him not long after I quit school and moved in with Buck Hamilton, a rising star in the Williamstown Football club, later the famous Collingwood ruck man and middleweight boxer. I called him my lover, but there was no love in involved. We just loved the sex. It was all Mum's fault. Really.

Buck and me were the talk of the town. I stayed in school for a few months more, but the incessant buzz of the rumour mill was so overwhelming I quickly realized that I could not stay in school. It was not so much that my friends—and I had plenty of them, boy and girl—were unbearable, I couldn't stand the looks and dirty smirks that showed all over the nuns' and occasional brothers' faces when they spoke with me. Besides, I had discovered that sex was an amazing way to get what I wanted. I could get Buck to do anything for me, anything. But school got in the way of us getting together, and since we lived in different houses, it was hard to find anywhere to come together. It was kind of sleazy to have to find a bush somewhere in the park, all the time knowing that nosey shits would be lurking around, hoping to get an eyeful of us, the dirty bastards. As well, Mum hated that I sometimes didn't come home at night—they were the nights when Buck's Mum and Dad were away and I could stay with him. So one morning, I got into my school uniform, sat at the table and ate my breakfast cereal (Vita-brits always with warm milk), then suddenly announced to all present, which were uncle Bobby and Dad and Mum, and I think Ryley was there too, "I'm moving in to my own place."

I hadn't the slightest idea of where I would go, but me and Buck had discovered an old abandoned house down near Gem pier. We had scavenged an old mattress to put in it, so for us it was comfortable enough.

"Buck and I have found a place down near Gem Pier," I said.

"The old empty house that's falling down?" asked uncle Bobby, not helpful.

"How'd you know that?"

"Everyone knows about that house. It's been a favourite hangout for years." He turned to Mum, "Sis, you can't let them stay there. It's a filthy old place."

"I s'pose you would know?" I said cheekily.

"Everyone knows," he said. And then he reached across the table and squeezed my hand. I still remember that squeeze, and I still love it when he does it. His dreamy dark eyes looked me square in the face, my bright blue-green eyes immediately turning away. I tried, half-heartedly, to withdraw my hand from his grip. He lightly rubbed his thumb on my knuckles.

"There's a flat going vacant down near Williamstown beach. It's one of those that they let out in summer. It would be a bit of a walk to school, but not too bad."

Mum stood, hands on hips and held forth. "First it's The Pill. Now it's a flat. What do you think, Bobby, that Sandy and me are made of money? She's only fifteen. She and that filthy bastard can't make it alone."

"We can and I'm going to whether you like it or not," I announced, defiantly.

Bobby squeezed my hand again then released it. He understood me immediately. "I'll help out if you like," he said.

"But she can't leave school. She's only in fourth form," complained Mum.

"She's just changing residence. She's still going to school, aren't you Lizzie sweet?"

"You left before that, anyway Mum," I said with derision.

"They were different times, dear. You wouldn't understand."

A voice came from the sleep-out. "If she wants to fuck that boy, let her. She'll soon get sick of it and come back home."

Major Mum, it was, her voice thin and croaky, no longer the powerful authority of the past, but still never minced words.

"You keep out of this, Mum! Do you hear?" answered Mum, getting angry again.

"As it's a holiday flat, it's probably furnished as well," said uncle Bobby.

"Are you sure it's available? It would only for be for this term until summer, right?" asked Mum.

"Yair. They rent it for double in the summer."

Not sure how much longer this service is going on for. Father Zappia is crooning away and others are coming in on cue. It's kind of a mixture of singing and chanting. The parents of the deceased stand up. Their heads are bowed, shoulders hunched forward. Father Zappia faces them, draws to a close. When will it end?

Bobby squeezed my hand a little more. I drifted back to the flat. Bobby talked to Uncle Lockie who talked to one of his many mates who owned the flat. By the end of the day, Bobby was back at my Mum's house where I had stayed, sulking and feeling sorry for myself. He walked straight to my room and I was about to say in my best sarcastic way, "you might have knocked," but I saw that he was jangling keys.

"Come on! Let's go see it!" he said as he waved the keys around, "coming Babs?"

I was up off my bed, grabbing at his arm, trying to get the keys.

"I don't want to be seen anywhere near it," cried Mum, "I wouldn't be seen dead in that place."

Bobby had borrowed Lockie's car of the week or month, seemed like he changed it so often. "Come on then, let's go," Bobby said, squeezing my hand and pulling me along.

Father Zappia is almost done. He's facing the audience now, the parents are seated, waiting for his next incantation. Four young men are waiting at the side, ready to come for the coffin. I don't recognize any of them. Bobby gives my hand another squeeze, and I suddenly find tears welling up. I want to sob. A terrible rush of sadness mixed with passion has come from somewhere deep inside me. I don't know what's going on. After all, I haven't a clue who this little kid is, or his parents. I shake my hand free from Bobby's and cover my face with my hands.

I need a handkerchief, and Bobby is there with one. Memories of the old flat rise up too. That's where it all started. Mum is kneeling joining in a prayer. I slip down and do the same, and when I feel Bobby at my side, it all comes back to me.

The flat was wedged away at the back of an old house that had been converted into four flats, on Twyford street at Williamstown Beach. Only about ten minutes' walk from the station or from school, so Bobby said. I fell in love with it as soon as we walked in the door. Just one bedroom, and a living room with tiny kitchen. But I went straight for the bedroom, grabbing Bobby's big hand and pulling him along after me. He held back a little, but gave in none the less. I let go his hand and made a leap for the bed, landing on my belly, snuggling into the pillow. Bobby edged forward to the side of the bed. I rolled over on my back, and smiled my biggest smile ever. In those days, I wasn't wearing my bright red lipstick that later would become my trademark. Never mind, though. Uncle Bobby was turned to jelly. I could see it in his flushed face, and besides I could see the bulge in his pants. I knew then that I had a special gift, one that gave me enormous power over all men. What I did not know was that I loved uncle Bobby in a way that I would not love any of the scores of men I slept with in later years. Being young, I went straight for the source, no fooling around. I reached for the bulge and unzipped his fly. Uncle Bobby mumbled something, I wasn't paying much attention. But his face was flushed, his trembling lips wet, eyes wide, devouring my image.

"Undress me," I said as I started to unbutton myself.

"Lizzie, we shouldn't…"

I grabbed at the belt on his pants, pulling myself up at the same time. I reached inside his fly and rubbed him some more. He was going out of his mind. I can't tell you the feeling of power it gave me. I was Supergirl. I could do anything! Why don't all girls do this, I wondered. By now, uncle Bobby was totally gone. He dropped his pants to his knees. I looked down and saw the start of his withered leg. He saw me, and went to pull up his pants again, embarrassed. "Don't," I said, "I love you the way you are, Uncle Bobby. I reached down and stroked the withered leg. And to my amazement, he started to cry!

"Uncle Bobby! What's wrong?" I asked, caressing his leg even more.

"You're so sweet," he sobbed, "I love you so much. I have since you were a little kid. You're the only one of my family who treats me like I'm a real person."

He stepped away and pulled up his pants. I started to take off my clothes. I wanted to try out my new powers. "Come on uncle Bobby, I'm here all for you," I said.

"It isn't right," he cried. "It shouldn't be me."

"If not you, who?" I said, lying there, on my back, stark naked, my legs crossed."

"You should have a boyfriend your own age. I'm too old."

"You're not. Anyway, why should that matter?" Now I opened my legs to see what that would do to him. "I've got a boyfriend anyway, don't I?"

"Lizzie! Oh Lizzie!" he cried, backing away from the bed. With two big hops, he rushed out of the bedroom and I heard the flat door slam shut. I've had sex with many men, but uncle Bobby is always the one I think about.

Buck and I, we lasted for about six months if that. He was my first, so I honed all my skills on him. But I quickly found out that my power was not absolute. Things that at first worked incredibly well, began to fade, and it became more and more difficult for me to get him to do what I wanted. The best way was to deny him sex, then he wanted it really bad. But the problem with that tactic was that it pushed him to look around for someone else. We lasted till the end of fourth form, and that was it. I told him to piss off. Besides, there were other boys buzzing around. Some of them had money. It didn't take much to separate them from it for services rendered.

The serious young men marched slowly out of the church, carrying the tiny coffin, led by Father Zappia, the parents and other mourners following. Mum got up and I followed her, pulling Bobby by his fingers. We stood outside the church and watched the hearse disappear in the direction of the Werribee cemetery.

Uncle Lockie appeared from nowhere. "Are you going to the cemetery? You can come with me, if you like. I have known the parents for many years. We went to school together."

Mum ignored him and went back into the church.

"No thanks. I have to get back to the ferry," said Bobby.

"Me too, I said as I squeezed his hand."

*

Thursday.

"I forgot the holy water," said Father Zappia.

"Don't worry, I have some left over from last time, I think," smiled Lizzie, "come on in and I'll have a look in my cupboard."

Father Zappia struggled up the steps of the Winnebago, fingering his collar with one hand, grabbing at the handrail with the other. In recent years his once slender body of an Italian youth had blown out into one of an older man who ate and drank too much, a round torso balanced precariously on rather long spindly legs. But his hair remained black, hardly a sign of grey, kept long and combed straight back so that it covered his collar by an inch or more. His face had also remained thin, lined deeply at the forehead, a frown for every sin, he joked to others. And today, another frown would be added, no doubt.

There was a slight jolt as the ferry chain tightened and the old diesel motor began to pull the ferry across the water. Bobby stood on the bridge, surveying the deck. It was a busy day today, the deck crammed with cars and a few small trucks.

"Here, let me help you up, Father," said Lizzie, dressed nicely as a choir boy.

"God has frowned on me, Lizzie, as you can see."

"Nonsense. You look the same as I remember when you Christened me."

"Now, my child, you mustn't lie-a, even out of kindness. You were only a baby then. You couldn't possibly-a remember how I looked."

"But you can, and you should think of your body as a temple of God, isn't that what you taught us?"

"My child, it is you who have not changed. You are as beautiful as ever. Let me look at you."

Father Zappia had the choir boy's robe made specially for Lizzie, a gown of the whitest cotton, finely spun, a thin red ribbon sewn into the edges, tied only at the top so that when Lizzie stood tall, the robe hung open from the sharp corners of her shoulders, revealing her *corpo splendido*, the round breasts partially revealed, her curvaceous hips and small triangle of reddish hair peeping out from below that belly that he, tongue between his teeth, would soon stroke lightly with his pudgy fingers.

Lizzie had worked all morning on her hair, to get it to look as short as a choir boy's. Father Zappia had pestered her to get it cut short, even joking that she should shave it bald, all of which of course she refused. She was very proud of her voluminous tea-blonde hair, flecks of crimson in places, especially when the morning sun reflected on it from the water as she stood at the edge of the ferry deck. She had tied it back tightly, revealing her high forehead, and shaved all her face to make it as smooth as could be. She did offer to shave off her pubic hair, but Father had said definitely not. He liked to play with the curls, winding them around his fingers.

Lizzie gently turned Father around so she could undo his collar. She then started on his vest, reached around to undo his pants so they dropped, slid her hands inside his underpants and squeezed the cheeks of his protruding buttocks, taking huge handfuls of flesh or fat that moved like jelly when she squeezed. And when at last she had him naked, she gently turned him around so that he faced her, his eyes, though, never looking into hers, always turned away; he couldn't bear to look at what he was doing, she thought.

"The holy water?" he whispered.

"Coming," she said, and reached over to the little refrigerator, retrieving a tiny glass bottle, once full of Haines liniment, now half full of Holy Water, filled on her last journey to St. Mary's. She helped him on to the bed where he lay, motionless, seemingly helpless, his eyes tightly shut, his breathing shallow, wheezing. She unscrewed the cap of the bottle and placed her finger on the nozzle as she tipped it up. She then began to lightly trace with her wet finger around his nipples resting on his fatty breasts, almost those of a woman, then slowly with a little more water, down to his forbidden parts. At this point, she sprinkled drops on to his rapidly rising organ pipe, the term he used when bragging. He stirred and wheezed, now small drops of tears appearing at the corners of his eyes, deep frowns on his forehead. He grabbed her hand and forced it on to him.

"Sing," he whispered, "sing." And she sang, in a light, falsetto voice, mimicking that of a choir boy, now putting aside the holy water, climbing up to sit astride him, "*O God, our help in ages past, our hope for years to come—*"

"Don't stop! Don't stop!" he cried, grabbing her hand, pushing it on to himself.

"*Our shelter from the stormy blast—*"

"Oh God! I have forsaken you!" he cried again, now his eyes open, trying to lift his head.

"*And our eternal home.*"

With both hands, Lizzie cradled his forbidden parts, squeezing lightly the soft, vulnerable balls, pulling him into a sweet taste of Heaven, savouring this moment, a fleeting moment when the power of God revealed itself, reducing His earthlings to a quivering mass of jelly.

"Do-a you have the bible?" asked Father Zappia.

"Of course. What reading do you want today?"

"The usual. Judah 38:8-10."

"Aren't you sick of that? I mean, you're not doing anything wrong by your church, are you?"

"The church doesn't matter. It's God. Now-a read it-a please."

Lizzie reaches for the bible and pulls it open to a well-worn page, so worn that it's loose and stained as well. She has let go of him, and he's now going at it himself.

"Onan knew that the offspring would not be his—"

"Go! Go!"

"so when he went in to his brother's wife—"

"O! Dio! O! Dio! Sono a vostra mercé!"

"he wasted his seed on the ground—"

"Aarrgh!"

"in order not to give offspring to his brother—"

"The whip! Get the whip!" he calls as he pushes Lizzie off him and curls up in a large hairy ball.

"The switch or the thin leather one?"

"Leather! Leather! O Father, I have sinned against You, stained my soul forever!"

Lizzie ferrets around in her cupboards and finally retrieves a whip of two strands of leather about a yard long. "Shouldn't we have started with this?" she says, unable to hold back a grin.

"The demons, the demons! Get them out of me!" he cries.

"You have to say the words, don't you? I'm not qualified, you told me that."

"In the name of the Holy Ghost, Jesus our Lord and Saviour, Satan! Get thee out of me! Get thee out of me!" He begins to whimper. "It's not enough!" he cries, "you must say it too! You have my blessing!"

Lizzie raises her arm, waves the whip above her head and brings it down with a sharp slashing motion. For a moment, the leather seems to stick to his rounded back. Father Zappia hugs his knees, winds himself into an ever tighter ball.

"Say it! Say it!" he screams.

"I command you," she says in her deepest voice, "in the Father's name, get thee out of him. Get thee out!" And Lizzie, unable to retain her detached demeanour, essential when dealing with excited clients, brings down the whip with great force and without her usual precision, so that the leather strands break across his shoulders and wrap around his head which he tries unsuccessfully to bury in his knees.

"Oh Lizzie! Oh Lizzie! You are the hand maiden *del diavolo!*"

"Get thee out!" she screams, "get thee out!"

And now she whips her quarry unmercifully, hard stinging slashes, leaving bright red welts on his back, arms, side of his face, and he cries and whimpers. The screaming has gone. Lizzie, now well into her character, raises her foot and gives him a push, which causes him to roll over and the human ball unravels and then come the swift stinging stripes across his bloated tummy, the tentacles of leather occasionally reaching his forbidden parts, causing cries of agony.

"Lord! You must forgive her! She does your doing! That I may be cleansed of the devil's temptations. Please Lord-a, hear me! Forgive her all her sins. She has a pure heart. She acts only ever in kindness. Do not-a punish her, Lord, she does-a your bidding every day! She bears the sins of us all, O Lord! It is such a heavy load to carry. The sins of us all! Hear me Lord! It is true! She does our bidding! Look what–a she does for me! All that I deserve! Her saintly heart is yours, O Lord! Only a Saint could do what she does, day after day, night after night. You know that, Lord. You know that. Take her into-a your arms and love her like the child that she is!"

Father Zappia has talked his way through the pain, Lizzie is getting tired, the strokes of the whip softer, she begins to slowly drag the strands of leather lightly across his emblazoned skin; skin made hypersensitive by the welts, so much so that he stops the whimpering and begins to breathe deeply, a faint wheeze squeaking out of his Italian nose.

Lizzie patiently awaits the second coming.

*

Tuesday. Two loud thumps on the Winnebago door and in comes Buck, full of smiles as usual. He hands me a small parcel.

"So what is it today?" I ask, unwrapping the parcel, "Collingwood lost I heard."

"Yair, it was the fucking umpire. He was against us."

"Never mind, Bucky, we'll fix that." I open the parcel and out fall these white shorts covered with green smudges. "How'd you get them?" I ask.

"Never you mind. The smudges were when I accidentally ran into the umpire and he fell down, poor bugger," grins Buck. He's already stripped down to his jock strap. "Put them on" he orders.

I slip them on, but they don't quite do up. My hips, shapely like they have always been, are too wide so I have to leave the fly undone, which Buck likes anyway. I can already see the jock strap bulging. To think I can do this to him after so many years. I reach up into my cupboard of knick-knacks and rummage around for the whistle. I've learned to blow it like the umpire does. It makes an ear splitting noise in the Winnebago. I give it my strongest blow and raise my arm. "Against you, Hamilton! Stay on the mark! Geelong's free kick!" I've no idea what any of this means, but it's met with a torrent of abuse from Buck who's ripped off his jock strap and plunges into me, the umpy's shorts ripped open, and he's got me in his beautifully strong hands, placed under my equally beautiful breasts, raised up and propped on his protruding body, my legs wrapped round him, and we're dancing in what little space there is in the Winnebago, and I'm blowing the whistle, and now he wants to bite my neck, but I blow the whistle some more then spit it out and it falls with a clank on the floor. "The flags! Get the flags!" he yells, and I reach for the cupboard and pull out two white flags. "Goal!" He gasps, "Goal! Hamilton scores again!" Buck slumps back on to the bed and I sit astride him waving the flags. "You bloody beauty!" he mutters, "you bloody beauty."

*

Lizzie almost burst into tears when she heard the familiar knock on the door. She knew it was Bobby.

"Come in," she called.

Bobby opened the door and looked in. "Are you ready?" he asked.

"Yep. Coming right away. So where are we going to look?"

"I'd suggest somewhere on Nelson Place, or maybe Douglas Parade. Not too near the ferry in case this bloody bridge they say they're going to build, gobbles up all the land around the ferry terminal."

Bobby looked up to her, as she stepped down to the doorway. "You look so beautiful," he said.

"Thank you uncle Bobby," she replied.

"You don't have to call me uncle, you know. I'd rather you called me just Bobby."

"I know. It's habit." She put out her hand and he took it to steady her as she took the last long step down on to the ferry deck. She locked the door and they stood hand in hand as they watched the cars drive off the ferry.

8. Tricks of the Trade

The door of the Winnebago shook on its hinges. None of Lizzie's clients ever banged on the door like that. She ignored it and continued to prepare herself for her next client who was due any moment.

"This is detective Striker," called the solemn voice, "police business, open up!"

"Who?" Lizzie of course knew quite well who it was. Though she had never met him, she heard well enough of his straight-arrow deadpan character, unsullied, incorruptible, dedicated to the truth, so they said, all of them hardly impressed, all of them convinced that behind such a brittle character must lie some juicy story.

"Detective Striker! Open up please. I am investigating the disappearance of Simone Stalinsky who I understand was last seen on this ferry."

Lizzie pushed opened the door so hard that it slammed into Striker's fist as he was about to pound it once more.

"Ouch!"

"Sorry detective, you shouldn't knock so hard," grinned Lizzie.

"Miss Malley?"

"You can call me Lizzie. Won't you come in?"

"I think it would be better if you stepped outside, Miss Malley."

"But it's so noisy out there. And besides you don't want people seeing us talk do you?"

"As you wish, Miss Malley. But I must apologize, I'm on my morning run, so I'm not dressed in my official work clothes."

Lizzie held open the door while Striker stepped past her, the entrance so narrow that he unavoidably rubbed against her body, hers, clad only in a light night gown, a body not giving way to his touch, a body sure of itself, unmistakably in charge. His, though, taught and stiff, his t-shirt clinging to his sweaty chest, Striker well aware of this odour filling the small space. She quickly closed the door and hurried over to the table on which sat a half drunk cup of tea and a bible, heavily worn, loose pages hanging out. She pushed it aside and reached for the kettle.

"Care for a cuppa?" she asked, but she noticed the slight movement of his nostrils, as though he had smelled something unpleasant. She was offended, naturally. She was careful always to keep her place tidy and spotlessly clean.

"No thanks."

"I'm not the kind of filth you think I am," she said, immediately regretting it.

"You do not know what I am thinking, Miss Malley and I do not think of anyone, even you, as any kind of filth."

Chastened, something that happened rarely to Lizzie, she sat opposite Striker at the small fold-down table. Her light gown hung slightly open as she sat, revealing the creamy white of her cleavage, one that had excited many men. Striker looked away, his eyelids fluttering. She wrapped her gown more tightly around her, trying to ignore the notion that she was sitting across from Cary Grant.

"So how can I help you, Mr. Striker?"

"I understand you know or knew Simone Stalinsky?"

"We have met a few times on the ferry."

"And her husband, Lennie Stalinsky?"

"I don't know him, but I've heard all about him. He's the commo, right?"

"Yes."

"So what's the problem, Mr. Striker?"

"His wife disappeared a week or more ago. We think she boarded this ferry late at night, Friday night, I believe."

"Oh, you mean the night they fished the body out of the Yarra?

"That's right. I spoke with the ferry driver, Bobby Malley, your uncle I understand, who said she came with him to the ferry."

"Could have done. I was in bed fast asleep that night, so I saw no one that late."

"You were asleep here, in the Winnebago?"

"What's wrong with that?"

"Just that if you were asleep, who would drive the Winnebago off or on the ferry?

"Mr. Striker. Please don't be an asshole. You know what I do here. The Winnebago stays on the ferry. It's where I have it parked. It's a deal I have with the ferry owners. I pay them a reasonable rent for the spot."

Striker looked perplexed. "Why the ferry?"

"Why not?"

"I could arrest you right now for what you're doing."

"Mr. Striker. I thought this was an investigation into the disappearance of Monie, not into what I do for a living. If the latter, then I suggest you leave right now and get your boss's permission to come back and arrest me."

Striker pursed his lips. Lizzie didn't like him at all. He was tight, buttoned up, dangerous, as far as she was concerned. She'd seen such men before. They were walking time bombs, that's what they were.

"Then you saw nothing that night? There was no knock on your door? Your uncle said she was very drunk, and he was sure she staggered on to the ferry."

"What time was it again?"

"Around eight thirty. I had an early night. I'd had a big day and went to bed very early. I heard nothing. And of course, I rarely go out on the deck, so I saw nothing."

"You're very sure about all that? You understand that it's an offense to mislead a police officer investigating a possible murder?"

"You think she was murdered?" gasped Lizzie.

"It's a possibility."

"So why don't you speak to her husband? They are always the number one suspect in my opinion."

"There's nothing more you can tell me?" persisted Striker.

"You never give up, do you?"

"Not when someone's life is at stake."

Striker slid out from behind the table.

"You're leaving already?" quipped Lizzie.

Striker hesitated, half out of the seat. "She was seen knocking on your door."

"Then I must have been out to it. I had a couple of brandies before I dropped off. It was a big day."

"A witness saw the door open."

"The witness was mistaken."

Striker left the table and turned to the door. "I'll let myself out," he said.

"You do that." Lizzie wasn't used to men not doing her bidding.

The truth was that Monie did knock on her door. Lizzie had tried to open it to see what the commotion was, but it wouldn't open because someone was leaning against it. She gave it a strong push with her leg and it flung open, and there was Monie flopped down on the deck. "The body's dead," Monie mumbled, "I saw the Commissioner."

"What? Who's dead? The Commissioner?"

Lizzie had rushed past Monie to the crowd at the front of the ferry. But she saw clearly the Commissioner shouting orders and Bobby was there too. She returned to Monie. "You're a stupid drunken bitch," she growled at Monie, giving her a slap on the face. Monie suddenly sat up then staggered over to the edge of the ferry where she added voluminously to the detritus of the river. That was the last time Lizzie saw her. She could have told all that to Striker, but she came from a family that never told the truth to a copper, unless he was one of their own, as was Shooter. There was a sudden jolt as the ferry banged into the jetty. Monie, bent well over the side of the deck was disgorging the very last drop of whatever had been churning around inside her, probably some of Babs's sausage rolls as well as her false teeth. The jolt caused her hand to slip from the low rail at the edge of the deck and she toppled over, falling ten feet into the murky waters of the Yarra.

*

Old flames never die, that's what they say. It's not quite right, though, when it comes to Buck. At the time, he seemed a lot older than me, I was 15 and he was 17 and obsessed with football. His Mum and Dad didn't like me and I ignored them like I ignored the rest of the busybodies in Willy. I loved to prance around the shops in Willy, down on Nelson Place, in my school uniform, hanging all over Buck, the picture of the sinful lascivious life they all wished they had. He didn't exactly move in with me, though. After a couple of weeks, I realized that I wanted my time to myself and getting up and looking at him over breakfast, just a glass of milk if one of us had remembered to buy it, wasn't for me. So I started sleeping in past breakfast, only went to school if I felt like it, whereas Buck was up early, went for his run, had to go to school or the coach at Willy football club would drop him off the team.

Then one afternoon as I was walking past St. Mary's on my way to the shops, this bloke comes out the church prances down the steps and nearly bangs into me.

"You're Lockie's little niece, aren't you?"

"What's it to you?" I say, with as much hostility I could muster.

"Your uncle Lockie doesn't lie, that's for sure."

"Oh yair?"

"You're even more gorgeous than he said."

"Oh, I know you. I've seen you at the barber shop," I say coyly, stopping, hands on hips, chest thrust forward, giving him my big smile.

"Harry Nolte at you service, my sweet."

"I'm no lolly, if that's what you're thinking."

"So where are you off to then? Shouldn't you be at school?"

"What's it to you? Are you the truant officer now?"

"Too bad you're so young," he says, reaching into his trouser pocket.

"Oh? I might be young, but I know what's what," I say, with lots of cheek.

"Would this help you out? He's holding a folded up $10 bill which he presses into my hand. "With the compliments of uncle Harry," he says. "I hear you've moved into a flat on Willy Beach."

"How'd you know that?"

"I'm running for state parliament; I know everything that's going on in Willy. Too bad you're so young, as I said, or you could vote for me in the next election."

I take the $10 and look him squarely in his moon face, his little moustache twitching away, his eyes squinting beneath bushy black eyebrows, showing flecks of grey. "I'm old enough," I say with a tilt of my head. "So have you got a car?"

"It's right here," he says, pointing at a VW bug parked right in front of the church.

"Can you give me a lift to my flat, then?" I ask.

He's already got the door open for me. I still remember that chance meeting. It's where it all began. The easiest $10 I ever made. Actually, it was the *first* $10 I ever made.

"It's our tenth anniversary," said Harry Nolte as he climbed into the Winnebago, "ten years since our chance meeting outside St. Mary's."

Lizzie extended her hand to help him up the two steep steps. Of all her clients, Harry was easily the most repulsive and certainly the most annoying. His little moustache continuously twitched from side to side, and now he had developed a new mannerism of licking it every now and then with the tip of his tongue, usually after he said something he thought was funny.

And he never looked you in the eye when he talked. Always furtively looking someplace else.

"Harry! How nice of you to come," Lizzie said, an affected voice, full of derision that only she knew.

"My darling. I've brought you a present to celebrate."

"Oooh! Thank you. What is it?"

"Open it and find out," replied Harry, excited.

About the size of a shoe box, it was wrapped in green and yellow-striped paper, tied with a broad, yellow bow.

"Don't tell me it's Italian shoes," she mused.

"Open it and see."

Lizzie tore open the wrapping and found a shoe box inside. She lifted the lid and there sat a splendid pair of stiletto heeled red leather shoes.

"Oh, Harry. You shouldn't have."

"Go on, put them on," he urged with great satisfaction.

She reached down to slip them on her feet, but there was paper in the right shoe, and it wouldn't slip on. She reached in and pulled it out, stiff paper not the kind they use to pack shoes. She pulled it out and was about to throw it in the bin when she saw that it was the colour of money.

"Harry, you devil you," she smiled as she unravelled four $50 bills.

"The pleasure has been all mine," he bragged, twitching his nose and cheeks, waiting, anticipating a kiss, which she forced herself to give him.

"You're so kind, Harry, you really are." She assumed that the shoes came from Bobby's stash. That's the only way he could have got her shoe size. Off Bobby. She looked at him, his eyes looking past her to the mirror on the Winnebago door. "I suppose you want special treatment, this morning?"

"What you do is always special."

"OK. Harry, so what is it you want?"

"I'm going to run for federal parliament. I'm too good for this little state."

"What's that got to do with me?"

"My advisers tell me that I have to look normal to have a chance."

"What does that mean?"

"I need a wife," said Harry, holding back a grin.

"Harry! You're a confirmed bachelor, you've told me that over and over."

"I know. But now I'm getting on a bit," he stretches his round dimpled chin up over his collar, "though I'm still looking all right. I need a wife to make me look normal."

"I'm hardly that," said Lizzie, taken aback, aghast at the prospect.

"I know, I mean, well, you know what I mean."

"The answer's no, Harry and here's your money back. Now let's get down to business."

Lizzie undoes his thin navy tie, undoes the collar, and begins to unbutton his shirt. Harry pulls back, still looking past her in the mirror.

"I'm serious," he said. "You have to marry me. I can't campaign as a bachelor. There will be talk."

"You think there wouldn't be talk if we showed up married? It's no secret what I do in Willy. Everyone knows except my mother, and she only pretends not to know."

"I'll make it worth your while."

Lizzie ignores him and continues to remove his shirt and singlet, which he does not seem to notice. The grey fuzz on his chest matches his grey moustache that is yellowed at the edges from smoking Phillip Morris cigarettes. His straight greying hair, what there is of it, is combed flat, stinking of hair oil, and he sports large unclipped sideburns as if to make up for the lack of hair on his head. He has begun to squint as well. Now, she undoes the belt of his grey Fletcher Jones pants, worn shiny front and back, thick and unappealing, the style from some ten years ago, straight and baggy. She unbuttons his pants and they fall away. She slides her hands inside his underpants and gradually pushes them down. He turns to look full in the mirror and watches them drop. He doesn't see his beer belly, his thin bony legs and arms, all pointy and bumpy, covered in scores of dark brown blotches. He sees a man at the height of his powers, that's what he sees, thought Lizzie.

"I can make you into a queen," says Harry, preening himself.

"You're full of shit, Harry," Lizzie wanted to say, but bit her tongue. "I'm sure you could, Harry, but where would you find the money? An MP doesn't get paid much, does he?"

"There are ways," he said with an air of mystery, "there are ways."

"Like what?" Lizzie, more than anyone else, certainly was wise to the ways of politicians. She had slept with many of them. And that was what Harry was counting on.

"With your help," he said, looking quickly at her, then back to the mirror.

"You want to use me?"

"Why not? That's what wives are for, isn't it?"

"So let me see," said Lizzie, thoughtfully, "you want to marry me then you will get, free of charge, everything you currently pay me for."

"And you'll be queen, wife of the future Prime Minister of Australia."

Lizzie suppressed a laugh. The thought of Harry as Prime Minister, what a joke! "You make it sound very enticing," she said.

"So, let's do it then," he said, looking once again in the mirror, eyes quickly darting to her face and back. "You've nothing to lose, everything to gain."

Lizzie grabbed at his quickly shrinking crown jewels, not that they were of much size anyway, though she was sure he thought he was the manliest of any. To her surprise, he stepped away a little and put his hands down to grab hers.

"Harry, let's get down to business," she said, stroking his hair with her other hand. But there was no action down there, nothing. She tried all her tricks, but there was little response.

"I'm serious," he said, no longer smiling or even twitching. "I'm going to be Prime Minister. I can't do it without you."

"Put your pants on, Harry. I think we're done. I don't want to be anyone's wife, otherwise I would have done it years ago."

"Will you at least think about it?"

"I don't love you, Harry. It's just business."

"There's no such thing as love, you of all people must know that. Getting married is a business relationship." Now he was really serious, all twitching was gone and for the very first time he looked her squarely in the face. Little did he know that he had touched a raw nerve that brought her to the brink of tears. She had been in love, was still in love, but could not find a way to consummate it.

"You sound like a desperate old man,'" she replied with derision that he did not detect.

He looked away and the twitches started again. Lizzie usually helped her clients get dressed, a way of saying come back again soon. But now she held back. "There's no way I'll ever marry you, Harry. Sorry."

He pulled up his pants, buttoned his shirt, tied his tie looking into the mirror. "One day you'll regret this," he said as he opened the Winnebago door.

"Here's your money back,' she said, expecting him to refuse.

"Thanks," he said as he took the money, "you can keep the shoes."

*

Striker's Friday run. This is the Shrine run, a big run to get rid of all the stress of the work week. Up Page Street, right on Albert Park Road, across the Domain, into the Botanic Gardens, around the Shrine of Remembrance, then back home. There was a lot to mull over. Another meeting with the Commissioner coming up this morning. Why the Commissioner should bother himself with this case, who knows; not that unusual for people to be fished out of the river or bay, so the only reason he can be interested is because he thinks Monie is a communist's wife. Of course, she's probably a commie as well. That she has survived, however, is a stroke of luck, at least if she regains conscious-ness, maybe she will be able to tell him what has happened, if anything, should it turn out that someone dropped or pushed her in the river, most likely her husband. This morning, on his big run, he would make a detour and swing by the Alfred hospital where Mrs. Stalinsky lay unconscious. He wouldn't be dressed for the part, in his running clothes, but for some reason people accepted that as OK, whereas if he showed up in his usual double breasted suit, but without a tie, people would think it disrespectful. What would be important to know, though, was whether there is any connection at all with the dead bodies: maybe her head will be shaven too? Obviously, her throat would not be slit.

9. Finding Monie

"Don't you think you should phone up your commie mate and tell him?" asked Babs as she plonked down a plate of bacon and eggs in front of Sandy, who sat reading the *Sun* and sipping a cup of tea.

"He has a radio too, you know," mumbled Sandy.

"I know. But you know what he's like."

"No, I don't. Not when it comes to women."

"Then I think I'll phone him," said Babs.

"Go right ahead. But it's none of our business."

"We all thought she was dead, for Christ sake."

"No we didn't. I didn't anyway," mumbled Sandy.

"He won't do anything. He's hoping she's dead, I bet."

Sandy looked up from his paper. "Babs, you don't know that. Stop making trouble."

"If doing the right thing's making trouble, then I'm it."

"Go on then, phone him," Sandy sighed.

"He's your mate, Sandy love. Come on, give him a ring."

Bobby appeared at the door of his bedroom. "I'll give him a ring," he said, "after all everyone thinks I'm the last person that saw her alive."

"And were you?" asked Babs as she plonked down another plate of bacon and eggs.

"That's what that protestant copper Striker thinks, I'm sure of it."

Bobby, rubbing his eyes, limped across and sat down in front of his bacon and eggs. "Can I get a cup of tea?"

"Get it your bloody self," muttered Babs, half joking, as she plonked down a cup and saucer and poured the tea.

"Pass the milk," he said.

At that moment the phone rang and Babs plonked the half full bottle of milk in front of Bobby and walked across the kitchen to answer it. "Just a minute," she said, and handed the phone to Sandy. "It's your commie mate," she muttered.

126

"G'day mate," said Sandy, "I s'pose you heard the news?"

"Striker came to my house and told me. This time it really is Monie. She looks bloody awful," said Lennie.

"Gees, I'm sorry to hear that, Lennie. Is there anything we can do here?"

"No, but I'd like to speak with Bobby if he's there."

"OK then. But is she all right?"

"Still unconscious, it's a toss-up if she'll make it," Lennie replied.

"So where did they find her?" asked Sandy.

"Somewhere near the ferry. That's why I want to talk to Bobby. I thought he might know something more."

"Bobby, he wants to talk to you. She's still out to it," said Sandy as Bobby took phone.

"Lennie? You OK?" asked Bobby. "I told that stinking cop all I know."

"I'm OK. They say a fisherman bloke pulled her out right near the ferry on the South Melbourne side of the river. So she must have fell off the ferry?"

"Last I saw her" said Bobby, "she staggered on to the ferry on the Willy side and it made one trip across and she was gone. I looked everywhere for her, I tell you. I did. It's not my fault, if that's what you're thinking."

"No of course not. It's just that you were the last one to see her, so Striker says."

"He's got it in for me, I know that. He's trying to do all of us Willy boys in, that's for sure."

"How do you know that? Striker is an asshole but why would he go after all of you?"

"You know, Lennie, for a commie you're pretty dumb. Who do you think was behind that put-up charge of animal cruelty against Sandy? And who do you think got Shooter banished to Geelong?"

"How do you know he was behind all that?" asked Lennie.

"I have my sources. Very reliable sources. I know everything that goes on in Melbourne and Williamstown. I'm the ferry captain you know. I see everything that goes on."

"I have no idea what you're talking about, Bobby. You're just a ferry driver."

"Are you saying I'm lying?" Bobby's face reddened.

"Bobby, here, give me the phone," said Babs with a worried look. Bobby gripped the phone and would have bashed it against the wall like he did in the phone booth a while ago, but for Babs pulling it from his hand.

"Lennie, this is Babs. I'm very sorry that Monie is out to it. But at least she's not dead like we all thought. It must have been awful for you when Striker took you to the morgue."

"Babs, thanks. It was. But now it could be even worse. They say that if she wakes up, she could be brain damaged, like a vegetable. I hope that Striker catches the bastard that did it."

"What do you mean? That bloody tight-assed copper still thinks that someone tried to kill her?"

"You should have been there. He's got all these bodies, four of them, and Monie would have been the fifth. They all have slashed throats and their hair shaved off."

"But the news said that there were no signs of foul play," observed Babs.

"I know. And as far as Monie is concerned, apparently that's true. But that doesn't stop cops like Striker from thinking otherwise."

"I suppose you're right. Do you want to come across and spend some time with us? You're always welcome, you know," offered Babs.

"Thanks, I think I will. I have some loose ends to tie up here because of the national strike ending, then I'll catch the ferry across. It will give me a chance to talk some more with Bobby. Maybe there's something he's forgotten."

"You're playing detective now?" asked Babs with a frown.

"No. I just feel like there's something missing. I know that Monie is a pain in the ass. I know that better than anyone. But I saved her from the street. I care for her, you know."

"Of course you do," said Babs, reminding herself that Lennie also lives nicely off the money Monie inherited from her family.

"If Lennie comes anywhere near me, I'll punch the bastard out," muttered Bobby as he chewed his bacon.

"Bobby, grow up. The bloke's upset. How would you like it if your loved one—perish the thought—nearly drowned, and was close to death?" Babs said playing her big sister role.

"I have a loved one, but I don't have her, everyone else does." Bobby growled to himself.

"Whatdja say Bobby?" Babs put her hand to her ear.

"Forget it. Nothing."

He pushed his plate away, limped out of the kitchen, hopped down to his Imp and drove away. Today was his tenth anniversary with Lizzie, except that she had forgotten it.

*

When Monie woke up she asked for a whiskey. It's what she did every morning she woke up, and Lennie was always standing there at the ready. Instead, detective Striker sat in the corner of the hospital room.

"Good morning Mrs. Stalinsky," he said, rising from his chair and approaching the bed.

"Who the bloody hell are you? Where's Lennie? Where's my whiskey?" she growled.

"I'm detective Striker, Mrs. Stalinsky. You've been unconscious for several days. You almost died."

"Detective? Where's your bloody clothes? The whiskey? Where is it? And where's my teeth?"

"My apologies, Mrs. Stalinsky. I just dropped in to see if you had come round. I'm on my morning run. I'll see if I can get you a cup of tea." He reached for the call button. "Maybe your husband can find a spare set of teeth for you. You lost yours in the river, I think."

"Detective who?"

"Striker."

"I've heard of you. Leave my husband alone. Just because he's a commo, you treat him like he's a criminal."

"We think someone tried to kill you," Mrs. Stalinsky.

"What? Why would anybody want to do that? I'm not worth anything to anyone."

"Not even your husband?"

"Least of all him." Monie almost grinned, but pains shot up the side of her face, so she grimaced instead. A doctor entered the room.

"Detective Striker," said the doctor, "I think you should leave off for now. I need to examine Mrs. Striker to see whether there have been any lasting effects of the drowning."

"Drowning? What are you talking about?" asked Monie, agitated.

"I am doctor Harlow, Mrs. Stalinsky, You almost drowned. We're worried there might be some collateral damage."

"I'm all right except for the pains in my face." Monie closed her eyes.

Harlow moved closer to the bed and leaned forward. "Your speech is a bit slurred, Mrs. Stalinsky."

Monie opened her eyes and licked the saliva that had accumulated on her lips and mumbled, "that's because I haven't had my whiskey. And I've lost my teeth. There's nothing wrong with me that a stiff shot can't fix."

"We'll see about that," answered the doctor as he reached down to pull back the bed covers.

"Good. Then get me a bloody whiskey."

Striker intervened "What is the last thing you can remember, Mrs. Stalinsky? How did you come to be in the river?" he asked

"What river?"

"The Yarra, of course. Near the Williamstown ferry," answered Striker.

"All I remember…no…there's nothing there. Where's Lennie? Has anyone told him I'm here, wherever that is." Monie drifted off.

"You're in the Alfred Hospital. I phoned your husband. He should be here soon," said Striker.

"Detective Striker. Would you please step back and let me examine her?" insisted Dr. Harlow.

"I don't need anyone poking me. I'm fine, I tell you. Get these tubes out of me so I can get dressed and go home."

Monie sank back into the bed. An orderly erected a screen around her. It was the signal for Striker to leave. "She's not to leave before I give the OK," Striker ordered, "I have more questions."

"Like what?" called Monie, "I'll leave when I feel like it."

"Just lie still, Mrs. Stalinsky, I need to check your legs. Can you feel this?" Harlow now had the covers back and stood at the end of the bad.

"Yes." Monie said in a faint voice.

"Can you wiggle your left foot? And now your right?"

Monie complied and murmured with her eyes closed again, "there, you see. There's nothing wrong with me."

Monie was exhausted. All the activity, talking and questions, then poking and prodding, the pain in her foot and the side of her face. The doctor had said both would go in time and that she must rest. She told him to fuck off and leave her alone. He had looked at her with disdain, a look that she was used to. Monie was born with a foul mouth, that's what her mother always said. "That filthy tongue of yours will get you into trouble one day," she said. But it didn't matter what they said, Monie always spoke her mind, that was her defence anyway. And she'd come in for a lot of abuse from teachers at school when she answered them back in no uncertain terms, abusing them like she reckoned all the boys in her class would like to do but weren't game. Instead, they teased her, making fun of her rough, reddened skin, her buck teeth and her gaunt body, so skinny that the boys called her "Bones." And her hair, that was what got her mother really upset. They took her to the hairdresser every couple of weeks, without fail, and for as long as she could remember.

Its mousey grey-brown colour wasn't attractive and Mum's hairdresser always wanted to colour it, but I wouldn't let her. Mum was OK with it, though. So I'd tell the hairdresser to fuck off too, and stalk out of the shop. Mum tried all styles, anything to keep my hair neat and tidy, cut short, shoulder length, tied in a bun, fringed, you name it, she tried them all. The trouble is that I had a mannerism that I constantly ran my hands and fingers through my hair, so no matter how well coifed it was by the end of the day it was a straggling mess.

I guess what I'm trying to say is that I was an ugly kid and I paid dearly for it, never understanding that my foul mouth just made things worse. And I know I'm still ugly and still have a foul mouth and that's why I'm amazed that Lennie picked me up. And I mean really literally fucking picked me up. He's the kindest bugger I know. He doesn't deserve me. Nobody does, come to think of it. Including myself, not to mention my poor old Mum and Dad, bless their souls, they're gone now. No, not what you think. They're alive and well, or at least I assume so, but they got fed up with me at long last and one day just took off up north to the Gold Coast to some kind of gated community and that was it. I remember the day well. I had just graduated from Monash Uni with my social work degree. I know, you can't bloody believe it, and Mum and Dad would have been so proud, but I had lost contact with them for some years by then having ended up in Turana Training Centre for delinquents because I was found drunk too often on the street in Toorak where we lived, and it wasn't the first time I'd been doing it since I was in high school. My parents really weren't responsible for my behaviour, they tried all they could to cope with me, but I was too much for them, too much for anyone. So when I was picked up, they told the cops and the social workers that they didn't want me back. They couldn't cope with me anymore.

I think I'm babbling. My mind's all fucked up. I know, it's the booze, it destroys brain cells. But I need the booze, without it I can't function. I kept abusing the teachers at the Training Centre with my foul mouth and they'd grab me, pin my arms to my side, almost squeeze the life out of me, a result I would not have minded all that much. I took to screaming in those days, and if I could get my arms free, I liked scratching whoever was bloody silly enough to get close. My counsellors at Turana—in those days, boys and girls were all in together—kept saying I made poor decisions. That was bull shit of course. I never made any decisions. I just did things. Thinking never came into it. That's all there was to it. In my days at Turana they'd send me off to some unsuspecting foster family and I'd last a couple of weeks at most and they'd send me back, or more often, the cops would pick me up off the street, drunk lying in a gutter somewhere. Or they'd catch me turning tricks on a street corner in St. Kilda.

On one famous occasion I managed to get some booze smuggled into Turana after we went out on an excursion. It was a bush walk. We had this new teacher who was enthralled with nature, "our mother" she called it. "Not my bloody mother," I'd say, and she would look at me as if to say, "Oh you poor little dear, it's not your fault you had an awful mother." Of course, none of this was my Mum's or my Dad's fault. I mean that literally. I know because around that time I was interviewed by a social worker (I'd had many such interviews) when she was called out of the room so I sneaked a look at my file—by this time a pretty thick file—and there it was right on the front page, adopted at 18 months, born of an alcoholic mother. But it didn't matter. It was taken for granted by all of us, including the teachers and social workers that everything bad we did was because of poor upbringing, the parents' fault. It was a most convincing excuse for everyone inside Turana. In a way it bound us all together, our wardens, teachers, custodians, men with the keys, had the terrible job of looking after a bunch of obstreperous defiant adolescents who had been mismanaged or spoiled by their parents. And when we acted up, we were routinely informed that we were "not at home now" and disciplined severely, and I mean severely, usually with a leather strap, and later when that was frowned upon, they took to squeezing the daylights out of you under the guise of preventing you from hurting yourself.

The bush walk wasn't really a bush walk. We just went out walking across the park near the zoo. Trouble was we all ran ahead and left mother nature's teacher behind. And a few of the boys took off across to Parkville and broke into a couple of houses while the rest of us kept cover and did what you'd never believe. We played a game of leaving a trail in the woods like in the fairy tale of Hansel and Gretel. And when the trail was set, I ran back to nature's teacher and said, "don't worry miss, we're all here, we've left a trail for you to follow," and ran off again well out of her sight. We waited until we heard a shriek and we knew that mother nature's teacher had found the trail. We all crept up to see the fun. The teacher and the custodian who had come as the enforcer were standing there, mother nature's teacher, her hands to her face, then throwing up and the custodian standing hands on hips, flabbergasted. Each of us had made a deposit along the path. That's right, we dropped a turd every twenty yards or so. And during the turmoil the boys who had gone off to rob a couple of houses returned carrying booze which they stashed under a bush and I noted carefully where. We had each been given little knapsacks to bring our lunch and a drink, so we had a convenient way to carry back the booze. In spite of all that, mother nature's teacher took us to the place that was the least natural of any environment, the zoo that was just across the park. Each of us got to take a swig of booze, brandy I think it was, maybe some whiskey too, and we all became pretty silly, one of the kids trying to jump into the lion enclosure but fortunately was so drunk he fell backwards and was carted off somewhere. One of the boys who was a bit too friendly with the custodian gave him a sip and they pissed off somewhere and we didn't see them again until we were going back.

They set up Winlaton School for delinquent girls and there, although I never lost my abusive mouth, they got me under control, and I mean bloody really under control, or at least that's what they thought. I ran away from Winlaton one night—the security wasn't all that tight—and went off to Carlton, hung around the pubs, and managed to get a couple of blokes hooked, socked down some booze, that's about all I remember of it. The next thing I knew, I woke up in a hospital room, all sore down below. They kept me there, tied down to the bed, only freeing me to eat the horrible food they served, until I had recovered. The fucking bastards. I kept asking them, in my abusive way of course, what they'd done to me, and the nurses, crabby bitches, kept saying that I'd done it all to myself. "Done fucking what?" I yelled. "What do you bloody think?" they answered. I was eventually transported in an ambulance back to Winlaton, where I was treated most kindly, confined to my room until I was completely recovered. It was not until I was in the interviewing room with "my" social worker, a very kind old lady, who was a volunteer, they said she was the wife of some big shot politician, whatever, who told me that for my own good, they had tied my tubes so I couldn't get pregnant, because if I did, I'd give birth to a child that was defective because of my alcoholism. So it was only the right thing to do, didn't I agree?

Well, I bloody did agree, because I thought now that this was what bloody happened to me, that I was defective too. It all made sense, and I had a most convenient excuse for what I was like. I had a defect. It never really occurred to me that what the bastards did, get inside me and cut me up, without asking me, not even my Mum and Dad as far as I knew, because they'd completely given up on me ever since they had me put in Turana. The effect of all this was to make me a compliant, withdrawn, pathetic little creature, spending almost all my time in my own single room, basically an isolation cell, only mixing with the others for evening meals.

The professionals, the psychologists and social workers said that this "time out" as they called it, finally worked with me. But it wasn't the time out, it was the dreadful deeply felt feeling of helplessness that overwhelmed me. If they could get inside me and cut me up, there was no limit to what they could do to me. I was transformed into a sickly adolescent with a severe mental and physical defect. I was still prone to outbursts, still had a foul mouth, but now it was all because I was a defective and my handlers, the teachers and social workers, became almost sympathetic, some even kind. They had teachers at Winlaton and some of them were OK. One of them took me under her wing and brought me along. She was the only one that saw, although I might be ugly and a bloody nuisance, that there was nothing wrong with me mentally, I mean I was not a mental defective like everyone else thought I was. She got me all the books, and got me to classes, and eventually got me to take some exam that was supposed to get me into university. And my getting that qualification, it was something that was a special matriculation exam they called it, that got me accepted into the social work program at Monash University, where they had a special admissions program for handicapped persons like me. And that was my downfall. Because they let me out thinking I was cured. And as everyone knows, no one is ever cured of alcoholism. A social worker found me a boarding house in Richmond and I even had a small scholarship to pay for it and some living expenses. For a student, it was supposed to be enough. And for most, it probably was. The trouble was that the boarding house was just across the street from the Bridge Hotel.

*

They got off on the wrong foot when Striker first called Stalinsky to tell him that Monie had come out of her coma.

"Why is this a police matter?" asked Stalinsky, "I want to talk to the attending doctor."

"I thought I was doing you a favour," said Striker with some restraint.

"What favour? Police interfering with a private citizen's concern about his wife's condition?"

"Don't you want to know where she is so you can come and visit her?"

"Where?"

"The Alfred."

"I'm on my way. And you had better be gone when I get there."

Lennie abruptly hung up. Striker didn't even have a chance to tell him what ward she was in, or even what her condition was, not even that she was awake and talking."

10. Lennie Finds Monie

It was a bright sunny day, a slight nip in the air, an excellent day for a brisk walk. Lennie decided to walk to the Alfred from his house in Richmond. Along the way, he would think over the past week's events. The great march forward, as some of his mates had called the march to free Clarrie, had captured the imagination of everyone, especially the press. Having Sandy's boys there along with all the other union reps from across the country was an amazing accomplishment. They had brought the government to its knees, a rare event indeed. It was his greatest achievement as chair of the Party, possibly the biggest win ever for the union movement, and certainly a step forward to the day when the revolution would come, just like Marx said it would, in spite of young Ryley's protestations about unions just being a tool of the owners of production. You could feel the consciousness of the workers in the air during the march. It was palpable. They were starting to see the injustice of their condition, the callous exploitation of their labour, soon they would feel it in their bones. He was already planning how he would take advantage of the next crisis that the stupid government would no doubt get itself into. Next time there would be violent protests as well, complete and utter disruption of the bourgeoisie. Their comfortable lifestyle made possible by their abuse of the workers, would soon be a thing of the past. Their greed and violence would bring on their own destruction. They would get at last what they deserved, just as would the workers when they rose up *en masse* and exerted their rightful place in a free and just society.

But what about Monie? She had been the bane of his life ever since he tripped over her prostrate body as he stepped out of the saloon bar of the Bridge hotel after a meeting of his Party executive. They had argued over whether or not to continue infiltration of the unions and that had devolved into a silly disagreement as to whether they should follow the party of Mao or stick with the Soviets. The fact was that the Soviets, as opinionated and narrow minded as they were, claimed to be the only ones who really knew what communism was, the only ones who had successfully put it into practice. There wasn't all that much of a difference, in Lennie's view. Both ended up using violence to their advantage, the numbers of people killed along the way were hardly any indication of success. It was what they ended up with that was important. Had they established a just society? Was everyone made equal?

"Watch it, you bloody idiot!" someone screamed from his shining new Holden, "it's a bloody red light, are you blind?" Lost in his reverie, Lennie managed to step back on the curb.

"Up you!" he muttered, only then noticing that he was at Church street bridge.

Bloody Monie. You know, I should have stepped over her right there and then and left her to rot. She was rolling over on the footpath, trying to stand up but falling down over and over, blurting out the foulest of language you ever heard from a man, let alone a woman. Everyone else, though, all blokes coming and going to the pub, just walked around her, or said something about screwing her. I tried to step over her, but she rolled against me and I nearly tripped. At the same time one bloke came up and said something abusive and spat on her. I think that's what made me lean down and help her to stand up. I didn't do it for Marx. As a matter of fact I was convinced at the time that she was just one of his lumpen proletariat, no good for anyone. Basically trash to be used if the occasion arose, but essentially to be thrown away, just like garbage.

"Get me a fucking drink," she slobbered, "if you want to fuck me you have to buy me a drink."

"I'm doing neither," I said firmly, and got her standing on two feet, then began to haul her along with me. I'm not that big a person, so it was a struggle to keep her walking.

"You got a fucking place?" she asks, her tongue hanging out the side of her mouth like a dog's.

"Shut up, and let's get away from here," I said, not having thought exactly what I was doing or where I was going, except that it appeared to me that I was walking in the direction of my house. "I'm taking you home."

"My fucking place or yours?" she grinned.

The walk home to my place was not easy, and it must have appeared to the passers-by who tried not to look, that we were both drunk. But home we went and I emptied the remains of a small bottle of brandy I kept for medicinal purposes into a glass and watched her sock it down. It had the desired effect. She calmed down and almost became rational.

"So where do you want to do it?" she asked.

I carried her into my bedroom and placed her on top of the bed, careful not to ruffle the sheets. She was slobbering all over the place, so I dashed to the bathroom, worried that she would throw up on my nice clean sheets. But by the time I came back with a towel she was fast asleep, snoring like all drunks do when they pass out.

I stood at the bedroom door, biting my bottom lip. I couldn't understand what I'd done. She was without any doubt a repulsive human being. Her rough reddened skin, not just her face but anywhere you could see her skin, was anything but inviting. How anyone could lie with her I could not imagine. One would have to be very drunk to make it palatable. And I already knew from having half carried her here that she stunk to high heaven, who knows where she had spent her last few nights. Or maybe she was homeless, which was a pretty good bet.

The walk was taking much longer than Lennie had antici-pated. But it was a lovely sunny day, an enjoyable day for a walk. He had stopped on the bridge to admire the Yarra, then crossed to Alexandra Avenue. He figured that he wasn't even half way, so decided to follow the nice walk along the Yarra to Punt Road where he would catch a tram to the Alfred. It had been a long journey with Monie, full of surprises. That first morning at home when Monie woke up her first thought was, "where's the booze?"

I watched her roll over and sit on the edge of the bed, having no idea of course, where she was. "What about a cup of tea?" I said, trying hard to smile, something I don't manage too often.

"Who are you, asshole?"

"Lennie. Lennie Stalinsky. And you are?"

"I s'pose you fucked me?"

"No I did not, though I can understand why you might think so."

Monie seemed to take this as a kind of apology. Usually when something like this happened the bloke would say—if they happened to be in a room and not under a bush somewhere—

"fuck you," and leave, or maybe wouldn't have stayed around till she woke up anyway.

"A cup of tea would be good," she said cautiously, "and I wouldn't mind a touch of brandy in it as well."

"No brandy, sorry. You drank it all last night."

"You're a really tight bastard, aren't you?"

"I hope so. It's what's got me through life so far."

"Oh, so you're going to tell me your sad story? Well, shut the fuck up. I've got stories of my own to deal with."

"But I can see that yours are self-inflicted. I've survived in spite of everything else."

"Poor fucking shit you are. Well, I'm getting out of here. Can't have breakfast without a shot of brandy."

"I've made you some toast. I expect you have your tea black?"

"What's it to you?"

"You still haven't told me your name."

Monie struggled off the bed and I guided her to the bathroom. "You better have a shower while you're in there. You smell to high heaven," I called, expecting to get a stream of abuse back. But she closed the door and there was silence until I called out again, "your tea's getting cold." I heard the shower. "I'll get you some clothes. You can't put those filthy ones back on," I called through the door. I rummaged through my drawers and dresser. It wasn't that I had all that many clothes myself. I found some pants and underwear and a shirt and passed them into the bathroom along with a towel.

"Get out you dirty bastard!" she yelled.

"Shut up and get yourself clean."

And that was the start of our relationship, if you could call it that. I had never talked to anyone like that. Never. I avoided talking to people as much as I could. I mean, I talked a lot with my party members, organizing our work, but that was as far as it went. There was nothing social about it. We never hung out together like people do, just for the fun of being together. I never found that much fun. That's why I never went to those Friday night shin-digs at Sandy's place, except maybe only once and that was to introduce Monie. And even then she had to nag me about it for a long time before I did it. She's the social one, if that's what you could call it.

She came out of the bathroom looking like a bloke. There was nothing feminine about her. I wondered immediately what my poor old Dad would have thought. Me having an ugly woman in the house. Though now, except for her protruding front teeth, she wasn't so bad, and I could see a hint of a nice figure hidden under my old clothes.

"How do I look?" she said with a big smile, a smile I was not prepared for.

"A very handsome proletarian," I said.

"Prola-what?"

And that was the second start of our relationship. I told her I was a communist and over several cups of tea and toast I gave her a lecture on Marxist thought. I could see, though, that she was having trouble keeping down the toast, but after a while, as I talked on, getting excited as I always did when I was preaching Marx, she sat there, entranced, at least that's what I thought. On that very day, I got her out of that rooming house across the street from the Bridge Hotel, and she moved in with me. And for the next few weeks I took her along with me to my Party meetings, and went with her to Monash University where she had enrolled in a social work degree (that's another story). By being with her constantly I was able to keep her off the grog and I even shifted our weekly party executive committee meetings to my house, instead of the pub. The comrades complained of course, but they went along with it, and I have to say, it had a very good influence on our conversations. We got a lot more done and there were far fewer arguments. The blokes were very curious about Monie, they kept hinting that maybe she wasn't a real communist and shouldn't come to our meetings. But I ignored them. She was by now as much of a communist as they were. In fact, I think I taught her lots more and got her to read lots more than any of the blokes in the party. They weren't thinkers, they were doers. Monie was—is—a thinker like me, even though the way she talks you wouldn't think so.

Lennie reached Punt road. The noise of the traffic and the approaching tram jolted him back to the present. It was a relief that at least Monie wasn't dead, although he had to admit to himself that, had the body Striker made him identify been that of Monie, he was well prepared to accept it. In fact he was anticipating a kind of relief, that her death would release him from the trials and troubles she had caused him ever since that first meeting. Honestly, though, she hadn't cause him all those troubles. He had brought them on himself. But life would be simpler without her. He was sure of that. It was why, when Monie disappeared for periods, sometimes several days, he never tried that hard to find her. He simply assumed that she had gone on a binge and would eventually show up, usually begging around Flinders Street station, and he would go down there and find her, sometimes under the Swanston Street bridge. And she begged, not because she had no money, well, temporarily she would run out of money but be too drunk to go to the bank and get more. And in her drunken condition, what bank would even let her in the door?

When Lennie finally arrived at the Alfred and found his way to Monie's room, who should be there but Ryley, and of course, Striker sitting in the corner. Monie, still hooked up to tubes and various apparatus, lay breathing deeply, eyes closed, mouth shut, her teeth for once, not on display. Someone had combed her hair and cleaned her face, maybe even applied a little make-up, which of course, Monie never used. She heard distant voices, familiar ones, and for once in her life just listened, not wanting to speak.

Lennie turned immediately to Striker. "What are you doing here?" he asked angrily.

"I'm doing my job," he answered.

"Like the lackey that you are," said Ryley with as much sarcasm as he could muster.

Lennie turned to Striker. "Get out," he demanded softly, but firmly, "get out."

"I'm going, but I will need to speak with both of you once you are done here."

"Get stuffed," muttered Ryley, inching towards him.

Striker stood at the foot of Monie's bed and said, "I'll speak with you later Mrs. Stalinsky. Maybe you can talk some sense into these fools." Then he left.

Monie heard it all but it didn't register, only that she felt safe knowing that now both Lennie and Ryley were there to watch over her. They cared for her. It was more than she could ever have asked for in her life. Someone who cared about her, in spite of all the trouble she caused them.

Why Lennie stays around, it's a mystery, one that I thank God for every day, every minute of my life, except when I'm on a binge, then it's not possible to care about anything but the booze. I know I'm a horrible person and don't deserve Lennie, let alone Ryley. Why on earth would he bother to come here? Oh but maybe it's because of his being a mate to Lennie. It's nice of him anyway.

Then again, maybe it's because of my money, thanks to my "loving parents." I know I drove them crazy and I don't really blame them for putting me away in Turana. And after I ran away a couple of times and turned up back home, they chose a different solution. They sold up everything and took off to Queensland so I had nowhere to run to. The poor things, they had been punished for all of their good deeds, adopting me, knowing that I had a defect, doing their best to raise me. But I was too much to raise. An incorrigible child and rebellious adolescent, a danger to myself and others. They couldn't cope with the unstated finger-pointing by my teachers and social workers that I was the product of their defective parenting. It was their fault, not mine. And for a long time I believed that as well, until I finally discovered the truth that they were not my real parents. Up until that time I suffered the guilt and shame of being an ungrateful child, adopted by well-meaning loving parents, saved from a life in institutions. Did I deserve what they did? I'm sure they could not live with their guilt and that's why they went off to Queensland hoping never to see me again, and as well, God Bless them, they set up a trust that guaranteed me a basic income for the rest of my life. And there's the joke. Lennie picked me up off the street, not knowing that I would be the one who would support him. So unlike my parents, his good deed was rewarded—with me and my antics.

Monie's eyelids flickered, then opened. Ryley and Lennie were deep in a debate about the finer points of Marx's paper on the Jewish Question.

"You buggers, can't you talk about anything else?" she barked.

They reluctantly stopped in mid-sentence and turned to her.

"You're awake again!" said Ryley. "Thank goodness!"

Lennie said nothing, but approached her and held her hand, no smile, no expression. Monie was used to that. It's what he was like and had always been so. Never showed emotion except when under real stress there were those little beads of sweat that showed up on his shiny bald forehead.

"Striker left you alone, I hope?" Lennie asked.

"Haven't a clue. Don't bloody remember talking to him."

"And the doctors? They said you're OK?" asked Ryley.

"They said I'm fine."

"Then let's get out of here," said Lennie.

"Only thing is, I haven't got any clothes," said Monie, "don't suppose you thought to bring some?"

"I'll have to go home and get some. Anything special you want?" asked Lennie.

"I could get a taxi and we could sneak you out in your hospital gown," offered Ryley.

"Only it opens wide at the back. I don't want people staring at my bloody ass," complained Monie.

"Since when did you care what people thought?" muttered Lennie.

At that moment, Striker entered the room and they all turned to face him. Monie was already sitting on the side of the bed, trying to cover herself up. Striker was once again transformed into his tightly sheathed self, his double breasted suit buttoned up, narrow tie carefully knotted against a bright white shirt with a cut back collar, the latest style.

"Not so fast," he said, "I have some questions for all of you."

"We're not answering any of your questions. You have no right to detain us. Get out of our way," warned Ryley.

"You heard him, asshole," added Monie, very much recovered.

"I am conducting a murder investigation and you are obstructing my inquiry. I could have you arrested."

"No you couldn't. You're bluffing. You're doing what your bosses told you to do, harass innocent citizens because of an imaginary communist plot," countered Ryley.

"Your little toe, Mrs. Stalinsky. "Does it hurt?"

"What's it to you?"

"For your information, we have three bodies in the city morgue, each of them with their little right toe sliced off, two of them with their throats cut, all of them fished out of the Yarra or Hobsons bay in the Williamstown area. We likely have a serial murderer on our hands. Now would you stop this communist nonsense and answer my questions. They're just routine. But I need to find out how you came to be found in the Yarra, drowning, Mrs. Stalinsky. If we could trace your movements up to that date, we might get an inkling of who you talked to or were accosted by."

"I've told you, detective, I remember nothing. I'm a bloody alcoholic, didn't they tell you? I don't remember what I do most of the bloody time when I'm on a bender. Now bloody go away and leave us alone."

At that point, the door opened and Bobby limped into the room.

"You're just in time," said Striker.

"In time for what?"

"You pushed Mrs. Stalinsky off the ferry into the Yarra, didn't you?" charged Striker.

"And tried to cut her toe off while you did it," intervened Ryley, with one of his big grins.

Bobby limped across to Monie. "You're alive!" he said, "thank goodness."

"Yair, so there's still time for you to fuck me!" she blurted.

"Monie!" cried Lennie.

"Did you push her into the Yarra, Mr. Frost?" persisted Striker.

"Fuck off!" said Bobby with as much hostility as he could.

"Then I'll have to arrest you and take you in for questioning," said Striker stepping forward.

"Over my dead body, you bourgeois asshole!" growled Ryley, stepping between them.

"Stay back, Ryley. I can take him on my own, no problem," said Bobby, turning away from Monie, stepping into Striker's way, pushing forward his chest, his huge arms and fists at the ready.

Striker pulled himself up straight, as though trying to grow taller on the spot. Lennie quietly shuffled to the other side of Monie's bed and reached for her hand. He squeezed it and got her to turn her head and look into his grey eyes. There were tiny little beads of sweat popping out on his forehead. Monie turned to Striker.

"I just remembered," she said, "I remember what happened at the ferry."

"You don't have to talk to him," said Ryley. "Tell him to fuck off."

Striker relaxed his stance. "What is it Mrs. Stalinsky?"

"I fell in on my own."

"Is that so?"

"I was pissed as usual. They'll all tell you that. Bobby was there, he was the one who had to put up with me."

Bobby relaxed his arms and stepped back. "That's right. She was a bloody nuisance."

"I saw the Commissioner," continued Monie, "I know what he was up to, don't I Bobby?" she said, and made a kind of witch's cackle. "Anyone got a cigarette?" she asked.

The three men looked at each other. None of them were smokers.

"Well, fuck you all!" she complained, "Doesn't any one of you have a smoke?"

"You weren't pushed off the ferry?" persisted Striker.

"I bloody fell in. I was vomiting over the side, that's how I lost my teeth, and the ferry jolted and I fell in. Simple as that."

Striker turned to Bobby. "And where were you all this time, Mr. Frost?"

"I was getting the ferry ready to return to the other side."

"You didn't push her?"

"She's a friend, you idiot. Of course not. You can ask Eurie, the other driver, anyway, he was there."

"I have talked with him. He says he left as soon as the body was pulled up and you took over the shift."

"Why don't you bloody ask that stuffed shit Commissioner? He was there, wasn't he? Come to think of it, I remember I was pushed after all," said Monie with a devilish grin.

"Monie! Shut up!" cried Ryley.

"It was the Commissioner, that's who it was. I felt his hot stinking breath on my neck. It was the Commissioner!" Monie stood up off the bed, the hospital gown falling open. "Now get the fuck out of here, copper, or I'll call the police!" she barked.

The sight of her misshapen, disgusting body panicked Striker who took two steps backwards to the door and departed without a word.

11. Web of Intrigue

It was usually Sandy who showed up at the police station on Nelson Place to get one of the wharfies out of the lock-up. Most often the charge would be "drunk and disorderly." Shooter only locked them up if they were bothering people in the street, or if there was a serious brawl outside one of the pubs, which happened fairly often. They were tough blokes, they worked hard, but they drank hard too. This time Sandy was the one locked up and there was no Shooter to get him out. The new senior constable Stanford Lane had even put him in handcuffs and left them on even when he was pushed into the cell. He turned to face him and copped a searing blow to his cheek, dropping him to his knees.

"Why did you torture that dog, you cruel bastard?" charged Lane.

Sandy said nothing. He wanted to say, "I tried to save it, you stupid bastard," but he made himself take the advice he always gave his mates, never answer a cop's question. Besides, it was obvious that he had been set up, probably by Lane himself. The constable placed his boot against Sandy's chest and thrust him backwards against the cell's only bunk, banging his head on its edge. Sandy sat, stunned, barely conscious.

"I'll be back in ten minutes, during which time I want you to read this confession and sign it," demanded Lane, motioning his junior to hand him a pad and pen. They turned and left. Sandy's head dropped, his chin resting on his chest.

Lane did not return. Instead his junior constable showed up after an hour or possibly more as far as Sandy was able to make out, jangling his keys.

"You weren't one of Shooter's boys, were you? I pity you if you were," said Sandy.

"Shooter? Who's that?"

"Never mind."

"I'll take that confession now," said the constable reaching for it.

"Sure." Sandy had signed it with "fuck you," but the constable didn't even look at it.

"You're free to go for now, but you better show up for the hearing or you'll cop it."

Sandy followed the constable out to the reception room, walking unsteadily, finding it difficult to keep upright with his hands still cuffed behind his back. Then he saw Bobby and Ryley waiting for him and he knew everything was all right.

"Take him out of those cuffs, you bastards!" yelled Bobby, red with rage, his huge fists clenched tightly by his side.

"Take it easy uncle Bobby," said Ryley, grabbing his arm.

The constable sensed the rage and quickly undid the cuffs. "Sign this and you can go," he said, handing him a release form.

"Fuck you," said Sandy and the three of them walked out of the police station.

They climbed into Bobby's Hillman and Bobby started off.

"Did you talk to Lizzie?" asked Sandy.

"Yes, no problem. She'll take care of it, with Lockie's help."

"Everything?"

"You mean getting rid of that pompous senior constable?"

"Yeh. And the merchandise secured?"

"Sort of."

"What do you mean?"

"Well, it's in my bedroom," answered Bobby, coyly.

"Shit! Bobby. What's it doing there?"

"The cops were on to us. We had to get rid of it out of the van that Banger swiped to move the goods."

"Is there a buyer?" asked Sandy.

"Lockie says he's working on it."

"So everything's under control then?"

"Sort of."

"OK. What is it?" asked Sandy.

"Well, Babs found the stash in my bedroom. She's bloody livid."

"I bet she is. Maybe we shouldn't go straight home. I could do with a beer anyway. Let's stop in at the pub then drop in at the barber shop and see Lockie."

"Won't Mum be worried?" asked Ryley.

"We can phone her from the pub," answered Sandy, having trouble staying awake.

"You need a brandy," said Bobby as they pulled up outside the Steam Packet.

*

Billy Boyle, Lockie's eager apprentice, applied shaving cream to his customer's sideburns. "Trim them up a little?" he asked.

"Just a little," was the answer.

Billy flourished his razor and expertly shaved that delicate part under the chin where hair turned to whiskers.

"You're pretty good for an apprentice," noted the customer.

"That's because of my boss's excellent training."

Billy looked up as Sandy, Bobby and Ryley entered the shop.

"I'll be done here in a minute, then I can get to you," said Billy.

"We're looking for Lockie," said Sandy as he lumbered into the shop, rubbing his back.

"He's not here. Off on one of his business trips," replied Billy.

"Where's he gone?" asked Sandy.

"I think he went to Werribee."

"Who in Werribee would want to buy a load of Italian shoes?" muttered Bobby impatiently.

"Shh. Not in front of the kid," said Sandy, nodding towards the apprentice.

"It's all right, Mr. Malley," said Billy with a wink, "I'm good. My Dad's one of your boys. Besides, Lockie's my uncle, didn't you know?"

"Oh, right. I forgot about that. Hope he's treating you like a good uncle should," said Sandy.

"We get along just great. He's the best hairdresser in Williamstown, and he's taught me everything he knows."

"Not everything, I hope," quipped Ryley, then turning to Sandy and Bobby, "but Mum's right. It's too big a risk to stash the stuff in your house."

"What about your house then?" asked Bobby with a grin.

"You know all I have is one room in a Spotswood commission house with space for a bed and nothing else."

"That's pretty much all I have in your Mum's house," answered Bobby.

"Do you know when Lockie will be back?" asked Sandy.

"He didn't say, but he usually likes to get back in time to close up the shop. He's been going down to Werribee a lot lately. He takes me with him quite a bit. I just love being his apprentice."

"He's up to something, no doubt," said Bobby. "Why don't we stash it here, upstairs in Lockie's hideaway?"

"You know that would be even more risky," muttered Sandy.

"You're looking tired, Dad. I think we should get you home to Mum. She'll be half crazy with worry, even though we phoned her."

Bobby moved to the door. "Come on, then. Let's get back home and get you into bed, Sandy."

*

Ryley kissed Babs on the cheek. "Got to run, Mum." See you all later."

"You can't go now," called Babs. "What about all these shoes?"

"I've done my part. And there's no room in my place."

"I wouldn't know. I've never been there, have I?" quipped Babs.

"Do you want a lift?" asked Bobby. "I'm going to the ferry to meet Lizzie, I can drop you off on the way."

"No, I'm right thanks. I'll take the train. I'm meeting a friend at the station."

"Oh really? Who?" asked Babs.

"None of your business."

"When are you going to bring her home?"

"None of your business, Mum."

"Isn't our home good enough for her?"

"Mum…"

"Sorry! Love you darl!"

"I know," Ryley called over his shoulder.

Sandy plopped down on the old couch. The physical exertion of the past twenty four hours had caught up with him. Babs busied herself making a cup of tea and rummaged around in her tins for some biscuits.

"You should leave Ryley alone," said Bobby as he filled the kettle and put it on the burner. Babs banged the cups and saucers as she arranged them on the kitchen table.

"I don't think that's any of your business," she said, immediately regretting it.

Bobby responded by going into the front room to see how Sandy was doing. "Sandy's out to it," he called. "Don't think he'll be having a cuppa. It's just you and me."

Babs sat down at the old table and stared blankly at the kettle, waiting for it to boil. Ryley was all she had left to hope for, she told herself. Why shouldn't she keep at him?

I wouldn't mind if he brought his girlfriend home. He's ashamed of me, or maybe all of us. It's not fair. You have two kids, bring them up and give them everything, and they turn around and leave you, treat you like you're some kind of grown up pet. I shouldn't complain I know. At least Ryley comes home to see me. Not like Lizzie. She might as well be dead. Never phones, never comes home. What kind of a life does she lead? Mixing with all those big shot clients, so she says. Or at least that's what Bobby says she does. But I know Bobby. He's the soft one of us. He's always protecting Lizzie. It's like he's in love with her, but I try not to think about that. I told it to Father Zappia once in confession and he told me off. Made me say two hail Marys to make up for it. We shouldn't have sent Ryley to university. It's taken him away from us. He thinks he's better than us. Sandy didn't want him to go. But I insisted. If he's smart enough to get in, why shouldn't he? I argued. And I was right. I thought it would open doors for him that were closed to the likes of me and Sandy. But so far he's just become a know-it-all communist, and where will that take him? To the bloody Soviet Union? And who'd want to go there? Or China? That would be worse! The chinks don't like us, I know. If they all came down here, and they will someday. Oh shut up Barbara! Shut up!

The phone rang. It was Lockie.

*

Rumour had it that Lockie was now the largest land owner in Werribee, though Lockie had said nothing to anyone about his big win, and certainly none of his guests would dare risk revealing anything about that eventful night. But sooner or later Lockie knew the news would get out, just because solicitors were now involved in formalizing the transfer of land owner-ship, so officials in the Werribee town office would sooner or later have to be involved. As it turned out, he had won two parcels of land from Harry Nolte. The main parcel was a track of probably useless land that ran down the coast from the southern edge of the Werribee sewerage farm and inland almost to the fringes of the Werribee township. An enormous tract of land that was, as Lockie would find out later, subject to flooding, whether from the overflow from the sewerage farm or when there were high tides and the bay returned to its former boundaries that once reached as far as the You-Yangs. The other property was the Werribee cemetery, the whole lot of it, including the burial plots, used and unused. This turned out to be something quite extraordinary that Lockie found out later. When he went to his solicitor and told him of his great win, his solicitor burst out laughing saying, "you can't own a cemetery. All cemeteries occupy Crown Lands and are run by Cemetery Trusts, according to the Victorian Cemeteries Act of 1958!"

He had been tricked!

But, no. Harry Nolte might be an inveterate gambler, but he wasn't a cheat. It turned out that the Werribee Cemetery was a private cemetery that the Cemeteries Trust law had not caught up with and likely never would because it would be a matter of grabbing private property and turning it back into Crown Land, a complicated legal undertaking apparently. The trouble was, though, the cemetery was almost full, so Lockie was faced with a hunk of land on which he would have to pay considerable taxes, but for which there would be limited income. Obviously, he could not get it designated as farm land and so enjoy the considerable tax advantages. He had won, in fact, a liability, the solution to which, according to his solicitor, would be to try to get the Victorian government to buy it off him and turn the cemetery into a trust in accordance with the law.

*

Shooter caught up with Lockie at the Werribee Racecourse pub.

"So what can I do for you?" asked Shooter.

"Well, it's more like what I can do for you," answered Lockie, "you want to come back to Willy?"

"Of course I do."

"And we all want you back too."

"And? Come on. Out with it!"

"So I can arrange it," said Lockie with a sneaky grin.

Shooter downed his glass of beer in one mighty gulp and complained, "for Christ sake, Lockie, stop stuffing around."

"You know I have friends, many friends…" said Lockie.

"You mean the poker game blokes?"

"Partly. I can also talk to Lizzie. She knows the Police Commissioner better than I do."

"OK. Then let's get it done. That bastard Stanford Lane. That shithead. They should send him off to the Mallee somewhere in the middle of the desert, the pompous prick."

Shooter pushed his pot forward and the barman filled it, producing a nice thick head.

"My best, just for you," grinned the barman as he collected the money on the counter. Shooter smiled back, but turned to Lockie and leaned into him. It was a familiar bow of his head, not one of submission since his chin was about level with

Lockie's receding hair line, but a familiar stance meant to remind Lockie of his second place in the pecking order.

"So, you own the Werribee cemetery?" he asked Lockie as they clinked their glasses and said, "cheers!"

"Seems like it. And everything that goes with it, the hearse, the funeral home, everything. How'd you find out?"

"I'm a cop, I find out about everything. Must have been one hell of a game."

"Unbelievable!"

"Is Harry OK with it? I mean, it must be the biggest gambling bet ever around here," said Shooter.

"He's a bloody good bloke. I almost feel sorry for him," grinned Lockie.

"So what do you want from me? I know you, Lockie. There's always a price for one of your favours."

Lockie leaned closer and whispered, "do you have any mates on the Werribee police force?"

"Yair. I know them all, especially the senior constable."

"I need them to turn a blind eye, just in case people notice what I'm doing."

"And what's that, exactly?"

"I'll be doing things at night that some people might ask questions about. I'll need the local cops to turn a blind eye. But I'll fill you in on the details when the time comes."

"Lockie, you're not doing something stupid are you? I don't know how many times I've saved your ass," warned Shooter.

"I know, I know. Don't get started. I've looked after our family pretty well, I think you'd have to agree."

Shooter stared into Lockie's face, a youngish face, barely a wrinkle, his deep blue eyes always darting here and there, blinking constantly, his cheeks flushed, set high above a classic square Irish jaw, closely shaved, nary a whisker in sight. "I don't think anyone told you that it was your job to look after 'our family.' I dunno what you mean by that anyway."

"When Tommy, bless his soul, took off to the war, it was left to me to support us all. You didn't do anything, except take Tommy's place and bully us like he did."

"Here we go. You can't get off it, can you? If I hadn't kept you buggers in line who knows where we would all have ended up."

"You could have got a job. But no, you had to become a cop to get out of going to war."

"And you? Do I need to say how you evaded the draft?"

"Shut up, Shooter, really. We always end up arguing like this. All I'm asking for is a very small favour."

Shooter downed another beer and stepped back. "I'm going for a piss," he said, standing tall, his chest pushed forward, head and shoulders pulled back.

*

Babs was waiting at the front gate, walking back and forth, pursing her lips, looking like the Major with every step, her still natural slightly dark blonde hair wound back and contained in a hairnet. She saw the Hillman turn the corner and walked to the curb to wait for it, hands on her hips, just like the Major. She was all set to give them hell.

Bobby pulled up at the curb. "You better watch out!" he said, turning to Sandy.

"It's you she's after," said Sandy.

"We're all in for it," muttered Ryley.

Sandy struggled to ease himself out of the little Hillman. His large frame and growing beer belly added to the difficulty, not to mention his stiffness from the bruising he received at the cops' hands.

"G'day luv," he said softly, his lips as usual hardly moving, "sorry I left you in the lurch."

Nellie raced forward, jumped up on him, licked his face.

"Nellie get down you silly bugger," she scolded, smiling all the while.

Sandy grabbed Nellie's head in both hands and ruffled her ears, "Oooh she's a good dog! Come on now, down you get!"

Babs stood back, hands on hips, "so what the bloody hell happened?" she asked, her smile gone, "what did they do to you?"

Sandy pushed Nellie down and extended his arms to Babs. She leaned forward and he hugged her lightly, just enough for her to then push herself away. "That new senior constable," he said, "he set me up. I dunno what's going on, now with Shooter is out of it."

"All the more reason why stashing those shoes in my house was stupid, you pack of bloody idiots," Babs growled.

"It was only temporary," pleaded Bobby, "we didn't have a choice, the cops were on to us."

"He's right, Mum," added Ryley.

"And you keep out of it!" snarled Babs, "we didn't send you to university so you could learn to be a crook."

"Nah, that's right Mum. They teach you how to be big crooks at the uni," joked Ryley.

Bobby limped around the car and tried to hug both Babs and Sandy. "I'm glad you're both all right," he said, tears in his eyes.

"Gees, Bobby, it's not that bad" scolded Babs, "don't go all teary-eyed on me now. Let's all go in and I'll make us a cuppa tea."

*

Bullies have a lot of trouble making friends and Shooter was a bully, not a merciless one, but a bully just the same. It was inevitable, growing up in a family that was run by a tyrant, Major Mum, herself bullied by a no-good heavy drinking husband who treated his animals better than his wife and kids. But it was probably also that Shooter was the second of the boys, lorded over by his big brother Tommy (Dago to those who were his mates), a primary school teacher. Who but a bully would want such a job ruling over a room full of little kids five days a week?

Poor Dago. He fancied himself the intellectual of the family, believe it or not, just because he went to Teachers College. But something must have gone wrong, or maybe bullying little kids wasn't enough for him. Shooter remembered the night Dago came home and announced that he had quit teaching and signed up for the army. "Any self-respecting bloke should do it," he announced, "we have to join the war and save ourselves from the yellow peril." Dad wasn't there, of course, he was down at the pub, probably getting into a brawl right then. And the Major, she said nothing, just busied herself around the oven, checking on the scones, rinsing a few dishes. It was left to sister Babs to express the family's unwavering support of Dago and how good it was that Australia had such brave blokes who'd go to war without hesitation in order to save their country. Babs, walking around the table, leaning forward to put down a plate of sausages and mashed potatoes for each hungry mouth, dropped Dago's down with a bang, splashing some of the gravy on to the table cloth.

"Watch it, Babs!" he scolded, as if he cared about the table cloth, he didn't have to wash it after all. Babs leaned over Dago's shoulder and tried to wipe off the smudge of gravy, but she just made it worse and spread the gravy out making a bigger smudge. "Here, I'll fix it," he said and moved his plate over to cover the smudge. "You see? Easy done!" Bobby, just a little kid, started to giggle. Dago reached across to him and clipped him over the ears with his open hand. "What are you giggling about? You're lucky I'm not your teacher. I'd soon straighten you out, you little twerp." Suddenly, Babs, still with the cloth in hand, and a plate full of sausages in the other, grabbed Dago by the ear and shook it fiercely.

"You stupid bugger!" she cried. "You're going to fight a war to save the pommies? Since when did they do anything for us?"

"Babs, you don't know anything. You better stick to cooking and the dishes," snarled Dago. Babs plonked down the other plate in front of Lockie, who sat, elbows pulled tightly into his side, looking down, fearful of what would come next.

"You think you're smart, don't you? Just because you're a school teacher." Babs cried out to the Major. "Mum! Don't let him go, Mum. Don't let him go!" She gave his ear a rough pull and pulled at his black wavy hair. He reached up and grabbed his sister's hand, squeezing it tightly. He was about to say something that he or she would regret, but the Major intervened. He grabbed Bab's hand and squeezed it tight.

"That's enough!" barked the Major. There was a clinking of cutlery as everyone stopped to listen. "You're all lucky your father isn't here right now. He'd beat the bloody daylights out of all of you!"

Dago slowly loosened his grip and Babs stood back, red in the face. The Major stood, hands on hips, staring at Dago. "You're not going to war, and that's that," she said slowly and with such authority all became dead silent. "You hear? You're not going!"

This was just too much for a bloke who had just signed up to go to war and who was a school teacher who all day gave orders, and never took them. The time had come for him, the eldest, to quit this family, free himself from the tin-pot tyranny of his mother, the physical brutality of his father, to free the country from a real tyranny, the Japs. But he didn't say any of this. He simply said, "I'll be drafted anyway Mum," looking around the table, then added, "Lockie and Mickie junior will have to go too."

It was right there and then that Mickie., only a few years younger than Dago, in fourth form at St. Mary's high, decided that he did not want to go to war to fight someone else's battle, which is what Sandy, his sister's boyfriend kept saying. Instead, he could do something better, he could become a cop, avoid the draft, and get to tell people what to do. And they would call him Shooter.

"What about me, can I go? I want to kill some Japs too!" chimed in Bobby.

156 COLIN HESTON

"You shut your little mouth," said the Major, "you're too young, and besides—"

"What?"

But there was no need for an answer, and nobody wanted to say it. Bobby knew why of course.

Within six months Dago had gone through training, was deployed to New Guinea, and within days of that, notice came back that he had been killed in action. Run through by a Japanese bayonet, that's what it was, said the Major, though there was no official statement to that effect. It was not long after that when the bully of them all, their father, was killed in a brawl outside the Steam Packet pub.

*

Tuesday. Striker packed his running gear, grabbed a quick crumpet and cup of tea and climbed into his unmarked police car, an aging souped-up Ford Falcon, always parked in front of his little house on Page street. Today was a Geelong day. He drove down Williamstown Road and joined the queue to the ferry. Eurie was on duty, did not appear to recognize him, and guided him skilfully to his spot on the ferry. On the other side, he would drop by the Williamstown yacht club, change into his running clothes and take a run around Willy, always a pleasant jog. Straight out of the yacht club on Nelson Place, down towards Gem pier, past the Timeball Tower, through Point Gellibrand park, along the esplanade to Williamstown Beach, rather too built up for his liking with cheap looking ostentatious mansions, probably by those who could not afford a mansion on the other side of the bay. Maybe a quick swim there, then on to Victoria Street, to Ferguson Street and finally back to the yacht club on Nelson Place. A quick shower, then back into his double breasted, narrow dark tie and fresh shirt, and off to Geelong.

*

Shooter pulled in to the small parking lot at St. Helens beach. There was a contingent of officers and ambulance men out at the end of the jetty. Apparently there was a body floating in the water and they were waiting for him to give the go ahead to haul it in. He picked his way along the dilapidated jetty, stepping over rotten planks, over large gaps where boards had fallen into the water below. Up close, the water was a murky, dark and dirty yellow, not the dark green like it looked from across Corio Bay. There were clumps of black seaweed caught around the pylons, lurching back and forth with the ebb and flow of the bay. The whole jetty swayed with the swell.

"What have we got here?" he asked when he reached the end of the jetty.

"It's a body, sir. Shall we haul it up?"

"Go ahead. Be careful not to damage it though," answered Shooter.

"It's small. Could be the body of a child."

Shooter frowned. "I hope not. Go ahead. Pull it up."

It was the body of a child, probably about seven or eight years old. Nicely dressed in short pants, a school shirt and jacket.

"Don't tell me," muttered Shooter, "it's missing its little toe on the right foot."

"Sir! You're absolutely right! You should be a detective!" joked the constable.

"That won't be necessary," came a strong, stilted and familiar voice, "I'm the detective."

Shooter looked around and there standing in his policeman's plain clothes, was detective Striker.

"Striker! Didn't expect you here so soon. Did someone in my office phone you?"

"Word gets around, senior constable Frost. Word gets around," answered Striker as he surveyed the scene.

"Do you want to take charge of the body, then?" asked Shooter, always keen to pass on a problem to someone else.

"Thank you, I will. I'll add it to my collection," Striker added wryly.

Shooter looked at him curiously. "There's more?"

"You already know of the one at the ferry, I believe," said Striker.

"Oh yes, forgot about that."

Striker continued, "and we have three more in the Melbourne morgue."

"Kids?"

"No. Two women and the other one you know about. The male pulled out from the ferry."

"Toes cut off?" asked Shooter.

"I'm not at liberty to say," said Striker with a hint of mystery. The embarrassing fact was that Cordner had never mentioned it and he hadn't noticed anything himself.

"Oh, right you are," said Shooter, winking at Bryan, his first constable who also happened to be his only child.

Shooter leaned down to look more closely at the child's face. It seemed familiar. An angelic face, but a horrible sight in death. He wondered what his big brother Tommy might have looked like, but quickly put it out of his mind. You had to be tough in this job, keep personal memories out of it. Very hard, very hard.

"He's a Willy kid, Dad, I reckon. Seen him around somewhere, I know," said Bryan.

"How many times have I told you, don't call me Dad when we're on the job and there's people around?"

But Striker was all ears. "So this is your boy?" asked Striker with a slightly amused grin.

"Pleased to meet you, sir," answered Bryan raising his hand in half a salute, extending it enough to shake Striker's hand.

"He's my boy," said Shooter. "Detective Striker meet constable Bryan Frost, Bryan meet Striker."

"Fine looking lad," said Striker.

They shook hands, Bryan a little uneasily, looking sideways to his Dad. The sun peeped through the clouds and lit up the small child's white face, sleeping, dreaming. The angel of the Lord has descended, Bryan thought. He took off his cap and ran his hand through his pale hair, strands of ginger sliding through his fingers. At moments like these, and there hadn't been many of them, he wondered if he was cut out for this job.

Striker issued orders and the body was wrapped up and removed. The small group dispersed, leaving just Bryan and his Dad standing there together at the end of the old jetty. Shooter moved to say something, but words were not there. Likewise, Bryan wanted to say that he saw the Angel of the Lord descend, that the little boy was in good hands now, but did not dare say it. Instead, he sniffed a little, the odour of seaweed causing him to wrinkle his nose. "This place stinks," he said.

"Yair. It's the meat packing plant just around that point." Shooter gestured towards North Shore. "They toss all their leftover bits in the bay. The sharks circle around for them. That's why I'm surprised I didn't see any bite marks on the boy's body."

"You suppose Detective Striker noticed that?"

"Who knows. But I wasn't going to tell him, was I? Not my place."

"S'pose not Dad."

Shooter glanced at his son, then looked across Corio Bay to Geelong and Eastern beach. The forced move to Geelong had taken the wind out of his sails. It should not have. Bryan had

been at the Geelong station for several years now, moved there
from his first post at Bacchus Marsh. It was uncomfortable,
that's what it was. They shouldn't have done it. And he knew
that Bryan blamed him for his mother's sudden departure.
When he was around fourteen, just starting to find his way,
looking to become a cop like his Dad, she took off back to
Mildura to stay with her aging mother on their small vineyard.
It almost broke Bryan's heart and he wanted to follow her there,
but Shooter had adamantly said no, and his Mum had also
insisted that he stay in Williamstown and finish his schooling.

She'd had enough, she told Shooter, and that was about all
she said. She never took to Williamstown, a little club that
didn't take easily to outsiders. And that's what she was, a rare
single Italian woman from Calabria. A good catholic, though,
yet even at St. Mary's the Irish who ran the place, kept her at
bay. Shooter had no patience with her complaints. Said she was
imagining it all. And Father Zappia was no help at all. Told her
she was intolerant and to get out and mix with the other women
of the parish. But then, he was from the north, Bologna, and
looked at her as some kind of primitive beast. She did try, but
her cooking was not all that good, most of it Calabrian which
the other women thought tasteless, especially her breads and
biscuits such as they were. And they wouldn't eat spaghetti at
all. Shooter especially made fun of it, insisted that she cook
meat and potatoes most days, shepherd's pie as well. He
couldn't understand why you had to eat all those slippery
noodles just so you could eat the meat. Meat and potatoes and
a good roast lamb on Sundays. That was all a man needed. And
she wasn't very good at cooking roasts either. Missed the out-
door brick oven they had on the farm. Babs didn't go out of her
way to help her either. But that was because she was so busy
cooking for her tribe, a tribe that often included Shooter. Not
that Babs didn't invite her. She went there on most Sundays for
the roast, and even took some of her own cooking for a while,
but nobody ate it, so she stopped. And the Major, when she was
in her prime, just scoffed at her, told her that she should go back
to the farm where she belonged. And finally, she decided that
the Major was right. She went to Father Zappia and told him
she was going to leave her husband. He gave her a dressing
down, all of which hardened her resolve. She didn't trust him.
He was often around at Babs's place, eating her roast lamb. And
it was obvious to everyone that Father Zappia was in cahoots
with the Major and Babs. They were always in a corner

somewhere nattering away to each other, as if they had some kind of secret the rest should not know about. It was of course clearly and forcefully stated by Father Zappia that she and Shooter could not get a divorce, ever. It was against Roman Catholic doctrine. Leaving her husband was a very serious sin, for which it would be next to impossible to obtain forgiveness. In her own way she made up for all this shunning by bringing Bryan to church with her several times a week when he was little, and made sure as he grew older, that he was imbibed with the catholic faith. Father Zappia, who was obviously attracted to young Bryan, perhaps a little too attracted, greatly approved of her devotion to her son's spiritual development. During confession he even informed her that the Pope considered that her devotion to her son's Christian life made up for the rest of her sinful ways.

*

Shooter turned, his hands in his pockets, a rare posture for a cop. He looked back over his shoulder. "You all right?" he asked.

"Of course I am, Dad, I mean sir," answered Bryan with a grin.

"We're OK then?"

"Yep. How about you?"

"I just got back from Werribee where I met with your uncle Lockie."

"Oh yair? What's he up to this time?"

"Don't know what he's up to exactly, but it looks like I might be able to get back to Williamstown pretty soon."

"You mean they're posting you back there? Pretty short posting here, then!"

"You know what these bureaucrats are like," said Shooter.

"What's uncle Lockie got to do with it?"

"Oh, nothing," lied Shooter, "you know what he's like. He knows everything before it even happens."

"So what was he doing in Werribee then?"

"He's come into a lot of land, owns half of Werribee now!"

"No kidding? How'd he do that?"

"I don't know. I never ask him. Would you like to get appointed to Williamstown too?"

Bryan stopped, then carefully stepped over a gap in the jetty. He did not answer. They walked in silence back to the shore.

"I take it you don't want to?" persisted Shooter.

"I kind of want to, but I don't think I should."

"OK then. Just thought I'd ask."

"I mean, I think I have to make it on my own down here. Besides, I like Geelong and the blokes here are cracker jack. And there's a really nice Irish priest at Saint Mary's of the Angels. I really like him, not like that Italian bugger Zappia at Willy."

"I thought he liked you?"

"That was the problem. He liked me too much."

12. A Family Business

Reluctantly, Lockie had agreed to meet Harry Nolte at the cemetery. He suffered slight—only slight mind you—pangs of guilt over his big win. Besides, one could not really trust Harry. You could never quite figure out what he was up to. Rather like myself, thought Lockie as he sauntered up to the large funeral home just inside the cemetery gates. There was a hearse parked outside, a youngish fellow dressed nicely in a black suit polishing it up with a big green cloth. Harry stood on the red brick steps to the home, a spectacle of sorts, for he was dressed in his farm clothes which consisted of dirty old khaki shorts and an old Geelong footy jumper.

"Gees, Harry, you shouldn't have got all dressed up to meet me," joked Lockie.

"Hey, you're someone special now that you're a big land owner."

"And do I own this as well?" asked Lockie as he gestured to the hearse.

"You do. Both of them."

"The driver too?"

"That's right. A bit of a liability, I admit," he grinned. "But he's an excellent driver."

Lockie reached out to shake the hand of his new possession.

"Roy Farmer, meet Lockie Frost, your new boss," said Harry.

"Pleased to meet you mate," said Farmer.

"Likewise. Keep up the good work," responded Lockie.

"Let me show you around," said Harry, "then we'll go down to the other parcel of land that's a lot more interesting."

Harry turned and went into the house. "You can use all this space for whatever you want. We do services in here for those that don't want a church."

"You're a funeral director?" asked Lockie, incredulous.

"Not exactly. Not licensed or anything, although I don't think you have to be especially licensed, if you see what I mean."

"Do you have to be on deck all the time?"

"Oh, no. I pay a manager to look after everything."

"And where is he?" asked Lockie, getting the jitters.

"You just met him."

"Harry, you bastard, what have you sold me?"

"I didn't sell it, remember?"

"Oh, yeh. What have you let me win, then?"

"That's not quite accurate, you bugger. I lost it fair and square!"

"OK. OK. So I've got a hearse and a manager to take care of and this whole lot of land full of graves and headstones."

"That's about it. I had plans, you can visit my architect, to add an extension on to the funeral home right over there." Harry indicated a blank wall on what Lockie reckoned was the eastern side.

"What for?"

"I was planning on building a crematorium."

"Shit! Glad you didn't. I don't think I want to mess with that. People will be calling me a Nazi, if you know what I mean."

"I would have gone ahead and done it, but they built one in Altona so I didn't think there'd be enough demand."

"That's the only reason?" Lockie asked, suspiciously.

Harry walked to the big glass northern doors and opened them up. "If you don't mind, I won't take you out there through all the graves. I don't like going there. But you can see from here that the cemetery is chock-a-block."

"Oh, so that's the catch. That's what you didn't tell me until we signed the agreement."

"Shit, Lockie, you're so suspicious. Don't be such a sore winner! The cemetery is a going concern. There's no problem. There's still room for another couple of years' clients, if you know how to manage it."

"Nice," muttered Lockie.

"Sarcastic bastard. You need to read up on how cemeteries work."

"Thanks. I didn't have running a cemetery in mind when I won this property off you. If I'd known, I would have played till I lost."

"It's all in the game," smiled Harry slyly, "besides, I think you're just the bloke to run this place. You'll figure out a way to make it work."

"I already have. The first thing I'll do is fire the manager."

"Your choice there. Shall we go look at the other piece of land?" asked Harry.

"We needn't bother. I know where it is. It fronts on to the bay, right?"

"It does. Of course, you don't own right down to the water. The government owns all land within a few hundred yards of any water-way, so I'm told. But you can act like you own it. Nobody knows. I built a little jetty out on it, as a matter of fact, to moor my boat."

"You mean the boat's not included?"

"Sorry, but you're welcome to use it, if you don't mind letting me drive through your land to get to it."

"Fair enough. What do you pay your manager? I'm having second thoughts."

"He's just a student at the university. Doesn't cost much. He only works maybe eight hours a week, at most. I pay the basic wage, whatever that is right now."

"And what's he do?

"Takes care of the hearse, keeps the cemetery tidy, handles the customers, organizes the funerals if they want. Keeps track of the accounts. Your choice, Lockie. You should keep him at least for a few months until you find your way."

"Maybe you're right." Lockie made to leave.

"So when's the next game?" Harry asked as they shook hands.

"Dunno yet. Everyone's a bit busy. Having trouble settling on a date."

"Well, let me know. I'm always up for it, as you know."

"I'm meeting with the Commissioner today. We'll try to get it set up then," said Lockie as they parted.

*

Sandy heard the phone ring. He was half conscious, dreaming, maybe. Lockie had called to see if he was all right, said Babs, hands on her hips, looking down on him, wondering what he was up to. His whole body shuddered as sometimes happens in a dream that isn't really a dream. It was enough to open his eyes and see Babs standing in front of him., talking to him as though he were awake.

"Lockie says he's got everything set up. Sandy? What's he talking about?"

"How should I know?" Sandy mumbled.

"He sounded very happy. What's he up to?" Babs knew that Lockie was always scheming and whenever he sounded as happy as he did right now, some kind of scam had gone down.

Sandy stirred, He ran his hand through his wispy hair, showing signs of grey, not much of it left on his smooth head.

He managed to smile up to her, his face and jaw line retaining their round, smooth contour. "The oven. The new gas oven, That's probably what he's on about."

"Well he could have told me," Babs complained.

"What?"

"Forget it. You want a cuppa?"

"Thanks, luv. That'd be good."

"Are you feeling better?"

"Think so. Needed that snooze. Sorry I scared you. It was that bloody copper."

"I know. Not to worry. So I'm getting my oven at last?"

"I hope so. Lockie knows a bloke."

"OK, say no more," Babs grinned as she handed him his cup of tea.

"You know what, Babs?" Sandy whispered.

"What?"

"I think it's time we unionized the police."

"Drink your cup of tea, darl. You're still dreaming."

"No, I'm serious. I'll talk to Lennie. We'll start a grass roots movement, get the young blokes to organize."

"This is all because of the one bastard that set you up over that dog?"

"It's what got me thinking."

"How will unionizing them make any difference. Cops are bloody cops, let's face it. They'll always be bullies."

"Does that include Shooter?"

"Of course it does. He's always been a bully. I've told you that lots of times."

"You ought to be a cop as well, then, from what you've told me how you had your brothers under your thumb."

"That's different. I was just doing what the Major told me. It's not a bad idea, though. But I'm too old for it now."

"Besides. They don't have any females in the force. How could they? They wouldn't pass the height test." Sandy grinned, then replaced it with a frown when he saw Babs's frown and the corners of her small mouth turn down. Then he sat up, excited. "That's it! That's what we'll do!"

"What? You want to turn the police force into a bunch of girls?"

"Exactly! I'll talk to Lennie. We'll campaign to unionize the force, claim that the administration discriminates against women!"

"Your union mates aren't going to be too impressed. They'll be scared you're going to campaign to have women wharfies."

"So what?"

"I think you better go back to sleep, darl. Drink your cuppa."

*

Eurie was about to raise the gang plank as Lockie drove up to the ferry. He wound down the window.

"G'day Eurie. Bobby not on today?"

"Lockie, you beauty! Great shine! It's about as black as I am!" joked Eurie admiring the hearse.

"It's my latest acquisition. Nicest hearse around, don't you think?"

"Smooth! But why are you driving a hearse? Someone died?"

"I bought a cemetery. It came with it."

"No doubt about you," cackled Eurie, "never know what you're going to do next."

"That's the way I like it Eurie. Is Lizzie still on board?"

"Yep, she is."

"Anyone with her?"

"Not sure, I think so."

"Thanks. See you later."

Lockie drove up the ramp and parked the hearse next to the Winnebago and knocked on the door, three strong slow raps.

"Just a minute," came a muffled voice.

Lizzie appeared at the door, and Lockie climbed aboard, pushing past her arm.

"Lockie! Watch it!" she cried.

There was hurried movement inside, the Winnebago rocked side to side. The fact was, there was nowhere to hide in the Winnebago. The closets were way too small, no bed to hide under. The Commissioner sat uncomfortably on the small bed, his uniform clenched in his hands, hugging it to his lower body, the nipples of his flabby tits pushing against his black singlet.

"I was just leaving," said the Commissioner, trying to smile.

"Gees, Commissioner. Sorry to interrupt. I thought Lizzie was on a break."

"We're done, I think, aren't we darling?" quipped Lizzie, leaning forward to stroke his cropped bullet head.

The Commissioner fumbled around with his pants, trying to find his wallet.

"You can fix me up next time, darl," said Lizzie.

"As a matter of fact, I was hoping to chat with you, Commissioner," said Lockie. "Do you have a moment?"

"What's it look like?" snarled the Commissioner.

"Good. Let me help you put your pants on," grinned Lockie.

"I think that's my job, uncle Lockie," said Lizzie thoroughly enjoying the occasion.

Lizzie reached for the Commissioner's pants, but he pulled them away. He rose steadily and tried to get them over his bare feet, then slipped off the bed on to the floor.

"You see? You can't do without me," she said, again stroking his cheek softly.

"I know," he said, sitting back, resigned.

"Here, lift your feet, that's right. Now your undies, there, we can pull them up, careful now. Next your pants, careful of that bright new zipper. We don't want anything catching in it do we?"

Now that the Commissioner had his pants on Lockie seized the moment.

"Commissioner, Lizzie and I have a few things we need you to take care of for us."

"If it's about that theft from the docks, not a chance. I won't condone that kind of criminal activity."

"We don't know what you're referring to, Commissioner."

"You don't say?"

"We want Shooter moved back to Williamstown. We take it that you were behind the decision to move him to Geelong?"

"He wasn't doing anything about the pilfering on the docks and other places," said the Commissioner abruptly.

"That's not why. You're trying to put my father out of action," charged Lizzie.

"Look, my sweet. I was under a lot of pressure. It came down from the highest level," complained the Commissioner, rubbing the back of his neck in an effort to remove his embarrassment.

Lockie was about to issue a threat, but Lizzie restrained him. It would not be good for business for either of them to lose the Commissioner as a customer.

"Uncle Lockie and I, we love and respect Sandy so much."

"He's a communist," that's what I'm told," said the Commissioner, looking down his nose.

"That doesn't make him evil, and so far at least, being a communist isn't a crime," answered Lizzie, all puffed up, trying to talk like Kewcy.

She reached over and stroked the Commissioner's cheeks again, this time running her slender fingers, those fingers that he so much adored, slowly down to his bare shoulder, her fingers following the edge of his singlet. "My darling sweetie-pie, you must do this for mummy's sake, don't you know?"

Lockie shifted on his feet, coughed lightly. He knew when to shut up. The Commissioner looked up, grabbed Lizzie's fingers and pulled them to his lips. The threat was there, lodged in her finger tips. A shudder broke them apart as the old diesel engine roared, slowing the ferry down as it reached the dock. The Commissioner was himself again. He methodically dressed, placed his watch on his wrist, looked at the time and announced, "I must go. Have an appointment with the mayor and can't keep him waiting."

"Are we right for another meeting of our club?" asked Lockie, also returning to his business-like manner.

"Soon as I can fit it in. I'd say probably late next month. I'll mention it to the others when I see them." The Commissioner reached into the inside pocket of his jacket and pulled out his wallet. "Here you are," he said to Lizzie, "this makes us all square."

"Indeed it does," answered Lizzie, taking the money and slipping it ostentatiously down her cleavage, a territory well known to him.

Lockie opened the door and stepped back to let the Commissioner past. "Looking forward to our next meeting," called Lockie.

"Likewise!" called Lizzie.

The Commissioner, his back turned, waved, his hand making a V sign as he hurried down the gangplank to the waiting unmarked police car.

Lizzie turned to Lockie. She was not pleased. "Next time you want to put the screws on one of my customers, don't do it in my presence," she growled.

"Lizzie, it needed both of us."

"Not in my office." Lizzie was very, very cross.

"It couldn't be in my office either. Anyway, the Commissioner wouldn't have come. We had to corner him here."

"Dad mustn't know anything of this," she said, still cross, but resigned.

"Of course."

"And Shooter? I suppose you've told him?"

"Not the details. I just said I would take care of it and that he should get ready to return to Willy. He knew better than to ask how I'd pull it off."

The ferry shuddered as it pulled away from the dock. Eurie looked down from the bridge. Something was going on. It was better he didn't know what. Lizzie got into the hearse with her uncle Lockie. First time he'd seen that. In fact, Lizzie only ever left the ferry with Bobby.

*

Lockie and Lizzie rolled up in front of the house on Cecil street. The hearse was just about as long as the house was wide. Lockie pulled up right behind Bobby's Imp.

"I'm a bit nervous about this, uncle Lockie" said Lizzie.

"You, nervous? I don't believe it."

"It's more than a year since I've dropped in on Mum and Dad."

"Babs will be so pleased I'm taking care of the shoes, she won't want to spoil it by growling at you."

The front door burst open and Nellie came running out to meet them, making a b-line to Lizzie, her paws reaching well up to Lizzie's chest.

"Now Nellie, you silly bitch, get down!" ordered Lizzie.

"Nellie! Get down now, there's a girl!" called Sandy, one of the few occasions on which he raised his voice.

Bobby ran past him to grab Nellie. "Sorry," he said to Lizzie as he grabbed the dog's collar and pulled her back. Lizzie extended her slender arm and patted her on the head. She felt Bobby looking at her and wanted to return the look, but in front of her Dad, didn't feel like she could.

"Who bloody died?" called Babs.

"G'day Babs. Nice to see you too," replied Lockie.

"She's a bloody beauty," admired Bobby. "A Buick, right? About 1950?"

"Dunno, I never asked. It came with the deal I made to buy property in Werribee."

"What are you going to do with it?" asked Babs.

"What do you bloody think?" quipped Lockie.

"Come on Lockie, don't be a bloody shit," sneered Babs in her Major Mum voice.

"Hello Mum. How are things?" asked Lizzie. Sandy was closest to her, so she hugged him first. His arms were still firm, reassuring. Things were all right with him, she thought.

"So don't I get a hug?" said Babs.

"Of course you do." Lizzie stepped forward, almost strutting, her stiletto heels struggling to find a secure footing. She extended her slender arms. Babs had already eyed her off. She wouldn't approve of the loose blouse, the collar undone to reveal her cleavage. And her slacks, black, tight around her thighs, pulled in at the waist to show off her figure, all that Babs had already taken note of, unhappily.

"I'm so happy to see you darl," Babs muttered with a smile, genuine but forced none the less.

"Me too."

They hugged each other and Babs held her tightly, not letting go. The others watched. Bobby went up and put his arms around both of them and said, "come on, let's go in and have a cuppa, then we can load the hearse, assuming that's what you had in mind, Lockie?"

"Won't the s notice?" said Babs, letting go.

"Let them," said Lockie, "it's not like they never saw something like it before. They're all mates around here, aren't they?"

"I'm not so sure now," said Sandy, "not after what happened when I was walking the dog."

"That wasn't yours," answered Lockie, "it was the bloody cops, and that's all taken care of now."

"What do you mean?" asked Sandy, "are they dropping the charges?"

"Better than that. They're bringing Shooter back from Geelong." Lizzie gave Lockie a bit of a look. After all, it depended on the Commissioner doing his part, and one never knew until it was done.

"Really?" said Babs joyfully, this time truly meaning it, "you are a wonder, Lockie."

"Don't mention it." Lockie wanted to say that it was really Lizzie who had pulled it off. Of them all, only Bobby probably had an inkling. He would already be suspicious that Lizzie had shown up with him.

The cup of tea and fresh scones were followed by a few beers, and eventually, Babs cooked sausages and gravy, mashed potatoes and peas, all-round favourites of their childhoods. They sat around the table shelling the peas, recalling happy events of the past. Bobby and Lizzie retired to the living room couch and sat silently, neither able to think of anything to say to each other. Sandy and Lockie went into Bobby's bedroom and counted up the shoe boxes. And when they came together at the kitchen table to eat, they all knew that Babs was worked up about something because the mashed potatoes were especially fluffy. She had violently attacked them, whipping the potato masher round with a speed and agility matched by none, banging the sides and pummelling the saucepan bottom, her lips pursed tightly in deep concentration.

*

It was late by the time they got the hearse loaded. Babs was worried the cops would come, but they never did. Lockie drove off, telling Sandy he did not need help at the other end.

"Where are you taking them?" Sandy asked.

"To my warehouse," answered Lockie.

"Have you found a buyer?"

"I think so. But it will take some time to set it all up. Too risky to keep the merchandise here in Bobby's room. In any case Bobby want's his room back, don't you Bobby?"

"It would be nice."

Bobby pinched Lizzie's fingers just a little. "I better get you home. It's already late for a beautiful young girl like you to be out."

"Thank you, uncle Bobby. We better be going."

"I could come too, if you like. Keep Bobby company on the way back home," offered Babs.

"It's OK sis. I'm on an early shift in the morning. I'll stay on the ferry tonight."

"On the ferry?"

"Yair. Eurie and me put a little bunk in the bridge."

*

"Mandrake, you're a wizard!" exclaimed Lockie.

"That's what I'm here for, Mr. Frost," answered Roy Farmer his inherited cemetery assistant.

"You don't mind if I call you Mandrake?"

"No worries, Mr. Frost. It's a pretty high standard for me to meet, though."

"Call me Lockie. Sorry to get you out so late."

"No problem, Mr. Frost. I'm a uni student, we don't keep to daylight hours. "

"So lead on!"

"It's over here." Mandrake flashed his torch and led Lockie down the steps at the back of the reception house, through a maze of graves and head stones, some hundred yards or more.

"Can we get the hearse down here?"

"That's a bit of a problem. I'd have to do a lot of work to clear the path."

Mandrake stopped in front of a large crypt, all built of local bluestone.

"This is a gargantuan crypt," exclaimed Lockie.

"There's two entrances. It's actually two crypts. One is in use, the other hasn't been sold, so it's empty."

"Which one is which? I hope you know Mandrake," said Lockie nervously.

"I think the one on the left is empty. We can use that."

"The keys? You have the keys?"

Mandrake jangled the keys. "Oooooo!" he called in a ghostly voice.

"Shut up Mandrake and open it!"

The crypts were only a few years old. Harry built them thinking he could sell them off to anyone who wanted to show off their wealth, and there were more and more of them showing up in Werribee these days. But the demand hadn't been quite as strong as he expected. Maybe he was charging too much.

"Here we go," said Mandrake as he pushed open the door, disappointed that there was no creaking sound as there would be in the movies. He flashed the torch around revealing ledges and alcoves, and lots of space.

"Looks good," said Lockie as he slapped Mandrake on the back. "Let's get the stuff."

"What stuff is it exactly?" asked Mandrake with a grin, wasted in the dark.

"Shoes. High class Italian shoes."

"Any to fit me?"

"Yes, if you were a girl. Are you?"

"Get stuffed, Mr. Frost!"

"Call me Lockie, remember?" They returned to the hearse, the back door swung open.

"We can't drive it down the track, Lockie. There's been a bit of rain. It will get bogged. The mud around here is awful. The blokes that dig the graves hate it. Anyway the track's not wide enough."

"Then we'll have to carry them," said Lockie.

"There's another possibility."

"Which is? Go on Mandrake, out with it."

"We could load up the trolley they use to carry the coffins."

"Don't pall bearers carry them?"

"Some don't like to. Scared they'd drop it and the body would pop out."

"We have a trolley then?"

"A couple. There's one in the hearse and one in the little store room next to the kitchen in the funeral home."

"Ah yes, the kitchen. Did you do that little job I asked?"

"Of course I did, Lockie. It's ready to go."

They managed to load both trolleys and a few trips did the trick. Unfortunately, not all the last load would fit in.

"We'll have to put the rest in the other crypt," said Lockie.

"Bugger you!" complained Mandrake, "I'm not going in there!"

"Give me the bloody keys," demanded Lockie, with bravado.

"Take them."

Lockie took them, but with some hesitation. "Got wobbly knees all of a sudden?" chided Mandrake.

Lockie turned the key and slowly pushed open the door. Mandrake stood rooted to the spot, Lockie the same. "Maybe we could use the storeroom next to the kitchen," he muttered.

"Good idea," said Mandrake who, suffering from what he called "irresistible impulse" a concept he had learned in his criminal law class, gave Lockie a decent shove and the door flew open, Lockie staggering forward, dragging Mandrake behind him.

"The torch. Where's the torch?" Lockie cried.

It was then that the stench hit them. The air was thick, a full-on soup of the dead, as Lockie described it later. Mandrake switched on the torch but dropped it as Lockie pushed past him to get out. They knocked over the trolley, Lockie, not so agile, falling down, the shoe boxes scattering everywhere, shoes falling out, one of the stiletto heels jabbing him in the ribs when he landed.

"Gees! You all right, Mr. Frost?"

"Never better, you bastard! And I told you to call me Lockie." He managed a grin as Mandrake extended a hand to help him up. "Stack them into the crypt right now or you're fired!" he ordered, trying to sound like Babs.

Mandrake wasn't sure whether Lockie was really upset with him or not. But he needed the money and didn't want to get fired. "OK. Mr. Frost, I mean Lockie. Sorry for that. I don't know what happened, really."

"I bloody do. You pushed me, you bastard."

"Not me, Lockie. Must have been a ghost."

There was plenty of room in the second crypt, so after haphazardly returning the shoes to their boxes, they quickly stacked them just inside the door and closed it, then wheeled the trolleys back to the storeroom.

"It's all ready for you, Lockie." Mandrake pointed at the kitchen stove. You probably should get a plumber to come out and check everything. I think I managed to turn everything off.

It's a pretty nice stove. Pity to pull it out of here. Nice kitchen too.

"Whoever heard of a kitchen at a cemetery?" said Lockie with more derision than was necessary. With considerable effort they managed to lift the stove on to one of the trolleys. It was probably about the weight of a body, though the trolley felt top heavy as they wheeled it to the hearse. Sandy would be off the hook, and Babs thrilled that she at last had a gas stove so she could cook her scones and sausage rolls, no more guess work putting her hand in the oven, no more having to stoke up the fire.

13. Family Affairs

Ryley road alone until his friend got on at the Willy north station. They would ride one more stop to Newport, then alight together. The problem was they could not meet in his rented room in the Spotswood house. The landlady would never allow it. There wasn't enough room, anyway, even less room than in Lizzie's Winnebago, which was where they were going right now. They had met on Williamstown Beach one hot summer day. "Met" was not quite the right word. They saw each other from a distance. A chance meeting of glances, their slender bodies, his tall the other less so, but stocky and muscular, glistening with oil, one deeply tanned, the other white, vulnerable to a merciless sun. Each turned quickly away, embarrassed, looking down at themselves, thinking of the other. Ryley wrapped himself in his big beach towel on which were stamped in big letters, the latest government slogan, LIFE BE IN IT.

The couple sauntered down North Road to the ferry. Ryley fingered the keys to Lizzie's Winnebago in his pocket. Neither spoke. Each walked at their own space, one on either side of the footpath. They reached the ferry car park and Ryley was relieved to see that Bobby's Hillman was not there. Nor was there a light on in the Winnebago. It was all clear. He could make out the dim image of Eurie, working on the moorings. They would go on the ferry separately.

*

As they entered the Winnebago, Lizzie immediately sensed that someone had been there. There was a very faint odour of lemon or something like it. It was familiar, but she couldn't quite place it. No doubt it would come to her. She looked at the sheets on the bed. They were fresh. Whoever it was thought a lot of her, or else wanted to cover their tracks. Bobby was right behind her, his hand resting lightly on her shoulder.

"What's the matter?" asked Bobby..

"Someone's been here."

"How do you know?"

"I can smell it," said Lizzie as she sniffed.

"Come to think of it, so can I."

"Not Lockie. He smells like a hairdresser," said Lizzie.

"Who else has a key?"

"No one, as far as I know. But it's a Winnebago. It's easy to work the lock."

"I hope you don't keep anything valuable inside," said Bobby.

"Nothing that's worth any money, if that's what you mean."

Lizzie ran her hands over the fresh sheets. She felt Bobby's other hand at her waist. Then his big frame was pressed lightly against her back. She pushed back a little and turned to face him. He needed a shave, she thought, the whiskers make him look older than he is. As tall as she was, Bobby towered above her, his head of reddish sandy hair almost touching the roof. He looked like her father when he was a lot younger, she thought. But not really.

I don't know why this is damn well happening, it's been like this since that time he took me to my flat. I can't help it. My knees go wobbly and my head swirls like I've been sniffing petrol. That day comes back to me every time I lay in bed on my own. And that's how I felt that time when I called out to him to come to me, a teenager for God's sake, lying flat on the bed, my legs spread apart, calling for him to come to me. And Bobby, his cheeks pulsing red, his green Irish eyes nearly popping out, a frown on his forehead trying to stop himself, his tongue pressing behind tight lips, was it only ten years ago? Ten years since I have been screwing every bloke around, all the time thinking of uncle Bobby? He's breathing in big pants, his cheeks are pulsing red, it's just like it was that day. Will he say no this time? We've come so close, so many times.

"We could get that place," he said.

I placed two fingers on his lips, flushed lips too they were. "I can't wait," I said, "I can't wait any more."

"Lizzie!"

"It's time!

He had gone over how he'd do it a thousand times, and so had I. We were one, like no other. One! And only! Our bodies forgetting who we were, all the gossip of a decade, suspicious looks, titters maybe, whispers and glances, we were at last who we really were, not what they said we were. No, we were at last who they wanted us to be, their poisoned lascivious minds revelling in the filth of our sin! How good we were! How virtuous we made them be! Let them know! Tell them what we are! Uncle and niece wedded into one! The lines blurred by love authentic and true, who could deny its beauty?

Bobby's huge naked frame fell on her, Lizzie opened her arms, imagined her body split in two. "Uncle!" she called, "Uncle Bobby!"

And now, he lay on his back, kissing her feet, feet that would look splendid in fancy Italian stiletto shoes, he grinned to himself. Lizzie at her end caressed his very large feet, lightly fingered his right foot where the little toe used to be. Bobby flinched.

"Oops, sorry! Does it hurt?"

"Nah. Tickles."

"Why do you limp then?"

"It's just the way I walked when I was little, I suppose, when it really did hurt. And my whole leg was weakened by the infection that nearly killed me. That's what Babs said anyway."

"You poor little darling. Mummy kiss it better?"

"That's the last thing I would want from my bloody mother," he joked.

"But not from me!" she said, and began to kiss him, slowly with each peck, moving up his white and freckled body. Half way up.

"That's far enough," he said, feeling a joy that he had pined for ever since he lost his toe.

And at the end, when they were once again who they were not, dressed, and ready to go, Lizzie said, "I'll sell this Winnebago, and we'll get that place we looked at."

"But what would people say when we moved in together?"

"Who cares? It's not people you're thinking about, anyway is it? It's Babs."

"I know. You're right."

"She's only your sister, it's none of her business."

"But you're her daughter. And she's been more like a mother to me, not a sister."

"God forbid!"

"You can't blame her, Lizzie. She only wants the best for you."

"And you're the best, Bobby. I've known it since that day at the flat when you ran away from me."

Bobby grabbed Lizzie's head between his mighty hands, twiddling her ears, looking into her green eyes, a perfect match for his. "I love you," he said.

*

"I've got a question for you," said Ryley.

Lennie had barely opened his door to the loud knock and found Ryley looking down on him from the top of his slender frame, a bit of a silly grin on his face.

"Ryley! What a surprise. What are you doing around this neck of the woods?"

"What do you mean? It's where all the workers live, isn't it?"

"Except me, I'm not what you'd call a worker. I don't really have a job."

"Well are you going to let me in or not?"

"Of course. Come right in and I'll get Monie to make you a cup of tea." Lennie stepped back, calling, "Monie, we have an early morning visitor."

"Bloody hell, Lennie, it's not even six in the morning," came a muffled cry.

"It's Ryley."

"What's he doing bloody here?"

"G'day Monie!" called Ryley.

"Come on into the kitchen and I'll put the kettle on," said Lennie.

Ryley followed Lennie down the dark passage to the kitchen just as Monie emerged from the bedroom, half asleep, looking like something the cat dragged in, thought Ryley.

"So what's the question?"

"Well, I'm sort of in a relationship and I wondered what Marx would have thought about it."

"I'm going back to bed," said Monie, "it's too early in the morning to be talking about Marx whose relationships began and ended with his prick." She pulled her ragged dressing gown around her and turned back to the bedroom. Ryley grinned at Lennie. He wanted to say "thank goodness, what a dreadful sight she makes during the day, let alone early in the morning," but resisted. How Lennie could go to bed with her was beyond all comprehension.

"And the question is?" asked Lennie, as he warmed the teapot. "Actually I should say, why is there a question at all? If it's a relationship thing, you should ask Freud, not Marx."

"Freud's dead," quipped Ryley.

"And so is Marx," responded Lennie.

"But Marx still lives through the great communist movements of the world," announced Ryley.

"That's true."

"He was married, wasn't he?" asked Ryley.

"Indeed, and she had five kids to him…"

"And he fucked the housekeeper as well," came a muffled cry from the bedroom.

"And what about his mate?" asked Ryley.

"Engels you mean?" responded Lennie.

The kettle boiled and Lennie poured the water into the teapot.

"Right. I mean, they must have spent a lot of time together, a very close relationship wouldn't you think?" asked Ryley.

"He wasn't a bloody homo, if that's what you think!" called Monie again, this time loudly in her rough, smoker's voice.

"I thought you went back to bed!" called Lennie.

Monie appeared at the kitchen door, wrapped once again in her dressing gown, filthy and ragged. "Give me a bloody cup of tea," she said to Lennie, "I can see that Ryley needs a woman's touch. You're not going to be any help if I think what's going on is what's going on."

"And what exactly is that?" asked Lennie, belligerently.

Ryley intervened. "I didn't mean to cause any trouble. I was just wondering. Anyway, I suppose I can go to the Ballieau and look it up."

"Look what up?" asked Monie, now getting into her stride, looking for a battle.

Ryley put down his cup and rose to leave."

"Ryley, don't go yet. You obviously are troubled. Let's have it out. I've read everything Marx and the rest of them ever wrote. You don't need to go to the library."

"Maybe I do need to read up on Freud," Ryley said as he backed out of the kitchen and strode with big steps towards the front door.

"Well, I admit I can't help you with Freud," said Lennie.

"I can," said Monie, "they made us read the crap in Psychology for Social Workers class. It's completely made-up bullshit."

Ryley, always courteous, stood at the front door, waiting for Lennie to open it. It had been a mistake to come here. He had forgotten how insensitive and obnoxious Monie was, not to mention her ugly horse's teeth and pock-marked face. And as well, he now understood that he wasn't sure what he wanted to ask anyway. Was he looking for some kind of approval? He was a grown boy. He didn't need anyone's permission.

"Well it was a quick visit, Ryley," said Lennie as he held open the door, "sorry I couldn't be of more help."

"You and Monie have been a great help, as it turns out. Oh and by the way, I think Dad is dropping by later this morning, isn't he?"

"Yes, he and Banger. We're hatching another communist plot," grinned Lennie.

"No doubt. Got to go. Have a poli-sci tute to run. I'd rather you didn't mention my visit to Dad."

14. On the Waterfront

Autumn was approaching. The leaves, golden yellow, fluttered like butterflies through the misty rain. There weren't many things in life one could say Striker really loved, but this time of the year was his favourite. It was kind of un-Australian, Striker thought to himself, to like autumn leaves, deciduous trees of which there were few natives in Australia. He grew up next to one, though, loved to sit under the only tree outside the Glastonbury Protestant Orphanage, a maple that glistened on sunny autumn days, a bright light that shone against the heavy bluestone monolith of the orphanage. There wasn't a lot to say about his childhood. He kept to himself, was known then, as he is today, as a loner. He had always been happy with that. He did play with a few of the other boys, joined in the exciting team sports, was popular because of his athletic ability. But he remained apart, not because of growing up in an orphanage, he had no complaints about that, but because, he was convinced, a loner was who he was and always would be. Provided they fed him and gave him books to read, which they did when they had them, he was happy enough and wanted nothing more.

Striker stood on the front porch of his little house and paused, hands on his hips, looking up and down Page street, admiring the bushy plane trees reaching their full autumn colours. He jogged out to the front gate and turned to admire his cottage. He had lived frugally, worked hard, and when he at last was appointed to the detective branch at C.I.D, Central Intelligence Division, in Melbourne, he bought this cottage, one he had admired for several years ever since he noticed it when he was on a police training run. They would run the 10k from the academy at Glen Waverly down to St. Kilda beach, dive off the end of the pier, swim to Middle Park beach, and from there wend their way back through the streets of old houses in Middle Park, across Albert Park, then back to the academy. It took years at various stations all over Victoria, some in the middle of nowhere, until he passed with flying colours, the exam that got him into the C.I.D.

This was the day to clean his mind, choked as it was with regrets and self-recriminations. Raining or not, chilly or not, he enjoyed the physical challenge. He jogged down Page street, turned the corner and headed for the beach where he waded into the murky water of Port Phillip Bay and swam across to the St. Kilda pier, then jogged from there back to his cottage. He ran every day, but this day he really needed the run. His last meeting with the Commissioner had disturbed him for many reasons. He couldn't get it out of his mind. He said things he wished he had not. Lost control of himself, something that he never, ever did.

"Why did you move Senior Constable Frost to Geelong and replace him with a protestant like yourself?" asked the Commissioner, leaning forward on his desk.

"Because those Catholics run Williamstown and they're all corrupt. They are the source of the rampant pilferage on the docks."

"Why did you not consult me first?"

"I thought it imperative to move immediately, given the mounting number of dead bodies showing up in Williamstown, and the complaints of theft from the wharves."

"A simple phone call would have been enough."

"I apologize, sir. It will not happen again."

"And why did you immediately target Mr. Malley, the most influential fellow in Williamstown?"

"I wouldn't say he was the most influential sir, but I do know that he runs the wharves and that nothing moves off those wharves without him knowing it."

"You have proof of that accusation?"

"Not exactly sir. But everyone who has lived in Williamstown for any length of time knows it."

"So you decided on your own that it would be a good idea to put him out of circulation by engineering a false arrest, a set-up?"

"You mean the animal abuse charge?"

"You know that's what I mean, Striker."

"I did not know that was how Senior Constable Lane would proceed. I did not order that. I ordered Lane to take immediate steps to reduce Malley's influence in the Williamstown community and on the wharves in particular."

"You thought he was capable of undertaking such a sensitive and difficult project?"

"I did sir. I've known him for a long time, we go to the same church, sir. He's a straight arrow, incorruptible."

"Entrapping a leading citizen of the local community does not seem like a sensible solution, does it?"

"No sir. I would not have done it like that."

"So you're not defending the action?"

"No sir. I apologize sir. I should have kept closer supervision of senior constable Lane sir."

"I want this entire episode erased from local memory. Start by bringing back Senior Constable Frost."

"Yes sir. And what about Constable Lane sir?"

"I'm bringing him here, at H.Q. where I can keep my eye on him, and will use him for special projects, and first up, to clean up that sordid mess of homeless beggars that hang around Flinders Street station, harassing the good people of Melbourne."

"Yes sir. I understand sir. I will have Frost reassigned back to Williamstown immediately sir."

"That won't be necessary. I've already taken care of it."

"Yes sir. Thank you sir. Is there anything else sir?"

"Yes. When are you going to solve the dead body problem?"

"I'm making slow headway, sir. It's hard to get people in that community to talk, sir."

"They do not trust us because we appear to them to act arbitrarily and without consideration of their welfare. We must not be bullies, Striker, you know that."

"Yes sir."

"Now. A piece of advice. Loosen up a bit. Make friends with Senior Constable Frost. If there's a serial killer in Williamstown, they should be just as concerned to catch him as you are."

"Yes, sir. I will do my best sir."

"You need to forget that they are Catholics. I know that they are a weird mob, but we have to work with them. Understand?"

"Yes sir. I do sir."

"Then see to it, Striker. Off you go!'

Striker climbed out of the water, up on to St, Kilda Pier. The few men fishing looked at him with wonder. It was pouring rain, in the 50s at most. They were crazy enough to be fishing. But to swim and jog in it? He ran bare foot as well, down the pier across to Beaconsfield Parade and back home on Page street. A quick shower, and he would be ready for a new day with the Catholics.

*

Sandy, as boss of the Waterside Workers Federation, ran the docks out of a small office that he and Banger set up in the end of one of the new containers they had managed to commandeer. He was known as the "quiet boss" all over the docks and stevedoring industry because he rarely spoke out to the media, nor did he visibly force any of the workers into compliance.

Wesley Simpson, the secretary of the WWF was its public face, a public school boy who had done law and commerce at Melbourne University and decided to make a career of serving the lower classes, as he called it. What he meant by "serving" was rather different from the usual do-gooder mind set. He wasn't beyond making a dollar or two on the side as he went about his good works. He saw it as his duty to the blokes in the working class who needed a bit of a lift up. In fact he was more than happy to leave running the WWF to Sandy, because it freed him up to pursue his vast business interests, which was the import of goods, preferably high end goods that he could pass on to his network of wholesalers. He and Sandy went through an amusing tussle each time about where they would meet, Sandy's office or Simpson's. To make matters even more confusing, he appeared to Sandy as a narrow minded protestant (Sandy's words), a stickler for correct procedures, an excessive and misplaced reverence for the law in every little detail. This was a wonderful front that Simpson and Sandy kept up, at times, Simpson not sure whether Sandy was taken in by it all or not. Sometimes he thought he over did it a bit with his reverence for the law, especially as Sandy and his mates on the docks treated "law" as a word they uttered rarely, and when they did, it was in reference to its overbearing use by the cops who picked on them at their every whim.

Ryley immensely enjoyed these meetings with Simpson to which Sandy always invited him. And after the usual tussle, the meeting would always end up at Sandy's office, and Ryley would always show up early and harass his Dad as to why on earth he allowed such a stuck-up prick from public school to be secretary of the WWF anyway. Sandy would listen quietly, then take a deep breath and almost in a whisper, a faint smile on his proud and pleasant face, "Ryley, my boy, go for a walk around the docks, talk to the blokes. Listen to them. And what do they talk about? They're trying to make a living, they have kids to feed, need a few bob to spend at the pub, and to watch the footy. If they can do that they're happy. They need a bloke like me to speak for them who's been through all that, who knows what it's like to be short of a quid."

"But why aren't you secretary, then, Dad? That's what I don't understand."

"This country is run by blokes who are just like Wesley Simpson. They're in top government spots and they mostly run all the big industries. Lennie's right about all that."

"So why do you let them? Why don't you all rise up and take over? There's more of you than them. Besides, Simpson doesn't run a business, does he?"

"Because we would lose. They have too much power for us. It's only when we are very careful and put on a good public demo like we did to save Clarrie, that we can have a win. And even there, it remains to be seen whether we have really won the battle. By the way, Simpson is a business man before anything else. We do a lot of business together."

Ryley shrugged his shoulders, making his slender tall frame seem even thinner. "Wouldn't the country collapse if all your blokes went on strike?"

"It would, no doubt about it. And we have that up our sleeve to fall back on if we don't get what we want."

"So why don't you do it?"

"Because it's not clear that we would win, and more importantly, it's not clear what we would end up with if we brought the country to its knees."

"It's obvious isn't it? We'd take over the country!" said Ryley excitedly.

"Well, I never read Marx and don't intend to. I know that Lennie has a lot to say about this. But I really don't think I'd like the blokes that I know from the docks running this or any country," said Sandy with a pained grin.

"I could," said Ryley, standing tall, his angular thin face contorted into a huge grin.

"That's what worries me," joked Sandy now laughing too.

"What business is Simpson in, anyway? He doesn't seem like the business type to me. And what business would you have with him anyway?"

Sandy looked to Banger and asked, "any sign of Lockie and Shooter?"

"Not yet."

"You didn't answer me, Dad," said Ryley.

Sandy looked across to Banger again and Banger grinned.

"Come on. What's going on?" insisted Ryley.

"Simpson is our middle man," said Banger.

"Yes, between you and the toffs and politicians," said Ryley, almost snarling.

"No, in business. Banger and I are part of his supply chain," answered Sandy."

"Supply chain? What the bloody hell is that?"

"Don't they teach you anything at the uni?" put in Banger.

Ryley shrugged again and rose to leave, just as the silhouette of a figure appeared at the door of the office.

"G'day mates," said Wesley Simpson in an affected working class accent, "am I too early?"

"Not at all, Wes," said Sandy, "I was just bullshitting with my son Ryley, here, who goes to Melbourne uni. He's going to be a doctor."

"I'm getting a doctorate Dad, it's different," corrected Ryley.

"Pleased to meet you, young man," replied Simpson, extending his hand, "we need bright young men like you at university and later to come work with us. Too bad you're not doing law or commerce or you might end up taking my place!"

"Pleased to meet you, Wes." Ryley shook hands, squeezing as hard as he could. "The law's not for me. Too much piddling detail. I'm an ideas person."

"Interesting," responded Simpson.

"And you know Banger." Sandy gestured towards Banger.

"Yes, we've met before I think," answered Simpson with a tiny wink.

Banger shook hands, his natural handshake also like a vice. Simpson's face reddened a little as he tried to suppress the pain.

Sandy continued, "I've also invited a couple more people to join us. They'll be here soon. Hope you don't mind."

"Not at all. Is there something special afoot?" asked Simpson.

"Only a national strike, probably," grinned Sandy with a nonchalance that would befit any corporate toff, "and a little supply chain work."

"A national strike? Really? And the issue is?"

"Well, let's wait until the others show up."

"A cup of tea, or something harder?" asked Banger.

"A cup of tea would be fine."

"Here, have a seat," said Banger, pointing to a wooden box beside. an old wooden packing crate taken from a container, cut down to size to make a table. The office was lit by one florescent light suspended from the roof, and a couple of rough windows cut into the metal sides. Old hessian bags hung over them to reduce the blinding rays of the daily sun. Banger walked into the gloom at the other end of the container to boil the kettle that sat on an old Coleman stove.

"Nice office you have here," grinned Simpson.

"We like it," called Banger from the gloom. Do you take milk?"

"No, just black."

"That's good, because we don't have any," quipped Banger.

"Yes, we do," said Sandy, "I put some in the beer fridge this morning. And I'll have my usual, just a touch of milk."

"OK. And what about you, Ryley?"

"Nothing thanks, unless there's a beer?"

"Coming right up!"

There was a metallic knock at the doorway and in came Shooter with Lockie at his heals, Shooter resplendent in his uniform, Lockie wearing the latest style in jeans and a garish fair isle jumper that Babs had knitted him for his 30th birthday, now long past. Simpson shaded his eyes as he peered at them from his seat at the crated table.

"You remember my business partners, my brothers-in-law Shooter here, and the smartly dressed one, Lockie," announced Sandy.

"Don't get up," said Lockie, dancing over to shake hands, Shooter staying back by the door.

"G'day to you both," smiled Simpson. "Quite a family gathering," he said, looking to Sandy.

"You should meet the Major," joked Lockie.

"A soldier?"

"Not exactly, they're talking about Babs my missus," said Sandy with a grin.

An awkward silence ensued, broken finally by Ryley.

"Another tea, beer anyone?"

"A beer would be good," answered Lockie.

"Nothing thanks. I don't drink on duty," mumbled Shooter.

Simpson coughed nervously, putting his fist to his mouth, his eyes darting from one to the other. "I'm not sure I understand why all you blokes are here," he said querulously.

Sandy replied, "Lockie is a businessman and friends with the Police Commissioner, and Shooter here knows how to manage crowds and demonstrations. The cops are crucial to everything we do. We have to keep them on our side. But I think you know all that. It's not like the first time you have met my blokes."

"Of course. And with their assistance are you planning a violent revolution?" chided Simpson.

"I wish!" exclaimed Ryley.

"No, not really. But it could lead to something like that," said Sandy looking around the group.

"So, lay it on me. Come on, out with it!" said Simpson, impatient and a little annoyed.

"I've had talks with the Seamen's Union secretary. We're going to merge with them. And we'll call ourselves the Maritime Union, and then when we've done that, we'll merge with the Stevedoring Workers union."

"So why all the drama? Nobody in the street will care less."

"You don't seem to know the government like we do," said Banger, a rare comment. "They'll use their thugs to infiltrate the wharves, incite the seamen, there will be violence, not of our making."

"What thugs?" asked Simpson, incredulous.

"The government has expanded its Federal Police. They're copying the F.B.I. They do undercover work, infiltrate unions, incite riots. Try to get union workers to break the law, then arrest them and claim conspiracies to overthrow the government," said Sandy.

"Gees, Dad, you sound like Lennie," joked Ryley.

Sandy gave him a look of disapproval, telling him to shut up.

"Are you sure about this?" asked Simpson, "maybe you've been watching 'I Led Three Lives' too much."

"A bloody good show," said Shooter, "I watch it all the time."

"But let me ask you," persisted Simpson, "why in fact you think these mergers are necessary? I thought things were going great after your big win over the Clarrie O'Shea case."

"The fact is," said Sandy, coughing to clear his throat, "we're losing members, because of containerization. There's much less demand for our labour."

"I hadn't thought of that. So what do you want me to do?"

"Talk with the secretary of the Seamen's union and see if he'll go with it."

"Why don't you?"

"I already have privately. But you're the public face of the WWF. You have to set it up. And while you're at it, test the waters with any of the other unions that might be interested."

"And what about the Trades Hall Council?"

"Yes, and those bastards too. They need to be right behind us. No sitting it out like they did with the Clarrie campaign."

Shooter and Lockie moved to the door.

"You're leaving so soon?" asked Simpson, "I'm sure we have lots more to discuss."

"I think we've heard all we need to hear; don't you think Lockie?" said Shooter.

"Shooter, before you go. There's one last thing I'd like you to think about. I mentioned this to Babs and she told me I was crazy," said Sandy.

"Must be good then," joked Shooter, "come on, out with it."

"It's time the police were unionized."

"Wow! Dad!" cried Ryley, shaking his fist up high.

Simpson shifted on his stool. "You've got to be kidding!" he said, eyes wide, a big frown on his forehead.

"There should be women on the force," said Sandy, feigning nonchalance. They all should get extra pay for weekends and Sundays, overtime. There are a lot of issues."

"Right on Dad! Let's do it!" cried Ryley again, shaking his fist.

"Not so fast!" exclaimed Simpson. "One thing at a time!"

"You old bastards! You stick-in-the-muds!" complained Ryley.

Sandy rose and walked around the table then stood behind Simpson. He patted him on the shoulder. "Take it easy Ryley, he's right," he said, "but it's something that we will be working for over the coming year or two."

Simpson placed his hand on Sandy's and looked up at Ryley. The boy had spirit, a dangerous amount, clever and impetuous, he thought. "Your doctorate, is it in political science?" he asked.

Ryley stared back. He was about to tell him to get stuffed. But he felt Banger beside him, grabbing his arm.

"Here's your beer," said Banger, taking his hand and pushing the stubby into it.

Sandy turned to Lockie. "Can you stay a few more minutes?" he asked, "we haven't got to the business items on our agenda yet."

"Uh, oh," said Shooter. "Time for me to go."

"Thanks for dropping by," said Sandy, "and think about it. I know you don't like politics, but I'd like to know what the rank and file might think."

Shooter nodded good-bye and left without a word.

Ryley went to leave as well. "Got to go Dad, sorry if I said anything out of place."

"Off you go, son. One day you'll be in Wes's place or even better," said Sandy, pride getting the better of him.

Ryley stopped at the door. "You know what Dad?"

"What?"

"We should take over that Trades Hall Council. They're a bunch of spineless dills."

"You know what, my boy? I think you're right. I'll talk it over with Lennie when we meet this afternoon. Will you be there, by the way?"

"I'll try to make it, Dad. Have to meet with my thesis adviser at two. The meeting's at four, right?"

"Yes. At Lennie's place in Richmond. You know where that is?"

"Oh sure. I'll try and get there."

Sandy quickly turned to Simpson. "So now Wes. We've got one small matter of business to deal with. Lockie here, is in charge of the goods right now."

"What?" asked Lockie, feigning ignorance.

"What do you have for me?" asked Simpson.

"Shoes, about 100 pairs. Fresh in from Italy," said Sandy.

"Are they any good?"

"The best," offered Lockie now fully on board. "They're mainly high end women's shoes, mostly those stiletto style. Bruno Magli, Alberto Fermani, and Elsa Schiaparelli. The very best."

"As you can see," said Sandy, "Lockie is the stylist of the family. If he says they're good, they are."

"Sounds very promising. The price?"

"We figure $20 a pair. They're worth close to $100 retail."

"They're genuine, right? Not fakes from Japan or Korea."

"We don't deal in counterfeits. We're not criminals," said Lockie, offended.

Simpson stood up from the table holding his teacup. He downed the last of his tea. "I have a wholesaler who may be interested. Have to test the waters. Otherwise it might be better to go straight to a couple of retailers. I know a buyer who contracts with Myers. That might work. I'll get back to you soon after I have asked around."

Sandy reached forward and they shook hands. "Thanks Wes. I really value our business relationship."

"Me too, Sandy. My best to the rest of your family."

15. Revelations

"Bobby!" called Babs. "Your bacon and eggs are ready."

"Coming sis."

Babs watched her young brother, her favourite she had to admit, so kind and gentle, yet so unhappy most of the time. That is, until now. Bobby bounced out of his bedroom, smiling, jovial, put his arm around Babs and hugged her.

"Gees, I'm popular this morning. It's only bacon and eggs. What have I done?"

"Nothing Babs. Thanks for looking after me for all these years."

"You're my favourite brother, you know that," she said as he squeezed her in another hug.

"And you're my favourite sister."

"Go on, get away with you," said Babs coyly. "You know what? I think I'll come visit you and see if I can meet up with Lizzie on the ferry. What about that?"

Bobby sat down at the table. "That would be good," he replied, "except that Lizzie doesn't take the ferry anymore."

"You mean she's moved to Melbourne?"

"Not exactly."

"Here's your cuppa."

"Thanks sis."

Babs sat down next to him and poured herself a cup of tea from the old teapot she inherited from the Major. "This old tea cosy, it's on its last legs. Remember when I knitted it from the wool Major Mum unravelled from your old jumper? You fell over and tore a big hole in it and she got into one of her tantrums and unravelled it and told me to knit it again, but I couldn't because it was too hard so I knitted the tea cosy."

"How could I forget, Babs? You were so good to us. I don't know how we would have survived without you."

Babs sipped her cup of tea. "Now tell me what's going on," she said.

Bobby had hardly eaten any of his breakfast. He nibbled at his toast. "Babs," he said, extending his arm, his big hand lightly touching hers as she put down her tea cup.

"Out with it," she insisted.

"Lizzie and I, we're buying a little house down near the ferry, just around the corner from it."

"What do you mean 'Lizzie and you'?"

"We're moving in together."

Babs pulled away, stood up and emptied her cup of tea into the sink. "I know what Lizzie does for a living, you know. I'm not stupid.," she said, her voice quivering, hand shaking, trying to hold back a tear.

"I've looked after her for so long, Babs."

"I know you have, darl. I know. You've been so sweet."

"She's about had enough of it, and we decided that it would be easiest if we pooled our savings and bought a place together."

"Together?"

"Yep. Together."

Babs pressed the small of her back against the kitchen sink. "I hope you'll be very happy," she said as she ruffled Bobby's hair and gave him a little kiss on the forehead. Bobby clasped her hand and held it to his cheek as she rested her chin on his head. A tiny tear dribbled down her cheek and on to Bobby's hand. She knew to say no more.

Babs saw Bobby off and returned to her kitchen. She washed every dish carefully, rubbing off the smudges of yellow from the fried eggs, rinsing them over and over, scrubbing the insides of the tea cups to remove the tea stains. She would go see Father Zappia, that's what she would do, and if that didn't help, she would go down to the bookbinders and lose herself in the glue and paper. Maybe do both.

It's my own fault I know it. God, I know you're looking down on me, but I tried my best, really I did. It's not fair if you make me suffer for a couple of mistakes I made, I mean it's what they chose to do, isn't it? I could have tried harder to stop them, but I know and surely you do too that it would only have hardened them in their ways. They've been doing it since Lizzie moved into that flat that Bobby found. I shouldn't have let them. She always denied it though, said she was with the bloody foot-baller. But I knew better and I should have spoken out.

Babs rounded the corner on her way to Parker street. The drizzling rain turned into a downpour, causing her to open her umbrella, adding to the weight of the sins that she carried. They were predicting abnormally high tides and floods. And one look up at the dark bluestone of the St. Mary's spire almost lost in the deeply ominous dark clouds above, was enough to tell her that God awaited her inside, his wrath, a putrid mix of lethal black clouds, seeping and oozing through the huge beams of the church roof, waiting for her, ready to pounce as soon as Father Zappia gave the word.

I'm not going in there, I'm not. I'm not that bloody bad, really I'm not. I've done my best for them all, cooked and served them my entire life, surely that's worth something. Took care of my brothers when they were little, raised my two kids pretty much on my own, struggling for the dough to feed them. I did them better than I got when I was a kid, that's for sure. And with Sandy it was boom or bust. We'd go for weeks without hardly any money, then all of a sudden he'd have lots of it and we'd spend up and eat up, and of course with the men, they'd drink it all up. I had to use all my wiles, and I've got plenty of them, to sneak some of Sandy's money and store it for a rainy day. And there were lots of them, just like today. I took some of Sandy's money, but God, that was all right, wasn't it? I had to feed my family, didn't I? It would be a worse sin not to, don't you think?

Babs turned to the church, looking up at its spire as she closed her umbrella. The rain drenched her hair and face. She saw God's face in the grey clouds, moving and swirling, descending ready to do His work. Her lips moved ever so slightly. "Jesus, please come to me today. If Your Father won't forgive me, I know You will. And maybe Saint Catherine, please Saint Catherine, you know how devoted I've been to you, please say something in my favour. Please!"

In response, the light drizzle turned heavy, the rain now drenching her head to toe, water trickling down her neck, but she refused to open her umbrella. She looked up and pleaded, "If that's what you want, Jesus, you know I'll do it for you. And Saint Catherine, if I must catch pneumonia for you I will. I know I deserve it."

Suddenly, a voice boomed behind her.

"You'll catch your death of cold! Put up your umbrella you silly bugger!"

She turned to see Lockie standing there, dressed all in black, a huge black umbrella held out high, his arm stretched out to drag her under and his hearse parked behind him.

"Lockie, where did you come from?"

"It's the hearse. Isn't she a beauty? Purrs like a kitten."

"I was just going in to see Father Zappia."

"Oh, that's a coincidence. So was I."

"You've been up to no good as usual?" quipped Babs, a smile even, hard to do in her black mood.

"Me? I'm the picture of righteousness, sister. You know that!"

"Yes darl, I know that."

"And what about you?" asked Lockie.

"I was dropping by to help Father rearrange his relics. He says he wants to get rid of some of the old stuff that he thinks aren't real relics."

"There won't be much left, then will there?" joked Lockie.

"So why are you here then?"

"I'm making donations to the church."

"You? You're giving money away? I thought you only did that with your gambling mates."

"Are you kidding? I only take money off them, never give it."

"What then?"

"Well, in my most recent acquisition I have acquired a large stock of coffins that I found piled up in one of the back rooms of the cemetery house."

"Empty I hope?" Babs joked.

"Now Babs, you're starting to sound like me!"

"So what's Father Zappia want with empty coffins?"

"He's going to bless them, and then he'll use them for poor people who can't afford to pay for fancy coffins."

"That's nice. I never thought of that. What do people do if they can't afford a coffin?"

"Father Zappia uses what little church funds there are to help them out. This way, he'll save that money and it can go towards the repairs for the church, of which it is in dire need."

"Lockie, you're so kind."

The rain stopped, a sign that they should go forward into the church. Father Zappia appeared at the door.

"Hello father," called Babs.

"What can I do for you today?" he asked, clenching his hands together, looking from one to the other.

"I'm here about the coffins, Father. Remember?" said Lockie.

"Yes of course. You have them in the hearse?"

"Jesus, er… excuse me, gees Father, a hearse is only made to take one coffin. You'll have to come out to the cemetery to bless them. There's five of them."

"Oh. I could come right now, if you like," said Zappia.

"Suits me."

"Just wait a bit and I'll get-a my holy water and a few other things."

"Father?" called Babs.

But Father Zappia had already turned back into the church and when he returned resplendent in holy robes and other paraphernalia, Babs had gone to her glue and paper.

*

Bobby sat in his car waiting for the crowd to disperse. While he watched Banger doing his job, calling the bulls, he was so glad he had refused Sandy's many pleas for him to join him on the wharves. Even with his limp, Sandy would say, he was such a big bloke that he'd make the bull's list every day. And today, Bobby was reconsidering.

There was the usual crowd of men, some slightly drunk and rowdy, others not drunk but belligerent none the less. All displayed familiar looks of desperation, clambering to get past the iron gate, on to the dock, to work. Banger stood on a ramp, a notebook in hand calling out names from a list. These were the bulls, the regulars who knew they would be called on first every time because of their sheer weight and size. You needed to be a bull to carry the huge loads, bags of wheat, bales of wool, not to mention bags of super phosphate, caustic soda and other dry chemicals that spewed from the hessian bags when stabbed by the grappling hook that pulled them from the pile. The government said it had banned this practice a decade ago, but it still persisted perhaps more so than before, because contain-erization had reduced the number of workers needed on the docks drastically. And even though, thanks to Jim Healy some years ago, the two competing unions, the WWF and the scabs union ("the temporaries and permanents") had amalgamated, their power had diminished greatly in recent years. Not only was the work hard, but the hours often unforgiving, up to twenty-four hour shifts when a ship came in; again, supposedly the government had passed a law years ago that twelve hours

was the maximum. But the owners of the shipping lines
demanded maximum efficiency, maximum output, and so did
the public who were fed a crock of lies daily by the press that
the wharfies were lazy good-for-nothings.

But what am I doing that's better than this? Bobby asked
himself. Back and forth on the ferry all day every day, me and
Eurie. And if Lizzie is right, they're going to build a bridge and
that would mean death to the ferry, my life of fifteen years and
counting gone. Lizzie was always right, she knew these things.
The blokes she serviced, they were all higher-ups, in the know,
each and every one of them. And now, we've made our pledge,
we've come together. She loves me, even minus my toe and
with my limp. She doesn't care that I'm a gimp. And that crowd
of blokes down there, the wharfies they'd call me worse names
than that. I'm a pathetic cripple to them, that's what. They might
be hard workers and hard done by like Sandy and his mates say,
but they don't care about the likes of me. I'm a cripple and it
wouldn't even matter if I showed them I could carry a 200-
pound bag of wheat on my shoulders for hours on end. It
wouldn't matter one scrap. It's not fair. I never asked to be a
cripple did I? I'm a cripple, thanks to… Well, I have to stop
thinking about it, don't I? That's what Lizzie does for me. She
knows what it's like to be different. And that's what makes her
my idol. I've worshipped her ever since that day I took her to
her flat. She opened her arms to me (well it was her legs to be
honest). She didn't care that I limped. And look how different
she is. And she chose to be that way. She chose it, mind you.
Would I ever have chosen to be a cripple? Cut my own toe off?
But look at Lizzie. She plies her trade and the blokes she serves,
they despise her for what she does for them, yet they can't stay
away from her, and they risk everything to be with her. What if
she had a hidden camera and told the world what her clients do?
But she doesn't. She gives her whole body up to them, she's
their Mother Theresa. Oh God! I think I've committed a blasphemy! What would Father Zappia say if I told him I thought
of Lizzie as Mother Theresa? Not only that but we want to get
married?
    Seriously, why not? But we can't. Maybe one day it will be
allowed. It's why after we consummated our "marriage" Lizzie
burst into tears. I still can't believe it. She cried and I took her
in my arms and I never felt so strong in my life. There we were,
lying naked beside each other, bathed in the glory of sensation,

lust at last put in its place, and Lizzie rolled into me, kissed the tip of my nose, tears streaming down her face. "Love, love me do," she whispered. And I took her in my arms and hugged her so close, no words were needed. The Beatles said it all anyway. But I did speak, meaning well, thinking of the future. And should not have done.

"I'll get a job and we can start a family," I said. "I'll talk to Sandy. I can work on the wharves."

Lizzie stopped crying, pushed herself back.

"What do you mean? We can't have a family, you're my uncle, you silly bugger."

"I didn't mean it that way," I lied.

"So what did you mean?"

"I, I, bugger it. I don't know."

"Then I'll tell you. You don't like what I do for a living. You're just like the rest of them."

Lizzie pulled away and started to get dressed.

"That's not true. It's different for me. I want you all to myself, you see. I hate sharing you with all the others."

She turned to me, stopped pulling on her blouse, left those wonderful nipples sitting pretty. "I know, sweetie, I know. I'm sorry I got cross."

"Maybe we could adopt a kid or something."

"Sweetheart. Let it go. I love you because you accept me the way I am. I'm not going to change, at least not until I'm too old to do it."

I was about to say, "I'm not one of your clients," but bit my tongue. It would have ended everything. She would never have forgiven me. Instead, I took her into my arms again, she half-dressed now, and me still naked, and hugged her tightly. "I'll always love you. I'll never let anything bad happen to you." I said, meaning every word.

The crowd dispersed and Banger came across to the car.

"Looking for work?" he asked Bobby who had wound down the window of his little Imp.

"Not likely."

"That's good, because there isn't any," joked Banger.

"I'm supposed to pick up you and Sandy, right? Take you to the ferry?"

"Sandy will be here in a few minutes. Not to the ferry. We're taking the train to Richmond to see Lennie."

"To the station then?"

"Right, unless you want to drive us to Richmond."

"Not today."

"I'll run down and tell Sandy you're here. He's probably a bit busy organizing the new blokes. Won't be long."

16. Dead Again

We'll take the tram to Richmond," said Sandy as he and Banger reached the top of the platform stairs of Flinders Street station. "We could walk along the Yarra, but to tell the truth I'm still a bit dodgy from the beating that cop gave me."

"You're getting too old for this," said Banger, "that was a couple of weeks ago, wasn't it?"

Sandy did not answer. The glare of Flinders street blinded him as his eyes, like those of everyone who came through this station, glanced up at the row of clocks that bordered the crescent spanning the broad stairway down to the street. They rounded one of the columns that supported the squat arches of the station when Sandy, not nimble on his feet at any time, tripped over a prostrate figure stretched out on the stone floor. Both he and Banger were big men, Banger less top heavy compared to his big brother, but both of them one could reasonably say were beefy blokes with big iron fists and beer barrel torsos.

"Look out!" cried Banger, but too late.

Sandy put out his hands to cushion his fall, but as he did so, the prostrate body roused itself into a sitting position, yelling, "Get fuckn off me! What the fuck are youse fuckn doing?"

He knew that voice and as he fell on to that body, he landed on none other than Monie, her red, leathery face glowing with the plonk she had consumed, her buck teeth bared like a dog's.

"Shit! Monie. What the hell are you doing here?" shouted Banger as he tried to help Sandy rise.

"It's her second home," mumbled Sandy, grabbing Banger's extended hand, struggling to stand.

"Youse fuckn tipped over me money tin. Where's me bloody money? Fuckn shits!"

Sandy stepped away, heaving a little, rubbing his hand that had taken the fall.

"You OK?" asked Banger.

"I'm OK. But feeling a bit wobbly."

They both looked down on Monie, her body twisted in all directions, rolling around extolling her streams of abuse at whoever came by. Her heavy rimmed glasses were broken in the middle and stuck together with sticky tape. Her old tweed suit, the one she had been wearing for the past couple of months had dark stains all over it, no doubt made by the plonk she had consumed, or in this case, not consumed. And there were yellowy streaks of slime where she had thrown up over herself. Sandy went to pull her up, but Banger intervened.

"I'll get her, Sandy. You need to take care of yourself," said Banger.

He leaned down and with his big wharfie's hands and arms, scooped her up and tossed her over his shoulder. Monie screamed louder abuse as Banger forged ahead, the crowds of busy commuters opening up to let him through. "Leave her alone, you bully," someone called. But none of the busy people made any attempt to stop him. Monie's kicking legs firmly in his grasp, Banger strode as if he were lugging a bag of wheat on the docks. Sandy hurried to keep up.

"We better get her out of here and on to a tram," he called, as they reached the top of the steps to Flinders street. But those steps were as usual, filled with people either coming or going as well as many hawkers and drunks sitting on the steps, asking for money.

"Out of the way," called Sandy, now in the lead. Banger was forced to a halt and now tried to pick his way around the bodies, their heads twisted up gaping at him. Then a loud deep voice came from the throng.

"Put that person down immediately!"

The voice was so deep, so firm, so penetrating that it seemed to stop everything and everyone in their tracks. It came from somewhere behind them, from within the cavernous station arches.

"Put her down, Malley! Put her down!"

Sandy turned and looked up the steps and saw, to his disgust, the cop who had beaten him, Stanford Lane. With agile leaps, kicks and pushes, Lane descended on them tried to drag Monie off Banger's shoulders. "Bullies both of you!" he sneered, "typical of you Williamstown mob."

By his side, his junior constable rattled a pair of handcuffs. "Want me to cuff them, sir?" he asked with glee.

Banger, trying not to drop Monie like a sack of spuds on to whoever it was sitting at his feet, tried to let Monie down gracefully. She at least had stopped kicking, but was now dribbling slime mixed with vomit down her brown tweed jacket some of it finding its way on to Banger's white shirt. He waited for Sandy to speak. Sandy was always the picture of serenity in the face of the cops, except Shooter, of course, but none of them really thought of Shooter as a cop.

"Constable,' said Sandy, "my apologies, we're trying to do the right thing and take Monie here home to her husband who is a good friend of ours."

"I'm going to have to arrest you," said Lane with a smirk of satisfaction.

Monie now sat quietly, hugging Banger's leg, her long pink tongue lolling about, trying to lick away the vomit from her lips.

The inhabitants of the steps began to back away. They sensed a fight was coming. There was now a clear path down to the street. A taxi pulled up to drop off a customer. Sandy nudged Banger, and nodded in its direction. He leaned down to help Monie on to her feet, wincing as he grabbed her with the arm that had just broken his fall. Banger stepped backwards up the steps, bumping into the junior constable who buckled and lost his footing and down he went backwards on to the steps, taking the fall with his elbows. By the time Lane was able to move forward—though Sandy had figured that the cop was all show and no action—Sandy had Monie under his arm, and like one would carry a child having a tantrum, pushed through to the open door of the taxi and fell inside, slamming the door behind them. Banger took off across Swanston street, weaving his way between the cars, all stopped anyway as people watched the spectacle of what might have appeared to some as a brazen kidnapping conducted right under the noses of two police officers.

"Jessie street Richmond!" called Sandy.

The taxi driver twisted around to speak. "Richmond?" he asked.

"Yes. Jessie street."

"She better not throw up on my back seat," warned the driver.

"Hope not. She'll fall asleep I think, if I know her."

"So where are you from?"

"Williamstown. What about you?"

"Naples."

"No kidding? How long have you been over here?"

"Twenty years."

Sandy strained to look out the back window, trying to find Banger who had taken off across Swanston Street and down the alley behind Saint Paul's Cathedral. The cops had shown no inclination to chase him. And with this traffic he'll probably get to Lennie's before I do, thought Sandy. He felt an elbow in his ribs and saw that Monie was settling down to a deep sleep. "So what brought you here, then?" he asked, turning to the driver.

"Naples was a shit of a place. No work, everything crumbling down, half the bloody city were bloody criminals, they'd pinch the shirt off-a your back."

"So how'd you end up doing this job?"

"They stuck me in a migrant hostel down there in Norlane and it was about as bad as Naples, without the bloody criminals. Then a mate I met at the local pub took me down to the wharf in North Shore and I got a job unloading the shit that came in from Nauru."

"You mean bird shit for the phosphate company?"

"Yair. Pivot I think it was called."

The cab reached Punt Road and sat waiting for the green light.

"How was it on the wharf?"

"Bloody no good, mate. The sulphur and bird shit, it was bloody poison. I stuck it out for six months or so till I had enough money to get up here and stay with-a me cousin in Carlton. And I helped him in his restaurant."

Monie gave a huge yawn and coughed a watery throaty cough. Sandy pushed her away and turned her head to face the window in case she threw up.

"Yair? Carlton's a nice place I hear. Lygon street, that right? I'd like to go there some day."

"There's lots of restaurants there now. The university types go there. I had a couple of restaurants there over the years, but-a the bloody government regulations got too-a much I gave it up. I'm happy to help out-a my cousin, and I make a little money on the side driving the cab."

The taxi turned into Jessie street.

"Thirty-six," said Sandy. He slid across the seat and opened the door, turned and dragged Monie out. She was half asleep, still floppy drunk, impossible to keep hold of. He rummaged in his pocket for money for the cabbie who now stood on the footpath waiting patiently. Then he felt a hand on his wrist.

"Don't worry Dad. I'll get it. Looks like you've had a bit of excitement." It was Ryley, his light slender frame looming above him, a wide sweet smile that Sandy cherished.

"Thanks, son. Just in time. My problem's not money though, it's Monie as you can see." She had flopped out of his arms and lolled half on the footpath and half in the gutter.

"Where'd you find her?"

"Fell over her at Flinders Street station. That bastard cop Lane tried to arrest us. Banger was with me. He ran off somewhere. He'll probably show up any minute."

"You mean the one that beat you?"

"Right."

Ryley paid the taxi driver who, much relieved, sped off. He grabbed Monie under the arms and pulled her up, but her arms just slid through his and she flopped down again. "Bugger her, Dad. Let's bloody leave her. Lennie can come and get her."

"Much as I'd like to. But the cops will come sniffing around if some neighbour complains. Let's take an arm each and we'll drag her up to Lennie's front door."

Ryley bounded up the steps and knocked on Lennie's door. They dragged Monie up and just as they got to the top, the door opened and Lennie's bald head appeared.

"Goodness! You've found her! She's been gone a couple of days again."

"No problem, Lennie. Where do you want her?"

"I think in the back bedroom on the cot. She can sleep it off there and then I'll clean her up."

"At your service, smiled Ryley."

"Is Banger coming?" asked Lennie.

"He'll be here soon. It's a long story," said Sandy.

They no sooner got Monie settled and sat down with a beer in Lennie's tiny front room, probably smaller than Sandy's, when there was a loud knock.

"That will be Banger," said Sandy.

And it was.

"You got a beer?" asked Banger, "I'm bloody thirsty. A hell of a walk, ran most of the way."

"The bastard cop never chased you, though, did he?" asked Lennie.

"Nah, don't think so. But I didn't want to take any chances."

"So let's get down to business," said Lennie.

Muffled moans came from the bedroom. All eyes turned to Lennie who ignored them. Instead he turned to Sandy. "What do you have in mind that you couldn't tell me over the phone?" he asked.

"I think we should plan for another national strike, but this time a really genuine national strike, with every single union in the country."

"That's impossible," said Banger, taking a deep swig of his beer. "There's scores of them everywhere and we can hardly hang on to our own members on the wharf." He spoke from grim experience, having had to strong-arm some blokes to pay their dues, and other scabs that offered themselves up to the shipping owners.

"I'm aware of that," said Sandy, "but it doesn't mean we should not try. Anyway, our own union is weak right now because we don't have enough members. There's not enough work for all of us because of containerization. They've been laying blokes off right and left for a year or more now."

"That's what they say," said Banger, who rarely disagreed, at least openly, with his big brother. "I think they're trying to whittle us down."

"Whatever the reason, Sandy's right. There's strength in numbers," said Lennie.

Lennie got up and put on the kettle. "Anyone for a cup of tea?" he asked.

"I'll have another beer," said Banger as he emptied his glass. Sandy nodded and Ryley followed suit. It was a bit early in the day to be hitting the booze just yet. Lennie handed Banger the bottle. "Help yourself," he said, "it's my last bottle." Lennie had not caught up with the times. He still bought his beer in the big bottles that were gradually disappearing from the shelves. It was another sign of Australia going Yank.

"A man-sized bottle, that's what I like," quipped Banger. "Have you seen those shitty little cans they're selling now and those little stubby bottles?"

"It's the Vietnam war," complained Ryley. "The Americans are everywhere making trouble fighting a war against imaginary communists."

"They're not imaginary," cautioned Lennie. "They're real and let's hope they win."

"Who, the commies?" asked Ryley.

"Who do you think? I'm a communist," answered Lennie, straight-faced, emotionless.

"That's a terrible thing to say, Lennie. I've got a couple of mates who lost the draft lottery and are now, as we speak, fighting in Vietnam, poor bastards," said Ryley, his angular body hunched over the kitchen table. "I'll have a cuppa too, please. I bet bloody Kerr's kids or grandkids if he has any didn't have to register for the draft."

"I wouldn't say so. The big shots love war. That's why they send their kids to public school where they're brainwashed by pommy teachers who make them dress up like soldiers and march them round and round. I've seen them," said Lennie.

"Then they go off to military academy or to the uni to become lawyers," added Sandy, "you must meet lots of them at the uni."

"I know them, stuck up shits. It's disgusting what Australia's doing in Vietnam. You'd think they would have learned their lesson from both world wars, following the pommies wherever they went, and now the Americans," answered Ryley.

The kettle boiled and Lennie poured the cups of tea. "Milk anyone?" All said yes, just a little. He then sat down at the end of the table and took on a posture of the chairman, which he was, of the communist party of Australia.

"The Vietnam war can work for us," he said as he looked at each of his mates, and they were his mates, he reminded himself. "I don't know if you have been watching the telly, but the Americans are beginning to tire of this war and I know from my sources over there, in fact there's a movie doing the rounds, I think at the university you may even have seen it Ryley, that shows very clearly the horrible dirty history of the Vietnam war, and why it is totally unjustified. A product of French and British imperialism, taken over with gusto by the Americans who would like to be the next imperialists of the world, if they are not already. But first, Sandy, what is it that you had in mind?"

"We should do two things; First, fix things here at home, in Victoria. We have to take over the Trades Hall Council. We found out what useless buggers they are when they stood aside during the Clarrie case." Sandy glanced at Ryley who sat across from him. "Putting aside the fact that he's my son, I'd suggest that we get Ryley elected as Secretary of the Trades Hall Council. It needs someone who knows how to talk like them, who's been to the uni, who's got those credentials. And we know that Ryley can also talk to us blokes as well. He's perfect for the job."

Ryley sat up straight, unusual for him and not at all easy given his spindly frame. His thin angular face lit up with a big smile, almost hiding his embarrassment. "Gees, Dad, I dunno," he muttered looking down at the table.

"That's the first time Ryley's been short of a few words,"
grinned Banger.

"But I've got my dissertation to finish. I'm only half way
through it."

"That can wait," said Sandy, "this is more important. The future
of all workers in Australia is at stake."

"Gees, Dad, you sound like Lennie. Maybe we'll make a
commo out of you yet!" he joked.

"Call me what you like. It's the workers and their families I
care about," retorted Sandy.

"Here! Here!" they chimed as one.

Lennie coughed a little to call his mates to order. As though
on cue, there was a deep moan and snort from the bedroom,
which he ignored. "There are going to be demonstrations at first
small, but they'll get a lot bigger, against the Vietnam war. The
BBC and American television are starting to report on it and it's
not favourable to the Americans. It's a vicious heartless war.
People don't know yet just how awful it is. They're indiscrim-
inatingly dropping napalm bombs on villages, incinerating
crops, jungle and people alike. We can use this to unite our
unions all over Australia. There's no one, once they see what's
going on and that our Australian boys are caught up in it, who
would support this war."

Sandy responded. "Which brings me to the second thing we
have to do. And that's set up a network with all the unions large
and small all over the country. And that's where you come in
Lennie. If you're what our government and you say you are, a
died-in-the-wool communist, I take it you have a network of
communist mates all over Australia."

"You mean Russian spies?" said Lennie with a slight twitching at the corners of his mouth. "It's what Striker and the federal
police think is what I am."

"I don't care what you are, Lennie. You're a mate and we
have the welfare of all Australian workers at heart," said Sandy.

"Here! Here!" came the affirmation of everyone around the
table.

Another loud groan followed by long rasping noises came
from the bedroom. Then came gasps then one loud squeaking
sound, almost a yell.

"Monie's coming out of it," observed Lennie, unconcerned.
"I'd say there are probably upwards of fifty or more unions
throughout Australia all trying to fight for their particular trade
or work, some of them even fighting against each other, and we

know all about that with the history of the docks here, don't we?"

"Can you contact them all, get them together?" asked Sandy.

"I can, and I will," replied Lennie.

"Do you have any mates in the Trades Hall Council?" asked Ryley. "I'm going to need a lot of help if I am to insert myself into their cosy operation."

"I know some people," said Sandy.

"As do I," said Lennie. "I think we can do this, and we can use the Vietnam war as our ally. There will be many demonstrations against the war. I will co-ordinate the demonstrations and try to get them put on the same day or close to it all over Australia, every capital city and of course Canberra, most important. In fact we should have some blokes camped out there in front of Parliament house all the time. And we might even think about doing the same thing in front of the Prime Minister's house. Come to think of it, the Governor General as well."

"Sounds good to me. Are you up to it Ryley? Think you can carry it through? Might take a couple of years to get you in there."

"My dissertation..."

"It's going to take all your time and energy. You need to forget about your dissertation for the time being. You can always go back to it."

"I'm all for it, but I think I had better talk to my adviser."

"There's a time for words and there's a time for action," pronounced Lennie.

"I know, I know, I agree," said Ryley. It's just that it's a bit sudden."

"I'm sorry, son, to have sprung this on you. And I haven't said anything to your mother about it."

"Nor should you. I want to do it, I just need a little time to adjust to the idea. Then I'll say something to Mum."

Lennie looked directly at Ryley and leaned over to do something he rarely did. He took Ryley's open hand, its thin long fingers, in both his hands, squeezed, and said, "Ryley, your Dad has a gift for seeing the way through. You are the future. You can make a better life for the workers of Australia, and who knows, you could make Australia a country we can all be proud of, no longer the lackey of imperialism.

A brief silence descended on the kitchen, broken suddenly by Banger who blurted, "Lennie, shouldn't you go in and check on Monie?"

"I suppose you're right. I'm sure she's fine. I'm used to these episodes. She always comes round. Lennie pushed back from the table and went into the bedroom. There was a long silence, and he did not come back. They looked at each other and all as one got up from the table and hurried to the bedroom. Lennie sat on the edge of the bed, Monie splayed out over it, on her stomach, her head hanging over the side of the bed. Her face was no longer that garish bright red, her mouth hung open, saliva and other viscous fluids extended down from her open mouth. Her eyes remained open, staring, lifeless. This time she really was dead.

"The fucking bastards!" sobbed Lennie, turning to his mates.

"Lennie..." said Ryley, attempting to put his arm around him.

"Get away from me! All of you!" Lennie's sobs turned into screams, his round face red, beads of sweat on his forehead.

"It's nobody's fault," continued Ryley.

Sandy gripped his arm and muttered. "Let it go, son. Let it go."

Lennie pushed Ryley away and threw himself on the bed beside Monie. He pulled her to him, her eyes fixed, staring like a child's doll. He leaned over and kissed her face, that horrible ugly horse's mouth, the saliva streaked with blood wetting his pale lips.

"We better go," mumbled Sandy.

*

Lockie stood by, dressed in his best dinner jacket, black pants with black satin ribbon sewn into the seams, black patent leather shoes, hair carefully trimmed, sideburns taken off, face freshly shaven with the closest of shaves by his apprentice. He stood at the entrance to his cemetery, awaiting the hearse. Sandy, Babs and Banger waited quietly together, Babs doing her best to make conversation. Bobby, Lizzie and Ryley pulled up in his Imp. The trouble was that the hearse had not yet shown up. Mandrake had been dispatched by Lockie to take the hearse, making sure it was nicely polished, to the city morgue to pick up the body, place it in the coffin then drive out straight to the cemetery. When exploring the funeral home, Lockie had discovered another ante-room in which there were several empty coffins. They looked a bit shabby, scratches and scuff marks, needed polishing up. But they would be OK after Mandrake had worked his magic on them.

Lockie was annoyed. Lennie had insisted on accompanying Mandrake to pick up Monie. and had also made it clear that he did not want Lockie along. What Lennie did not tell him was that he planned, once he had Monie on board, to drive by Flinders Street Station and pick up as many of Monie's reprobate mates as could fit into the hearse and bring them to the funeral. And when the hearse finally arrived, parked expertly by Mandrake its rear facing the cemetery gate, Lockie stepped forward to open the rear door, and was met with calls of abuse and a horde of drunks falling out of the wagon, dragging the coffin with them. He deftly stepped aside, worried that his dinner suit would be torn or dirtied by these filthy creatures.

"Where's the booze you bastards?!" they shouted abusively. "This is Monie's bloody send-off! Get outa the bloody way!"

The trouble was that there was no booze. Lockie had not got around to setting up a bar in the kitchen. There was nothing to give them. The rabble was starting to stagger forward, climbing over the coffin that lay on its side on the orange gravel path to the entrance, tripping over themselves and others. Banger was edging closer, ready to herd them like stray sheep. He looked to Lockie, as if to say, "give the word." But he did not.

"You blokes! Grab the coffin. We're going in!" Lockie commanded, looking in the general direction of Sandy and Banger. At that point, Father Zappia appeared at the entrance. He raised both hands, palms facing forward.

"Oh Lord and Saviour!" he called, looking up at the cloudy sky, "hear us O Jesus! It is time to submit our dearest Monie to your loving care! May you have-a mercy upon us all," and looking down at his supplicants, he spread his arms as if to embrace them and in his deepest most serious voice, boomed, "behold! We beseech thee! We bow before you! Take into your bosom our dearest Monie, whom in your infinite wisdom, you have chosen on this day to join your loving disciples."

The immediate effect was to quieten the beggars who by way of habit were taking up their places against the rough concrete and stucco wall each side of the gate, holding out their hands, a couple even with small cups in which they had placed a penny or two so that they would jingle. "Alms for the poor! Alms for the bloody poor, you bastards!" they shouted. Lennie walked up to each of them and with a flourish, at least as much as he was capable of, gave each of them a ten cent piece. He then produced from his hip pocket a flask of Corio whiskey that he handed one of them, with strict instructions to pass it around.

Father Zappia turned quickly, walked through the gate and into the reception hall to await the procession that would follow. Sandy, Bobby, Shooter and Banger stepped up, effortlessly raised the coffin on their shoulders and marched slowly towards the cemetery entrance. Lennie followed, Babs and Ryley, arm in arm, then Lizzie, dressed in her only black outfit, which consisted of tight fitting slacks, and a loosely woven black sweater, poised on her brand new red Italian stiletto shoes. She was there under sufferance, complaining that she did not really know Lennie or Monie. She was there, really, for Bobby's sake. Father Zappia stood, awaiting the procession, beside a vase of white lilies sitting on a small coffee table that made up an altar, of sorts. Babs had picked the lilies from her garden and arranged them herself in a vase she had borrowed from her boss, Phil. Mandrake had put out a couple of rows of folding chairs and placed the trolley beside the flowers, awaiting the coffin. Lockie and Mandrake took up positions each beside the coffin as Sandy, Banger and Lennie carefully placed it on the trolley.

There had been a bit of a disagreement. Lockie had ordered Mandrake to dig a grave, but Mandrake reasonably pointed out that there was no room and besides nobody had stepped up to pay for it. Lockie, for his part, accused Mandrake of being a lazy student who didn't want to dirty his hands with a shovel. Mandrake was deeply offended and sulked for a day or so, not showing up to carry out his chores. Lockie even offered to borrow a digger from the wharf where they were doing some construction work, but Mandrake pointed out that neither of them knew how to drive one. In the end the problem was solved by Lennie who insisted that Monie be cremated. Trouble was that Lockie's cemetery did not come with a crematorium. However, trying to relieve Lennie of the stress of finding the money and arranging for her to be cremated, Lockie had generously told Lennie that of course his cemetery could manage a cremation, leave it all to him. And as far as everyone was concerned, that was how it appeared. Mandrake, true to his name, set up some heavy drapes just behind the double doors to the kitchen, so their plan was, while Father Zappia said his piece, to slowly wheel the coffin away from the altar and through the open kitchen doors sliding through the drapes as though it was on its way to cremation. Later, they would bury her on his other property, the Annex he called it, down by Hobsons Bay.

The appearance of Father Zappia was quite a surprise to Lennie, especially as he had draped the coffin with a flag of the hammer and sickle. It was his way of paying Monie back for all the trouble she had caused him, trouble he admitted that he had asked for, no doubt about it. The fact was, he had no idea what her religious beliefs were, just assumed her atheism because she went along with his Marxism. But there was no sense complaining now. What was done was done. Of course, it was Lockie and Babs who had conspired to have Father Zappia present. Who else among their little group was qualified or experienced to deal with death?

With all seated, Father Zappia sprinkled a little holy water on the coffin, then turned to the little group sitting patiently on their fold-up chairs.

"Réquiem ætérnam dona eis, Dómine; et lux perpétua lúceat eis," he boomed in his deepest voice starting high, finishing low, then in English, "Eternal rest give to them, O Lord; and let-a perpetual light shine upon-a them."

Lizzie tried not to look directly at Father Zappia whose gaze, whether conscious or not, came to rest on her, staring at her shoes. Babs nudged her with her elbow. For some silly reason, both started to giggle and it took a great deal of effort to contain it. Bobby glanced sideways and squeezed Lizzie's hand, hard enough for it to hurt, hoping this would help her control herself. They both covered their faces, and bowed their heads. They were about to get up and rush out when the door to the hall opened behind them and in walked Striker. Father Zappia stopped briefly, then continued, sprinkled a little more holy water on the coffin, which was his signal to Lockie and Mandrake to gently wheel the coffin away.

As far as the little group was concerned, Monie was gone. And that was that.

17. Striker Moves In

Much to the amusement of his colleagues and the chagrin of his superiors, Striker still insisted on wearing a double breasted suit. He kept it tightly buttoned up at all times. Some joked that it was his corset and that underneath there lurked a huge beer belly that would pop out over his trousers if he unbuttoned his jacket. He could have rebutted that theory by pointing out that he was a teetotaller, but then, nobody would believe that either. He chose, instead, to interpret the fun they made of him as terms of endearment, let them have fun at his expense. He had no need of friends anyway. He had his work, all encompassing, and he had his faith. That was more than enough to get him through life and its challenges. He lived alone, and never felt lonely. A few acquaintances, some from police academy, tried to befriend him, but they gave up trying after a short time. Then they felt sorry for him, which did annoy him a little. But the fact of the matter was that he cared not a drop what others thought of him, good or bad. He was a completely self-contained person, all of it wrapped up inside his double breasted suit. Naturally a dark grey suit, sometimes with a faint stripe, mostly full coloured dark grey, of the best quality Australian merino wool.

Striker, having dealt with the rowdy mob outside by the cemetery gate, the result of which they had run off in zig-zag formation across the open fields that abutted the cemetery, some of them wandering in amongst the graves, but scattered far and wide, who knows where they would end up. It didn't matter to Striker, and mattered probably far less to the hobos themselves, though they did depend on finding places where there were lots of people from whom to beg. And of course, there were plenty of pubs in Werribee, they would end up hanging around there until the publican chased them away, or one of the drunk customers beat them up.

Standing taut and straight at the back of the hall, Striker watched with amusement the little group, such a tight group it was, their king-pin Sandy Malley quietly sitting beside his wife, the others buzzing around him. One could understand why communism had so far not worked out too well, at least that's what it looked like, if this bunch was typical of ordinary everyday communists who were Catholics none the less. And having Father Zappia run the service out here and not in a church was such a joke. Who are they trying to fool? They're communists the whole lot of them, even if they say they're not. And who knows? Striker had heard of red priests in South America, Father Zappia could quite easily be one of them. Anyway, this lot were all as Irish as they come, even if Babs insisted that they were Scots, and even if they went to church every Sunday—they were practicing communists as far as he was concerned. Maybe Stalinsky was the only one who knew what he was doing exactly, and most likely he was spying for the Soviets or even the chinks. He was a Jew after all, he said to himself.

It was time for Lennie to give the eulogy. It was brief. A eulogy really wasn't necessary, according to Lennie. Monie's life had been one long series of disasters and the whole thing had been a tragedy. In fact as far as he was concerned, she was better off dead, and, though he didn't say it, so was he better off without her. Lennie cleared his throat, stepped up beside the coffin, and with a bright white handkerchief, patted the drops of sweat that always formed on his shiny forehead. Lennie began:

"Comrades, and my dearest Simone." Lennie turned to the coffin, placing his hand on the lid. "I was not truly prepared for this day, even though I have been expecting it to occur ever since I met Monie, tripped over her, as a matter of fact, when she lay drunk outside the Bridge pub. I am a communist, a dedicated communist, as you all know—and that includes you too Mr. Striker—so I felt it my moral duty to pick Monie up and take care of her. We communists care for our fellow man, care for the poor. We save the detritus that is cast off by the greed of the capitalists and their lackeys, especially the police. I know that many of you found Monie hard to tolerate, her foul mouth, her lack of social graces. But in spite of the trouble she caused me for many years, she also taught me what it was like to be one of the downtrodden, the people she routinely lived with *and* for. Her adoptive parents—nobody knows who her real parents were—tried their hardest to raise her, give her a decent home, but the odds were stacked against them. Monie's life had been set in stone long before she was even born. Her mother, forced into alcoholism by the grinding poverty and desperation thrust on her by the evils of capitalism, gave birth to a baby under appalling circumstances, guaranteeing that she would be born into a life of misery, flawed in every respect, a creature who at times would seem hardly human. What kind of God is it that allows this immoral capitalistic system to mutilate His creatures in such a heartless and degrading way?"

Lennie glanced across at Father Zappia, who had stepped quietly down to sit in the audience, embarrassed to stand beside this rabid atheist. Lennie continued. "Capitalists have but one God—Money! I say," staring fiercely at Father Zappia, "get thee behind me Money! Get thee behind me!"

Father Zappia looked stonily at the floor. Babs of course was outraged and had to be restrained by Sandy who put his arm around her and held her close to him. Lizzie and Bobby were amused, though Lizzie felt it necessary to restrain Ryley who kept muttering under his breath, "go for it, Lennie! You beauty! Right on!"

Lennie licked his lips, stood briefly in silence while he awaited his audience to digest his challenging remarks. His mouth was dry, and with his white hanky he patted down more drops of sweat from his forehead. "My dearest Monie," he cried, "I can only guess at what your life has been like, what you have lived through, the cruelties large and small you have endured, but also your kindnesses that you would have, did make with some of your clients and certainly your drunken hobo friends. I know they will miss you deeply. You have made a difference in this life, and that's what matters. Our world is a lesser place without you, as am I a lesser person."

Lennie stepped down, head bowed, a quick glance at the coffin. Ryley, breaking away from Lizzie, stood up and app-lauded. He quickly sat down when none joined him. People just shifted nervously in their creaking chairs The drizzle of rain that had been with them for weeks now, turned into a downpour, pounding the tin roof above. Father Zappia stepped up again, looked to the ceiling and raised his arms as if acknowledging God's will. In his most sonorous voice, he delivered the bene-diction to the departed:

"Come, you who are blessed by my Father, says the Lord; inherit the kingdom prepared for you from the foundation of the world."

The service was very short for a catholic service, probably because Sandy had told Father Zappia to make it short and because he expected Stalinsky's eulogy to be so offensive, and it certainly was. Striker stayed back, waiting for all to leave, nodding courteously to anyone who acknowledged his presence. He beckoned to Shooter when he came by. "Constable Frost," he called.

"At your service sir."

"Could you remain here with me? I will need your assistance."

"If you need me, sir. However, I am the only means of transportation for my sister and brother-in-law."

"You mean you use your official police vehicle as a taxi?"

"Apologies sir. It's just that when you're an officer in the community, sir, it's important to help out where you can. I'd do this for anyone else I knew in Williamstown if they needed my help, sir. What was it you wanted me to do sir?"

"Search this place. I have a search warrant."

"Search for what, exactly, sir?"

"I won't know until I find it," said Striker evasively.

"Then it seems like I wouldn't be much help, sir?"

"You're probably right. On second thoughts maybe I don't need you."

"Thank you. By the way, sir. I don't know if you had anything to do with it."

"With what?"

"My getting me back to Williamstown."

"I am not involved in assignment of officers."

Shooter shot him a fierce look, as if to say, "liar." But Striker had already turned away and was approaching Lockie, his real target for today.

Mandrake, standing to the side, muttered, "I could take some people back, there's plenty of room in the hearse now, without the coffin."

"Thank you. I don't think we've met?" said Shooter, extending his hand. "I'm Shooter Frost."

"Pleased to meet you Mr. Frost. I'm Roy Farmer, but Lockie calls me Mandrake."

"Mandrake? What the hell for?"

"You'd have to ask him."

"And you can call me Shooter. That's what my family calls me, and looks like Lockie has made you one of us."

"Thank you Mr. Frost. It's a privilege."

"If you could hang around a bit, it might be a help. I should really stay and see what Striker is up to," said Shooter.

"Who?"

"Striker. That's the detective from Melbourne. He's a tight-ass, investigating the murders."

"Murders?" asked Mandrake in disbelief.

"Yes. The bodies that have been fished out of the Yarra and Hobsons Bay in recent weeks."

"I thought he might have been looking for the... oh it doesn't matter," said Mandrake

"Go on, Mandrake. We're family here. What?"

"Well, I don't know. You better talk to Lockie."

"It's the shoes, isn't it?"

"I don't know what you're talking about, sir," replied Mandrake, defensively.

Shooter grinned. Mandrake stood, shifting from one foot to the other, nervously.

"I know my brother," said Shooter.

"If you'll excuse me, I have to clean out the hearse after those drunks messed it all up," said Mandrake as he slipped away.

*

Father Zappia nervously tugged at his collar as Striker approached. He and Lockie were deep in conversation. Striker was sure they were up to something. Priest or no priest, anything was possible in Striker's view.

"Mr. Lachlan Frost?" he addressed Lockie with exaggerated formality.

"Detective. What can I help you with this time?" Lockie smiled.

Father Zappia nodded at Striker, smiled briefly then sneaked away.

"I have a warrant to search the premises," said Striker.

"What is it that interests the Victorian Police force in my collection of dead bodies?" asked Lockie cheekily.

"Never you mind. I know what you and your tribe are up to."

"You mean us Micks," replied Lockie sarcastically.

"I didn't say that," retorted Striker.

"What am I supposed to be hiding, then?"

"You'll see when I find it," said Striker, projecting an air of confidence..

"Aren't you legally supposed to have a reasonable suspicion of something before you go invading someone's private property?" asked Lockie, trying not to sound too hostile.

"Since when did you care what the law said or didn't say?"

"I care a great deal. If I didn't I'd be in gaol, unless of course I was railroaded like you bastards did to my brother-in-law Sandy recently."

"I don't know anything about that. What's behind that door over there?" Striker pointed to a door leading to a room next to the kitchen.

"It's just a store room."

Striker went in, followed closely by Lockie. There were various cleaning supplies and brooms, along with five coffins, one of them a child's size.

"Open them," ordered Striker.

"Open them your bloody self," answered Lockie, "what do you think, I'm burying bodies in my storeroom? You cops…"

"I'd shut up right there if I were you unless you want me to take you down to the station for questioning," warned Striker.

Striker opened one of the coffins. It was empty. It looked used. There were scuff marks on the outside but the inside bare, no plush satin materials that were typically used to line a coffin. The other four coffins were in the same condition. "So what's this then? Where are the bodies?"

"What bodies?" asked Lockie, the picture of innocence.

"The ones that were in these coffins."

"How should I know? They came with the property and were here when I took it over. You'd have to ask the previous owner."

"Who was that?"

"Harry Nolte," Lockie said with smug satisfaction.

Striker tried to keep a straight face. "He said nothing to you about them?"

"Nothing"

The only other room was the kitchen in which lay the coffin containing the body of Monie. Striker pushed his way through the drapes and went in. "So what's the body doing here?" he asked Lockie who stood in the place where the gas oven used to be.

"Lennie wanted her cremated. We will be taking it to the crematorium in Altona shortly. I suppose you want to look inside it too?"

"That won't be necessary. Which way to the cemetery?"

"You mean you want me to dig up all the graves?" asked Lockie, faking incredulity.

"How long have you known Leonard Stalinsky?"

"What business is that of yours?"

"Answer the question."

"None of your business."

Striker was now walking through the double doors that opened the way down to the cemetery. He followed the track marks of the hearse with his eyes. "What are those at the end of this track? I see tread marks."

"We had a recent burial, detective."

"I'd like to see inside."

"Do you have a warrant? Not to mention that you would be disturbing the dead," chided Lockie.

"I have a warrant, as I said."

"But not to open these graves that are owned by individuals who have bought their plots or in this case crypts. I do not have the keys to them. The owners have them."

"So now you are stickler for the law," said Striker, annoyed.

"Just like you," answered Lockie.

Striker surveyed the cemetery. Then looked back at Lockie. "You'll be hearing from me again," he said, then left.

The small group of Frosts and Malleys stood by the hearse awaiting Lockie. Striker walked past them, sullen. Ryley called out something abusive, but Striker did not seem to hear.

"Ryley!" scolded Babs, "don't! You're only asking for trouble."

"I know Mum. That's why I do it," he said with that big devilish grin she loved.

Bobby took Lizzie's hand. "You coming with us, Ryley?" he asked. "I'm due back at the ferry for my shift in half an hour."

Ryley followed them to the Imp, Babs watching Bobby and Lizzie holding hands like young lovers. Lennie stood apart, alone, hands in his pockets, watching Striker drive off.

Lockie hurried over, Mandrake in tow. "OK. We need to get a move on. Can't keep Monie waiting too long," he said jokingly, then regretting it when he saw Lennie looking so alone. "We can all fit in the hearse, I think, then Mandrake and I will have to come back and pick up Monie."

"Where's Father Zappia?" asked Babs, then answered her own question. "Someone must have picked him up. He has lots of admirers in his parish who take care of him." She smiled. She was one of them after all.

They piled into the hearse, and as it passed through the cemetery gate, there was Father Zappia happily waving. He had remained behind to watch over Monie. It was the least he could do, under the circumstances, he told Lennie.

*

Mandrake turned into Cecil street and rolled the hearse to a stop in front of Sandy's house. Babs was first out. "There's party pies, sausage rolls and sandwiches all ready. I just have to heat up the pies and sausage rolls in my new oven," she said. "That won't take a minute."

Sandy followed saying, "and there's plenty of cold beer." He waited for Lockie to slide out of the passenger seat. "Lockie, phone this number," he said as he handed him a small piece of paper. "I've heard back from Simpson. He's found a buyer. You better take care of it today if you can, but watch out for Striker."

"OK. Will do." Lockie turned to Mandrake. "We'll have a quick couple of beers then we'd better get back to the cemetery. Father Zappia will be waiting for us too. There's a chance we will have to empty out the crypts in a hurry."

"Do they have any red in there?" asked Mandrake.

"Wine you mean?"

"Yeh."

"Bloody university students. Don't know what's happened to them these days," muttered Lockie, half joking.

"I could skip the booze, if that's what you want," said Mandrake, annoyed.

"There's always time for a drink," said Lockie, winking and slapping Mandrake on the back. "I appreciate all you do. I'm going to give you a raise."

*

Striker had never put a foot wrong, was well liked by his superiors and his subordinates. Destined for greatness, that's what people said, would undoubtedly be the Commissioner one day. Perhaps for that reason the Commissioner did not like him, or at least that was the impression Striker had. Nor did he much want to become a Commissioner, because truth be told, he did not like politics. He liked clean, pure police work. And there were submerged political elements surrounding all these goings on in Williamstown. It was an intensely political place, political with a small "p" though. It was just a small step up from small time hoodlums, as far as Striker was concerned. A hotbed of Catholics flaunting the law, doing what they wanted, with a strangle hold on the local community that was made up of mostly union workers on the wharves. The odd one out was Stalinsky, hailing from Richmond itself a hotbed of communists and their sympathizers, who did not fit in at all with the closely knit Willy Catholics. And there was that young firebrand Ryley Malley whose head had been filled with all kinds of communist theories. Most likely by Stalinsky, not to mention all those commo sympathizers at the university.

As for himself, Striker liked Australia the way it was. He thought that, by and large, everyone got a fair go if they pulled their weight. He couldn't see what the unions were always complaining about. The owners had to find the money to run their businesses. Without them, the workers wouldn't have any work, would they? Truth was, though, he didn't really give much thought to these things, he was a simple man. He liked his job, his police work. He was good at it, and most importantly never gave up on a case until it was solved. His bosses knew that, which was why the Commissioner did not interfere too much, except that this time he felt his heavy breathing on his neck all the time. The Commissioner was no doubt doing what his bosses, the politicians, the likes of Harry Nolte and the mayor, told him what to do, or couldn't do more likely. Why Lockie Frost bought that cemetery from Nolte was a big puzzle. And he didn't dare interview Nolte without the Commissioner's blessing.

When he phoned the Commissioner's office, he got the usual run-around, until he mentioned Harry Nolte. Then suddenly the Commissioner was available. He would meet with him later in the afternoon. There would now be time to swing by the city morgue and have another look at the bodies.

*

Striker stood with the medical examiner, surveying all the bodies. He had asked Cordner to lay them out together yet again so that he could look more carefully and compare them more easily. To the row was now added the body of the child from Geelong.

"With the exception of the child," said Cordner, "there's one thing that is very significant."

"Which is?" asked Striker, impatiently.

"They have been dead for quite some time, I'd say probably up to a month or two. And there's also traces of embalming fluid in them."

"And the rest? The shaved heads and the slit throats?"

"Definitely done after they were dead," Cordner answered.

"What does that mean?"

"It means that whoever is doing this probably isn't a murderer. You can't murder someone if they're already dead, can you?"

"So we've got a sick-o hanging around a funeral home defiling corpses?"

"That's my guess. We've got a serial defiler, not a serial murderer on our hands."

"And what about the child?"

"He was also defiled after dead, though not that long, in fact could have been just after he died. As well, the body has severe lacerations to the chest and head, as you can see. Those lacerations were the cause of death, most likely from some kind of accident, probably run over by a truck or something."

"The head's not shaved and the throat not slit like the others though."

"Right. Of course, there's the other common feature we have observed on them all."

"The toe?"

"Right. The little toe of the right foot has been sliced off on everybody."

"What do you make of that, then?" asked Striker.

"That's your department, isn't it? I'd say you are looking for a ghoulish hairdresser," grinned Cordner.

"How funny you are. Maybe a ghoulish communist?" joked Striker in return.

"I'm sure the Commissioner would like to hear that!"

An orderly appeared at the doorway. "Senior constable Frost is here to see you, detective," she said.

"Show him in."

Shooter appeared at the doorway, clearly not wanting to enter. "You wanted me to see you sir?" he asked.

"Yes, Shooter, I mean Constable. Come right over. I want you to look over all these bodies and tell me if you recognize any of them."

"I don't know, sir, I'm not used to this."

"Come on, Constable, they won't bite you. They're very dead."

"Why me? Why are you picking on us blokes from Williamstown?"

"I'm not. I'm asking you to do your duty as a police officer," said Striker, pulling rank.

Shooter edged forward. Cordner looked on, amused.

"Can you identify any of these people?" asked Striker. "Look carefully at each one. The child, especially, do you know him?"

Shooter moved quickly past each body and stopped at the child's. He was visibly upset, on the verge of vomiting. The smell of embalming fluid didn't help either. He put his hand to his mouth and ran out.

"Constable!" called Striker. "Come back!"

Striker followed him into the toilet and waited for Shooter to finish. "You recognized the child?"

"Don't know any of them, sir. Sorry."

"You've never seen any of them before?"

"The boy of course. You were there."

"Where did Lockie go after the boy's funeral?"

"I wouldn't know, would I? You sent me away to Geelong," answered Shooter, trying very hard to keep his cool.

"But you met with him in a Werribee pub, did you not?"

"So what? We're brothers after all."

"It was just after Lockie took over Nolte's cemetery."

"So what?"

"Something is going on and I'm going to find out what it is," said Striker with a deep frown.

"Can I go now?" asked Shooter, "I've got a community to take care of."

"I expect you to keep me informed as to Lockie's whereabouts and what he's up to."

Shooter walked past Striker and out the door.

18. A Shallow Plot

Left on his own, Father Zappia sat forlornly on a hard chair in the kitchen, fingering his embroidered travel bag that he bought at a shop for priests in a little street that ran from Piazza Navona down to the Campo dei Fiori. It brought back many memories. He pined for those carefree times in Rome, his simple acolyte's robe, under which, in the summer, he wore nothing—naked beneath mind you! He was sitting in the back of the 69 bus on his way to the Vatican for a meeting with Cardinal Rose. But that was the furthest thing from his mind right then, for there sat a vivacious, if a little garrulous, young woman, all of probably 40 years old, beautifully dressed in an expensive light flowing gown, almost translucent, her shapely figure pressing to come out from under, the skin of her face tight and radiant, lips—O those lips!—fluttering, racing ahead of her brain as she smiled and chattered, and it was all directed at him! She looked down at his feet, and he followed her eyes. He had seen a painting in a tiny room somewhere in the Vatican, of Christ sitting at the table of the last supper. It showed, as the famous painting of da Vinci didn't because of damage, Christ's feet, wearing delicate leather sandals. In a moment of self-indulgence, no, more precisely a forbidden lasciviousness, he decided that he wanted a pair of sandals just like those. He justified this urge to possess a material object on the grounds that in his role as a priest he would be a *sacerdos alter Christus* so he had every right to emulate Him. The cobbler, whose workshop was just around the corner from San Giovanni in Laterano where he stayed with the other acolytes in the attached seminary, obligingly made him a pair according to his specific instructions. He paid the cobbler with several blessings written only for him and his family, and a special ticket to enter the restricted rooms under the altar of Saint Peter's.

"Father," she said, raising her eyes slowly from his feet to his closely shaven boyish face, "those are beautiful sandals you have."

He sat up straight as could be and raised his chin so that he looked down his nose just a little. A controlled smile followed. "I am not a Father, as yet," he said with a blush.

"Oh I'm sorry. What should I call you then?" her red lips said.

"Peter, just call me Peter," he replied, more blood rushing to his ears and neck.

"I'm Lucy, Lucy Valentino from Philadelphia," she answered in such a loud voice that the clutch of people jammed into the bus turned and stared as one. She put out her hand, perhaps a give-away to her age, the blue veins visible leading up to her knuckles, as though he should kiss it.

And he did. Without thinking. Just took her hand in his, the other held against himself to make sure his robe did not flop open, tied down after all only by the gold cord that was wrapped twice around his slender waist. He took her hand lightly to his lips, barely if at all touching.

"A pleasure to make your acquaintance, Madam."

"Oooh, thank you Father, I mean Peter. And are you on your way to the Vatican?"

"I am."

"You sound Godly already," she said mischievously.

"Thank you. May I call you Lucy?"

"Oh yes you can! And your sandals, they didn't come from Via Condotti, I'm sure."

"They did not. A wonderful cobbler whose workshop is just around the corner from our seminary made them specially for me."

"If you don't mind my saying so, Father, I mean Peter, they look like Jesus's feet."

Titters arose among the crushed onlookers. As if on cue, the bus suddenly jammed to a halt. Not at a red light, but a pedestrian who had decided to walk out in front of the bus. A stream of abuse could be heard from the bus driver.

"Lucy! Such sinful flattery!" he replied, almost slipping off he seat as the bus stopped.

"Could I perhaps have the address of the cobbler? Do you think he would make a pair for me as elegant as yours?"

"I'm sure he would for the right price." The young Father-to-be Zappia smiled from ear to ear, revealing resplendent white teeth, though a little irregular.

"May I have the address?" Lucy produced a notebook and pencil.

"It is in the little street just behind St. Giovanni in Laterano, but I do not remember its name."

"Perhaps you could take me there?" asked Lucy, coyly.

"I would be pleased to do so. But I could not do it until later this evening after I am through with my student chores."

"Would seven be OK?"

"That would be fine. We can meet in front of the altar in the church of San Giovanni. Do you know-a how to get there?"

"Yes, Father, I mean Peter." She put out her hand again, but this time the young Zappia took it in his and helped her step down to the curb. The bus had reached its destination outside the Vatican.

The rain outside continued to pound the tin roof of the funeral home. A clap of thunder woke him from his reverie. Shaking his head, he shifted on the hard chair and stared blankly at Monie's coffin. He heard another loud crack, but this time it was not thunder.

Striker had not quite done his job on the homeless rabble who had poured out of the hearse and ran helter-skelter through the cemetery and in and out the funeral home. He had chased them away, but like flies, they inevitably found their way back. If not booze, there was food in the kitchen, or so some of them thought.

The loud crack that Father Zappia heard was a rock that someone had thrown at the front door, trying to force it open. He struggled up from his chair, clutching his embroidered case and went to the door. It was unlocked. He opened it and there before him was a rowdy, rain-sodden bunch of homeless un-shaven louts, the likes of which he had not seen in his thirty years of priesthood, not even in South Philadelphia. No longer staggering, but looking bedraggled and tired, they dragged themselves past Father Zappia and wandered around, making gurgling, coughing and screaming noises, until they found the kitchen.

"You can't go in there!" cried Father Zappia.

But they were already in there, rifling through the cupboards, and then they spied the refrigerator.

"Get out! Get out!" he yelled again, running to the refrig-erator, pushing his way through the stink of unwashed bodies and rain soaked clothes, banging them away with his embroidered bag, then standing against the refrigerator facing it, his arms outstretched in an embrace, his back to the mob. They banged at him with their hands and fists, but he would not let go. Things had reached a level of frenzy that only happens when people are angry, tired and hungry. "Scum!" he cried, "scum!" and began trying to kick them away with his feet, kicking with considerable difficulty backwards, but landing some blows none the less. He heard a big crash, which was undeniably the sound of a cutlery drawer falling to the floor. He managed to twist his head around to see out of the corner of his eye what had happened, only to see a large oaf of a man poised above him, holding a fork.

"Get away!" growled the oaf, "get away or I'll stab your eye and swallow it whole, you fuckn cunt!"

"Lord have-a mercy!" moaned Father Zappia, "forgive them for they know not what they do!" At which he felt awful pains in his head, not from the fork, but from the dreadful feeling that he had just taken the Lord's name in vain.

"Ya fuckn shit priest. Get away! We want food!"

The great oaf brought down the fork, but by now there was bedlam in the kitchen and he was bumped by another of the half crazed mob, and the fork rammed into the refrigerator door, and ricocheted onto the Father's embroidered bag that was wedged between his body and the refrigerator. This was too much for the Father. He looked down and saw the fork sticking out from his bag, having pierced the cover. A hole in his priceless Italian leather bag! Father Zappia was now in a rage of his own. He let go of the refrigerator, grabbed his bag, pulled out the fork and turned around, jabbing at the mob with fierce thrusts of the fork and even using his bag like a whip to belt them. Like crazy goats, the bunch of idiots ran this way and that, eventually finding the door out of the kitchen, all trying to squeeze through at once. Unable to do so, they turned as if one, and all fell silent. The rabble now swayed a little, the oaf standing before them, his hands rubbing his neck and pulling on his ears, peering at Father Zappia from beneath eyebrows that even Santa Claus would envy.

"Let's get 'im, mates! Let's get 'im!" growled the oaf.

Father Zappia did not try to run; there was nowhere to run except through the door that was blocked by the stinking bodies of the ruffians. He would protect the refrigerator at any cost. That was what he must do!

*

Lockie and Mandrake were not especially sober by the time they got back to the cemetery. Which was fortunate. They arrived to see the homeless dills running hither and thither in all directions, banging on doors and windows of the funeral home.

"Fuck off you shits!" yelled Mandrake.

Lockie was stunned. "You talk like that at university?"

"Not really," said Mandrake, "I just thought it would be the language they would understand."

Lockie grinned. The mob had not responded.

"Just pick up a stick or something, here this umbrella will do, and chase them with it. They're used to being beaten. They'll run away."

Mandrake did as he was advised and sure enough, they ran off, rather like the goats they reminded him of, stopping at a safe distance among the graves, some hiding behind head stones. The rain seemed to have taken note and rained even harder. Lockie went inside but quickly returned. "You've got to see this! Quick! I need help!" he said.

Mandrake sprinted as fast as he could, holding the umbrella. What is it?"

They ran over to the kitchen door and saw the oaf and a couple of other reprobates stuck fast in the doorway, Father Zappia hugging the refrigerator, his embroidered bag once again snuggly tucked away between his belly and the fridge door. The oaf scowled and tried to free his arms and hands, but each time he tried the poor couple of blokes who were jammed, one curled up on the floor in between the oaf's legs, thus pinning them against the doorway, the other, a small joker, crammed up against the door jamb, his head squashed against it, arms flailing around trying to get a hold of something that would loosen him. But to no avail. The more any of them struggled, the worse the jam became.

"Please, Lockie, come and save me!" whimpered Father Zappia.

Lockie turned and ran back to the hearse.

"What are you doing, Mr. Frost? I can't do this on my own!" complained Mandrake.

"Don't worry I have a non-violent solution," called Lockie.

He returned just as Father Zappia called out, "is Mrs. Malley with you?"

"No, but I have the next best thing," grinned Lockie. He opened a large cake tin full of Babs's party pies and banged on it with the lid. "Come and get it!" he shouted. "Free food!"

It worked like magic. The tense bodies in the doorway relaxed and, presto! They suddenly broke out and rushed to Lockie as did the many others even from far away in the cemetery.

"I'm going to call you Mandrake from now on," joked Mandrake.

"Here, you better put the pies out on the trestle over there, otherwise they'll knock you over fighting for the morsels. Wish I'd brought more!"

*

Father Zappia plopped down on a chair in the kitchen, staring blankly at Monie's coffin. He looked up at Lockie. "Is Mrs. Malley with you? He asked again.

"I told you, no. Why would she be?"

"Oh. No reason. She had mentioned that she wanted to talk with me."

"If only this rain would stop, we could get the merchandise from the crypt," muttered Lockie to Mandrake.

"We could fill the coffins up then trundle them back here and load them in the hearse."

"But the hearse wouldn't take more than a couple of coffins and we have enough merchandise to fill a half-dozen of them." Then, turning to Father Zappia, he said, "we really need your help, Father."

"I'm not-a helping you move your stolen goods, boys. That's not what priests are for," he said crossly.

"Father, I wouldn't ask you to do anything like that. What I was going to ask you was to say a prayer to stop the rain!"

"I'll do that, but you understand that you can't just expect God to grant you what you want. You have to lead a good Christian life."

"But I do, father, I do. Look how I help those in need. The free coffins, free cemetery service for the poor. Free burials."

"Yes, my son. I do recognize that. It's just that…"

"OK. I know I haven't been to confession for quite a while. I promise I will next week."

Father Zappia rose from his kitchen chair, leaned over Monie's coffin, then raised his arms to the ceiling, and said:

"Lord, I remind you of James 5: 17, Elias was a man subject to passions as we are, and he prayed earnestly that it might not rain: and it rained not on the earth by the space of three years and six months. I say unto you, O Lord, forgive us our sins, hold back your rains that we may worship you ever more."

There was no bolt of lightning, no clap of thunder. Mandrake grinned and nudged Lockie who held back a chuckle. "Thank you Father, I think the noise of the rain has lessened already. Let's go, Mandrake, get the other trolley and we'll load up the coffins."

"But what do we do then?" asked Mandrake. "If Striker shows up again, he'll find them sitting in the coffins."

"You're right as usual, Mandrake. I'll phone up Bobby and ask him if he could come out with Lizzie's Winnebago and collect the lot."

Lockie went off to the office to make the call and shortly returned carrying two umbrellas. "Found them behind the office door," he said, "Harry thought of everything."

They put Father Zappia on umbrella duty while they pushed the coffins down the grassy track to the crypt and loaded them with boxes. Father Zappia held the umbrella, not very effectively. He was more concerned to keep the rain off himself, than Lockie or Mandrake. Eventually, the rain did stop, though not completely. By the time they were done, the grassy track had turned into a bog of thick sticky, black Werribee mud.

"I've done my part," said Father Zappia, scraping the mud off his once shining black shoes. "Now can you get me back to my parish?"

The coffins, loaded with boxes, were stacked at the entrance of the reception hall, awaiting Bobby's arrival.

"As soon as Bobby gets here," said Lockie, and as an afterthought, "while you're waiting, you could say a prayer over Monie's coffin to send her on her way."

"I already did that," replied Father Zappia, full of resentment and feeling guilty because of it.

"I could make you a cup of tea," said Lockie in his best suave voice, "oh, but I forgot, there's no gas stove. I gave it to Sandy for Babs. Now if you'll excuse us, Father, Mandrake and I have some business to discuss in the office."

He nodded to Mandrake who followed him to the office. Father Zappia was left watching over Monie. Lockie closed the door behind them. "We have to decide what we're going to do with Monie," he whispered.

"I thought you were going to take her to the Altona crematorium."

"Are you kidding? You know how much that costs?" complained Lockie.

"So what then? I don't think we have any room left here in the cemetery, unless we start burying them one on top of the other. They do that in Europe, you know."

Lockie frowned. "This is Australia. We can't do that here."

"We can just do what Harry did."

"What was that?"

"Depending on who it is, start burying them down at the other property, the one by Hobsons bay. The annex he called it. You won that too, right?"

"I did. Haven't got around to looking at it yet."

"It's huge. And best of all the ground is sandy and easy to dig," observed Mandrake.

"Has Harry buried any there?"

"Oh he started only a few months ago. There's probably half a dozen or so buried down there."

"So we'll just take Monie there and dump, I mean, bury her there?"

"Except that you told him she would be cremated," noted Mandrake with a smirk.

"Oh. Right."

"We could just put in a little head stone and tell him that the ashes were buried there. There's a small section of the cemetery, the section just right next to this house, that's on rocks and can't be dug deeply enough for a proper grave. We could turn that into a section for little headstones for those who were cremated."

"Great idea Mandrake. No wonder you're at university. That's what we'll do."

"No worries!"

                                        *

"We'll quit and drive around Australia, that's what we'll do," said Lizzie as Bobby drove the Winnebago to a halt outside 68 Cecil street.

"I'd have to give up my job on the ferry," complained Bobby.

"So what? There's all of Australia to see. I've hardly ever been outside Williamstown," replied Lizzie.

"But I like my job running the ferry. And what would Eurie do without me?" Bobby complained.

"They'll find someone else, no worries."

Bobby sighed. "But what about our little house on Douglas Parade?"

"We'll rent it out to someone," said Lizzie, all business-like.

"I don't think we can afford it, Lizzie, seriously."

"Oh, stop whining," said Lizzie, immediately regretting it.

Bobby did not answer. He switched off the engine and stepped out, waiting at the curb for Lizzie. She came up to him and
put her arms round his big waist. "Sweetie, I know this will
upset you even more, but, if you're worried about your ferry
job, what are all my clients going to do without me?"

Bobby looked at her, struggling to find the right words. "I
need a cup of tea," he said, a little smile on his big face.

And what will you do without your sister? thought Lizzie.
His sister, like a mother to him. Always inside his head. For
sure, she said to herself, I've never had a mother, only Bobby's
big sister.

Bobby pulled her arms from his waist and kissed each hand
as he held them together, then gently pulled her along to the
house, limping a little more than usual. "Come on, let's go see
Babs. She'll be happy to see us."

Babs, all smiles as usual, met them at the door. "Just in time
for a cuppa, and Lockie's on the phone he wants to talk to you,"
she said.

"Who, me?" Bobby asked.

"Who else? Why would he want to talk to Lizzie? You know
Lockie, he only wants to talk to you if he wants something."

"Babs, don't say that," said Bobby with a frown.

"Say what? I didn't say anything."

Bobby hurried to the phone where it dangled off the hook in
the kitchen. Babs looked up at Lizzie, trying to penetrate, see
beyond those lovely red lips and into her green eyes, the colour
of her mother's before she got sick, looking, looking for a hint
of love, just a little. "Come on, darl, I've got a nice cuppa waiting and I baked some yo-yo's in my new oven just for you. I
know they're your favourite."

"Gees, Mum, you're a marvel. Always cooking something. I
don't know how you do it."

"I could teach you," suggested Babs, cautiously.

"I know Mum. I'm sorry, I was never interested in kitchen
stuff."

"Well, what are you and Bobby going to do once you move
into your new house and you become a housewife. Live on pies
and pasties and sausage rolls from the bakery down on Nelson
Place?"

"Oh no Mum. We'll live on bread and butter and Vegemite,"
quipped Lizzie with as big a grin as she could.

"All right, all right. I'm sorry, darl. It's just that…"

"I know. You'll always be there when I want to learn."

Babs turned away and walked to the kitchen. Lizzie stayed back, surveying the room, remembering the times she played on the floor with her little doll's house that Sandy had made her, and the dolls that Babs had made on her old Singer. She heard Bobby raising his voice, to be expected if it was Lockie on the phone.

"What is it Lockie, what do you want this time?" yelled Bobbie into the phone.

"Hey, Gimpy, you're in this with all of us." said Lockie.

"I'm not a gimp, all right? You're an asshole!"

"Bobby, I didn't mean anything. I'm sorry. You've got all sensitive these days. What's going on?"

"Lizzie and me are going on a big trip around Australia in the Winnebago."

"You're kidding!"

"No, really. I'm quitting my job and so is she. We're eloping together."

"Eloping? What do you mean, little brother?"

"What I said."

Lockie held the phone away from his face and stared at the receiver as though he could look into Bobby's face. "Gimpy, I mean Bobby…"

"So what is it you want?" asked Bobby, still angry.

"I need you to come out here with the Winnebago and load up the shoes. I've found a buyer, or at least Wes Simpson has. Mandrake and I also need some help with cemetery work, but that can wait until you get here. You better wear some old clothes and old boots. It's pretty wet out here and lots of mud."

"Why can't you load them into the hearse?"

"Because it's conked out. Won't start. All this bloody rain. Bobby, please. Sorry I've been an asshole. I promise I won't mess with you again. Besides, I've got Monie to dispose of as well."

Bobby had that urge to bang the phone against the wall, a habit that he had fallen into lately. He gripped it tightly and replied, his teeth almost clenched, "OK. Lizzie and me will be out there as soon as we finish our cup of tea." This was enough to annoy Lockie. He always expected people to jump and do what he wanted immediately.

"Thanks Bobby. You're a terrific brother," he said, laced with sarcasm.

Bobby hung up the phone and turned to Babs who was all ears and asked, "you're going around Australia? You and Lizzie?"

Lizzie came to the kitchen door. "I wish you hadn't told Lockie," she said, quietly, angry.

"I didn't mean to. It just came out. He makes me mad."

"Well, good luck to you both," said Babs.

"I hadn't really said I agreed," said Lizzie holding back a tear. "I don't know if I'm ready to settle down, as they call it."

Babs came up to her and took her by her wide shoulders, standing on tip toe, looking into her eyes. "I know what you're going through, darl. You don't want to give up your job and be stuck in the kitchen like I was all my life."

There, she had said it.

Lizzie looked for a moment, startled, then her red lips turned into a big grin. "Mum, you're the greatest. You do understand."

"Of course I do, darl. You do what you want. Don't let the men boss you around. You're still young. You can do anything," she said getting a little carried away.

"Anything" was right, thought Lizzie. If only she knew!

"Sweetie, we have to take the Winnebago out to the cemetery. Lockie's got a bit of a problem with the hearse," said Bobby as calmly as he could.

"You mean he wants to move those bloody shoes," said Babs.

Bobby downed his cup of tea and munched a yo-yo.

"Do you need me?" asked Lizzie

"I always do, sweetie."

"Did Lockie say whether Father Zappia was still there?" asked Babs.

"No, he didn't. Why?"

"He was supposed to meet me in the sacristy this morning, but he didn't show up."

*

"Have we got any shovels?" asked Lockie.

"Only one. I think Mr. Nolte kept it in the empty crypt. He had a mate with an excavator who dug all the graves. Only took ten minutes," said Mandrake.

"Then we'll have to buy some shovels on the way. There's a hardware store not far from here."

"I'm not digging any grave. I told Mr. Nolte from the start. I'll do anything, but I'm not digging any holes."

"Fair enough, Mandrake. You don't have to."

Lockie ran to the hearse and returned with another tin full of Babs's morsels. He stood by the hearse and banged the lid on the tin, calling, "food! Sausage rolls! Come and get it!"

The oaf emerged from somewhere behind the house, and a few others came out from behind gravestones to join him. They descended on Lockie, grabbing frantically for a sausage roll.

"Where's the bloody sauce?" complained the oaf.

"Shut up and get in the hearse, you assholes!" answered Lockie, "we're going to dig a hole." He beckoned to Mandrake to get into the driver's seat as he opened the back door of the hearse and climbed in, holding the sausage rolls. The bedraggled lot followed, dribbling slime down their chins in anticipation.

"Where's the bloody beer?" someone asked.

"Come on! Get in!" ordered Lockie as he maneuvered himself to the back of the hearse, dropped down, and closed the door behind him.

"Hey, what about me?" cried Father Zappia, standing at the entrance.

"Wait here! Bobby and Lizzie will be here shortly to get you."

"What about Monie?"

"Mandrake and I will be back for her once we get the hole dug."

"Which way?" asked Mandrake.

"Out the gate and left, straight down Railway Avenue then the hardware store will be on the left." He turned to the greedy passengers. "We're going to dig a hole and you'll all get two dollars each, then I'll drop you off at the Werribee pub. Alright?"

There was no answer. Just the noise of growling and slapping of lips as the sausage rolls were consumed. His passengers were an unruly mob still. Lockie thought of stopping by a pub and buying them some plonk. It would make them much easier to manage, but the trouble was they would do nothing until it was completely consumed, and by then they'd all fall asleep, even in the rain, which continued unabated.

Lockie bought three more shovels and after a little difficulty, they finally came upon the lot. It was flat and soggy, covered with thick grass, an occasional sheep browsing. Seagulls flew overhead, danced around the grassy tussocks, fought over small scraps of whatever it was they thought was food. And they quickly swooped down on the hearse as the door opened. They knew where the food was. They had come to the wrong place, though, because the homeless scavengers had devoured every crumb. Lockie surveyed the land, a huge expanse of flat stony paddocks, no fences in sight, except along the orange gravel road from whence they came, the property apparently extending for miles all round. And it extended right down to Hobsons Bay just a hundred yards away, the grey murky water lapping the shore. He turned to Mandrake. "This is the place, right?"

"Yes, this is it. You see those dark reddish patches? That's where Mr. Nolte had some graves dug. Can't see the tracks of the excavator, though. Had so much rain, I guess it washed them away."

Lockie waved some dollar notes in front of the homeless. "OK. Out you get. Take a shovel each and follow Mandrake here. He'll show you where to dig."

He opened the back of the hearse and started tugging at his workers, waving the money in their faces. They struggled out, the oaf falling down, getting mud on his hands. "Do we get compensation for this?" he asked cheekily, showing his muddy hands.

"How deep does it have to be?" Lockie asked Mandrake.

"Depends how long we can get them to dig, doesn't it?" answered Mandrake with a smirk.

Mandrake marked out the size of what he thought should be the grave and they started digging. The first couple of feet went pretty well. But gradually, the workers began to complain, asked for water and were told to turn their heads up to the rain and to drink that. In the end, Lockie called a halt. His diggers became a cantankerous lot, a couple of them losing their tempers and throwing their shovels away.

Lockie sighed. "All right," he said, "I can see it's no use. Get in the hearse and I'll take you to the pub."

This was an order that was obeyed instantly. He opened the back of the hearse, and they piled in without one word of abuse or complaint.

"We'll drop them off at the Racecourse pub, then go back and collect Monie. Maybe Bobby will be there and he could help us finish off the grave and send Monie on her way."

"Why would Bobby do it, if we don't?" asked Mandrake.

"Because he's my little brother and always does what his big brothers tell him."

"But doesn't he have a gammy leg or something?"

"That's nothing. He just uses that as an excuse for all his failures," replied Lockie.

"He seems like a nice bloke to me," Mandrake chided.

"He is, too. It's just that he's a whiner. Don't you have any brothers or sisters?"

"No. I'm an indulged only child, like they say," said Mandrake with some pride.

"If so, why are you working for me? Don't they give you money?"

"I won't take it. I want to make my own way."

"Fair enough."

*

The rain had let up at last when Bobby and Lizzie arrived at the cemetery, but now a cold blustery wind blew across the flat paddocks of Werribee. Bobby, Lizzie on his arm, walked to the waiting Lockie, all smiles at the entrance to the funeral home.

"Thanks, Bobby. Don't know how I'd manage without you two. Is your leg acting up? Your limp seems worse than usual."

"It's the cold and the wet. Always does this. But it's nothing. I'm OK, aren't I sweetie?" He turned to Lizzie and gave her a little peck on the cheek.

Lockie looked on in amusement, Mandrake peeping over his shoulder, almost gawking. Fortunately, Father Zappia had stayed in the kitchen with Monie, so was yet to learn of the unofficial public joining together of Bobby and Lizzie.

"The good news is that Mandrake here, thinks he can fix the hearse but it will take him a half hour or so. In the meantime we can load the shoes into the Winnebago, and I'll take it into Melbourne to deliver the shoes to the buyer. And, if it's all right with you, Bobby, once Mandrake has fixed the hearse, maybe you can take Monie down to the cemetery annex and bury her there."

"Why can't you load up the hearse with the shoes while Mandrake is fixing it?" asked Lizzie, always suspicious of Lockie's ulterior motives.

"I suppose we could do that, but we need to act while the rain has stopped. It's a bit hard to dig a hole deep enough when it's pouring rain, you know."

"You haven't dug Monie's grave?" asked Bobby, incredulous.

"We got it mostly done, but the rain got in the way," replied Mandrake, who now had raised the hood of the hearse and was tinkering underneath it.

"Bobby's not going to dig your bloody hole, Lockie, you can see how painful his leg is," said Lizzie in her strongest Major Mum voice.

Lockie was about to say something he would regret when Father Zappia emerged from the kitchen.

"Father Zappia," called Lizzie, "how lovely to see you. Do you want a ride back to Willy? Bobby and I were just going."

"Thank you. I really have to get back. I know I was supposed to have an important meeting with Babs. She will be cross with me."

"She mentioned that," said Lizzie, "but I know she will forgive you."

Father Zappia smiled approvingly. "Your Mum is a wonderful person," he said, "and so was her Mum."

"That might be stretching it a little bit," said Lockie, "but let's get the Winnebago loaded. What about it Bobby?"

"OK. If that's what you want. We do have to get the merchandise delivered," he said with a quick glance at Father Zappia. "Father Zappia will have to come with us while we get Monie buried. There won't be room in the Winnebago once it is loaded."

Lizzie squeezed Bobby's arm and pulled him aside. "Are you sure you want to do this? Lockie's taking advantage of you, as usual," she whispered.

"I know, but let's get this all done so we can get away from this crowd, get away together, for good, and maybe never come back!"

"Lizzie, maybe you could go inside with Father Zappia and say a prayer over Monie while we load the Winnebago," said Lockie solicitously.

In short time, the Winnebago was loaded and Lockie drove off. This was the signal for Mandrake to pronounce the hearse fixed. He started the engine and called out to Bobby. "Mr. Frost! All set. Do you want to load the coffin now?"

Bobby stood watching, hands on hips. "OK. Where's the trolley?"

They loaded Monie into the hearse. Mandrake held back. Lockie had cunningly maneuvered him into a position where he would have to do some digging, but he had made it plain enough that digging graves was not one of his duties and never would be. Bobby did not know that, of course.

"So are we going?" asked Bobby.

"We better bring the shovels," said Mandrake coyly.

"Two should do it, then. Do you have that many?" asked Bobby.

"What about four?" said Mandrake.

"You mean…?"

"Why not? It's in my contract with Lockie that I do not dig graves. It's the one thing I steadfastly refuse to do, and he agreed with it."

"But he's not here now, is he?"

"No, the bastard."

"Tut, tut! Mustn't talk about your boss like that!" kidded Bobby. "Can we fit four shovels and the four of us in the hearse?

"If we squeezed in. Lizzie could sit on Father Zappia's knee."

"Father Zappia's going to wield a shovel too?"

"If he comes, he works," pronounced Mandrake.

"You tell him then," said Bobby, "and what about Lizzie?"

Mandrake went back to the kitchen where Lizzie and Father Zappia stood facing each other, having what looked like a very serious conversation. Father Zappia was in his usual place in front of the refrigerator, clasping his embroidered bag to his chest, holding forth. "It would be a grave sin," he said with a deep frown, "a grave sin."

"No more sin talk. Sorry to interrupt, but we have to get going. Father Zappia are you coming for the internment of Monie?"

"You're burying her? I thought she was to be cremated?"

"Change of plans according to my boss," said Mandrake.

"Yes, I will come. I just need to get my holy water," he said as he turned to the refrigerator.

"What about you, Lizzie? Are you staying here?"

"I'm not staying here on my own among all these dead people. I'll come," she answered.

"It might be a bit muddy," warned Mandrake. "We'll have to squash in a bit. Not a lot of room in a hearse once you have a coffin in it."

They squeezed into the hearse, Mandrake revved the engine bragging how he had fixed it, then drove down to the cemetery annex.

The wind blew off the bay bringing with it a light spray, but nothing like the rain that had kept up the last several days. When they got to the half dug grave, Mandrake was thankful that the water had subsided, though someone, not he, would have to get down in it to dig the grave any deeper.

Lizzie remained in the hearse while the others alighted. Mandrake unloaded the four shovels and said, "all right. Let's get started."

Bobby alone stepped forward and took a shovel. Lizzie sat hunched up in the front seat of the hearse. She was not getting out under any circumstances. Father Zappia, without thinking, took a shovel but then handed it back. "I am here to deliver the last rights. Not to dig," he said curtly. Stepping aside, Mandrake did not take back the shovel so Father Zappia, annoyed at this affront and insult to a venerable priest such as himself, stepped up to the edge of the grave and threw in the shovel. Bobby, also annoyed at having been conned into digging the grave jumped in to retrieve the shovel and handed it up to Father Zappia who reflexively grabbed it. It took only the slightest tug from Bobby to cause Father Zappia to lose his balance and he slipped into the grave, up to his ankles in mud.

"Thanks Father, I knew you were a good bloke," said Bobby with a devilish grin. "Mandrake hand me my shovel. Let's get this done."

Mandrake leaned over here and there and scooped up a few shovelfuls of mud. Father Zappia slopped around, unable to lift the shovel when it was full of mud. Eventually, Bobby called to Mandrake to pull the Father out, which he did. By now the hole was about four feet deep, still a long way to go. It wasn't possible to get it any deeper, the water just kept seeping back in.

"That's it!" called Bobby, "there's no way we can get it any deeper. It will have to do. We can bury her here and when everything dries out, have the expert gravediggers move her to a deeper grave."

"Whatever you say, boss," answered Mandrake. He leaned over to give Bobby a hand up. They unloaded the coffin from the hearse and managed to get it to the edge of the grave. They had forgotten to bring anything to help lower it, so in the end they dropped it in. Under other circumstances this may have caused the body to pop out of the coffin, but because the bottom of the grave was full of water, the coffin landed with a soft thud. But now the sight of the coffin in the bottom of the grave brought a calm over them all and Father Zappia immediately fell into his proper role. Bobby signalled to Lizzie who came and stood by him, arms around each other.

Father Zappia scooped up a handful of mud, then stood tall, and said simply, "goodbye dear Simone," and recited from the book of Revelations:

"Blessed are the dead which die in the Lord from henceforth: Yea, saith the Spirit, that they may rest from their labours; and their works do follow them."

He flicked the sticky mud off his fingers into the grave and it landed with a "plop" on the coffin. Bobby moved forward and began filling in the hole. Mandrake was even moved to help him. The wind was cold and the rain was coming back. The sooner they could get away from here the better.

19. Deliverance

Lockie waved to Eurie as he drove the Winnebago on to the ferry. "This is not what you think it is," he said, "I'm driving off the other side."

"That's OK. Where's Bobby?"

"I don't know. Didn't he quit the ferry?" said Lockie.

"I thought he was going to stick around for a little while longer while we train the new bloke, my mate here." Eurie nodded towards a dark skinned fellow, a head of thick black hair, a toothy smile. "What are you doing in the Winnebago, anyway? Bobby said that he and Lizzie were going to take their honeymoon driving it around Australia."

"Honeymoon?"

"That's what he said." Eurie shrugged.

"I never heard that. I'm just taking it over to the garage to have it checked out. Last I heard Bobby was going to start work on the wharf with Sandy. OK if I park it away from its usual place?"

"Go anywhere there's space."

Lockie pulled up on the left side and waited. He was annoyed with himself for not having settled on the price with the buyer when they spoke on the phone just before he left the cemetery. Trouble was that he couldn't understand what the bloke was saying half the time. Sounded like a Chink, talked too fast. Should have known, the address was in Little Bourke street after all, right in the middle of Chinatown.

Suddenly there was a tap on the window. He looked out and saw none other than Harry Nolte. He wound down the window.

"You're not Lizzie!" Harry joked. "What are you up to, Lockie?"

"Running a few errands, mate. I s'pose you heard that Bobby and Lizzie are shacking up together."

"I did. Weird arrangement if you ask me," said Harry with a hint of nastiness.

"I wouldn't know. Staying right out of it all."

"So how are you managing my old property?" asked Harry, curious and amused.

"Great! If only the rain would let up."

"Don't suppose you'd like to sell it back to me, would you?" Harry said with a devilish smile.

"What? Harry, what are you up to?"

"I came into a lot of money at the racecourse. And sold one of my horses for a mint."

"Yes, but why buy this property?" asked Lockie, suspicious.

"Tell you what. I'll buy half and we can go into business together. I've had a huge offer from a developer for the parcel of land down by the bay."

"And what about the cemetery?"

"I've got a mate in the government lands department. We can sell it off to them and they'll turn it into a trust. It's what they're doing to all the cemeteries these days, you know. It's the new Victorian government. They're taking over everything."

"Maybe. I'll think about it. Sounds interesting," said Lockie cautiously.

"Great! Give it some thought and then we'll talk over some numbers."

"Are you still going to run for parliament?"

"Who told you that?" Harry was not a little annoyed.

"I hear every whisper in Willy, you know that."

"Probably not, if this deal goes through. And how's my young nephew making out? He's a smart young fellow you know."

"He's doing fine. Can't believe Billy learned so quickly. He's only been on the job for three months. It's like he's been clipping and shaving all his life. He can even cut women's hair, which is more than I could."

"Taught by the best of them, no doubt," said Harry with a grin.

The ferry shuddered to a halt. Lockie started to wind up the window. "See you Harry," he called as Harry waved and picked his way through the waiting cars to his new Thunderbird convertible.

Little Bourke street was impossible to drive down any time, but in a lumbering Winnebago, it was a tall order. Lockie slowly made his way down the block from Russell street, the way the buyer had described. He got as far as Dean Alley, squinting, looking this way and that for a bald Chinese bloke. "They all look the bloody same," he muttered to himself. And if he didn't find the bloke he would have to drive around the block again.

Suddenly, a small fellow, bald and gaunt, appeared in front of the Winnebago waving frantically, directing him to turn into the alley. He did so, and pulled up where directed, in front of a garage entrance.

"You the shoes?" ask the Chinaman.

"You got it!" answered Lockie.

"Fie dollars."

"What?"

"Fie dollars!" came the yelling reply,

"Five dollars? You're crazy!" complained Lockie.

"Not crazy. Hard to sell so many good shoes. Fie dollars!"

Lockie stepped out of the Winnebago and looked around. There were cars everywhere, a couple honking their horns at him to let them past. Crowds of people walked to and fro. It was overwhelming, too many people, too many cars. Too much for a bloke from a sleepy place like Williamstown. He just had to get out of there. "The traffic! Can't you get them to go back?"

"Traffic? What traffic? Nothing! I fix, I fix. Fie dollars!"

Lockie stepped out of the Winnebago and yelled back at the honking cars. "All right! All right! Can't you see we're doing business?" The haggler suddenly appeared at his elbow, nudging him.

"Fie dollars!"

Lockie opened the door to the Winnebago. "You take them all?" he asked.

"All! All! Fie dollars!"

"Take them then. Damn it!"

"How many?"

"One hundred."

The haggler counted out five one hundred dollar bills and handed them to Lockie. Three children, no more than ten or twelve years old scurried like ants into the Winnebago and retrieved the boxes of shoes. In no time they had them all. "You back out that way into Little Bourke Street, is best way," directed the haggler.

There was no way Lockie was going to back the Winnebago into Little Bourke Street. He climbed back into the driver's seat and drove forward but came to a narrow end of the alley. There was no way forward. He climbed out, hands on hips, incensed. He felt a tug at his elbow again. The little haggler grinned. "I drive it for you," he said.

"Go on then, bugger you! You do it!"

And he did.

*

Lockie couldn't wait to get back to Willy and vowed that he would never venture out of it again. Why anyone would want to live in Melbourne with its narrow streets clogged with cars and trucks he could not imagine. He pulled up at the barbershop to check on Billy, not that it was necessary. Billy had taken to his job like a fish in water. Learned the skills in a matter of months, and best of all was amazingly friendly with his customers. A kid that age, just out of tech school, you never know what they will get up to. Lockie had his own adolescent exploits to remind him of that. In any case, there was always, or mostly, Babs next door in the bookbinders, who would look in on the shop whenever she was there, just to see if things were going OK. He knocked on the storefront window and saw that someone was there.

"Hello, Phil. Is Babs there?"

"She's out back, working hard as usual."

"Mind if I drop in?"

"Of course not," said Phil, "I was about to make a cup of tea."

"That sounds good. Has she been next door at all?"

"I think so. She's quite taken with that apprentice of yours."

"As is everyone else!"

Lockie followed Phil through to the back and there was Babs, sitting on a high stool at the workbench, a huge flat table, sewing the signatures of a new book. The smell of freshly heated glue filled the room. Babs didn't look up. "Where's the rest of you?" she asked in her most unfriendly manner. "And where's Father Zappia? Have you brought him back yet? I waited for him nearly all day. Don't tell me he's still at the cemetery."

"Gees, Babs, I don't know. I left them attending to Monie's burial. I had some business to do, a delivery to make, so I switched the hearse with Bobby and Lizzie's Winnebago."

"I thought the Winnebago was Lizzie's?"

"Ok, Ok. Take it easy, Sis. I just assumed, now that they're a couple," said Lockie defensively.

"They're not, as far as I'm concerned." Babs carefully examined the signatures and cut the gauze that would hold them together.

"Sis, what's done is done. I don't want to get into it. He's my brother and she's my niece and I love them both, and so do you surely."

"Of course I do. But they'll go to hell! They'll be damned to eternity! That's what Father Zappia will say I know."

"And what do you say?" The question came from an unexpected direction. "Having just lost a loved one, the love of my life," said Phil, "I know that you should treasure your loved ones no matter what they do."

They both turned to Phil and Lockie said, "Phil's right, Babs. Accept them for what they are." He placed a hand gently on Babs's shoulder.

Babs looked up and cried, "But Father Zappia said…"

"Bugger Father Zappia! He just says those things because he thinks he has to. He doesn't believe them, or if he does he's a bloody idiot," said Lockie, getting himself worked up.

Babs carefully applied the hot glue and attached the gauze to make the spine. She sniffed a little and pulled out her little floral hanky her mother had embroidered many years ago, and dabbed a few small tears that had formed in the corners of her eyes.

Lockie squeezed her shoulder a little and said, "anyway, I'm guessing that Father Zappia will be back any minute. It can't have taken them all that long, especially as the rain let up in time for them to finish digging the grave."

"You left them to dig Monie's grave?" asked Babs, incredulous, setting down the book and grabbing the hand that rested on her shoulder. "Lockie! You are unbelievable!"

"Why?" asked Lockie, grinning down at her. "Someone had to do it."

At that moment the phone rang and Babs answered it. "It's Bobby. He says they're at our house and wants to know where is his Winnebago."

"What's he doing there?" asked Lockie. Babs held up the phone for all to hear.

"We're both soaked," said Bobby, "wanted to get cleaned up and put on some dry clothes. What about coming home and making us a cup of tea, sis?" and he hung up.

"What about Father Zappia? Did you bring him back?" asked Babs, too late. She dropped everything and rushed outside, and at that moment, the heavens opened up and the rain came down yet again. She turned to Lockie who had remained inside.

"Lockie, take me back to the house," she ordered.

"I have to get back and check on Billy," said Lockie as he hurried past Babs to the barbershop.

"But I'll get drenched!" complained Babs. "Take me in the Winnebago!"

Lockie had left her standing in the rain. She looked up at the dark bluestone sky, hands on hips, then shook her fist.

*

Father Zappia breathed a sigh of relief when at last Bobby and Lizzie dropped him off at St. Mary's. They were all shivering with the wet and cold, though Father Zappia was not quite as badly off since he had his various extra vestments pulled around him, and of course his embroidered bag to hug to his chest. He hurried straight to his house next to the church where Mrs. Sullivan his housekeeper had a hot bath ready for him and fresh clothes laid out on his bed.

"Oh dear, Father! I hope you don't catch the death of cold! I've made some nice tea and cinnamon that will warm you up and the cinnamon will keep the cold away." She spoke with a lilting Irish brogue.

"Thank you Mrs. Sullivan. I don't know what I would do without you."

"Shall I take your bag?"

"No thank you, Mrs. Sullivan. I have a few things I have to put right, some papers to go through. Best I keep the bag until I'm warm and cosy."

"Just as you wish. I'll be going now, my hubby will be looking for his dinner. I've left you some shepherd's pie in the oven. Oh and a parcel arrived for you. I left it in the study. Felt like a very heavy book."

"Thank you again Mrs. Sullivan," he called as he pushed his bag into the refrigerator. He had been waiting for the book for several months. He was about to step into the bath when the doorbell rang. He had a mind not to answer it, but thought better of it. Never know, it might be Babs who must be furious with him by now.

But it was not Babs, it was her husband Sandy.

"Why Mr. Malley. What a surprise. My apologies for being in my dressing gown. Just getting into the bath. We got a bit wet and cold out at the cemetery this afternoon."

"Father, sorry to trouble you. I'll come back another time."

"No, please come in. The Malleys are always most welcome here."

Father Zappia led the way into the grand old study. Mrs. Sullivan had just cleaned it up. He could smell the polish on the furniture. He motioned Sandy to a chair and sat behind his desk. "What can I help you with? Planning another march?" he asked cheerfully.

"No Father, or well, we are, but that's not why I'm here."

"Go on then."

"I'm not sure if I should even have come." Sandy got up to leave.

"Please, Sandy, it must be important if you've come all this way and in the rain as well."

"I wanted to talk to Babs about it, but I couldn't bring myself to do it."

"It's about Lizzie? If it is, I know all about it. Word gets around a small place like Williamstown-a, you know."

"No. It isn't about her. You mean her and Bobby?"

"Yes. God works in strange ways. He brings people together, and when they love each other as much as I understand Bobby and Lizzie do, it's best to leave it all to Him. When two people are in love, Jesus loves them too."

"I've never seen Bobby so happy," smiled Sandy.

"So what is the trouble, then?"

"I think Ryley is a homo, I mean, homosexual, he's…"

"Now why would you think that, Sandy? And if it's true, what can I do about it?"

"He always pretends he has a girlfriend, he's twenty five going on twenty six, I think. But he never brings one home, never been seen with a girl."

"That's hardly enough to assume he's homosexual, Mr. Malley."

"Well, my friend, you know him, Lennie Stalinsky, Monie's husband, suspects it."

"Why?"

"He says Ryley went to him for advice."

"Advice? What kind of advice?"

"He asked Lennie what Marx, you know, the communist, thought about it."

"What exactly?"

"I'm not sure of the details. Lennie just mentioned it to me when we were talking about other union things. Said Ryley was asking him about Marx's sex life."

"Marx was not a homosexual, as far as I know. Though as you could guess, my knowledge of Marx is rather limited," said Father Zappia, looking down, perhaps a little guilty.

"Anyway, Lennie—and Monie too, she was there—told him about Marx's dalliances, how he treated his wife, had a mistress and the lot."

"And on that basis you suspect that Ryley is homosexual? Mr. Malley, that's very flimsy."

"I could tell from the way Lennie told me that he suspected it too."

Father Zappia got up from behind the desk and stood by Sandy's chair, looking down on what he now saw anew, a solid middle-aged man at the peak of his powers, now anticipating the downward slope. He had seen this so many times before in strong men of Sandy's age. They were ripe for God's picking. "I'm glad you didn't tell Babs. She would have been in confession in a shot and I would have had to console her every day. She has enough guilt to bear as it is."

"Babs? Guilt? She never had a guilty thought in her life!" joked Sandy.

"And you?"

Sandy looked up at Father Zappia, the corners of his mouth turning slightly up, a grin slowly appearing on his fair, round face. "I've worked and cared for other people all my life," he said, "if you call that guilt, so be it."

"Not at all. I'd say it was God's work," quipped Father Zappia.

"So what if he is?' asked Sandy as he pushed himself up out of the chair, now making his physical presence felt.

"So what if he is? It's 1969, people are changing," answered Father Zappia in his most authoritative tone.

Sandy looked Father Zappia right in the eyes. "But the Roman Catholic Church is not. It never changes. That's what I like about it," he pronounced almost as though he himself were a man of the church..

"You don't come to church enough to make that determination." said Father Zappia sternly.

"Maybe not, but all right, I will start coming more often."

"Even once would be a good start," said Father Zappia indulging in sarcasm for which he would have to confess tonight when he said his prayers. "The church is changing rapidly. Pope Paul has already changed the Mass, and there will be a lot more, believe me. I could even tell you something of Pope Paul... and about Monte Caprino in Rome." He crossed himself and muttered, looking up, "forgive me."

"Father Zappia, you mean the Pope says it's OK?"

"I didn't say that."

"Thank you father. I'm leaving now. You've helped me a lot." Sandy got up to go.

"I think I've said it's nothing to worry about, unless…"

"Unless what, Father?"

"It becomes public. It's best not to talk about it." Father
Zappia lightly held Sandys arm, guiding him gently towards the
door.

"Pretend it's not happening?" asked Sandy with a quaint smile.

"Yes. Make it easy for him to keep up the pretence, if, in fact,
he really is homosexual," answered Father Zappia, looking
away.\

Sandy shrugged. "I'll let myself out. Your bath will be getting
cold."

"Tell Babs I will meet with her tomorrow morning," called
Father Zappia.

"You better tell her. I've never been here," called Sandy
forcefully.

Sandy left Father Zappia and walked straight to the Steam
Packet pub. He looked at his watch and saw that it was almost
five. After a brief period of sunshine, the drizzling rain had
returned, and he pulled his collar up around his ears. He would
be a little early for his meeting with Lennie and Banger, maybe
Ryley too if he showed up. He had dropped in on Father Zappia
on a whim, and now wished he had not done so. Zappia's advice
was what he would have done anyway. Pretend there was
nothing to it.

*

"You're welcome to stay here, of course," said Babs to
Bobby and Lizzie. "The mob will be here, though, since it's
Friday night."

Lockie looked across at Babs. She was puffing on one of her
Dunhills, which meant that she was up to something. Babs
made a cup of tea for him as soon as he came in, and called to
Bobby and Lizzie to join them at the kitchen table. They
emerged from Bobby's room, hand in hand. Lockie tossed the
keys of the Winnebago across to Bobby.

"Thanks,' said Bobby.

"And my hearse?" asked Lockie, officiously.

"Oh. I think I left the keys in it."

"Bobby, you're such a bloody gimp. Someone might have
stolen it."

"Steal a hearse on this street? Lizzie and I cleaned it up, I
hope you noticed."

"I did, and thank you. Don't know if it was worth it though
with all this rain. And here's your share, by the way."

Lockie passed over a one hundred dollar bill.

"It went OK then?" asked Bobby.

"Didn't get as much as we asked, but at least got it off our hands. That bastard chink pulled a fast one and there was nothing I could do about it. The Winnebago is a bugger of a thing to drive in the city. I'm never going back there ever again."

"Now, now, Lockie," said Babs as she took a big draw on her cigarette, "never say never." She looked across to Lizzie. "Can I warm your tea up a little love?"

"No thanks. We'll be taking off in a minute. Where's Dad?"

"He and Banger and Ryley went down to the pub to meet Lennie. They're up to mischief again. Planning something big. Something about the Trades Hall."

"Thanks for the dough, Lockie. Lizzie and I will be on our way."

"You're not staying, then?" asked Babs, butting out her cigarette in the ashtray.

"No. We're going to spend the night on the ferry in the Winnebago. Then the Winnebago and I and Lizzie will say good bye to the ferry."

"You're quitting your job, then?" asked Babs.

"Tonight is my last night."

"Then what?" asked Babs, trying to hide her disapproval.

"We're going away."

"Going away? Going away where?"

"We haven't decided."

Lizzie remained silent. If she spoke, she would lose her temper. The whole scene at the kitchen table brought back her teenage memories that she would rather forget. She squeezed Bobby's hand under the table. Gritted her teeth.

"We're going to take the Winnebago around Australia," said Bobby.

"And what will you live on?" asked Babs.

"We've got money and I'll do some shearing or something if we need more."

"You shear a sheep? You wouldn't know a sheep from a goat!" put in Lockie, "you're a gimp and always will be!"

Bobby would have leapt up and grabbed him, but Lizzie held him firm. "And you wonder why we're going away," he muttered. "Let's go Lizzie."

But Lockie continued. "What are you going to do with your little Hillman? Leave it in the street to rust away?"

"Babs can have it for all I care." Bobby tossed the keys across the kitchen table.

"I don't want it. I can't even drive anyway," said Babs, sensing that she had started something she could not stop.

"Then give it to Sandy, or Ryley. I don't care," said Bobby, fed up with the lot of them.

Bobby and Lizzie got up to leave. Lizzie held back. She had told Bobby that she did not want to leave on bad terms with Babs. She had pictured a little gathering outside on Cecil street, all the family and friends waving good bye, sending kisses, as they drove off.

"You're a pair of bloody dimwits, that's what," said Lockie, stoking the fire.

"Lockie, you shut your mouth. You're not helping any," snapped Babs. She had come to her senses and had a great idea. "Tell you what," she said, "let's have a send-off party. The two of you can invite all your friends and we'll have a great party here and send you on your way!"

It was now Bobby's turn to squeeze Lizzie's hand. She squeezed back, then pulled him to her. "I think that would be wonderful, Mum," she said as she pulled Bobby down to her and planted her best juicy kiss on his lips. Bobby looked into her eyes, those wonderful wide green eyes now with a touch of blue, rather like his own when he was a little kid. He could say nothing. She had silenced him.

Babs couldn't believe that she said what she did, but her tongue was waggling away, out of control. "And I'll make Ryley bring his girlfriend too. It's about time we met her."

Lockie stood up, annoyed. "I better be going. By the way, Babs. Father Zappia sent his apologies for not meeting with you. He was stuck out there at the cemetery. But I suppose you knew that."

"I guessed it. But I waited a long time."

"What do you need to see him for, anyway?" asked Lockie.

"That's none of your business," retorted Babs.

20. Catholics and Communists

Striker stood at the door to the Commissioner's office, awaiting the nod from his secretary. All the way from the morgue, to the police headquarters, then his own office and on to the Commissioner's office, he had lectured to himself, over and over, that he must not lose his cool, that he must speak in a measured, careful manner, choosing his words with precision. He was agitated, hadn't gone for his run for a couple of days. His routine all out of whack. Hadn't been able to sleep. Kept waking up, those damn bodies. There had to be a simple solution. Probably staring him in the face.

The door to the Commissioner's office opened and Stanford Lane, the senior constable Striker had sent to Williamstown to replace Shooter Frost came out, all smiles. "Good morning," said Striker. Lane nodded and walked quickly on. He was in plain clothes. The Commissioner was up to something.

"The Commissioner will see you now," said the secretary.

"Thank you, Miss."

Striker went in, the secretary hurried around her desk, a large metal monstrosity, and closed the door after him. The Commissioner leaned back in his chair, his feet on his desk, hands behind his head. Striker always found this offensive and promised himself that when he had that job, he would never do anything like that to demean the office he held. He stood at attention.

"Morning sir."

"Sit down, Striker. I take it you have made no progress on the bodies case?"

"I wouldn't say that exactly, sir," and remained standing.

"Then what progress have you made?"

"No new bodies have surfaced, at least. Still trying to figure out how or whether the bodies are connected."

"And what about the body of that disgusting woman?"

"You mean Simone Stalinsky?" asked Striker, eager to leave.

"Yes. Didn't she die too, after having nearly died when she was fished out of the Yarra?"

"The two events were unconnected, sir. She died of pneumonia, sir, choked on her own vomit when she was in an alcoholic stupor, according to the medical examiner, sir."

"And her toe?"

"Not cut off, sir. There's no connection."

The commissioner shuffled some papers on his desk. "I'm putting Stanford Lane on the case."

"You mean the bodies case sir?" Striker's fists tightened.

"Not exactly. I'm having him tail Stalinsky. Which will no doubt lead him to Williamstown, the suburban hotbed of communists and Catholics."

"This is what you called me in to tell me?" asked Striker, already angry. He had missed his morning run because of this.

The Commissioner pulled his legs from his desk and sat forward on his chair. "Detective Striker, I am doing this to help you. He's a strong catholic, he'll be able to blend in with that Irish crowd, especially that Malley and his wharfie cronies."

"But they have nothing to do with the bodies, as far as I can see."

"It's obvious to me that they do, and Lane agrees with me," said the commissioner with an air of superiority.

"How's that sir?"

They were all pulled from that ferry. And the ferry is run by the Frost boy, what's his name, the one with the limp?"

"Bobby Frost, sir. I've interviewed him and his niece Lizzie Malley. And not all the bodies were pulled from the ferry."

The Commissioner reddened, leaned forward, elbows on his desk. "And what did you find out from the loving couple?"

"Nothing sir. They knew nothing."

"Of course not. They wouldn't tell you anything. You don't know how to work these people, that's why. They know you're a protestant, it sticks out a mile."

"My religion has nothing to do with it, sir. I do my job regardless of what church anyone goes to."

"I want you to play back-up to Lane. Keep your distance, but be ready to help him if something happens."

"You mean I should tail senior constable lane, sir?"

"That's exactly what I mean. But keep your distance from the Irish buggers down there. Understand?"

"Yes sir." Striker was already planning his run. He would take the ferry to Williamstown and run all the way down the shore line to Gem pier, continue round all the way to Williamstown Beach, cut back across the park and drop in at the Steam Packet pub to see what was going on. If Lane was tailing Stalinsky, that's where they would all be. It was Friday. They would all be there by five. He looked out the Commissioner's window. The sun had finally come out. It would be a good run. "Anything else, sir?"

"Solve this bloody bodies case by Tuesday of next week. If you don't show me good progress, I'll send you to bloody Woop-Woop. Understand?"

"Right you are sir." Striker stood up, snapped his heels to attention, and left.

*

Senior constable Lane received a message from his informant, one of the Queensland louts from the march for Clarrie, that Lennie Stalinsky and the young firebrand Ryley Malley had just entered the Flinders Street station.

"Step on it!" he ordered his young driver who was waiting for him outside the Commissioner's office. With siren blaring, he had Lane at the station in no time. He bounded up the steps and made straight for the platform for Williamstown bound trains. His informant met him at the top of the stairs. "They're on the platform. Train coming in a few minutes," he said with a smug grin.

"Good work, Peters, good work. Stay with me. Are you alone?"

"Me other two mates are down the end of the platform, if we need them."

"Good job. We will need them if they go where I think they will go."

"Where's that?" asked Peters.

"It's five on Friday. They'll go to the Steam Packet pub."

"I could do with a drink and a punch or two," grinned Peters.

"You'll get the chance. But make sure you and your mates wait until I give the signal."

"What's the signal, captain?"

"Not captain. You can just call me Stan."

"OK. Stan."

"The signal will be when I punch Malley in the eye. Got it?"

"Pretty good signal, Stan old mate."

The train pulled up at the platform. Lennie and Ryley, deep in conversation, stepped on, Lennie glancing up just briefly at the mirror advertisement for Haig's whiskey and its border of nude nymphs entwined in vines.

"It has to be a complete and total national strike," said Ryley. "Total and complete. Everything has to be brought to a stop."

"Easier said than done," replied Lennie as they sat in a corner of the carriage together.

"It will bring the country to its knees. There won't be any food in the shops, no petrol for the cars. There'll be bedlam!" Ryley grinned with pleasure.

"I hope you realize what we are doing," said Lennie, always the cautious one.

"It's a revolution. That's what we're doing."

"Ryley, you should know better. We are not making a revolution. We are creating the conditions under which a revolution will inevitably arise."

"You mean dire economic conditions?"

"I mean that the masses, the workers, have to realize as they suffer for want of the basic needs for their survival, that their only recourse is to attack the bourgeoisie, the owners of production, and create a completely new social order."

"Violence!" growled Ryley brandishing his fist.

"We don't want violence and we are not advocating it. But it's necessary," insisted Lennie in a firm voice.

"Of course. It's not our doing, not directly. Only when all the economic conditions are right—like an eclipse of the sun," Ryley replied, waving his arm up high, as though reaching for the sky.

"The workers will come together as one, just as Marx said. They'll rise up and destroy the bourgeoisie," continued Lennie.

"A sudden insight! An epiphany!" sang Ryley, turning to look at the nymphs in the mirror.

"It will happen all at once, en masse," preached Lennie. "Look what happened in Cuba. Not to mention the Russian and then the Chinese revolutions. The masses rose up together!"

"But they had great leaders who led them. Who will it be here in Australia?" mused Ryley, a glint in his eyes.

"Maybe it will be you," smiled Lennie, gripping Ryley's arm.

"Now you're getting really carried away, Lennie," Ryley said, his long angular face lit up with a huge grin.

*

Sandy and Banger sat in a corner of the saloon bar, away from the din of the public bar. The barmen never charged them the penny extra, usually levied on saloon bar customers. They were union men after all, and union men looked after each other.

"Did you see those bastards?" asked Banger.

"The banana-benders, you mean?" muttered Sandy.

"Yeh. What are they doing here?"

"Sent here, no doubt, by their boss Bjelke-Peterson," said Sandy. "They must know we're up to something. If Lennie has been doing his part, rounding up the unions, word has probably got out from the scab informers in Queensland."

"You want me to go over and get rid of them?" asked Banger.

"No. Not yet. But I've no doubt they'll try something. We need to do our business with Lennie and Ryley first," said Sandy, "and speak of the devils, here they are."

"Ryley! Just the man I wanted to see," said Sandy with a bigger smile than usual. He got up and hugged him even, something men on the wharf never did.

"Gees, Dad. Are you all right?" asked Ryley, as he hugged him back.

Sandy pulled back and turned to Lennie and Banger. "I've been waiting till you got here to tell you the big news."

"Go on then," said Banger, "out with it."

"I talked with Wesley Simpson this morning. It's all set. He has the votes to get Ryley elected Trades hall Council secretary at the next meeting."

"This is the start of something big," said Lennie as he grabbed Ryley's hand and shook it harder than ever before. Ryley's was a familiar loose and floppy handshake.

Banger gave him a pat on the back as well. "This calls for a round of whiskeys," he said, as he took off to the bar to order the drinks. "Four whiskeys and four beers."

"Coming right up, mate."

Banger put up a five dollar bill and as he grabbed the change he caught a glimpse of the banana benders across the other side of the bar. There was a familiar figure hovering behind them.

"You know who I just saw in the public bar?" Banger asked as he distributed the drinks.

"You mean the banana benders?" said Sandy.

"Yeh, but someone else. That cop, the one that beat you up, Sandy. I'm sure of it."

"But I thought Lockie got him moved away somewhere," said Sandy.

"I'm sure it's him," said Banger.

"To hell with him! To the revolution!" Sandy muttered with a determined look, and raised his whiskey.

They all downed their whiskeys in one gulp and followed with the beer chaser. Lennie immediately announced that he had to go to the toilet. He wasn't up to this kind of drinking..

"It's through the public bar and down the alley," called Banger.

The others carried their beers over to the bar where they stood more comfortably, within sight of the banana benders.

"So what's the plan?" asked Ryley.

"We need to wait till Lennie gets back. The plan is that we go into action as soon as you are officially Trades Hall secretary. You're OK with it, Ryley?" asked Sandy, a very proud father.

"Too right!"

"You'll have to stop with your uni work for a while, who knows how long."

"Till the revolution, of course," grinned Ryley.

"Well, that might be a while coming."

"Not if we get all the unions working together, Dad," smiled Ryley, revelling in his new role.

"We have some powerful enemies, Ryley. It's going to take a lot of time, which fortunately you have a lot of."

Sandy bought another round of drinks, and another.

"Lennie's been gone a while. Hope he's all right," said Ryley. "I'll go look for him."

"I'm coming with you, Ryley," said Banger.

"I can handle those bananas, no problem," bragged Ryley.

"But two of us can demolish them," quipped Banger. "Let's go."

Sandy watched them saunter through the wide opening that led to the public bar. There was tall, lanky Ryley, one well-placed punch to the gut and he'd fold in two. And Banger, getting thicker and rounder with every year, measuring up to Ryley's shoulder, beefy arms and fists like all his mates on the wharf. He could pack a wallop. And he was quick too, you wouldn't think it by his size and his slow canter when he walked. Sandy and Banger had been in many fist-fights together. He downed his beer and started towards them, but he was a little too late.

A stocky figure, about Banger's height, wearing a greasy white singlet and old work pants leaned into Ryley's path, and Ryley bumped into him, spilling his beer. The figure turned and to Sandy's horror it was Stanford Lane, the copper. He had only ever seen Lane in uniform and thought him a puny little bloke for a cop. But dressed down like this he could see that he was all muscle, stocky like a middleweight boxer.

"Asshole! You spilt my bloody beer!" snarled Lane. He dropped his beer glass to the floor, and swung a haymaker with such celerity that Ryley had no time to duck and it landed on his eye. Ryley wobbled backwards, just as Banger stepped in and landed his favourite opening punch to Lane's solar plexus. Lane doubled up, gasping for air. Sandy looked around for the pub bouncer, but he was nowhere in sight. It was a put-up job, he now realized. Lane had paid the bouncer off. He raced into the public bar in time to see the three banana benders pushing their way through the crowded bar, eager to lay in.

"Outside! Outside gents! No fighting in the bar!" called the publican in despair.

But it was too late. The entire bar erupted in a violent melee, just like in a Western movie, but with real blood. Brawlers smashed beer glasses to turn them into lethal weapons, and the barmen ducked down behind the bar. They knew from experience that they should not get involved because it would be remembered on whose side they fought.

Sandy, still stiff from his beating at the hands of Lane, limbered up by picking on a few of the smaller blokes to thump. It felt good to be back in action again, he thought, standing mostly in one place, his favourite corner of the bar, waiting for fighters to come to him. They were easy meat especially when he upended a bar stool and jabbed it forcefully into their bodies, followed with a good whack with his clenched fist right to the face.

At last, there came the faint sound of a police siren. The publican must have called them, worried about his furniture. The fighters were getting tired, some already sneaking away, Stanford Lane one of them. He had taught them a lesson, sent them a message, he thought. It takes one Irishman to know another. Violence is the only thing they understand. As for Stalinsky, he got what was coming to him. If you hang around violent people, you have to expect to be hurt. He's a Jew anyway, you'd think he'd stay away from the Irish and likewise the Irish keep away from him. Just shows what nasty underground communists they are. How all they know is booze and violence. They're no communists. They're just common louts, the dregs of society. We should get them off the streets and off the wharves, that's what I think. I've told the Commissioner that over and over, and only now has he started to see the light, he's such a protestant shit-head. The protestants. They think they're tough and superior. But they're neither. None of them would have made it through Christian Brothers school that I went to in Geelong. There the whip and the rod worked its way, taught us real discipline, taught us how to endure pain. We're the tough ones. Not pampered like the other Catholics that went to the Willy catholic high. It was just another state school, as far as I could see. That Father Zappia, the weak Italian dingbat, just let them do what they liked. No discipline at all. And now you can see the results of it in the bar. It allows blokes like Sandy Malley to bully people around and take over half of Williamstown, that's what. The Malleys give us Catholics a bad name.

The police siren became louder. Senior constable Stanford Lane had done his duty. He sneaked away into the dark of the night.

Shooter rushed out of his police car accompanied by two other officers he had called on for help. Each held their favourite truncheon in their hand, each eager to use it, not having had much chance to do so in several months. Things had been too quiet. Shooter was very experienced in quelling bar brawls, though it was unusual for them to occur within the pub. Usually the bouncer managed to push them out on to the footpath. He had brought with him his umpire's whistle. It always got attention. That was all it took, but he always allowed his men to strike a few blows for the fun of it.

Sandy punched someone, backing out the door on to the footpath as he did so, just in time to bang into one of the cops who was about to bang him with his truncheon until Shooter grabbed his arm and said, "not him! He's one of us! Go on in. You'll see who they are, banana benders from Queensland. Get them!" Shooter stood just inside the bar one hand holding the whistle to his mouth, the other holding his truncheon up high. He waited for Ryley to land a couple of feeble punches and for Banger to clout someone so hard he collapsed in a pile. Then he blew the whistle. It made an ear-splitting screech and brought everything to a stop. He waved his truncheon. "See this?" he yelled. "You're going to get it if you don't get the hell out of here right now!"

The banana-benders immediately obeyed. Crouched over, they slunk out of the bar and disappeared into the night. Shooter walked over to Ryley who seemed to have gotten the worst of it. "You OK mate?" he asked.

"I'm good. Probably got a black eye though. That bastard Lane. He'll pay for it."

"You leave that up to us," said Banger. You're above all that now. Just wait until you're secretary."

"Secretary of what?" asked Shooter.

"The Trades Hall, that's what!" said Banger.

"My congratulations, Ryley, I didn't know," said Shooter, a big smile.

Ryley gently rubbed his swelling eye. "It hasn't officially happened yet. Ask Dad."

"Well if your Dad said so, it's going to happen. He never fails," said Shooter.

Ryley looked around the bar. "Gees, where's Lennie? I was going to find him when all this happened."

"Well he went to the toilet, didn't he?" said Sandy.

Ryley rushed out the side door to the alley where the toilet was. And as he stepped out, he almost tripped over Lennie, sitting against the wall, his head between his hands.

"Gees, Lennie. What are you doing here? Are you all right? We were worried about you," said Ryley, leaning down.

"I'm OK." Lennie looked up. He had been crying.

"You don't look OK, Lennie. Did that bastard Lane clock you? Look what he did to me, that shithead," Ryley pointed to his already black eye.

Lennie looked down. "No, I was on my way back from the toilet when I heard the fight start. I couldn't go in. I'm sorry. I should have helped you all, but I couldn't. I was just frozen."

"It's all done, now. We showed them a thing or two. And that bastard cop Lane slunk off, his tail between his legs," bragged Ryley.

Lennie continued to sob. "I'm sorry. It's just that…"

Ryley tried his best to comfort him. "I know, Lennie. I know. Don't worry about it."

Stanford Lane and his louts met up in the alley behind the Steam Packet. Lane was sober, his banana benders very drunk. "We have one more thing to take care of, then we're finished with Williamstown for a while," he said as though making an official announcement.

"What's that, captain?"

"Follow me."

*

Father Zappia dried himself off in front of the lovely open fire that Mrs. Sullivan had set for him in the study. He sat in his pyjamas sipping a nice hot cup of tea and munching on the tomato sandwiches she had left for him. It had been a horrible day, no doubt all God's work to remind him of his sins and responsibilities. But he wasn't feeling especially guilty. On the whole he had done the right thing by his flock, some of whom were heathens of the worst order. That Stalinsky the communist for one, but he wasn't one of the flock anyway. And his poor pathetic wife, Simone. Saint Peter had done the right thing by calling her to him, she had suffered enough. The wind had died down outside, though the shrubs around the cottage were still rustling, the rain beginning once again to come down hard. He placed his cup on the saucer and took up the parcel Mrs. Sullivan had left for him. It was battered and worn, stamps stuck all over it, having come all the way from the Vatican. It had taken a year or more of correspondence to convince them to send him the book on loan from the Vatican library. In the end, his old friend Bellarmino had dug up a facsimile of the book, so if it were lost in transit, it would not be so bad. He carefully tore off the brown paper wrapping, saving the Vatican stamps, which he would add to his collection. And behold, he held in his hands the book, black leather bound—Mrs. Malley would be impressed with it—and in gold letters stamped on the front cover, *Disputationes de controversiis christianae fide.* He thumbed through the pages, all five hundred of them, their edges painted in gold. A beautiful resplendent book! Too bad he could not keep it! Though it would take him a couple of years to read it. In any case, he knew roughly what it was about, knew all the arguments between Protestants and Catholics, goodness knows he heard enough of them from his own flock, but it would be most satisfying to see what the arguments were way back in Saint Robert's time. Though it was a little daunting to think that it was the last of the three volumes Saint Robert had written back in the sixteenth century.

The wind blew up again. The noise of the rain pelting against the window unsettled him. Perhaps Saint Robert was sending him a message! Suddenly he heard a loud bang that seemed to come from the kitchen. He wrapped the shawl that Mrs. Sullivan had left him on his easy chair around his aging and aching body and made his way to the kitchen, careful to switch off the lights as he went and switch on the lights as he went forward. His parish overseers had scolded him for using too

much electricity, the parish could not afford it! All the lights
were on in the kitchen and he felt cold air blowing through.
Someone had come in the back door.

"Who's there?" he cried.

"It's Senior Constable Lane," came the voice. "We had a
report of prowlers in the area."

Father Zappia entered the kitchen, and to his horror, there sat
two drunken louts helping themselves to whatever Mrs.
Sullivan had left in the refrigerator, his embroidered bag lying
on the floor.

"What's the meaning of this?" cried Father Zappia, "get out
of my house!"

"It's not your house," mumbled one of the louts, "it's the Pope's
isn't it?"

"Constable, what's the meaning of this? Get these louts out
of my home!" cried Father Zappia.

"It's not a home!" chirped Peters as he chewed away on a
piece of bread and cheese.

"My apologies, Father Zappia. These men must be the prowlers. I thought they were your guests," replied officer Lane.

"Certainly not. Please get them out of here." Father Zappia
lunged forward to grab his embroidered bag from the floor.

"Grab him!" yelled one of the louts. "What's he doing with
all this food when we poor buggers are out on the street wet and
cold and hungry. Jesus will punish you for this," the lout said
with a sneer as he grabbed Father Zappia by the ear and pulled
him up.

"All right!" cried Lane, "that will do!"

But it would not do. The lout hauled him by the ear, pushing
his head into the refrigerator, kneeing him in the backside as
well.

"Please! Constable! Help!" Father Zappia cried, still holding
his bag.

"Father?" called Lane. "I have a couple of questions for you."
He grabbed the lout's arm and pulled him back. "You two boys
wait over there and don't do any more damage, you hear? Father
and I must have a little talk."

Father Zappia held his bag even tighter to his chest as he
staggered back from the refrigerator. "What's all this about?"
he asked deeply frightened.

"Those spare coffins out at the cemetery. Do you know anything about them?"

"Why? What's it to do with you?"

"Answer my question."

"Mr. Frost told you, I believe. He donated them to the church. We use them to bury the poor if they cannot afford a coffin."

"But they're second hand, aren't they?"

"What? Of course not. How could they be?"

"I'll ask you once again, Father. Where did the coffins come from?"

Father Zappia was about to collapse in tears, he'd had such a trying day, felt weak at the knees. But at that moment there was a knock on the kitchen door and in walked Striker.

Stanford Lane stepped back. The louts looked up, grinning as only drunks can do.

"You banana benders get out of here," ordered Striker in his most officious voice.

"Wait for me outside," ordered Lane.

"And you can join them," ordered Striker giving Lane such a withering look.

Senior constable Lane stood stock still. He could take Striker on, he thought, even though he gave Striker maybe six inches in height. "Make me," he said, trying to stare through Striker's solemn, straight face, thin mouth, cold eyes, like all protestants.

"I don't think you mean that, Senior Constable. You have a career to think about. Do you want a future or don't you? I'm here by the Commissioner's order."

"To follow me, not interfere with me," answered Lane, "you've bungled this case from the start. You don't know how to deal with Catholics."

"And you are not a detective. Now get out!" ordered Striker.

"I'm staying. I want to hear your interrogation," persisted Lane.

"Interrogation? I'm under investigation?" complained Father Zappia.

"Of course you're not," said Striker. "Lane, if you want a future on the force, you had better leave now, and take those louts with you. I just came from the pub. You've created enough trouble for one evening."

Lane licked his lips nervously. He looked at Father Zappia and said, "I'll be back."

Striker watched him go and at the same time Father Zappia noticed that the rain had abated and the wind died down. It was an undeniable message. "If you don't mind, detective, I've had a long trying day and would like to get some sleep."

"So I can see. I'll come back tomorrow."

"What was it you wanted to speak to me about?" asked Father Zappia in his most friendly voice.

"It can wait. In the meantime, try not to have anything to do with Senior Constable Lane. He is not on this case. He is just trying to cover for himself because he knows that I could start an inquiry concerning the beating of Sandy Malley, in which Lane was involved. But that doesn't concern you."

"Mr. Malley is one of my parishioners, detective. It does concern me. In fact it had a terrible effect on his wife who came to see me soon after the event."

"In any case, Father. Please keep things to yourself for the time being."

"Don't worry. I don't want those louts anywhere near me!"

"And just to confirm. Those coffins Lane was asking about. Lockie Frost donated them to the church, didn't he?"

"Yes. When he took over the cemetery from the honourable Harry Nolte, he found them stacked in a back room of the funeral home."

"I see. Thank you Father. Get some sleep and have a good night."

*

"Sandy, won't you come with me?" pleaded Babs.

Sandy sat at the end of the old kitchen table, sipping his cup of tea, his empty plate pushed away, every trace of egg wiped up with the piece of toast that he was now slowly chewing. His jaw was a bit painful from a knock he had copped at the pub last night. There was union trouble in Queensland, it said in the Sun. He heard Babs, but turned the page of the Sun to the business section.

"Sandy? Won't you come?"

Sandy rubbed his jaw. There was quite a bruise. Babs had of course noticed.

"You're getting too old to be rough housing it down at the pub. What was it all about this time? Somebody bump someone else's beer?" asked Babs, of course, not expecting an answer.

"I'm not going."

"But it's about Bobby, my little brother."

"What about him?" Sandy buried his nose further into the paper.

"About his leg, and well, about Lizzie."

"I dunno what you're talking about, Babs."

"Father Zappia says he can help. I've been worried about those two for a long time. You know that."

"There's nothing to worry about. You worry because you want to worry," mumbled Sandy.

"Then you're not coming?"

"Saturday morning is my time with my papers. Zappia is a fraud, anyway."

"He's been very good to me."

Sandy sighed. "Then if it makes you happy, go on then."

"I'm going. And see that you do the dishes while I'm gone."

Babs strutted out the door and marched straight down to the church. There were puddles of water everywhere so she had to step carefully, even leap over the occasional deep puddle. She was glad she kept her hairnet on, her hair would have flopped all over the place. She marched right across the green grass, sloppy and spongey to her steps, that lay between her and the Father's cottage. She was about to the ring the bell when Mrs. Sullivan opened the door.

"Good morning Mrs. Malley. The Father isn't here. He finished his breakfast early and hurried off to the sacristy. He was very excited about something. But he said to send you across to him."

"Thank you Mrs. Sullivan."

Babs hurried across the grass again to the church, and the side door that led to the sacristy. She could hear Father Zappia humming a hymn.

"May I come in?" she called softly as she knocked lightly on the door that was slightly open.

"Mrs. Malley! Of course. Please come in. I am just dusting off our relics and rearranging them a bit. Mrs. Sullivan wanted to do it, but I thought you may like to help."

"Oh, thank you Father." She put her handbag down on the leather covered chair. The sacristy was a small, musty room, filled with paraphernalia, relics of all kinds, photographs of previous priests, old bibles locked away in glass cases, rusted metal objects whose sacred characteristics were long forgotten. Babs approached Father Zappia who was cleaning a shelf with a feather duster on the other side of the room. She paused a moment on her way to cross herself in front of the small altar.

"In the cabinet by the chair there is a pair of cotton gloves for-a you to wear," said Father Zappia, nodding to the cabinet.

"Thank you, Father."

"No worries-a Mrs. Malley."

"You know, you could call me Babs, we've known each other for a very long time."

"I know I could. But it just wouldn't feel right," said the Father piously.

He stepped down from the small three-step stool, itself a well-polished piece of fine rosewood, then stood back, hands on hips to admire the shelf. There were three glass display boxes, one very new by the look of the clean pure translucence of the glass and the brand new shining polished brass frame that made up the structure of the box, about the size of a small fish tank, and with an ornate lid fashioned into a pyramid. The other two boxes sat to the side, roughly the same size, but the brass of one of them darkened with age, and the other most likely the frame was of lead, its overall design like that of a stained glass window, except that the glass was clear and unstained, in places opaque from aging. "Mrs. Malley," he said.

"Yes, Father?"

"You know the story of Saint Robert of Bellarmine?"

"I didn't know there was such a saint."

"Then you will after I tell you what I have discovered. He was born on October 4, 1542."

"But that's, that's," stuttered Babs.

"Yes. It's-a your brother Bobby's birth date."

"What a coincidence," smiled Babs, her first real smile for the day."

"No coincidence, Mrs. Malley."

"What do you mean?"

"Saint Robert was also crippled," said Father Zappia in a solemn voice.

"He was born a cripple?"

"No. It seems that when he was a young child, he was in the barn learning to milk the family cow and there was a storm and a loud crack of thunder that frightened the animal. It lunged forward knocking little Robert off-a his milking stool and trod on his foot, breaking the ankle. In those days there were no doctors to go to, his family could not afford it anyway. His big sister—his mother died from complications at his birth—bound up the foot and made him a crutch from an old stick she found in the barn. He hobbled around with the crutch for-a many months until one day, when he was again milking the family cow, there was a storm and a crack of lightning that set the barn on fire. Robert threw down his crutch and ran for help. The barn burned down and the cow died in the blaze. But all fell down and worshipped Robert, because he was walking as though there was-a nothing wrong with his foot. It had been miraculously cured."

"You're kidding me, Father. Really? A broken ankle cured? It set properly on its own?"

"It seems that-a way. I have a friend who searched many old manuscripts in the Vatican library. He insists that it is all true. Though, he did find one letter written by one of the Cardinals who knew him well—Robert became a cardinal you know—that on cold mornings, Robert limped a little until he warmed up. He would often soak his foot in-a hot salt water."

"So I should tell Bobby to soak his foot in hot salt water?" asked Babs, half joking.

"No, you should-a not. The Lord will tell him what-a to do, when it is time," said Father Zappia, his bringing the fingertips of his hands together.

"Then He works in strange ways, as they say," said Babs.

"If I may-a presume, you are referring to Bobby's cohabitation with your daughter?" asked Father Zappia, ignoring her implied question.

"Yes, Father. Yes."

"But let's not-a go there yet. The important thing to remember about Saint Robert is that your brother was born on the same day, and that Saint Robert was ordained a Saint for his amazing work for the church. He was-a probably the most clever, erudite Cardinal of his time. Other Cardinals came to him for advice."

"Father, I don't know what erudite means, make it simple please."

"Oh, Babs, I am so sorry. I didn't mean to…"

"Forget it. What else were you going to say?"

"Let-a me show you. Look in this new display box. You see in the smaller glass box inside?"

Babs had to stand on tip toe to see inside. "I can't really see anything," she said.

"Here, use the stool."

Babs stood up and peeped into the bright new box. There, inside a smaller glass box, built without a frame, pieces of glass stuck together, was a withered, dark grey looking object.

"What is it?" she asked.

"It arrived last week by special courier, straight from the Vatican. They made a special dispensation for our church," announced the Father with great pride.

"What is it then?" Babs looked down from her stool, perplexed.

"It is the little toe of Saint Robert's right foot. A relic that was hidden away in the dusty bowels of the Vatican museum."

"And they let you have it and display it here?"

"Yes."

"I don't believe it!" muttered Babs, in fact, not knowing what to believe.

"They had one condition," said Father Zappia slowly.

"Which was?"

"That we rename our church the Church of Saint Robert of Bellarmine."

"And you said, yes?"

Father Zappia shrugged and said with raised eyebrows, "what else could I do?"

"What about the parish? Won't they be upset when you tell them?" asked Babs, her hand covering her mouth.

"Probably. But the more difficult problem I may face is that-a many will not believe that this toe is that of Saint Robert."

"So, it's about five hundred years old?" asked Babs, proud of her quick calculation.

"That's right. And you see, there is still flesh on the bone, and the toenail is also visible. It's a miracle."

"Can you take it down so I can look closer?"

"I will, but I have more to show you, Mrs. Malley."

"My toe? The one you have been keeping for me? Bobby's toe? Where is it? It's not this one, is it? You're not pretending that it's Saint Robert's toe are you?" Babs was all a flutter.

"Mrs. Malley. You're not-a being very understanding. I have spent a lot of time researching and thinking and most important praying to Jesus about your brother's toe."

"Oh I'm sorry Father. You know me. I don't beat about the bush. I'm like my Mum as you know. No bloody mucking about. So is it? Is it Bobby's toe?"

"Not at all. Not this one."

Father Zappia reached up and lifted down the oldest of the boxes and held it out to Babs.

"Take a look."

"Father it looks so old, I'm not game to touch it. Better put it on the table there, and you can open it. Can't see through the old glass, can't see what's inside."

Babs came down from her perch on the stool. Father Zappia placed the old display box on the small table, it also of polished rosewood. He opened the lid, and there inside was a brand new small glass box, similar to the other, all glass stuck together, no frame. And inside was a pink-looking toe, looking as though it had been freshly cut off a live body. Babs caught her breath and swayed backwards. Father Zappia caught her in his cotton-gloved hands, and held her until she steadied.

"Father! I don't believe it! It's not! It can't be! Father!"

"It is, it is that same toe. It's your brother Bobby's."

"But it looks like it was cut off yesterday!"

"I know. It is a miracle. Your brother is truly blessed."

"But Father. It can't be true. What have you done?"

"I have done only what you pleaded with me to do. To take care of it in the sacristy, to keep it among the other relics. And when I opened the old-a box planning to remove the toe and put it in the new box I had specially made, I almost fainted when I saw it."

Babs dropped down on her knees, Father Zappia holding her cotton gloved hands.

"Oh Father! Oh Father! I am so undeserving! Why has God done this?"

"It is Jesus' work-a I'm sure," purred Father Zappia. "Bobby has suffered the burden of his crippled leg. He has become the kindest of all your family—even you have always said that—and you have also often told me that you feel so ashamed of the way his brothers treat him, as a cripple, not as a true brother to be loved. Yet he loves them."

"Oh Father. I don't know what to say. What to think."

Tears now trickled down Babs's cheeks. She licked them, tasted the salt, thought of Saint Robert soaking his foot in salt water.

"Say nothing, my dear. Pray to Jesus and-a thank him for his kindness, for thinking of us, we tiny specks in the sea of sinners. He is full of forgiveness, Mrs. Malley."

"And what about Bobby and Lizzie?" Babs asked suddenly, drying her eyes and standing up with Father Zappia's help.

"What about them?" answered Father Zappia, sounding like a psychiatrist answering a question with a question.

"They, they've been living in sin, and now even more so. They're going away together, live as husband and wife. They won't have children will they?"

"One thing at a time, Mrs. Malley. This message from Jesus, this toe, is clearly a sign that He forgives you, and by extension, forgives your brother who, as we know, is linked to you not only through blood, but through a common traumatic experience."

"Traumatic what? I don't understand what you're talking about, Father. All I know is that I worry and cry at night in bed over Lizzie and what will become of her."

"Have you tried praying to Jesus? Jesus forgives, and clearly with the sign of the toe he has forgiven and gone beyond that. He is asking you to forgive too. Forgive your brother and daughter first, then forgive yourself."

"I've tried to forgive, Father. I truly have."

"And now you know that someone is listening to you. Pray to Jesus and the forgiveness will come."

"I will, Father. I will."

*

"I talked with Father Zappia," said Babs, cheerfully to Sandy, who was on his way out the door. "On your way to the pub?"

Sandy looked at his watch. "It's five o'clock. Where else would I be going?" he said with that faint smile of his. "Sounds like it was a good meeting."

"We're going to throw a party."

"A party? What for?"

"A going away party for Bobby and Lizzie."

"That's what you went to Father Zappia for?" asked Sandy.

"Not exactly, but that's how it ended up."

"That's great, Babs." Sandy leaned down and gave her a peck on the cheek then continued down the front step, on his way.

"We're having it in the church hall. The one next to the sacristy."

Bobby stopped in his tracks. "That was Zappia's idea?"

"No. But he went along with it. When I started thinking of all the people I would like to invite, I realized that we wouldn't have enough room here."

"All right, luv. Whatever you want to do. I've got to get going. The boys are expecting me.

"We'll have it on Friday night. Make sure you tell your boys to come. It's not far from the pub to the church anyway."

"We can also celebrate Ryley." Sandy grinned.

"What? Is he going away with his girlfriend too?"

"No, not as far as I know. They voted this morning. He's been appointed the new secretary of the Trades Hall Council."

Babs grabbed Sandy's hand. "Is that good? I mean, I don't know if I want him to get mixed up in politics. It's such a horrible business."

"Babs, my luv. He's been up to his ears in union politics as long as I can remember. He's a chip off the old block, sorry to say."

"Well, if he turns out half as good as you, that will be all right with me," said Babs as she pulled Sandy to her and gave him a sweet little peck on his bruised cheek. "Go off and have a good time with your mates. I'm going to invite half of Williamstown to the party."

"Do Bobby and Lizzie know yet?"

"Nope. I'll tell them when they come by tonight."

"I had the feeling that they were going to elope, if you could call it that, and sneak away without anyone noticing," said Sandy, revealing his thoughts, a rare occurrence.

Babs chirped up, "I already talked to Shooter. He's going to talk with Bobby. And Lockie is going to talk to Lizzie."

"Well I hope they haven't already left."

At that moment, Bobby and Lizzie pulled up in the Winnebago. Sandy pulled away from Babs and hurried off to the pub. He waved from across the street to Bobby and Lizzie, who walked up to Babs, holding hands, like young lovers.

"We've come to say good-bye, sis," said Bobby. "We're on our way."

Babs stood up straight, hands on hips, Major Mum style. "You can't go yet. I just talked to Father Zappia."

"Mum! What's that got to do with it?" cried Lizzie.

"He said I should accept it all and go on loving you both, and…"

"That's great Mum, but…"

"We decided to throw a big party for the two of you. A going away party."

"But sis, we're all packed ready to go," complained Bobby.

Lizzie, trying very hard to keep her cool, complained, "Mum that's really nice of you, but…"

"No buts. You're staying a few more days. Anyway, I bet they need you on the ferry to teach the new hand," said Babs. "And Lizzie, luv, you can invite all your friends, the ones you know from the other side. All of them! It will be the biggest party and I'm inviting half of Williamstown and we're having it in the church hall that's just off the sacristy."

Lizzie tightened up, squeezing Bobby's big hand. Bobby returned the squeeze. "Sis, I know you mean well," he said softly.

Babs kept talking. "Father Zappia convinced me. I have to do this. Not just for myself but for the two of you. Surely you don't want to slink away, feeling like you can never come back here. We all love you and accept the choices you have made."

"Mum, Father Zappia has done a job on you I can see."

"He has, thank goodness. I would otherwise continue crying myself to sleep for the rest of my life, because that's what I have been doing."

"Gees, sis." Bobby's kind heart rose up, causing his lips to quiver, "if that's how you feel…"

Lizzie pulled her hand away from his. She was angry, though at the same time, she had to admit she had never seen her tough Mum cry. The thought of it disturbed her. "Bobby, please. I don't know," she whispered.

Bobby reached out to her. "We could do with a little more time. It would give me time to sell the Imp. We could buy a few things for the trip. And I haven't really done the right thing down at the ferry. They do need my help with the new hands."

"I'm sorry, dears. But it's for the good of all of us. You don't want people talking behind your backs for the rest of your lives, do you?" Babs responded happily.

"That's why we decided we would never come back here," said Lizzie, cooling down.

"With the Father's blessing, and he will give it, I know he will, it will make things all right."

"Isn't it against the church?"

"Father Zappia says that Jesus' love is more important than silly old church rules."

The loving couple looked at each other. Lizzie didn't want to say yes, Bobby could see. But then she spoke up in a quivering voice.

"All right, but on one condition."

"Oh darling, thank you so much. You won't regret it!" Bab's reached for her hand and squeezed it.

"And what's the condition?" asked Bobby.

"That Father Zappia presides over a ceremony in which we take vows of devotion to each other," said Lizzie, full of mischief.

"At the party?"

"I don't care. But if he's serious, that's what he has to do. Otherwise it's all a farce," said Lizzie.

"I know he will. It will be like you were getting married."

"That's right. Marriage is sacred, isn't that right Bobby?" said Lizzie with a twinkle in her eye.

21. The Confession

Striker did not spend much time in his office. He liked to be out and about. But this time he'd had enough. After the encounter with Stanford Lane and his louts, he decided to confront him. The same went for Shooter Frost. Williamstown was a nest of scheming small time communists who happened to be mostly Irish Catholics, as far as he could see. And Lane had not helped. He was just like them but not one of them, at least not yet. Shooter on the other hand was not a cop at all, he was just another of their crooked players. He was too much a part of the community, he was compromised every which way and that. This latest nonsense about police being part of their communities. If you're too close to them how do you do your police work, tell them what to do, or arrest someone who thinks he's your friend?

He crossed St. Kilda Road and entered the park. It was a big run this morning, so he stepped up the pace and kept it up all the way through the park and into his office, where he found Lockie Frost waiting for him. He had decided to take the leap this morning because he thought he at last had figured out what was going on. So he had contacted Lockie and demanded that he show up at HQ. Lockie had bitterly complained, saying he hated going into Melbourne with all that traffic, why couldn't they meet in Williamstown. But that was just what he did not want. He wanted Lockie nervous, on the defensive.

"You're late," said Lockie, looking up at Striker's taut body, his muscles pressing against every part of his t-shirt and his shorts.

Striker ignored the remark. "Thank you for coming in," Mr. Frost.

"Lockie, you can call me Lockie, they all do."

"Just a moment Mr. Frost while I get my colleague to join us." He poked his head out the door and beckoned to Stanford Lane who was chatting with one of the other officers. "Lane? Come right in."

"Mr. Frost. How long have you owned the Werribee cemetery and its annex?" asked Striker.

"Annex? What annex?"

"The stretch of land down by Hobsons bay."

"How do you know about that? I only just looked at it the other day."

"The city of Werribee keeps public records, Mr. Frost."

"So you know how long I've had the cemetery then, so why are you asking?"

"Don't be a smart-ass," said Lane, standing in the corner of the office.

Striker continued. "We are going for a drive this morning, Mr. Frost. First we will visit the morgue where I will show you three bodies. Then we will go to the cemetery and I will search it for more bodies."

Lockie burst out laughing. "What else do you expect to find there?"

"With you Willy blokes, who knows?" said Striker suspiciously.

"I don't know why you brought me in here. I know nothing about your bodies."

"We'll soon see. And your apprentice. How long has he been with you?"

"You mean young Billy Boyle?"

"Yes."

"Not quite six months. He's a smart young fellow. Picked up the trade as quick as a wink."

"Maybe a little too quickly?"

"What do you mean by that?" asked Lockie, genuinely puzzled

"I'll tell you after I have spoken with him."

"Leave him alone, detective. Are you telling me he's got something to do with your bodies?"

"Anything is possible in Williamstown, wouldn't you agree?"

"No it's not! He's a bright young kid. Are you suggesting he's some kind of serial murderer?"

"Anything is possible," repeated Striker, eyeing Lockie carefully. "Senior Constable Lane, do you have anything to add?"

Lane took this as an invitation to get rough. He stepped over to Lockie and grabbed him by his collar. "What are you bloody mob up to?" he muttered in a deep guttural voice. Striker let him go on. Lane pulled Lockie out of his chair and pushed him against the wall. "Come on! Out with it!"

Lockie, a young tough when he was a teenager, abhorred violence. He had long ago, after his big brother had given him the hiding of his life for nothing more than being a smart-ass, decided that being cunning was a much better way of getting even or getting what one wanted. "You know that I only took over the cemetery a couple of weeks ago. So if you want to know what's going on there, I'd suggest you talk to its prior owner, Harry Nolte. But before you do so, I recommend that you check in with your boss the Commissioner. Just a bit of friendly advice."

Striker and Lane stared at him. Lockie stared back defiantly. He had put them in their place. Striker could think of no other retort than to change the subject. "And your brother, Shooter they call him, what is his part in all this cemetery business? You were seen talking with him at a Werribee pub soon after you took over the cemetery."

"My! You have been busy. Is this a free country or isn't it? What are you doing spying on a couple of brothers having a friendly beer?"

Lane pushed Lockie harder against the wall. "Do you want me to slap him sir? Just to get him talking straight?"

"No. Let him go. I think what we'll do is talk to his apprentice. He'll tell us what we want to know. Mr. Frost, I know what you've been up to. You may as well tell me now."

"If you know, then you tell me," answered Lockie defiantly.

Lane pushed him back down into the chair and raised his fist.

"Let him go," said Striker. "I'll take a shower then we'll all go for a drive, first the morgue and then the cemetery."

"Are you coming to our party on Friday?' asked Lockie mischievously.

"And what party is that?" asked Striker.

"Oh, if you know everything, I thought you would know all about that. In fact consider this an invitation. Better you come and be seen than you have your weasel here snooping around."

"That's the party at the church hall?" asked Lane, a shifty glance at Striker.

"That's right. The whole of Willy will be there. We're celebrating Bobby and Lizzie who are getting married, well not exactly, and then going off on a round Australia trip. And as well, Ryley Malley's appointment as the new secretary of the Trades Hall Council."

"Perhaps senior constable Lane may like to attend?" said Striker staring at him.

"Maybe."

"But why don't you attend, detective Striker," said Lockie, "your boss the Commissioner will be there. He's such good friends with Lizzie as maybe you know? And you know Lizzie too, don't you?" added Lockie with a sneaky smile.

"You know what? This interview is over," said Striker. "Tell your apprentice I'm coming for him. And Lane, contact Nolte and set up an appointment. "You can go, Mr. Frost." Striker gathered his things and made for the shower.

"You're not taking me to the morgue?" called Lockie after him.

"You better get out of here or I'll knock your block off," warned Lane. "Go on! Get!"

*

"What have you been up to?" asked Lockie.

"What?" answered Billy, defensively.

"I just was interviewed by those bastards Striker and Lane. They made me go all the way to their headquarters in Melbourne."

"What for?" Billy tried to look as innocent as he could.

"Answer me!"

"Leave the kid alone," said Harry Nolte as Billy trimmed his eye brows.

"You know what this is all about, Harry?" asked Lockie. "Striker said he was coming for you too."

"It's nothing. It's just a little arrangement I had with your young apprentice here, a wonderful young barber I'm sure you would agree."

"What arrangement?"

Billy put down his scissors and comb. "You remember the first day I tried out with a razor on the balloon that you covered with shaving cream?"

"And it burst and we all had a great laugh. You just couldn't get the knack of it," said Lockie.

"And I was here too," said Harry.

"And I was almost crying with embarrassment, I don't know how many balloons I burst," said Billy, a little redness in his adolescent cheeks.

"So I took him under my wing," said Harry.

"You're no barber, Harry. What are you getting at?"

"You tell him Billy."

"No, you! He's going to fire me anyway," cried Billy.

Harry nodded and sat forward. "Well, owning a funeral home and cemetery, as you will quickly learn Lockie, you naturally find yourself having to deal with dead bodies."

"I've already found that out, Harry, believe me," said Lockie.

"Anyway, it was sort of part of a deal I had with Father Zappia," said Harry, an amused look on his face.

"What do you mean?"

"He, well, he likes…"

"…to look at dead bodies," finished Billy. "He's a weirdo."

"We've known that for a long time," came the familiar voice of Shooter, sitting in a corner his head buried in the Sun. "I'd have thought Lockie would have warned you, Billy, to stay away from him."

"I would have if I'd known," answered Lockie," but I didn't! So fill me in, Harry. What was going on?"

"Well, I'd just come away from the shop here after Billy had burst another balloon and I was on my way to pick up a body from the church after a funeral"

"And?"

"Father Zappia always kept the body in the sacristy. A spooky place, I can tell you," said Harry, grimacing.

"And?"

"This day I went into the sacristy and there he was with a body, kissing its feet."

"So he pulled it out of the coffin?" asked Lockie.

"The lid was open and he pulled up the feet so they were hanging over the side of the coffin."

"Wasn't he embarrassed or anything?"

"Not really. He just looked up and said with a kind of sheepish smile that he was just blessing the body, giving it the last rites, and he pulled out a little vial of holy water that he always carried with him, and sprinkled some over the feet."

"That's all?"

"He mumbled something about how important feet were to Jesus. You know, that woman who washed his feet, don't remember who."

"It was Mary," said Billy as he reverently crossed himself.

"How do you know that?" asked Lockie, stunned.

"I've been taking my catechism with Father Zappia. He tells that story over and over. But finish the story, Mr. Nolte."

"Well, I looked and I thought that here was a good body going to waste. Why not have Billy practice his shaving on the bodies just before they were buried? I mean, there was no real harm in it was there?"

"So he came and got me from the barbershop and had me bring my shaving gear," said Billy as he waved his arm with a flourish, ready to apply the razor to Nolte's cheek.

"And that's how it started. At first, I had Billy try shaving the face, but he had a hard time with that."

"Yeh. I couldn't get at the face properly because it was deep down in the coffin. And the skin on the cheeks and under the chin was especially hard to get at, too many furrows to shave over. So we pulled the body up as best we could, which was pretty hard because it was all stiff, you know, so Father Zappia had to hold the coffin with his foot against the wheel of the trolley, while Mr. Nolte and me pulled the body up so the shoulders rested on the edge."

"Then Billy lathered up the face and got to work."

"It was much easier than shaving a balloon, and much better because if I made a mistake and cut the bloke, I could just keep going until I got it right."

"I could see it was working," added Harry, " so when he was done with the face and neck I said, why not shave the hair off as well?"

Billy continued. "Turned out that was about as hard or harder than doing a balloon, because the skin on the scalp was really hard and there was no give at all. Lucky the body was dead, or there'd have been blood everywhere!"

"And what was Father Zappia doing all this time?" asked Shooter.

"He was fussing around with his jars and relics, and every now and then he'd come over and kiss the feet of the body and mutter some kind of prayer," answered Harry.

"You going to tell Striker?" asked Billy, turning to Shooter. "I mean I wasn't doing anything wrong, was I?"

"I don't think Shooter will turn you in, will you Shooter?" asked Lockie menacingly.

"I don't think there's a law against being weird. But once that bastard Lane gets wind of this, he'll make trouble."

"Only if someone here tells him," said Harry, with not a little menace.

"Oh, no. He will find out. Striker already suspects something and said he and Lane were coming here to interview Billy," said Lockie. He looked across to Shooter thinking to himself, there were only two bullies at Christian brothers High school, his own brother Shooter and Stanford Lane. Both of them Irish, but Lane kowtowing to the protestants.

"Gees, Mr. Frost. We only did three bodies and by then I was an expert."

"With that, we all agree!" said Harry. "Don't worry, Billy, Lockie and me, we have contacts, there might be a bit of trouble from Striker and Lane, but it won't go very far, will it Lockie?"

"We'll fix it all up at the party on Friday," said Lockie.

"How come?" asked Shooter.

"I invited both of them to our big party on Friday night."

"That was a bit risky, wasn't it?" asked Harry.

"Maybe. But the Commissioner will be there, I'm sure. It will be enough to send them both a message."

"You mean the Commissioner of police?" asked Billy, incredulous.

"Stick with us, young man, and you'll go a long way!" said Harry, just as Billy lathered up the razor and began to shave the back of his neck, displaying an elegant wrist motion and supple fingers grasping the razor, a style that Lockie admired greatly.

"You're going to go a long way," said Lockie smiling with admiration.

22. St. Robert's Toe

Things got a little hot in the kitchen. Sandy announced that there was no room for him there and went off to the pub. Lizzie looked up at the old clock above the refrigerator. Bobby had gone down to the wharf with Sandy to meet one of Sandy's boys who was interested in buying the Imp. Babs had nagged Sandy to buy it, but he wasn't interested. They had no need of a car, he said. Willy was just right for them wasn't it? Why would they want to leave it? Babs pointed out how much easier it would have been for them if they had been able to drive to the Werribee cemetery on their own rather than having to wait around for Lockie or Bobby to drive them. And so on, and on. Babs had insisted on doing all the cooking for the party, dozens and dozens of party pies, sausage rolls and huge bowls of fruit salad. But when she sat down and counted up all the people she had asked, and then thought of all the people who had come up to her down the street saying they were looking forward to it, she realized that there was no way she could make enough, even with her new oven. And Lizzie wasn't much help. She had never learned to cook, wouldn't listen to her Mum. She tried to help, but Babs turned into Major Mum, barking orders, so Lizzie in the end retired to the Winnebago that was parked outside in the street. She wanted to tidy it up anyway, make sure there were no embarrassing items lying around. She went down to Douglas Parade and bought all new sheets and pillow slips for the bed, all new cutlery and crockery, and even some saucepans and a kettle. And Bobby had spent a lot of time going over it, making sure the engine was in tip-top condition, the little refrigerator working well, and the stove too. Lizzie was so fed up with her mother, though, that she wanted to retire to the Winnebago and not come out. She did run out on a couple of occasions, but came back again because she had this silly feeling that when

Bobby and she went off after the party, she wanted it to be spick and span, like a new Winnebago.

Neither Bobby nor Lizzie had wanted this party. They were all set to drive off a week ago, run away, elope, call it what you like. But in the end, they felt sorry for Babs, believe it or not. They didn't want to leave under a cloud, feeling guilty about her. She had been very good to them and was trying really hard to do the right thing. The party was a kind of salvation for her. And Babs and Sandy were right, it was better to have everything out in the open, instead of having to put up with people whispering behind their backs every time they saw someone down the street.

At last, as she stepped out of the Winnebago, Lockie rolled up in the hearse, all nicely polished, Mandrake at the wheel. And behind the hearse came Bobby and Ryley in the Imp.

"Just in time!" called Babs from the front door, holding an armful of pies.

"G'day, Mum, said Ryley with a big grin. "I'll take them."

"Thanks darl. Have you got the drinks?"

"We've got everything in the back. And I've got plenty of Red Army choir LPs," he said.

"You can't dance to that!" complained Lizzie, joining the group.

"Dance?" said Ryley, "who said anything about dancing? This is a booze-up isn't it?"

"There won't be room. It's not that big a hall and there's going to be a hundred or more people," said Babs.

"Then they'll just have to make room," said Lizzie. "Bobby and me are going to dance, aren't we Bobby?"

"I'll try," Bobby said, looking away.

Lizzie went to him, giving him a big hug. "I know you will," she said, kissing him sweetly on his lips. But then she noticed the Imp. "I thought you went down to the wharf to sell it?" she asked, with a frown.

"I couldn't bring myself to do it," Bobby answered sheepishly.

Lizzie stood, Major Mum-like, with her hands on her hips, about to hold forth.

Babs quickly spoke up. "I've hired a singer anyway," she said coyly.

"You have?" exclaimed pretty much everyone in unison.

"Who? What?" asked Ryley.

"I'm not telling you. It's a surprise," said Babs, savouring the moment.

"Oh, come on Babs, let it out, said Lockie."

"Nope! It's my big surprise and my going away present for Bobby and Lizzie." Babs turned to Mandrake. "Can you drop in at Freddy's Pastry shop and pick up my order and drop it off at the hall? I'll be down there as soon as I tidy up here."

"OK. But I have to pick up what's-his-name?"

"Lennie," said Ryley, "Lennie Stalinsky, and I'll come with you."

*

Babs finally got Sandy to stand at the door of the church hall to greet everyone as they came in. He had resisted right up until the last moment, saying that it was a lot of silly nonsense. Bobby had been the same, and Lizzie too, but in the end they gave in. Ryley, though, held fast. The party wasn't really for him, he insisted. It was Bobby and Lizzie's night.

Father Zappia, resplendent in his robes, a whiskey in his spare hand, was up front, shaking hands with each and every guest. Bobby and Lizzie had insisted on no gifts, but people came with them anyway. Sandy had suggested that instead of gifts, guests could give a donation to the wharfies' benefit fund, but nobody took any notice of that. Lizzie, resplendent in a long gown that seemed to cling to every part of her body like plastic wrap, stood there with Bobby, a pile of gifts beside her on a table.

Inside, Sandy's boys were hard at it. Banger had set up a keg and a large number of wharfies stood around it, in serious discussion about the best way to pour the beer. They insisted on filling their glasses directly from the beer tap, no beer from jugs for them. Banger agreed, but pointed out that there were lots of guests and you couldn't make them stand in a line, could you?

"This is my mate Tony from the uni," said Ryley as Tony shook hands with everyone standing around the keg.

"Tony, huh?" said Banger. "Italian, right?"

"Yair, that's right. Me Dad and Mum came out in 1947."

"Youse lost the war and then you won it," joked Banger.

"We Italians, we like to be on the winning side," joked Tony.

"Fair enough. There's lots of you down on the wharf. Your Dad on the wharf? I might know him."

"No, he's up at Mildura. Works on a farm that grows lemons and grapes. He's always where the vino is."

"Fair enough, mates, right?" said Banger, "we wharfies, though, we like our beer. Not like your mate here Ryley. He goes for the red. I s'pose that's why you two are mates."

"That's right," said Ryley quickly, "the red is over there behind the keg."

Tony followed him and out of the slowly building crowd Lennie emerged to follow him.

"Tony. This is Lennie, Australia's leading commo, and a good mate," said Ryley, full of joy.

"G'day Lennie."

Lennie did his best to give Tony a strong hand shake. "Very pleased to meet you, mate. Ryley's told me all about you."

Tony looked to Ryley. "Really?"

"Here, get this into you," said Ryley, handing Tony a large plastic cup filled to the brim with red wine.

*

With some trepidation, Lizzie looked forward to meeting her clients somewhere other than in the Winnebago. She still doubted that any of them would show up. They all said they would when she asked them after each of their performances, but that was then. After they cooled off, surely they would not risk stoking the fires of the local chatter of Williamstown. She was surprised at how they reacted to her news that she was retiring from her business to lead a normal life—that was how she put it. They all seemed relieved, not terribly disappointed as she expected.

"Good evening, Commissioner," Lizzie smiled and offered her hand to him, her tall, imposing, triangular figure sparkled beneath the light chenille gown. Her lips, no longer exaggerated with full, bright red, but a darker tone of red, almost mauve, blended into her well powdered face, cheeks touched ever so lightly with rouge. The Commissioner took her hand lightly in his and lifted it to his mouth to place a heavy noisy kiss on her long fingers. "It is such a pleasure!" he pronounced. "Such a great and historic occasion!"

Lizzie withdrew her hand from his and only then realized that his wife, a much older woman, older than the Commissioner, looking as though she could be his mother, stood beside him, awaiting introduction.

"And may I introduce my wife, Solace."

"Good evening Mrs. Trinity."

"I am so pleased to meet you, Elizabeth. Gordon has told me so much about you. I just love Williamstown."

Lizzie was about to respond when Babs chimed in.

"Thanks for coming Commissioner. I love uniforms and yours is the best I've seen!"

"This is my Mum," said Lizzie, shyly. "And this is for you," she said to the Commissioner, handing him a small box tied with a ribbon. "It's not to be opened now, but when you get home," she said with a small wink.

And so it went. The mayor came, alone, with great fanfare, dressed formally in tails, bow-tie, the works. Buck arrived, gorgeous young beauty in tow, taller even than Lizzie, dressed in skin tight black nylon stretch tights, a top made of the same fabric, a blazing red silk scarf tied carelessly around her neck. Lizzie handed him his present, in a tiny box tied with a satin red bow. He took it and knew immediately what it was. They didn't need to shake hands or do anything else. They knew each other inside and out.

Father Zappia was full on. He had already spilled a little red wine down his white vestry gown, but no one would tell him so. He stood at the doorway holding a cup of red, then suddenly turned to Lizzie.

"Where's my gift?" he asked mischievously.

Lizzie had debated whether to give him the whip or the bible. She decided on both. "Here," she said, "you are not forgotten, Father, you will never be forgotten," a wry smile on her face.

"Oh! Thank you. Shall I open it now?"

"That's up to you." Of all her clients, Lizzie was most surprised at how relieved Father Zappia was when she told him that she was retiring. It was as if a huge burden had been lifted, a cloud soaring into the heavens.

Babs, always attracted to Father Zappia, leaned across Lizzie and said, "go on Father, open it!"

Father Zappia took a slurp of his wine to empty it and dropped the plastic cup on the floor. He grabbed the present and tore it open and out fell the heavily used bible, some of its pages falling out as it fell, and the two stranded whip, which on closer inspection, showed the stains of dried blood.

"Father! Lizzie! What on earth is that?" cried Babs, putting her hands to her mouth.

"It's nothing Mum. It's just a private joke that Father and me have between us, isn't that right Father?"

Father Zappia didn't quite comprehend the moment. Babs had been around after all. She knew very well what this present stood for and was shocked. Not surprised, but shocked because it confirmed what she had long suspected Lizzie did for a living. She turned, looking for Sandy for consolation, but Sandy had long gone from the reception line to join the blokes around the keg.

The judge and Q.C arrived together, rather late, and quietly stood aside, supplied amply with beer by Banger who at the behest of Lizzie was looking after them. After the spectacle of Father Zappia, she had decided not to continue with her present-giving, or at least to put it off until a more private opportunity arose. She noticed though, that the only client who had not shown up was Harry Nolte.

The hearse rolled up and out stepped Lockie. "It's about time you showed up!" called Babs, "you're late for the reception line."

But Lockie went straight to Lizzie and gave her a ten dollar bill. "Harry Nolte sent this," he said with a mischievous grin.

Lizzie's face reddened. "Get stuffed!" she said, and Bobby raised his fist as if to punch him.

"Where's Father Zappia?" Lockie asked looking into the hall. "Oh, there he is. I have to speak with him. He's on the edge, I know it."

Puzzled, Bobby and Lizzie looked at each other and at Lockie who quickly ran inside.

Father Zappia caroused around the hall, always a drink in his hand, placing his other arm around anyone who was slow enough to remain in his grasp. The small hall was now full of people so it was hard to avoid him. His Italian accent was getting much stronger, as though he had only just got off the boat.

Bobby, himself a bit tipsy, limped up to his sister. "I thought you said you hired a singer?" he asked. "It's time we had some music."

"I'll take care of it," called out Ryley above the din as he fiddled with the PA system. And then there was an ear-splitting blast of the Red Choir.

"Oh No! Turn it off! Turn it off!" cried Father Zappia. "It's blasphemy! I will not have it played in my parish. Don't think I don't know what it is. We'll have nothing of those atheists here!"

Babs called out to Ryley. "Switch it off, darl. Our singer will be here any minute."

*

Babs stood alone at the door to receive the stream of people, many of whom she had never met. The others had gone off to chat with friends, the men especially to congregate around the keg. Father Zappia floated around the hall, moving from group to group. Laying on his blessings, kissing his fingers and touching them to random guests. Babs watched him disappear into the sacristy and worried that he should not be left alone in there in his drunken state. But she was eager to receive the singer she had hired, nervous about his reception. And at last, just as Ryley was about to have another go at playing his latest Red Army Choir record, a taxi drew up and out stepped the singer, guitar in tow. They had met once in Coles restaurant where Babs bought him a chocolate milk shake and gave him half his money in advance, a fact that she did not dare mention to Sandy. She was a little startled when he stepped out of the taxi, a squat, rotund man, a light gingery beard and beady eyes that squinted out over rimless glasses. The guitar, she could see, would rest easily on his belly when he stood to sing.

"Burl Ives at your service ma'am!" he announced jovially.

"You sound just like him!" said Babs, very pleased.

"I should, I am him!" Ives answered with a practiced smile.

"Come in and I'll introduce you to the mob. They've all had a few, I'm afraid. Hope they will quiet down for you."

"Ah, that won't be necessary. They can sing along with me. It's my forte!"

"All right you lot!" yelled Babs in her Major Mum voice. "Listen up!" Babs turned to him and asked, "are you going to stand, or will you need a chair?"

"Is there a stage?"

"Well. A bit of a one next to where they've got the keg."

"Then I'll go over there and sit on a chair to start with. Later, I'll join the crowd and walk through them as we sing along together." Babs took his leather coat and he proceeded to tune his guitar.

"Listen up! Welcome everyone!" called Babs. "Sandy and me are very happy you've all come to our little party to send off our happy couple Bobby and Lizzie!" Sandy tried to hide behind the keg while everyone cheered and clapped. Lizzie grasped Bobby's hand and they smiled the best they could. They had both dreaded this moment. All they wanted to do was get in the Winnebago and get the hell out of Williamstown. "And now I want you to meet our singer who has come all the way from America to sing for us tonight, Burl Ives!"

Some clapped, but many did not. The hall became strangely silent. Ryley almost dropped his glass of red. Undaunted, the singer impersonator set off across the hall on his way to the stage, strumming his guitar, and singing his first song. It was, of course, Waltzing Matilda.

"What's a bloody yank doing singing our bloody song?" muttered Banger, already slurring his words.

"It can't be bloody Burl Ives," said Ryley, "it couldn't be. But if it is, I'm going to strangle that bloody mother of mine!"

"Gees, Ryley, it isn't that bad. I mean, I don't really care if he sings Waltzing Matilda," said Banger, sobering up.

"What he's saying is," interceded Lennie, "the bastard is a scab, a scab of the worst kind!"

"Gees, Lennie, I never heard you talk like that. What's the bloke done?"

Ives was now circling back through the crowd. He had decided that the stage was not for him, too close to the keg anyway. "He sang as he watched and waited 'til his billy boiled," then swinging his guitar above his round head, his beady eyes squinting out over his scraggly beard and red cheeks, "You'll come a-Waltzing Matilda, with me."

"Like bloody hell I will!" called out Ryley, "Scab! Coward! Asshole!" He turned up the PA system and dropped the needle on the Red Army Choir. Two hundred voices, all in unison, blasted out, must have been heard as far away as Gem Pier. People covered their ears, Babs put her hand to her mouth. What had she done? It was all she could do now to stop herself from throwing up. And she would have, except that Sandy suddenly appeared beside her, his face slightly amused, but his heavy presence a consolation. "Darl! What have I done? He's just a singer impersonator!"

"I know luv. Trouble is it's Burl Ives. He ratted on his commie mates in America, and they all got put on the black list."

"But it's not really him!"

"I know, I know. It's bad luck." He signalled to Banger and pointed to Ryley. But Ryley was having none of it. He tossed down a cup of wine and started towards Ives who was reaching the climax of his song, seemingly impervious to the crowd's angst, the screaming of the Red Army Choir.

But Ives would not let up. "You'll never catch me alive, said he…"

Banger was now trying to keep his mates under control. The poor singer was in for a beating. Banger grabbed at Ryley's arm and tried to pull the needle off the record. Ryley's mate Tony grabbed Banger and pushed him away. The Commissioner stood erect, to the extent that he was able, in his splendid uniform and strutted into the centre of the hall, his wife on his arm. "Order please! Order!" he called, with little result. In fact, his wife tugged at his arm, looking towards the door. A retreat was in order.

But at that very moment, at the point of the choir's crescendo, as Ives sang, "And his ghost may be heard as you pass by the billabong…" the door of the sacristy burst open and out charged Father Zappia, carrying a small fold-up table, and several other items hidden under a white cotton cloth edged with cream satin ribbon. He charged straight for the centre of the hall, right where the Commissioner and his wife were standing, and set up the table, covered it with the white cloth and arranged the items, a highly polished brass cross, a bible, and a small square object of some kind that was covered by an embroidered cloth. Impervious to the impending chaos, he announced in his most sermon-like voice:

"Ladies and-a gentlemen! We are gathered here today," he crooned, "to celebrate the joining together of Lizzie and Bobby in holy matrimony."

A hush suddenly came over the crowd. Ryley switched off the Red Army Choir. "Did he say what I think he said?" muttered Ryley to his mate.

"You'll come a-Waltzing Matilda, with me," sang Ives, his voice trailing off.

"Lizzie and Bobby, please come forward!" called Father Zappia.

Unable to think under the circumstances, they came forward, holding hands, Bobby trying not to show his limp.

Father Zappia produced a little bottle of holy water, a bottle with which Lizzie was well acquainted, and sprinkled it over their hands clasped together, as they now faced each other. He then put his hand on theirs and asked:

"Lizzie and Bobby, do you each promise to love each other in sickness and in health, until death do you part?"

"We do," they whispered, bamboozled, unsure whether this was real or not.

"In the name of-a God the Father, the Son and-a the Holy Ghost, the spirit of-a Saint Robert, and the authority invested in-a me by his holiness Pope Paul, I now pronounce you man and wife."

Sandy put his arm around Babs, and said, "you didn't set this up, did you?"

"No, I promise you, darl. I had no idea. I think Father must be drunk."

"And what was that about Saint Robert? Who's he? I never heard of him."

"It's a kind of private joke between the Father and me."

"I won't ask what."

"That's good, because I'm not telling you anyway."

And as if on cue, Father Zappia, with a great flourish, whipped away the embroidered cloth to reveal the glass case that held the toe of Saint Robert. Babs put her hands to her mouth to cover a gasp. "We are in the presence of a Saint, my people," crowed Father Zappia. "Hold out your hands, Saint Robert." He pulled Bobby's hands, limp with confusion, away from Lizzie and placed the relic box in them. "I return unto you what is rightfully yours," he said. "May you live forever, Saint Robert!"

Babs fainted, falling to the floor with a flop. Bobby and Lizzie stood frozen to the spot. Bobby looked into the box and saw a pink toe, its end still bloody where it had been cut off. Lizzie, no longer confused, was now enraged. "We're getting out of here, now!" she growled. She grabbed the box and banged it down on the table, then pulled Bobby behind her as she made for the door. And they would have left, but they could not.

Striker was in the way.

*

After his morning run Striker, instead of donning his usual civvies, put on his police uniform. He planned a grand entrance and that is what it was. They pulled up to the church hall, Nolte, handcuffed in the back of the police wagon, screaming obscenities, threatening dire consequences from the Commissioner. Lane pulled Nolte out of the wagon and told him to shut up.

"You'll never get away with this!" threatened Nolte. "You've got nothing on me!"

"If you'd confess, we wouldn't have to go through all this," said Striker in his most officious voice.

"They're all my mates in there. Wait till I tell the Commissioner about this."

"You can do that right now. I'm sure he's in there as well, your mate the Commissioner," said Striker with too much sarcasm.

"You could at least take off these stupid handcuffs," complained Nolte.

"You're under arrest. It's the rules," said Striker.

"You haven't even told me what I'm supposed to have done, bastard."

"We know what you've been up to with Father Zappia," said Lane, pulling him by the arm.

"What? Him? You're idiots both of you."

Lane prodded Nolte forward. But then Striker hurried ahead. A huge din had suddenly erupted from inside the Hall, screaming, the sound of a record player turned up to ear-splitting levels, shouts and bangs, the typical sounds of a pub brawl. Striker booted the double doors of the hall open and rushed in, Lane following close behind, pushing Nolte before him. Striker saw Father Zappia snatch up the glass box and hold it to his breast. "Give me that!" he yelled, as Lane blew his police whistle, not exactly a police whistle, more like one that footy umpires use.

"Get them, boys! Get them!" yelled Banger.

Striker stopped dead in his tracks. Lane kept going. He had expected this and brought his favourite truncheon with him. He waved it around while he held Nolte by the scruff of his neck.

"Come on, scum! Come and get it!"

They were vastly outnumbered and were no match for the brawn of the wharfies. They would get the beating of their lives.

"Uncuff me!" cried Nolte.

Babs, still prostrate on the floor, tried to sit up and Sandy put out his hand to help her. But she no sooner came to and saw the pandemonium than she fainted again, flopped into Sandy's arms.

"Come on, mates!" yelled Ryley. "Let's teach these bourgeois lackeys a lesson!" He grabbed a wine bottle and lunged forward, smashing it against the keg, leaving the broken end in his hand, a lethal weapon. Tony stood back, aghast. "Ryley, don't!" he pleaded. "Please don't!"

Banger, ever the bouncer, rushed over and grabbed Ryley's arm just in time. "No, mate, we can't cut coppers, even though we'd like to. Give me the bottle."

Ryley gave way. He wasn't sure that he would really have gone ahead and done it anyway. But this incident, almost a disaster, gave notice to all. The hall went quiet, just for a second or two. Burl Ives thoughtfully strummed a chord or two on his guitar. A signal to all the inebriated that normality had returned. He even began a refrain, one of his signature pieces.

"Jim crack corn I don't care,

Jim crack corn I don't care,

Jim crack corn I don't care..."

The hall fell silent. Ryley was even more incensed, now he had to put up with a yank song. "Sing something Australian," he grumbled, "none of that bourgeois American shit!"

Striker held on to Lane, who was eager to make another arrest. Nolte flopped down on the floor and sulked. The Ives impersonator stopped and turned to face Ryley.. He knew his stuff. "Young man," he said, "it's a Negro song, the slaves sang it. Hardly bourgeois."

Striker walked softly over to Father Zappia who stood frozen to the spot, clutching his relic to his breast. He made the sign of the cross as Striker approached him.

"I'll take that," said Striker softly, reaching for the relic box.

"As a matter of fact, it's not the Father's. It's mine," said Bobby as he limped forward, still holding Lizzie's hand, pulling her along with him. "He gave it to me. After all, it's my toe."

Striker tried to pull the box from Zappia who would not let go. Another brawl was in the offing.

"It's my toe and you have no right to take it," insisted Bobby.

"It is evidence in my inquiry," retorted Striker.

"What inquiry?" asked Bobby, his fists already clenched.

"The serial murders, the bodies that have been washed up, a couple of them by your ferry."

"How could my toe have anything to do with that?"

"How could it be your toe?" countered Striker.

"I limp, don't I? You want to see where it was cut off?"

Bobby started to remove his shoe.

"Then how did your toe get into that box?" asked Striker, nonplussed.

"My mother cut it off when I was six years old and gave it to Father Zappia."

"I don't believe all this nonsense. Let me see the toe." Striker tried to move Father Zappia's hands away from the box so he could see inside. "Let me see," he insisted.

"Go on Father. Let him see," said Bobby. Lizzie started to giggle and Bobby squeezed her hand tightly.

Father Zappia swayed a little. He was still very drunk. He licked his quivering lips, tried to talk, but words would not come. He timidly moved one of his hands away, and made the sign of the cross as he did so. Striker peered into the box.

"It's a freshly cut toe!" exclaimed Striker.

"It is not!" cried Father Zappia. "It's a miracle, don't you see? It's a miracle! O-a Jesus! Thank you O Lord!" And he dropped down on his knees, pulling the relic with him. Striker let him go. Arresting a priest while he was praying to Jesus wasn't a good scene.

Lane let go of Nolte and jostled forward. "Let me take care of this silly bastard. These Catholics. They're half crazy" he said, much too loudly, foolishly ignoring the fact that most if not all the people in the hall were Catholics, not to mention himself.

Striker grabbed Lane. "Take Nolte out to the wagon. He's served his purpose."

Lane tapped his truncheon against his leg. Striker looked him in the eye and Lane thought better of it. He turned and tried to pull Nolte up, but Nolte would not comply. "He won't budge," said Lane, "you want me to drag him out?"

Things had not turned out the way Striker had planned. He had lost control of the situation. Now it seemed as though his venture into the party made little sense. Yet he was sure that the whole business of the bodies involved Zappia and Nolte. And the strong piece of evidence was now before him in the freshly cut toe.

"You cut that toe off a body, didn't you Father Zappia?" charged Striker.

"How dare you! It would be a grave sin to defile a body."

"Then where did you get the toe?" insisted Striker.

"I told you. It's a miracle!" Father Zappia remained on his knees, and once again made the sign of the cross.

"Father, I have to take you and the toe down to headquarters for questioning," announced Striker, unaware of how silly it all sounded.

"You're arresting me?"

"No, I'm asking you nicely to accompany me. And you can keep the toe with you for now."

"It isn't his toe, copper. It's mine," said Bobby belligerently.

"Then you'll have to do without it for now. After all, you've done OK without it since you were six years old, so another few days won't hurt, will it?"

Bobby reached down to Father Zappia and grasped the box. Father Zappia, on the brink of collapse, let it go.

"I'll take care of it, Father. Don't you worry," Bobby said softly.

"I'll take that, now, if you don't mind," said Striker, sensing an opportunity.

"I don't think so,' said Bobby.

Lizzie squeezed his hand, pulling him towards her. "What are you doing?" she whispered. "You don't really want it do you?"

"I don't know. I just don't want the cops to have it." He looked around the hall. "I wish Shooter were here. Come to think of it, why isn't he?"

Striker made a move towards him. Bobby pulled the box away. "Let's go," he said to Lizzie. "We're out of here."

"If you leave with that toe, I will arrest you for obstructing a police officer in the line of duty."

"You and who else?" asked Bobby defiantly.

"Give him the bloody toe and let's get out of here," growled Lizzie.

Once again, a tense moment. The wharfies had been slowly nudging forward. Striker looked around the hall. There was no way they would make it out without getting beaten up, and it would be one hell of a beating. He looked for the Commissioner who he had thought would be here, but he was nowhere to be seen. He saw the Mayor trying to be inconspicuous in a corner, and a few other celebrities he thought he recognized. But now he saw that Lane was the problem. He was red-faced, clenching his truncheon for all it was worth. He would use it and once he started all hell would break loose. An impatient, hot-headed fool, that's what he was.

"We're going," said Bobby. He turned to face the crowd and waved to them all. "Thank you so much for this wonderful memorable send-off," he said in a steady voice. "We love you all!" Lizzie blew them a kiss and they made for the door, Bobby still clutching his toe.

"You're not going anywhere!" cried Lane who let go of Nolte and swung his truncheon at Bobby. It glanced off the side of Bobby's head and on to Lizzie's shoulder. She gave a little scream, and that was it. Bobby swung the relic box hard at Lane and connected it right on his temple. The glass relic box incredibly did not break. Lane dropped to the floor unconscious. That left Striker, alone. He quickly picked up Lane's truncheon.

There was a stand-off. Bobby was much bigger than Striker, but Striker could no doubt move more quickly. But he was outnumbered by the many wharfies who were approaching him, grinning to each other. There might even be a fight over who would get to throw the first punch. They sensed a bloodbath. Striker edged his way to the door. Bobby was prepared to let him go. He did not want his send-off to be a bloodbath.

"Good riddance copper!" came a gruff voice. It was Babs, she had just come out of her faint.

Her cry was taken as a signal. The wharfies rushed forward bent on beating Striker to a pulp. He ran for the door and Bobby after him. But just as he made it to the door, it opened, and in walked Shooter.

23. Monie Resurrected

"Would someone get us a beer?" asked Shooter, Eurie standing beside him, water running down his face and dropping on the floor. Shooter too was drenched. The rains had returned. He had thought it would be a nice gesture for Bobby if he went down to the ferry and brought Eurie back to the party. But when he got there, Eurie was alone, struggling with a boat hook, fishing around in the water. The rain was pelting down, there were no cars in the car park, none on the ferry.

"There's another body. Eurie was fishing it out when I got there to bring him to the party," announced Shooter.

"Who is it?" asked Striker.

"How would I know? We haven't pulled it out. The rain was too heavy and the water too rough. We didn't want to risk falling in."

"The tides have been really high," said Eurie, "floods everywhere. Is someone going to get me a beer?"

"What happened to him?" asked Shooter, amused, pointing to Lane who lay groaning on the floor."

"God struck him down," said Bobby with a smile.

Lizzie came up to him and hung on his arm. "Can't we go?" she asked.

"Is the Commissioner here?" asked Shooter.

"He was, but I saw him and his missus slip out the back door quite a while ago," said Babs who now stood between Shooter and Striker.

"And the body? Where is it?" asked Striker trying to reassert his authority.

"It's still in the water," said Eurie. "I managed to tie it to the ferry."

Father Zappia, who had been sitting on his haunches fast asleep, suddenly awoke and began to crawl towards Lane's prostrate body to retrieve the relic box.

Striker leaned down. "I'll take that," said Striker. Father Zappia came to his knees, his arms reaching up to Striker, pleading. "You can't take it! It belongs to the church and the Holy Father," he pleaded.

"It's actually mine, as you said, Father. I'll take it," said Bobby, Lizzie trying to pull him back. He grabbed the relic box with both hands as did Striker.

Stalemate.

"What the bloody hell is it?" asked Shooter. "What are you two fighting over?"

"It's my toe," said Bobby.

"What?"

"My toe. The one Mum cut off, or maybe it was big sister here that did it?"

"Shut up Bobby, you know that's not true," said Babs.

"I don't neither!" He tugged at the box as did Striker.

"It's evidence," insisted Striker. "Give it up!"

"Maybe the body in the water is more urgent?" asked Shooter.

Striker let go the box in exasperation. Banger handed Eurie a beer. Lane sat up, still groaning and Lennie gave him a handkerchief to wipe off the blood that was trickling down his forehead. Bobby helped Father Zappia to his feet and gave him the box. "Look after it for me," he said, patting him on the back. People began to murmur; things were returning to normal. The singer pretended to tune his guitar. Ryley walked over to him and whispered into his ear, "if you sing another song I'll take that guitar and smash it over your head."

Shooter took Striker aside. "I'll get Lennie and we'll go back to the ferry," he said.

"Officer Frost, I don't quite follow."

"I think I know whose body it is," said Shooter.

"Then why didn't you tell me?"

"Because I didn't want to spoil the party, and because Lennie is a friend of the family."

"Are you saying…?"

"Yes. I didn't see it really close up, and I may be wrong, but I think it was his wife Monie."

"But I was at her funeral. I saw her coffin taken away."

"I know. And that's why I didn't want to say it out loud to everyone. I could be wrong. But then, she's got such an ugly face, I'd really know it anywhere."

Unfortunately, Lane was now fully conscious and overheard them. He struggled to his feet and called out, "you bastards! It's that commo's wife, it's her body!"

All eyes turned to Lennie who stood rooted to the spot. The thing is, he was so used to Monie getting herself into all kinds of crazy situations he was not all that shocked, at least not as shocked as those now staring at him expected. "Wouldn't you know it?" he said with a wry smile.

Striker stood tall. He now understood everything. He turned to Shooter. "Take me to the ferry," he ordered.

"You'll have to wait, sir. I'm drenched and I'm going home to shower and put on some dry clothes. Eurie probably wants to do the same."

"After I've had a few more beers," joked Eurie.

"Let's all go!" called Bobby. "I can say my last good-bye to the old ferry!"

"The party's over!" cried Babs, tears running down her face.

Bobby, Banger, Sandy, Lennie, Ryley pulling a reticent Lennie along all headed for the door, pushing past Striker. "Do not touch the body!" he cried, "I warn you all, it's a crime scene, you can be arrested if you interfere with it."

"Lockie! Where's Lockie?" called out Nolte running to and fro, his hands still in handcuffs. "Get me out of these!"

Striker looked at Nolte and smiled. "Let him go," he said to Lane who was now upright and almost able to walk.

Lockie sidled up and took the keys from an unusually compliant constable Lane. He undid the cuffs, handed them back to Lane and grabbed Harry. "This way, Harry, we've got a few things to do and talk over, don't you think?" He pulled him to the back door. "The hearse is out behind the church," he said. "We're going for a drive."

Now the hall was almost empty save for Lizzie, who also was on the verge of tears, a rare occurrence for her, Babs sobbing into her handkerchief, and Ryley's friend Tony standing awkwardly beside her offering her another handkerchief. The Q.C, the Mayor and the judge had long ago slipped out the back door following the example of the Commissioner.

"These men," snivelled Babs, "they're like children and that's how we should treat them."

*

Lockie drove as far as Williamstown Beach, then pulled up, overlooking the bay. The wind blew and the rain pelted into the windscreen of the old hearse. A spooky night by anyone's account.

"And what are we going to talk about?" asked Harry in an uncharacteristically sober voice. "I've had a pretty hard day of it with those two coppers," he whined, "putting me in handcuffs, I tell you. They only did it to scare me. They've got nothing on us."

"What do you mean 'us' Harry?"

"The cemetery shenanigans. Fooling around with the bodies. You know what I'm talking about. Billy Boyle told you everything."

"You mean they would arrest you for that? You're the serial murderer?"

"Stop shitting me, Lockie. You know nobody killed anyone. How can you kill them when they're already dead, you silly bugger?"

"They don't know that."

"Of course they do, unless they're really dumber than I thought," grinned Harry.

"And the throat slitting?"

"We just did that for effect. Billy's got a great sense of humour you know. He's a good kid."

"I know he is, said Lockie, "that's why I hired him. But how did the bodies get into the Yarra and Hobson's bay?"

"I put them there. Well, not exactly."

"What do you mean?"

"I made this deal with Father Zappia. Each time he did a funeral, he'd recommend me as the funeral director and after the funeral service, we would take charge of the body and Zappia would do his thing with it and I would let Billy practice his shaving. Father Zappia, he's a weirdo as you know. He's in love with Billy, I'm sure of that, but don't worry I took care of him and didn't let him out of my sight."

"So why did you let Billy be there in the first place? You're as crazy as bloody Zappia."

"Because we had a deal that I'd take the bodies in their coffins out to the cemetery, then I'd bury them in a grave dug at the cemetery annex, except that I wouldn't bury them in their coffins. I'd just have Mandrake drop them in the grave and fill it in and that was that. And that's how I was able to donate the spare coffins to Father Zappia's church."

"The room full of coffins at the cemetery. No wonder Striker was sniffing around there. He suspected something even then."

"Right you are, Lockie."

"But you haven't said how they got from the cemetery into the Yarra."

"You've been down to the cemetery annex haven't you?"

"Of course. We buried Monie there..."

"And the rain and record high tides?"

"Oh no! You mean?"

"Right. The water came up so high it flooded the graves and washed some of the bodies back into the bay and a couple of them floated on the tide up the Yarra."

"Oh no! That means that the body by the ferry really is Monie's? We didn't bury her all that deep either. It was raining too hard and we just couldn't get the hole deep enough. But we did bury her in her coffin."

The rain eased a little and Lockie rubbed some of the condensation off the windscreen so they could see down to the beach. And to his horror, there on the beach was a coffin. He jumped out of the hearse and ran down to the water. Harry walked slowly after him.

"It's hers! It's Monie's coffin!" Lockie cried.

"Well, that's good, isn't it? We can bring it to the ferry and put her back in it."

*

Bobby turned into Douglas Parade and only then came to his senses. He put his hand out to grab Lizzie's and realized that she was not there. As he took the corner, the Winnebago swayed unnervingly, top heavy with its load of drunken passengers, all crammed in, only room to stand. Banger had grabbed a flagon of red on his way out of the hall, and passed it round for each to swig. The only person sitting was Lennie who sat crouched down on the bottom step of the Winnebago, bald head in his hands. The police siren blasted away as Striker's police car zoomed past, its flashing blue lights, Lane with his arm out the window, giving them the finger.

Sandy peered out at the car. "You know what?" said Sandy, always cool in a crisis. "They don't have Harry! The bastards left him sitting there in handcuffs."

"Don't worry," said Banger. "Lockie will take care of him."

There was an awful screech as Bobby turned the corner into the approach to the ferry. The Winnebago swayed so much, pulling them all towards one side. It must have been very close to tipping. "Wow! What a great ride!" yelled Ryley, enjoying a return to his childhood.

Bobby pulled up under the one light of the parking lot, the rain continuing its drizzle, shimmering in the light. Shooter and Eurie were already there, Striker and Lane barking orders.. They had arrived just in time as the rope Eurie had used to tie the body to the ferry had loosened quite a bit in the stormy water. Poor Monie had gone stiff and she was, as always, difficult to get a hold of, the grey skin covered with a kind of slime that made it slippery to grasp. They hauled the body up onto the gangplank

"Her hair? Is it shaved?" called Striker.

"No!" Called Shooter "It looks just like it always did," he chuckled.

"And the throat, is it slit?" asked Lane.

"No. All's well there. I guess our serial murderer didn't do this one," said Shooter, full of sarcasm.

Striker now took over. "Pull it right up, please, right up out of the water. I want to see the feet."

Eurie and Shooter did as requested. They heaved together and the body landed with a plop on the gangplank.

"The toe!" called Striker. "The toe of the right foot has been sliced off, just like all the others."

"Some weird serial murderer," muttered Shooter.

"I tell you, I know exactly where that toe is," said Striker. "We need to get back to the church."

"You mean?" asked Shooter, "you mean Father Zappia?"

"Who else? And he had some help from Nolte and maybe your gambler brother," said Striker.

"Pardon me," said Bobby, "But wouldn't I know whether or not that toe Father Zappia had was my toe? And I say it is!"

"Nonsense. Where's Stalinsky?" said Striker, now in command.

"He's in the Winnebago. He didn't want to come out, couldn't bear it, he said, and I don't blame him," said Bobby.

By this time everyone was milling around poor Monie's body. Drunk as they were, they couldn't help cracking jokes. It was after all the first time they had seen Monie naked. Striker ordered Lane to take charge of the body and keep the drunken idiots away. It was now a declared crime scene. They walked quickly over to the Winnebago where Lennie sat on the bottom step, head in his hands.

"Mr. Stalinsky," Striker asked quietly, "I need you to come and identify the body. The right little toe has been cut off like all the others,"

"I can't do it, Mr. Striker. I can't do it. You don't need me anyway. You all know Monie. You can identify her."

"I will need you to come with me to Father Zappia. I think that he is the one who has been defiling the bodies. He cut off your wife's little toe. I'll need you to identify the toe."

"But we already know it's not her toe. It's Bobby's."

"Not true. Think, Mr. Stalinsky. You're a communist after all. It would be a miracle if it were Bobby's toe."

Lennie looked up at Striker, his eyes full of water, tears ebbing over his pale cheeks, disappearing into his beard. He pulled himself up and, standing on the bottom step of the Winnebago, he looked straight into Striker's cold protestant eyes.

"I might be a communist," he said, "but I'm a child of the holocaust."

"What is that supposed to mean?" Striker eyed him belligerently. His impulse was to grab Lennie's thin arm and pull him off the step, drag him to the police car. But he resisted. It was a communist trap. Stalinsky would scream Nazi pig and it would be all over the papers in the morning.

"I'm not moving off this step," mumbled Lennie, "you can do what you like to me, I've known far worse."

"You heard him!" called Ryley, "back off and go back to the Gestapo where you belong!"

Ryley stepped between Lennie and Striker. Tony timidly tugged at Ryley's elbow. "Ryley, come on, let's go," he whispered.

"That's right," muttered Striker with a snigger, his fists clenched, "do what your poofda mate tells you."

Lennie sat back down on the step of the Winnebago, his head in his hands. "Don't, Ryley, don't!" he cried, "he's not worth it!"

Ryley's leg shot forward, aiming at a good kick in Striker's balls. But Striker was more than ready, grabbed his foot, twisted it and thrust it up, upending Ryley who fell down with a plop, Tony still tugging at his elbow.

"Nice try, son," smiled Striker, as he placed his foot on Ryley's chest and pushed down. "Too bad they don't teach you how to fight at the university. This time I won't arrest you for assaulting a police officer." He pushed down harder and Ryley gasped for breath. "Next time…"

"There won't be a next time," called Bobby emerging from the shadows. "It's Monie all right. Now fuck off and leave us alone. And if you as much as look at my nephew again I'll beat you to a pulp."

"You and who else?" quipped Striker, foolishly.

"Don't need anyone else, but if you look around, there's plenty who'd love to help."

Striker slowly lifted his foot off Ryley. Tony helped Ryley stand, and struggled to hold him from lunging forward.

"Shooter!" yelled Striker. "Get over here!"

"Stay where you are," ordered Bobby, "if you know what's good for you and your boss, here."

Striker stepped back. He saw in the gloom beyond, a dim silhouette of a mob framed against the one street light, heavy rain once again falling.

Bobby stood tall, stretched his leg, feeling a twinge where his little toe used to be. He reached out with his open hand and tried to look Striker in the eye, thinking all the time of Lizzie and what she would want him to do. Striker stared back at him, puzzled.

"Let's call it a day," said Bobby calmly. "Why don't you go back to your side of the river and let us deal with our own problems over here? I mean, it's not like there's been a horrible murder or anything. Why don't you just leave us alone and let us sort it all out? You know our Sandy, he's the one who'll fix it all up. You know that, don't you?"

"Bodies have been stolen and defiled. It's a crime," lectured Striker.

"Maybe. But there's lots of crimes that people do that's best kept to themselves. Haven't you got murders or something more serious to attend to over there?"

"Mr. Stalinsky is from my side of the river, and he's a known communist," insisted Striker.

"He only works on the other side. He's really one of us over here, you know that. And being a commo isn't a crime, is it?" said Bobby, surprised at how calm he was.

Striker peered into the gloom, and saw Lane staggering backwards, facing the mob, now much closer. He looked back at Bobby, slowly stretched out his hand. "Maybe you're right," he said slowly.

They shook hands and Bobby tightened his grip. "You're a decent bloke," he said, and maybe even meant it.

Striker looked Bobby in the eye, then turned and quietly walked off to his police car, its motor still running, lights flashing. His double breasted suit suddenly felt too tight. He ripped off his jacket as he walked, then ran, to the car. The quiet of his St. Kilda house beckoned.

*

"Ryley, run over to them and call them off," ordered Bobby. Ryley hesitated, Tony nudged him forward.

"All's good!" yelled Bobby to the mob. "Let's all go home. Lockie and Mandrake will take care of Monie."

Thereupon Lennie stood up once again on the bottom step of the Winnebago. "I want to be with Monie," he cried. "It's the least I can do."

"Struth Lennie, haven't you had enough of her?" complained Bobby, wishing he hadn't said it.

Sandy emerged from the mob. "He's right. We need to take care of this ourselves like Bobby said. Let's put her to rest tonight." He turned to the mob. "Where are you Lockie, you there?"

Lockie emerged from the shadows, holding an umbrella to keep the rain off his expensive suit. "We can do it. There's an open grave out there, I think. And if not, she can be deposited in the empty vault. You know, the one with the shoes…" he said with a grin. "Mandrake, where are you, mate?"

"I'm right here," said Mandrake, calling out from the open window of the hearse. He drove slowly forward to the gang-plank. "Let's load her up."

"We found her casket on Willie beach. So we're all set," said Lockie.

"Bobby, you and the rest can follow in the Winnebago," said Sandy. "We'll have to stop by the church and pick up Lizzie and Babs, if they're still there, that is. They might have gone home. And Father Zappia too."

Lennie flinched. He would like to throttle Zappia, the creep. "You better keep him away from me, or I'll kill him," growled Lennie.

"Lennie, take it easy," said Sandy, patting him lightly on the back. "What you need is a drink to calm you down." He called out to the mob, "did anyone bring any booze?"

"There's still some red left here," called Banger. "Let's all take a swig to see us through. We can pick up some more at the church.

The mob formed a kind of circle and passed the flagon around until it was empty.

"Shit, that didn't last long," complained Eurie, rarely sober. "Got any more?"

"Check the cupboards in the Winnie. There's sure to be some there," said Bobby. "Here, Eurie, here's the keys."

"You mean I can drive it?" asked Eurie.

"Yair. My leg is acting up and I'm just about done for. That red doesn't agree with me."

Eurie rummaged around in the Winnebago and found a couple of bottles of whiskey. "Here you go, mates," he called.

Suddenly the old Winnebago sputtered to life. Eurie revved the engine.

"Take it easy!" called Bobby. "The old girl hasn't got much of a charge left in her. And it's Lizzie's, you know. She won't be too happy if something happens to it.

As if on cue, there was a crunch of gears and the Winnebago lurched backwards. Eurie had no idea how to drive it, and this was not helped by his inebriated state. The Winnebago lurched again, then picked up speed. Eurie had hit the accelerator in his confusion. He frantically searched for the brake, pushed the gear stick in whatever direction and there was a sickening grinding of gears. But it was too late. The grand old home, the repository of so many memories and so many other deposits made one final lurch, tipped over the side of the peer and hung precariously balanced on its undercarriage.

Bobby's jaw dropped. He stared speechless. The rest of the mob cheered and passed around the whiskey. Sandy was the only one who appreciated the seriousness of the situation. If it went over and into the Yarra, Eurie would surely drown. He called to Eurie to get out of the Winnebago right away, but the engine roared so loudly he could not be heard. He stepped forward, calling to Bobby to help. "You blokes!" he yelled. "Everyone, sit on the front bumper. Got to old it down, stop it from sliding into the river!"

At this point, the engine stopped revving. At last Eurie had taken his foot off the accelerator pedal. The rear wheels, though, continued to spin in the air. The trouble was that Eurie would have to step back to get out the door, and that would tilt the weight and risk the Winnie sliding off the pier. Bobby stood to the side and stretched out his hand to the door. "Come on Eurie, get yourself to the door and I'll grab your hand."

Eurie, now in a panic, leaped out of the deep seat, scrambled over the gear stick, and thrust himself head first to the doorway. He landed on his elbows on the bottom step. Bobby leaned as far forward as he could, but could not reach Eurie's now outstretched hand. Ryley ran forward. "I've got longer arms than you," he said to Bobby. He leaned out well over the edge of the pier and managed to grasp Eurie's hand. Bobby and Tony pulled back on his other arm. The Winnebago gave one final lurch, then slowly slipped into the Yarra, leaving Eurie hanging on for dear life to Ryley's slender arm. Tony leaned down and grabbed him. Bobby remained the anchor as if in a tug of war. Eurie was saved. But the Winnebago was not.

24. Escape

"Children, Mum! That's what our men are!" Lizzie put her arm around Babs' shoulders and gave her a little hug.

"Who knows what will happen next?" she sniffed as she dabbed at the corners of her eyes with her hanky.

"It was a great night, Mum. Be happy. Bobby and I, we're Ok if you are. These things, you know…"

"That Father Zappia, he promised me, he fed me a lot of bull shit and I was stupid enough to believe it."

"Well, Mum, what can you expect? He's a man like the rest of them."

"What kind of man would cut people's toes off?"

"Mum, best not to go there. You know?"

"Lizzie, my luv. Are you sure you and Bobby…?"

"Yes, Mum. We're sure. It's not like it's something that happened all of a sudden. Everyone suspected, even you, but none of us, including Bobby and me, wanted to accept it."

Babs turned to look up at Lizzie's face. The rain was coming down again and she felt a shiver. "I know, luv, I know. All I care about is that you are happy."

"We are, Mum. Or at least we will be once we can get away on our honeymoon."

Arm in arm they turned to the hall door. The door had stayed open, the coloured lights of the party pushed through the drizzle. A hunched figure struggled through the opening, clutching something to its chest, its cape wet and limping down the watery steps.

"Well if it's not St. Robert himself," cried Lizzie, full of sarcasm.

Babs squeezed her arm. "Lizzie, you mustn't. He's our Father, you know, even if he's mad."

Father Zappia remained stooped, a grovelling crumpled figure.

"The Lord has transformed him into a hunchback for what he's done," thought Babs.

He struggled to raise his head to speak, but could not. Looking at the wet steps, the rain now pelting down, he managed to mumble, "the phone. Bobby's on the phone. Something terrible has happened. Says you have to get there right away."

Lizzie glared at him. "Get where? What?" she sputtered. "Where's the phone?"

"It's in the sacristy," said Babs. "I'll show you. And you, you silly bastard, Father, come on and we'll get you into some dry clothes."

Father Zappia hugged the small box to his chest. "Don't you touch it!" he cried, as he cringed even more into a hunched ball. He dropped down on his knees.

"Father, come on now, be a good boy. I forgive you. I know you meant well," said Babs as though she were petting a cat.

Father Zappia shook his head. "You cannot forgive me. Only the Lord can do that. I don't deserve His forgiveness. I have sinned, I have sinned! Oh Lord Take me! Take me! Throw me into the pit of Hell!"

Babs, getting stronger by the minute, leaned down and gently grabbed him by the ear. "Come on now, let's go inside and I'll get you dry and make you a nice cup of tea." He had no choice but to comply. Babs let go the ear and he struggled up, still clutching the box with his free hand. They stepped into the hall just as Lizzie appeared, flushed and a big grin on her face. "You'd never believe it," she said.

"What? What's happened?" asked Babs.

"You're right, Mum. They are little boys. Eurie drove the Winnebago off the side of the ferry pier. Don't worry, they saved him before it went down."

"Oh my God!" cried Babs, putting her hand to her mouth, letting go of Father Zappia.

"Leave God alone," counselled Father Zappia, "he has enough on his plate right now." It seemed that the Father was coming to his senses.

Babs gave him a little push towards the sacristy. "Off you go. Put your little box away and get into some dry clothes," she ordered as though she were his Mum too. He meekly complied, brushing past Lizzie without even a nod.

"I've got to get Bobby. The Imp is parked back home, I think. That's what Bobby said."

"You don't seem that upset. I thought you and Bobby were going for your honeymoon in the Winnie," said Babs, a twinkle in her eye.

Lizzie stood back, her hands on her hips, just like the Major. "To tell the truth, I'm glad. All its secrets can stay at the bottom of the Yarra."

"Secrets?" asked Babs, mischievously.

"Shut up, Mum!" grinned Lizzie, "I'm off. You'll be all right with Father Creep?"

"I'll be OK. Someone has to clean up the hall anyway. I'll make him a cup of tea and he'll be right as rain."

*

Sandy could hold his grog, everyone knew that. His big hulking body soaked up the alcohol, and it seemed that the more he drank, the more sober he became. Always a quiet presence, his heavy frame, big round face, a very faint smile conveyed a permanent state of bemusement. That was the Sandy that all acknowledged and that Babs loved. She nestled in beside his elbow, head on his shoulder as they sat together in the back of the hearse, flanked on one side by Father Zappia and on the other by Lennie. Lockie sat in the front, giving orders to Mandrake. Not that he needed them, but it was Lockie, after all.

It was a very long night, a night that did not want to end. Monie lay in the back in her coffin, the lid tightly closed, Lockie made sure of that. And Winnie lay at the bottom of the Yarra. Dawn was approaching and at last the rain let up. The street lights had just turned off and the grey shapes of the new houses as they passed through Williamstown Beach emerged in the dull light. Soon they were in the flat, thistle-covered fields, a dull green, interspersed with new shoots of grass brought on by the rain of the past few weeks.

"Keep the lights on," Lockie ordered Mandrake. He looked back to see if the small procession of mourners' cars, mostly taxis that picked the blokes up at the ferry pier, had theirs on too.

Bobby and Lizzie took up the rear in the Imp. Lizzie was in the driver's seat. Bobby sat sprawled out, the seat pushed way back, giving room to his ever painful leg. He noticed that they were falling behind.

"You OK?" he asked.

. "Never better," grinned Lizzie.

"Shouldn't we be keeping up?"

"So you're a back seat driver now?" Lizzie joked, and slowed down even more.

"Lizzie?" called Bobby, resting his hands behind his head.

*

If Lockie would not cremate her, Lennie insisted that Monie be re-buried. He would have none of putting her into the almost vacant vault. Lockie had become annoyed because it meant that he had to make phone calls and arrange for a couple of grave-diggers to show up. Mandrake, of course, insisted that digging graves wasn't part of his deal.

"Where do you want it?" asked Mandrake.

Lockie peered into the gloom of the cemetery. The fresh sunlight warmed the gravestones and a foggy haze hung above them. "Go past the reception house, down to the right. It's the oldest section, so I'm told." He looked back and saw that the other cars were filling the car park. The fact was there was no room in the cemetery. He was going to put Monie on top of another old grave. "Down there," he said, "there they are. Looks like they're done."

Mandrake rolled the hearse slowly down the track, softened by the constant rain. Only the thick green grass held the mud together. One sudden stop or turn would cause the wheels to slip and they would be bogged. As it was, the squelch of the mud could be heard as the wheels rolled forward. "We're going to get bogged," he muttered. He pulled up slowly by the mound, the gravediggers, dishevelled, probably some of Lockie's cohort of homeless alcoholics, chatting and laughing to each other as they each took a swig of Corio whiskey, their arms and legs covered in mud.

"You blokes all done?" asked Lockie as he stepped carefully out of the hearse.

"Yep, gonna cost ya, though."

"Here's a tenner, and I'll give you another tenner after you fill it in."

"Right-o mate. Got any more where this came from?" The digger raised the bottle of whiskey, almost empty.

"After you're done. I got some up at the reception house."

Lennie stepped out and walked to the back of the hearse and waited for Mandrake to open it. Father Zappia, still clutching his little box, walked to the edge of the grave, hunched over, staring into its darkness, his damp cape fluttering in a light breeze that came off Hobsons bay.

Sandy stepped out on to the soft grassy mud, Babs holding on to his arm. "Babs, luv, stay in the hearse if you want, while we get the coffin out."

"It's not a coffin, it's Monie," muttered Lennie.

"I know, I know," said Sandy. "We're all very sorry for it all."

Lockie looked across at the gravediggers. He had no intention of lifting the coffin himself, but he didn't trust them to help. That left Mandrake, Sandy, Lennie and Father Zappia. But Mandrake sat motionless at the steering wheel, showing no indication of getting out.

"Mandrake," he whispered. I'll double your money for today if you'll help with the coffin.

"I've got my best shoes on," complained Mandrake, I only drive, remember our deal?"

"I'll give you an even better pair of shoes," said Lockie with a grin.

Father Zappia inched away, on to the other side of the grave.

"Father!" called Lockie, "we need you here, need help with the coffin."

Father Zappia, in an increasingly loud voice, began uttering various incantations, now raising his little box, along with the small vial of holy water, looking to the sky, brightening into a rich blue even as he spoke.

"Forget it," called Sandy. "Lennie and me can manage it, can't we Lennie? You take her feet and I'll take the heavy end."

Lennie looked forlornly out across the cemetery. He was not a big man, nor was he especially strong. But he would do anything to help Monie on her way. Sandy pulled at the coffin and it began to roll out.

Monie came out feet first and Lennie managed to hold her. Sandy reached in and grabbed the other end with his massive arms, conditioned by many years on the wharf. But Lennie struggled, and swayed sideways, unable to carry the load. Babs hopped out of the hearse.

"Hold it!" she cried. "I might be little, but I'm a major!" She spritely danced across the mud and took her place beside Lennie and the three of them lay the coffin on the slats that had been placed across the grave.

"Well done, mates!" called Lockie.

Father Zappia's voice reached a crescendo and he at last looked up, raised both arms high, the box in one hand, holy water in the other.

"Santo Spirito! Holy Father! We are sinners all! Have mercy! Take this sinner into your arms, may your Holy Son forgive her!" He sprinkled the holy water, but at that moment, Lennie leaped across the grave and grabbed his hand.

"Stop it! Stop it!" Lennie yelled, enraged. "She was no sinner, She was a good woman and meant well to everyone!" He shook Father Zappia so violently that he dropped the holy water and his little box into the grave. He gasped, unable to breathe. He pulled his hand out of Lennie's grip and fell to his knees, sobbing, his head in his hands, his cape now hanging into the grave, mud everywhere. "Jesus, I love you, I live every day with your miracles! Please forgive me!" he sobbed. "Raise Monie! Please raise her up!" But as he muttered and mumbled and sobbed, the gravediggers came over with ropes and with Sandy's help they slowly let the coffin down into the hole. Lennie stood beside Father Zappia, his hands clenched tightly together, tears in his eyes, beads of sweat on his bare forehead. His knee pressed hard into Father Zappia's back. It was all he could do to stop himself from pushing him into the grave. It was only the horrible thought of him lying on top of Monie that stopped him.

Babs skipped across one of the slats that lay across the hole and put her arm around Lennie. He was a cold fish, she thought, but he was one of them. "Lennie," she said as she gave him a hug, "let's go home to my place and I'll make you a nice cup of tea and bake some scones." She looked across to Sandy who stood there, a big hulk of a man, his arms crossed, his sweet faint smile reaching across to her, his feet planted firmly in the muddy ground. "You are my pillar," she said quietly to him, hoping he could read her lips. And as she spoke she pressed her knee against Father Zappia's back and he fell into the grave. He immediately scrambled around looking for his little box.

"Leave it there!" barked Babs in her Major Mum voice.

"And get away from my Monie!" called Lennie, hands on hips, aping Babs.

Sandy appeared at their side. He leaned over. "Take my hand, Father. There's a good bloke."

Father Zappia looked up, his eyes squinting against the now bright blue sky. There was nothing for it but to take Sandy's hand, and leave the relic with Monie. It was hers, after all, he had to admit. He felt Sandy's firm, reassuring grip, and suddenly he had a vision of a new life ahead, a new church, flowers by the altar, a richly painted crucifix above it, an overflowing congregation. He stared into Sandy's placid eyes. The hand of God had truly raised him from the grave.

*

Lennie hung on to the leather strap as he stood across from the Haig's Whiskey mirror on the Williamstown train. It was rush hour and people were jammed into the carriage. Monie would be giving someone hell if she were here, telling them they should go on strike for whatever reason. She loved the Friday nights at 68 Cecil Street. She loved her grog, loved her smokes, but most of all loved to argue with anyone, her rough gravelly voice tumbling out of that horse's mouth, her red rimmed eyes, watering all the time behind her thick glasses, spit and dribble coming out of her mouth as she held forth on Marx or anyone else for that matter. But Marx was her, and she really knew her stuff. She loved everyone, even though it didn't seem like it, the way she talked. But nobody loved her, not really, but on Fridays they loved to argue and booze with her, especially Ryley.

The train pulled into the Williamstown Beach station and the last of the commuters rushed out, mostly all men all in a hurry to make it to the pub for a few quick drinks with their mates before closing time. Lennie rubbed his fingers against the red brick of the station house, down the steps and headed to Sandy's for their weekly Friday night binge. He had thought seriously of not going tonight. Monie would not be there. No good reason to go. He wasn't much of a drinker anyway, didn't like to lose control of his mind, the one and only great thing he had, now that Monie was gone. He worshipped his consciousness, the consciousness in which Marx put so much store. And to lose it, the way the working men of Williamstown and everywhere else for that matter in Australia, happily did when they boozed up every weekend and many nights on weekdays as well, how could they ever achieve the state of consciousness that Marx said they would because of their exploitation, the forced drudgery of their working lives? The terrible conditions that the wharfies laboured under? And then staggering home drunk after the pubs closed, home to their wives who sat waiting patiently with their dinner on the table, only to be upbraided for letting the dinner get cold? What lives were they?

Lost in thought, Lennie almost walked past Sandy's modest little row house. It was only the noise of the front screen door as it swung on its broken hinges that woke him up from his obsessive thoughts. The sound of the Red Choir rose above the squeaking door, accompanied by a chorus of rough banter and argument, though a little thin without Monie there to orchestrate it.

Sandy came to the door, his mild grin a welcome sign. "Sorry you couldn't take the ferry," he said, "I heard it's not running."

"Yair. I think it might be a sign of the future," mused Lennie. "Bobby's gone?"

"Yair, he quit and he and Lizzie, they ran away together, can you believe that?"

"I can, I can. And I don't blame them," said Lennie, trying to overcome his feeling of sadness, a sadness about the world in general.

Sandy failed to mention that Bobbie and Lizie had not made it to Monie's burial. Lennie did not seem to have noticed.

Lennie wanted to say that if they love each other why not? But he wondered about it, he had to admit. What would Marx have said? And Monie, what would she have said? In Marx's time, cousins married, that was true. Didn't Darwin marry his cousin? But an uncle and a niece? Weird, that's what it was. And then he realized that if he thought it was weird, Monie would have embraced it. She understood these things. She had lived in a world that he had not.

They shook hands and Sandy took the bottle of red he had brought and guided him through the crush of bodies, all sweating, all with glasses in their hands, most drinking beer, except Ryley with his mate Tony, drinking red. Babs emerged from the kitchen holding a tray of sausage rolls. "Who's for a sausage roll?" she called, "fresh from my new oven!"

Lennie's mouth watered. Now this was consciousness! He took one and dipped it in the tomato sauce. Ryley pushed a glass of red into his other hand. "Bottoms up!" he called raising his glass, Tony at his elbow.

Lennie took a bite of his sausage roll, followed by a sip of his red.

"They're a little bit over cooked," said Babs, a glint in her eye that in some ways reminded him of Monie, always looking for an altercation.

"They're delicious," he said with the biggest smile Babs had ever seen.

"They oughta be," she said, "I've been cooking them for fifty years and then some."

Lennie grinned again. He felt a presence behind him, Babs looking a little past him, he thought. And all of a sudden, his mouth started talking, saying something he would never have said on his own volition.

"Get thee behind me Satan!" he hollered in a loud deeply exaggerated voice.

"I hope-a you are not referring to me?" came a thin, accented voice from behind him.

Lennie turned, his mouth full of a sausage roll, and there was Father Zappia, no longer hunched over as he had been since that night of the party. He stood, almost as tall as Lennie, resplendent in a new cape, black with thin red satin trim. Lennie was so taken aback, the sausage roll caught in his throat and he coughed it up, splattering it all over Father Zappia's face. Babs dropped the tray of sausage rolls and Ryley, a devilish smirk on his face, called out, "A miracle! A sign from God!" He grabbed Father Zappia's cloak and started to wipe the tomato sauce and half chewed sausage roll from his face.

"Get away from me!" Father cried, "you heathen! God will not forget your blasphemy!"

"Fuck off, you little creep!" scorned Ryley, giving the Father a little shove that was enough to topple him over the arm of the couch where he ended up blubbering behind it.

"Father!" called Babs, "Father!"

"He'll be all right," said Sandy, amused as usual, "I'll get him another white wine."

Lennie stood rooted to the spot. Was he the only one who noticed that Father Zappia had taken Monie's place behind the couch? He blinked, trying to force his consciousness to obey his will, his free will. Why must it do this? It was only a coincidence. Stop it! He muttered to himself. Stop it! He would not accept the thought, he would not say it. He would not! Against his will, he leaned over the couch to look down on Father Zappia's pathetic figure. The crumpled, blubbering idiot looked up, licking the tomato sauce from his lips and even off his cape. He had a stupid grin on his face as if he could read Lennie's thoughts, no not thoughts, inclinations, whatever they were. Yet he looked so pathetic, and, yes, reminded him of Monie when she lolled around there behind the couch, totally drunk, incoherent, just like she was often when he found her with the homeless on one of her benders. She needed to be scooped up and brought home. And that's what he did. And now what was left? A replacement by a fallen, pathetic Roman Catholic priest whose drug was not booze, but religion. Ah! There, Marx was right. But try as he might that idea quickly slipped away and was replaced by the one thought that would not leave him. He pushed it away, but it came back. He pushed Father Zappia down, calling out "Stop it! Stop it!" But that thought would not go away and would stay inside his head forever. If he had been there, if he had stayed with her instead of remaining in the kitchen with his mates. So cocky, so full of himself. He should have been by her side. "I killed Monie," a voice spoke clearly within him, inside his head, deep inside. And now, it was not so much a thought but a vision. He saw her, laying on her back, gasping for breath, the vomit choking the life out of her, he watched her roll over on her side, but it was one last fling, her body convulsed, her eyes bulged and she was dead.

He replaced that nightmare every sleepless night with an endless incantation that he had learned when he was a small child. It came to him out of nowhere, initially only the first two words, then the remaining two:

"Shema Yisroel, Adonai Elohainu, Adonai ekhad. Shema Yisroel, Adonai Elohainu, Adonai ekhad. Shema Yisroel, Adonai Elohainu, Adonai ekhad. Shema Yisroel, Adonai Elohainu, Adonai ekhad. Shema Yisroel, Adonai Elohainu, Adonai ekhad. Shema Yisroel, Adonai Elohainu, Adonai ekhad. Shema Yisroel, Adonai Elohainu, Adonai ekhad. Shema Yisroel, Adonai Elohainu, Adonai ekhad. Shema Yisroel, Adonai Elohainu, Adonai ekhad. Hear, O Israel, the Lord is our God, the Lord is one…"

Thus, each night, his consciousness exhausted, sleep helped him forget, until, much too soon, she left and he awoke to another remorseful day.

*

Lizzie slowly brought the Imp to a halt, pulling into a half made driveway to one of the many new houses in Altona. "You see those lights over there?" she pointed across the fields to a mass of lights, and many moving lights among them.

"So what? It's the refinery and the new motorway" said Bobby.

"You know where they're all going?"

"Who knows. To work, I suppose."

"What about us?" Lizzie said, pouting a little.

"What about us?"

"Where are we going?"

Bobby looked across at her, cupping the nape of her neck in his big hand. "We're going to a funeral, sort of," he answered.

"And then what?" Lizzie asked, grasping his hand.

"Our honeymoon. But we lost the Winnebago, I'm sorry, Lizzie."

Lizzie took his hand from her neck and turned to look into his big, kind eyes and a face that knew only good. "I love you, uncle Bobby, and I don't care about the Winnebago. I'm glad it's gone."

"But I thought…"

"…we were going around Australia," Lizzie finished his sentence.

"Aren't we?"

"Who cares where we go? Let's just get away from here and see where we end up," chirped Lizzie.

"Like where?"

"I know a short cut across to the motorway. Let's go there and follow it where it takes us."

"But it just goes to Melbourne or Geelong."

"And after that?"

Lizzie pinched Bobby's chin and pulled his face close to hers. "I don't know. All I know is that we have to get away, honeymoon or not. And right now!"

Lizzie backed the Imp out of the drive and took a small gravel road in the direction of the motorway. The sun had at last appeared and the rain stopped. She pulled off to the side of the road and they embraced. The fields glistened as the sun's rays bounced off the dew drops clinging to the thistles. And splashes of fresh green grass announced the coming of a new day.

THE END

Other fiction by Colin Heston

9/11 Two.
It's politics as usual when criminologist Maciver tries to thwart a terrorist drone tack on New York City. Harrow and Heston Publishers. 2016.. E-book and paperback. Amazon. Special Australian edition coming in 2020.

The Tommie Felon Show and other outrageous stories.
A collection of stories ranging from the absurd to the improbable, with a cynical twist. Harrow and Heston Publishers. 2017. E-book and paperback, Amazon.

Miscarriages
A young adult love story of James, a teen who grows up in a pub surrounded by alcoholics, and his homeless underage girlfriend Iris, who is illiterate, having never been to school. A denizen of violent pub life, James finds solace in Iris's irascible ways, but when she disappears without a trace after an abortion, James devotes his life to finding her, and gradually begins to wonder whether she ever existed at all.

About the Author

Colin Heston is the pen name of a criminologist of international repute. He has written nonfiction books on the history of punishment and torture, edited a four volume encyclopedia on *Crime and Punishment around the World,* and regularly contributes to a variety of criminology and criminal justice periodicals. His forthcoming fiction includes, *Holy Water* a satirical farce, about a Mexican drug lord who corners the market in Holy Water, and *MONA* a collection of Australian short stories, both available in 2020. He is currently putting the finishing touches to his next nonfiction book, *Civilization and Barbarism,* for release by SUNY Press, 2020.

HARROW AND HESTON
Publishers

AUSTRALIA, NEW YORK & PHILADELPHIA

www.ingramcontent.com/pod-product-compliance
Lightning Source LLC
Chambersburg PA
CBHW050013120726
47903CB00006B/1756